Within the Light's Shadow

Within The Light's Shadow

Shadows of Peace

Kenneth Kirkwood

Library of Congress Control Number:		2023900969
ISBN:	Hardcover	978-1-6698-5091-5
	Softcover	978-1-6698-5090-8
	eBook	978-1-6698-5092-2

This is a work of fiction. Names, characters, places and incidents either are the product of the author's imagination or are used fictitiously, and any resemblance to any actual persons, living or dead, events, or locales is entirely coincidental.

Any people depicted in stock imagery provided by Getty Images are models, and such images are being used for illustrative purposes only.

Print information available on the last page.

Rev. date: 01/18/2023

To order additional copies of this book, contact:
Xlibris
844-714-8691
www.Xlibris.com
Orders@Xlibris.com
842782

CONTENTS

DEDICATION

I am dedicating my book to my family. My wife, whom I will always cherish, for sticking with me through my journey as she, my son, and my daughter, granddaughters, and my daughter-in-law, along with several of my students and friends, were all contributors to our first poetry book *Poetic Inspiration—Peace Wisdom and Treasure*, which was published in 2009. My eldest son has been one of my most avid supporters, constantly pushing me and doing whatever he can to help me. My daughter has been my inspiration as I have watched her grow as a writer, and she challenges me to be more expressive in my writing. My youngest son has always pushed me with his musical talents, helping me to become more creative with my writing. As he has helped hone my poetry skills, hopefully, one day, we will collaborate to use my poetry to create music. I am excited as I continue my journey, completing my second book in *Search for the Light Series, Within the Lights Shadow: Shadows of Peace*. I hope everyone enjoys my writing, and I am grateful to those who have supported and inspired me to express myself and never give up, knowing that your voice can be heard no matter how small or big the scale of your writing is.

CHAPTER I

Graduation

My name is George Cantwell. My story begins the day I graduate from high school. After my final exam in Mr. Peterson's class, my best friend Scott Beaman and I were about to change the world. It was 7:30 AM when the bell rang, and I entered my homeroom. Immediately after the bell rang, Mr. Peterson ordered everyone to take their seats. I was so glad this would be the last time I had to sit at my old, dilapidated desk. Every time I would sit in the hard wooden seat, pain shot up my spine.

However, when I looked around the classroom it seemed like everyone was totally focused on the exam and they were glad it would be the last English exam they would ever take at Westwood High. In less than a week we would all be graduating.

The longer I sat in the classroom the more the pressure began to rush through my veins. It was beginning to feel like I was in an oven; the hot humid air in the classroom was suffocating me and my mind was more focused on joining the Navy with my best friend Scott. As my mind to drifted in and out of reality.

I truly could not understand why Mr. Peterson made me take his dumb test anyway. Last year he let all the seniors who had a 100 percent in his class skip their finals he called it their graduation gift.

However, this year I had 99.5 percent in the class, so he made me take the exam. It made no sense I understood the material. To me it seemed like he was punishing me because I had been late to his class four times during the school year. And he docked my grades by a ½ of percent and made me take the final exam.

I had already proven I understood the material and even turned in several extra credit assignments hoping he would excuse my tardiness. To me the exam was unfair. I had more important thing to do than to play games with my English teacher and his exam was just an exercise in futility.

The more I thought about it the more excited I became. That's when the pressure began to rush through my veins, and I felt like I was in an oven as the air in the classroom was nearly suffocating my soul. The streams of sweat were pouring down my face and dripped onto my exam and made my words unreadable. I wanted to scream!

All my mind could focus on was that Scott and I would celebrate after the exam. Both of us had decided we would navy and sail the seven seas. It would be the biggest adventure of our lives.

While in the navy, we would take some online college classes, thus ensuring that when we decided to go to college, we would be ahead of the game. Since we were assured that we would be stationed on the same ship near our hometown, everything seemed perfect. I could hardly wait for the fun to begin. I knew Scott would be with me every step of the way. What could go wrong?

No one understood our relationship. While Scott was rougher around the edges and seemed to make decisions spontaneously, I was always laid back and took things methodically. However, I was sure our adventure in the navy would change everyone's mind about our friendship.

They said it was Scott's crazy idea for us to join the navy. I knew the truth. I had decided this was the best way for us to show the world our true potential. Suddenly Mr. Peterson tapped me on the shoulder. "George," he whispered as he firmly placed his hands directly on my shoulder. "Remember, if you don't pass this test, it will be nice to see you in summer school."

I looked at Mr. Peterson with disdain and nodded my head. Then I took a deep breath and stared out the window.

Wow, what crazy joke was Mr. Peterson trying to play on me? He sure knew how to break through the pleasant memories of my time in high school. Why was he torturing me? My mind nearly snapped. I had to poke myself with my pen before I realized I was still taking my final exam

Soon the doors would open, and I would be free from this jail. Sure, Mr. Peterson had the upper hand because he knew I had received scholarship offers from three prestigious universities. All the scholarships were based on my 4.0 GPA.

Thus, he intentionally made me feel like I was the dumbest person on the planet. Yet, I still could not stop daydreaming about the rest of my life, even though I knew he was right.

When Mr. Peterson told my parents at their card game this weekend that I would be receiving a B, it ruined my 4.0-grade average. They would go into panic mode and force me to take his class over. That was the only reason I decided to take my final test; I did not want my parents to have a heart attack.

Meanwhile, Scott was patiently waiting for me to finish my exam. His patience started to wear thin, and he decided to peer through the window to see how I was doing. When he saw the grimace on my face, he almost felt the excruciating pain shooting up my spine because I could barely move in the small, hard wooden seat.

When Mr. Peterson whispered to me, he quickly stepped away from the door and began anxiously pacing back and forth down the hallway. He was going bonkers in the hallway.

"Wow!" Scott thought to himself.

It was utterly crazy how Mr. Peterson had approached me and whispered loud enough for the entire class to hear. Since I was the only person Mr. Peterson called out, it made me seem like I was the dumbest person on the planet.

Then, to top it all off, Mr. Peterson was so smug as he slowly made his way back to his desk. Scott became desperate. He could not let Mr. Peterson ruin our chances to take the naval entrance exam at the end of the week. He felt like Mr. Peterson was playing mind games with me.

Scott blamed himself. He realized that he should have never told Mr. Peterson about our plans to join the navy. Why should his best friend suffer because of his error in judgment? The more he thought about it, the angrier he became. Mr. Peterson had no right to call me out, which was unfair! Finally, Scott could not take it anymore. That's when Scott decided he would not let anyone hold us back. He channeled his anger and created the perfect plan to stop Mr. Peterson.

Scott suddenly started banging on the window like a maniac. When Mr. Peterson saw Scott, he angrily went to the door and pulled down the shade. Then he pushed the door open. "What is wrong with you, Scott," he said as he grabbed him and threw him against the wall. "I don't care who you think you are; no one messes with my class."

Scott looked at Mr. Peterson and started stuttering, "I'm sorry, sir; I thought I heard the bell ring. I was trying to tell George something important about our graduation plans." Mr. Peterson regained his composure. "Son, unless you want me to fail you for insubordination, I suggest you mosey along. Since you are done with your exam, you must wait outside with the rest of the students."

Scott stood there laughing. "Sir, I appreciate your concern. I am going to see Mr. Dobbins. I am not sure he will be happy about you assaulting a student. However, if you stop, I may let you slide if you stop bothering my friend. Then he turned around and started walking toward the principal's office.

Scott shocked the entire classroom as he turned the tables. I was snickering inside as I saw the worried look written all over Mr. Peterson's. Then he slowly walked to the front of the room and addressed the class. "Sorry for the interruption, class; everyone needs to return to taking your exam. You only have twenty more minutes." Then he sat at his big brown desk in the front of the room.

I felt sorry for Mr. Peterson. It was not his fault that my parents had convinced him that I would be a failure if I didn't go to college. The whole incident made me start thinking about how I would tell my parents that I would not be going to college until after I enlisted in the navy. It was scary to think about how they would go crazy when they learned about my decision.

Finally, I could shut my mind down and stop doubting my future. I was satisfied with my decision, and my life was about to start. Others might be upset by my choice. None of that mattered. I was going to enlist in the navy; I knew it was my only option to be free.

For better or worse, this time, I would stick to my guns. As I stopped looking out the window and buckled down. I looked at the blank piece of paper and crumpled up my exam. When I started, I knew I could finish this exam with my eyes closed. Once I took another stab and began to concentrate the game was over, and I would get my A.

It was nothing short of a miracle. In less than twenty minutes, I had mustered enough concentration to finish the exam; seconds before the final bell rang, I answered the last question. I did not even hear the final bell ring because I had been concentrating so hard.

Before I could put my pencil down, I heard Mr. Peterson. "George, you must turn your test in now. Class is over, and I must get your final grades in before the end of school today." I handed Mr. Peterson my pencil and quickly raced to the door.

Before I reached the door, Mr. Peterson put his hand firmly on my shoulder and stopped me. "George, I owe you an apology. Just so you know, I would have still given you an A, even if you got 0 percent on your final.

I should have never made you feel uncomfortable today. That was not my intention. However, when Scott told me last night that you would join the navy, it was my responsibility to steer your mind back in the right direction. George, you are like a son to me. I hated to see you wasting your talent by joining the navy."

Then he lowered his head. "Yet, if that's your decision, I support you. When Scott interrupted the class, I saw how stupid I had been trying to separate the two of you. Scott is a loyal friend, and he would do anything to protect you. He knew that he'd face suspension if I turned him in, yet he interrupted the class anyhow. Please ask Scott to forgive me. And if you need any help in the future, please don't hesitate to let me know."

While Mr. Peterson was talking, my mind went blank. As I stared at him, I wondered why everyone was so concerned about my life. They had eighteen years to pump their ideas into my head. Yet, no one even considered it was my life, and I must do what I feel is right for me. Trying to explain to Mr. Peterson and my parents that I wasn't ready for college was a moot point.

My parents had already chosen my path for me. All I had heard for the last year was the constant sound of their disappointment because I hadn't chosen my career or college.

When Mr. Peterson finished his confession, I was stunned. And I wanted to get out of the classroom as quickly as possible. When I tried to open the door, it was as if someone else was holding the handle on the other side. That's when I kicked the door with all my might.

The force from my shove broke the door handle, and the door flew open. I did not realize my strength. The crazy thing was that Scott had been trying to open the door simultaneously. Thus, Scott flew across the hallway, tumbling backward and hitting his head on the floor.

"Scott," I shook my head, "when will you learn to stay out of people's way? I thought when Mr. Peterson pushed you into the wall; it would knock loose the marbles in your head," I said, laughing as I reached down to grab his hand.

Scott smiled. "It's over, my friend. It's finally over. We are about to graduate from high school. You don't have to worry about Mr. Peterson because I turned him into the principal."

I conked Scott on the head with my backpack. "What have you done? Mr. Peterson made a simple mistake. He apologized to me and explained why he was so upset. Scott, Mr. Dobbins might fire Mr. Peterson because of your bogus attitude. Sometimes you infuriate me. You seem to feel like I can't fight my own battles."

When he stood up and rubbed his head, he looked like he was still in a daze from hitting the floor. Then he spoke up. "George, I thought if I reported Mr. Peterson, it would take the blame off you. I made a big mistake. After Mr. Peterson shoved me, I ran straight to Mr. Dobbin's office and started banging on his door.

When he opened the door, I began to panic. I did not know if Mr. Dobbins would even believe me because he was always so mean to me. To my surprise, he put his hand on my shoulder and led me to the couch. 'Son, who did this to you? Normally you are sent to my office because you have been cutting up in class. Whoever shook you up is going to pay. I don't care what you did; they have no right to mess with my students. Now, I want you to calm down and tell me what happened.'

When I told him that Mr. Peterson had yelled at me and thrown me into the wall, Mr. Dobbins became incredibly angry as he walked over to his desk, picked up his phone, and smashed it into the wall. Then he turned to me and said in a thunderous whisper, 'Scott, you don't have to worry about Mr. Peterson anymore because I'm about to suspend him, pending a review. If all goes well, the school board will force him to retire. Son, Mr. Peterson will never walk the floors of this school bothering fine, upstanding students like you again."

I shoved Scott out of the way and said, "Scott, we must get to Mr. Dobbins before he meets with Mr. Peterson. Mr. Peterson may have his issues, but he is one of my parent's best friends. I don't want to be the one responsible for getting him fired. Hopefully, we can calm Mr. Dobbins down before he goes completely nuts on Mr. Peterson."

He shook his head and promptly raced after me. "I'm with you, man. Mr. Peterson was one of my favorite teachers before he pulled that stunt with you today. I just wanted to teach him a lesson. I didn't think Mr. Dobbins would get so fired up."

As we rounded the corner, I ran headfirst into Mr. Dobbins. We would have been seriously hurt if it had not been for Scott's quick reaction. Mr. Dobbins looked at me. "Son, what is wrong with you? Haven't you learned you can get seriously hurt running through the hall?"

"Sir," I said, "can I talk to you?" Mr. Dobbins looked at me and said, "Son, you don't have to say anything. I will fix the issue before it gets out of hand."

"Sir, Mr. Peterson made a mistake. He had my best interest at heart. Please don't fire him."

Scott was puffing loudly as he chimed in. "He is right. I overstepped my bounds."

"I may not fire him. However, he's going to pay for his actions. I don't care what you did, Scott; teachers don't have the right to push students forcefully as he did." Then Scott replied, "Sir, you are right, but I think I should also take some of the blame for my actions. If you are going to fire him, you should punish me. Mr. Peterson upset me. He's not the only culprit, but I should share some blame."

"Scott, as far as suspending you, it ain't going to happen. I wanted to suspend you six months ago. Mr. Peterson talked me out of it. I guess both of you get a pass today." Mr. Dobbins chuckled. "Nice try! It looks like you two really like Mr. Peterson. It may all be a misunderstanding, yet I cannot let an angry teacher rough up any of my students, mentally or physically. I don't care who they are." Mr. Dobbins looked at both of us. "Boys, you know I must do something about this incident. I cannot have teachers roughing up my students,"

Mr. Dobbins was silent for a second; then, he looked at us. "Boys, I am glad you brought this matter to my attention. I have never seen a student stand up for a teacher like the two of you. Mr. Peterson is very well-liked. I may cut him a little slack, although he will have to pay the consequences for shoving a student. I cannot let Mr. Peterson go free. I will not fire him. He will be reprimanded. And if he ever touches another student, he will be fired. Please move out of the way. I have business to discuss with Mr. Peterson." Then Mr. Dobbins went straight to Mr. Peterson's classroom. "Robert, we need to talk. I have received several complaints about a disturbing incident that happened earlier this morning between you and Scott Compton. We can go to my office. However, I feel like we can hash things out right here," Mr. Dobbins said as he slammed the door.

While Mr. Dobbins met with Mr. Peterson, Scott and I stood in the hallway, hoping everything would be all right. Although we were both still upset with Mr. Peterson, neither wanted to see our favorite teacher fired.

About twenty minutes later, Mr. Dobbins came out of the classroom. He was shocked to see both of us sitting on the floor. "What is wrong with you two? I told you I would take care of everything. Since you are here, you need to talk to Mr. Peterson. He has something he needs to tell you." Mr. Dobbins chuckled as he turned around and walked back to his office.

When we opened the door, Mr. Peterson's back was turned away from us, staring out the window. It sounded like he was crying. When he heard the door close, he alertly turned around. "How are you, Mr. Peterson? Mr. Dobbins said you wanted to see us?"

He looked at Scott and me. "Boys," he said in a disgruntled voice, "I have been better. Thanks to your actions this afternoon, I nearly got fired." Then he dropped his head. "Scott, can you please forgive me? I overreacted to your joke, and I should have never shoved you."

"Sir, I overreacted also. I hope you didn't get into too much trouble because of my foolishness."

Mr. Peterson smiled. "Son, you had every right to interrupt my class when I spoke to George the way I did. I should not have betrayed your trust. Mr. Dobbins told me he would not have mentioned the incident to me, but several other students also complained. And since you were not the only student to complain, he had to deal with the incident. Many of his students felt like his behavior was inappropriate, Mr. Peterson should have shown a little more restraint, and they were thankful that no one got hurt.

"After talking to Mr. Dobbins, I started to seriously think about retiring, yet both of you showed the true meaning of courage. And even though my behavior was unacceptable, your actions are the only reason I am not retiring. I hope to use you as an example for my new students next year. Mr. Dobbins has agreed not to transfer me. He told me this was a personal warning, but if I ever touch another student, he will have my head on a platter. He said he would make a note in my record and that I should personally thank both of you. Because if he had not run into you in the hallway, he would have fired me. He told me you both showed incredible courage by sticking up for me."

Then Mr. Peterson turned to me. "George, as your teacher, I have failed you. I had no right to get involved with your choices. I should have respected your decision and never interfered. It does not matter if I do not understand why the two of you want to join the navy. I must learn to respect my students' right to make their own choice.

"George, I was going to talk to your parents about your plans during our card game on Saturday. However, I changed my mind. It is up to you to tell your parents your decision, and I have no right to interfere with your life. I realize I have been too biased on the subject. However, I don't think your parents would believe me.

After seeing your actions today, I am sure they will get over your decision once they see the benefits you will receive from joining the navy. I'm sure your father will have some feedback because he would prefer you join the army. That way, you would still be able to go to college, and be stationed close to home."

Once he finished talking to me, he turned away and said, "Boys, before you leave, I must once again beg you for your forgiveness. And I want you to know that I am upset at myself for not allowing you to make your own choices. If either one of you ever needs advice in the future, I am here for you."

When he turned away from us, we heard him weeping. We could not take his tears. So, we went over to him and hugged him.

"Sir," I said, "we respect you very much and are glad to have someone like you in our corner. I know that sometimes, it may seem like your students don't appreciate your concern. Scott and I are glad to have had you as our teacher and mentor."

"That's right," Scott softly replied, "I appreciate you talking to my father. I don't think I would have the nerve to explain my decision to him. Sometimes he can be tough on me. But due to your support, I will be fine. I am sorry for the ruckus earlier today."

"Thank you so much for understanding and trusting me as your teacher. I believe in both of you and know that you will succeed at whatever you choose to do. Now it is time for you to celebrate your graduation. And as I stated before, if you need anything in the future don't, hesitate to let me know.

1 Then, he sat at his desk and continued to grade our final exams.

While we slipped out of his classroom and made our way to Scott's car. However, as we walked down the hallway, I suddenly became confused. What if I was not making the right choice by joining the navy? How was my choice going to affect my family? Did I have what it takes to push away my parents and step out on my own? Why was everyone so concerned about my life?

I felt like I was in limbo. My entire life, my parents and teachers had pumped into my head that I had to get a college degree, or I would be a failure. I was slowly beginning to feel like I had become a traitor. If I didn't go to college immediately after I finished high school, would the sky crack.? Slowly my mind began to level out, and I realized that I was not a traitor.

How could I be a traitor to someone else's viewpoint of my life? They never asked me what I wanted to do with my life, nor did they care. They just figured that I would fall in line with their dreams. My parents did not realize that the more they talked, the more they pushed me away. Why couldn't they see that I had been given enough information to make an informed decision about my destiny? I had to do what I felt was right for me.

At one point, my Dad went to the local college and had the Dean contact me as a favor. When I asked the Dean why my parents were sticking their noses into my life, my parents were upset. All their friends' children had already picked their careers and chosen their colleges, and all I could do was lay out one of my dad's friends. To them, I was a lone wolf and needed guidance to ensure I made the proper choices. I was trapped, and my life was over before it even started. It was silly for my parents to expect a me to bow down to their demands without consulting with me to see what my choices were.

I was slowly beginning to realize that trying to explain to my parents or any other adult that I wasn't ready for college was a foreign concept to them. I thought to myself how silly people get. The world is full of viable opportunities that do not include attending school. Some of my parents' best friends never went to college, yet they owned their businesses and had become valuable members of the community. Why couldn't I be like one of them?

All I could think about was how my dad would react to the idea of me joining the military. I knew he would blame Scott. My mind felt like it was about to explode from all the pressure. I stood in the middle of the hallway for a couple of seconds, looking at Scott; I wondered how he could be so calm. When we reached Scott's car, I realized the showdown was about to begin. How would my parents react when I told them to lay off?

Suddenly, Scott nudged me back to reality. "George, why you gotta space out all the time? Remember, we will take the navy exam in two weeks."

I just shook my head and agreed. "You know, you're right, Scott. Why don't we take the exam and enlist tomorrow? I have always wanted to travel the world and sail the seven seas. I am going to tell my parents my plan tonight.

They should be proud when they find out I found a job traveling the world. Plus, the military offers many great online educational programs. After my four-year enlistment, I can decide if I want to make the navy a career or finish my schooling.

"Scott, it is time for us to stand up. We cannot, and we must not let anyone else dictate how we should live our lives. It is our choice. And if our parents can't understand, shame on them. You just stick with me to the end of the bargain, and together we will overcome our parents and doubters. We are going to take the test tomorrow, and both of us will be able to finally have a little peace of mind, knowing we stood up for what we believed was the best choice for our lives."

Scott looked at me harshly for a moment before he let his guard down and calmly stated, "Are you sure this is what you want to do? You know I am 100 percent with you. However, I realize your emotions are out of order knowing you are about to face your parents.

Let's talk to our parents tonight before we make any drastic decisions."

Then I looked at Scott. "You are not letting the pressure get to you, are you? Remember, we are in this together. I have always been ambitious, but I have never had a chance to show the world my true potential. However, you have always been more laid back.

Many people do not understand why we are such great friends because our personalities are opposite. Yet, none of those things matters. In less than a week, we will be walking across the stage and graduating from high school."

"I assure you; my life will be changed forever after I talk with my parents tonight. I cannot allow them to choose my path without even consulting me. I know I will regret it for the rest of my life."

"Scott, you are my best friend. You know how my parents can get. Sometimes I feel like they never listen to anything I say. However, this time after I explain my plan, I hope they will understand that I can still work on getting some college credits. And I will be able can have fun while traveling the world. If they must listen, cause if they don't, it will cause a permanent rift in our relationship for years."

"For the past year, I have dreaded talking to my parents. The more they talked about me going to college, the more they pushed me away. I'm tired of the two-hour lectures from my dad about a job and the responsibilities I am about to face. And I closed my parents out, put on my best face, and dried to act like everything was cool. But it wasn't! I did everything I knew to explain to them that I'm not like other people. Somehow, I must get my point across to my parents or, I will explode.

CHAPTER II

Facing the Music

Then I stared at Scott. "I must be honest to myself and my parents because I will never forgive myself or my parents if I don't have the chance to prove that I can take care of myself."

"That is why we must take the test tomorrow. And since Mr. Peterson has already talked to your father, it is time that I face the music and confront my parent's regarding my decision. Once I tell them my decision and why it is the best choice for me, I will finally have a little peace of mind."

Then I paused for a moment; looked Scott in the eyes and shook him. "You may not be sure about joining the navy, but I must remind you we are supposed to be enlisting under the buddy plan. You are supposed to be with me every step of the way. And unless there are some unforeseen circumstances, we will be going to boot camp soon.

Scott was relieved when I put my hand on his shoulder and firmly said, "Scott, remember our friendship will never be torn apart. You just stick to your end of the bargain, and together we will overcome our parents and all our doubters and move on to higher heights."

"Your friendship has given me the strength to go full steam ahead, no matter how much my parents put me through the wringer.

I am determined to tear down all the barriers and fight for what I believe."

"I am terrified that I must face my parents and tell them about my plans. I know it is time to travel the world and enjoy my life before I become all dried out from the so-called knowledge, I was supposed to learn by going to college. I can no longer allow others to control my destiny."

The idea that I had to be like everyone else or that I was a failure was driving me berserk. That's why this last year I closed my parents out., I knew I had to get away for a while to get my head together or I would, explode. Most of all, I did like the constant lectures on getting a job and the responsibilities that I was getting ready to face

Scott pulled up to the curb in front of my house and shut the engine off. He looked at me for a minute, and I could see he was frustrated. There was nothing that he could say to ease my pain. He knew I was upset about having to talk to my parents again, and wanted to comfort me, yet he felt so helpless and there was nothing he could do to stop the train wreck.

"Scott, I have been swept to the side for too long. I can assure you that I will talk to my folks tonight. Once I let them know how I truly feel about college and that I had decided to join the navy, they will understand me or shove me further away.

Then I shook Scott and forcefully said, "are you ready to sail across the wild blue yonder."

He was shocked because he had never seen me talk with such fire. And the authority in my voice sent chills down his spine. The strength I was exhibiting let him know that I would not bend. I could tell by the crazy look on Scott's face that I might have taken things too far. What could I say? It was my life.

"George, I am with you 100 percent. I am glad you will stand up and tell your parents the truth. We have both let others make our decisions for us without ever considering who we are or what we want. They've failed to listen to you for far too long."

"Scott," I said as I saw my house, "Wish me luck! Remember, whatever the outcome, I hope one day I'll be able to live in peace with those I love the most. Even if something goes wrong during our enlistment and subsequent tour of duty in the navy. I believe that by sticking firm to our decision, we are making one small step toward ensuring that our bond with our parents and friends will become stronger."

"Slow down, George," Scott said, "stop letting the pressure get to you. You are my best friend, and I know how your parents can get. In the end, they will come around. When they see our plan, they will understand that we can still get college credits and we can have fun traveling the world. I have no regrets, and neither should you our life will only get better from here."

Scott smiled as he watched me open the gate and silently make my way to the front door. Then he yelled at me, "Good luck, George," as he revved up his engine and took off into the night.

That's when I started to panic as I turned around, hoping to see Scott's car again before I faced my parents. However, he had already disappeared, and I was now alone. I felt so lonely as I slowly strolled down the driveway toward the front door. I wondered if I should talk to my parents now or wait until after dinner.

When I turned the handle and the door and tried to open the door silently, the loud creaking was so eerie it made me want to run and hide and never tell my parents that I was going to join the navy.

Yet, the house seemed empty as I silently made my way to the front room. When I poked my head into the front room, I was surprised to see my father sitting in his favorite chair, watching the six o'clock news. Everything was out of order because my father should still be at work. Where were Billy and Sally? They were usually waiting in the front room begging me to play a game of ping-pong or chattering about what they had been doing all day.

I had been waiting for this moment for over a year. My mind had been stretched to the limits I needed to get my head on straight. it did not matter how strange I felt. It was time for me to tell him my parents my plans without anyone else interrupting our conversation.

I realized it was now or never as I tapped him on the shoulder; I said, "Dad, can we talk? I want to discuss my plans."

My dad put the paper down. "Sure, it's always good to talk to my favorite son."

"Sir," I slowly began. "What I am about to say may be shocking to you. Before you jump to any conclusion, please hear me out," I said. "I will be taking the naval entrance exam tomorrow. I'll be going to boot camp at the beginning of next week. You may have reservations about my decision. I know you thought I was going to college; however, I am not ready to go there until I've traveled.

"Before you say anything you might regret, you must remember I am the one who must live with my decision. If you want to continue to be a part of my life, you need to stop telling me what you think is best for my future. Once I take the exam, I will be picked up by my recruiter, who will be taking me to Spokane to take a physical and sign all the proper documents needed to be inducted into the navy. After being inducted into the navy, I'll report to the Great Lakes facility for three months of training. I know you assumed I'd go to college after graduation, but you failed to ask me what I wanted. The navy has great educational benefits. And after I have finished my tour of duty, I will be able to continue my education.

"All of our conversations over the past year, you've stressed that I needed a job. Well, this is it. I will be traveling the world while taking some online college classes. Then after four years, I may consider attending a traditional school.

"You have failed to listen to me. All you ever say is how great it makes you feel knowing I will be going to college soon and how you regretted not going to college when you graduated from high school."

"Dad, I am not ready to be tied down at any college until I travel the seven seas and seen the world. I want to be able to enjoy my life. And the best part is I'll be getting a jump on my education by taking online courses and placement tests. By the time I finished my first enlistment, I will have completed my core courses. And when I do begin my studies on campus, I'll start with my accounting and business classes.

"I believe my decision will make me become a more well-rounded person. I'll be able to get some work experience and have some college under my belt. You may think I am messing up my life because I am not going to college after graduating high school. However, I did not take this decision lightly. Sir, I may make some mistakes along the way, but this is not one of them.

"You have always taught me to be an ambitious person. I have a chance to show the world who I am. I plan to do important things with my life; joining the navy is just the beginning of my adventure. I promise you don't have to be concerned about my life. Like you have told me since I was a little boy, I must live life to the fullest.

"I will enlist under the buddy plan; Scott will be by my side. My recruiter assured me that we'd be on the same ship near our hometown. Dad," I said in a resolute voice, "please don't make this any harder than it already is. I don't want to end up drawing a wedge between us that we may never be able to recover from. Try to consider one thing. I am the one who must live with my decision, and if you want to continue to be a part of my life, you need to let me go.

"I hope you will get on board with my decision. I'm willing to start my life without your support. I know you may not understand my choices today. I am asking you to trust me. Hopefully, one day, you will get on board. I'll always love you, and I am sure my life will turn out fine."

When I looked into my father's eyes, I could see he was upset with my choice to join the navy and my decision not to go to college. I could see that he was taking it extremely hard, and it looked like I had just broken his heart. Therefore, I felt like it was best for me to stop talking and see what he had to say.

"Son you know how much your mother has been looking forward to you attending college. Your decision to join the navy will break her mom's heart. I realize it is your choice, but you will regret not attending school."

Before my dad could get another word in, my mom burst into the room. I could see she had been weeping and it was driving me crazy. My Father looked at my mother, trying to console her as he told her to have faith in me.

"Dear, I'm sure he will make the right choice."

He turned to my mom and said, "Don't worry, dear, I will make a call in the morning to my army buddies on the base and stop all this nonsense."

My dad had not heard a single word I said as he thought he was consoling my Mom, but his words only made the situation more tenuous. I said angrily, "Don't worry about making any phone calls, I'll be fine. I know you wanted me to go to college right after graduation, but I never told you what I wanted before today. I'm asking you to understand that I must get away for a while. I love you both, but it is time for me to get my life together. I know I am not ready to go to college. I know my decision may shock you, but I am hoping you will eventually support my decision."

This is my life you are talking about; please stop worrying. "Whatever plans you have in store for my life will not happen. I suggest you give me a break with my decision to join the navy. I don't understand why you're getting so emotional. Is this a trick? Do you think by getting all emotional, Mom, I will change my mind and forget about joining the navy?

"I love you both very much. However, it is my life, and I am not the type of person who can be cooped up in a classroom. I have up my mind, and nothing you can say or do will change my mind. I'm going to enlist in the navy after I complete exam tomorrow morning.

"Dad, you know the educational benefits are great. After my time, I will be able to continue my education and my GI grant, which will, pay for the remaining school expenses. Plus, I will get a stipend every month. If I stay in the reserves, I will be able to have a retirement plan by the time I am forty.

"I'm going to be a sailor, and I'm willing to start my life without your support. I love you very much. However, I cannot let your emotions control my life's narrative.

"You cannot decide how I should live my life without consulting me. You can make all the phone calls you want; I'll be on my way to Spokane before your friends return your call. If you don't open your ears and listen to what I've been trying to tell you for over a year, you are going to need more than words to console Mom because it may be years before I ever step foot in this house again."

"Now, if you don't mind, I need to get some rest. I will see you in the morning." Then I turned around and went to my room.

I woke up early the following day in a cold sweat. I had been tossing and turning all night as I dreamed about my mother freaking out over me enlisting in the navy. All I could hear was my father saying, "George, you broke your mom's heart. Now you will pay the consequences."

I could hardly wait for Scott to pull up the driveway and beep his horn. I even thought about calling Scott and asking him to pick me up early. I dangled my legs over the side of my bed, put on my slippers, and slowly made my way to the bathroom to finish my shower eventually made my way downstairs to get something to eat. I was thankful everyone was still asleep, and I could eat in peace. The oatmeal in my stomach felt like up in a knot. As I began dozing off, I thought I heard Scott beeping. I jumped up and raced to the door.

When I opened the door, I was staring at the dark streets. I shook my head, must have been dreaming, and walked back into the kitchen.

Before I could make it too far, I heard a horn beeping again. What was going on? Was I going crazy? I should wait to take the exam until I felt better.

When I opened the door, I almost had a heart attack; Scott was standing at the entrance.

"What is wrong with you? I have been calling you since about four this morning. Why didn't you answer your phone?

"I had to sneak out of my house because my father was furious. Last night, when I told him I wanted to take the naval exam in the morning, he nearly took off my head. I have never seen him that angry before. Finally, around 4:00 AM, my father fell asleep on his favorite couch in the front room. So, I snuck out of the house and went to Denny's to get something to eat I tried calling call you to join me, but you wouldn't pick up your phone."

Once I got myself together, I looked at Scott. "Sorry about that, my friend; I must have been in the shower when you called. I left my phone in my room when I came downstairs early this morning."

Then I raced back up the stairs to get my phone.

When I returned, I patted Scott on the shoulder and said, "Let's get this exam over with. It does not matter what people think. The process has already begun."

When Scott saw the determination on my face, he smiled as we jumped into the car and raced to the exam center. We were the first ones to arrive at the exam center. When we tried to open the door, it was locked. I read the note on the door. The exam center had moved to 2100 Center Street.

"It looks like they tricked us. They have moved the test to Center Street, and the time of the exam is 9:00 AM instead 8:00 AM."

Scott looked at me. "It's a sign. Should we wait before we take the exam?"

I looked at him strangely as we walked toward the car. I had never seen him give up so easily. Something was happening inside his head. I could not put my finger on it. Was he going crazy? Why was he freaking out about the exam? I began to wonder, was joining the navy going to change our friendship? Although I felt strange, I kept it to myself, because I knew we had been through worse. And no matter what obstacles got in our way, we always remained together. Was I overthinking the situation or was Scott suddenly becoming a stranger?

"Scott," I said. "Are you out of your mind? We have come this far, and it isn't time to stop now. Don't worry about it, my friend; they just tricked us. It's only a small roadblock, and we have time to make it to Center Street."

When we finally reached the exam center, there was a line of over a hundred people slowly being ushered to the exam room. It seemed like none of us were prepared for what was about to happen as we were crammed into a small space and ordered to take our seats.

The last recruit entered the room. The recruiter slammed the door before standing the front of the room, yelling, his voice roaring like a lion's as he said, "Everyone needs to remain seated until I come by with your exam.

Once you receive your exam, I'll tell you where to go to complete the examination. For your safety, I want you to understand that I will not be calling your names because this exam is being recorded and I have been requested not to state your names."

The man next to me jumped up and said, "Are you people crazy? I just want to travel the world; I don't want to be in a secret group." Then he got up and walked out of the room. "Ladies and gentlemen, now is the time for you to leave if you do not think you are cut out to serve your country; remember you have been hand selected to take this special exam; due to your specific interest and set of skills the navy feels you can become a valuable asset to our government."

Another man raised his hand. "Sir, can you tell me exactly what we are getting ourselves into" "Son as I explained earlier this exam is recorded and highly classify; I cannot divulge that information Everything you need to know is on the test" After the recruiter finished several more recruits walked out of the room.

I became extremely nervous after the recruits walked out. I did not know what to expect as I silently waited for the recruiter to hand me my exam. He had already dismissed fifty recruits, and I began to wonder if I was in the right place. When he got to the man in front of me, he turned to him and said, "Son I am afraid you have not been picked for this special exam. You need to report to 104 for your exam.

Then he went to every recruit and shook their hands, wishing them the best of luck in their endeavors. After shaking everyone's hand, he stood in front of me and stared for a few minutes. "Congratulation, you have been chosen to take the exam." Then he handed me a piece of paper and ordered me to take my seat.

Once the recruiter handed me my security forms, he returned to the front of the room and called everyone to attention. "Ladies and gentlemen, I will give you one final chance to walk out of the room. If any of you decide this is not the right place for you, then I suggest you leave before I turn back around." Suddenly several more recruits jumped up and ran out the door.

Then he turned around and laughed, "Now the rest of you need to buckle down and get ready for the exam."

Then, to our surprise, the recruiter orders the MP to guard the door. "Ladies and gentlemen, once you read and sign the security document, you are bound to secrecy." After the MPs picked up the security documents the recruiter started passing out our exams. Then the recruiter looked at Scott and asked him to stand up. "Son are, you sure you want this, because we don't allow any yellow belly cowards in our group, and I can tell you are one of them mommy's boys who ain't cut out for anything but sitting behind a desk the rest of your life"

Scott's face was red as he stood up and began to challenge the recruiter, "How dare you talk about my mother like that. If you say another word about her, I will be forced to show you what this mama's boy is made of. Then he tightened his fist and was ready to pounce on the recruiter." However, before he could say another word two, MP s came up behind him and restrained him.

After they forcefully escorted Scott out of the room, the recruiter smiled, "Well at least we got that out of the way. We truly don't have any tolerance for little pipsqueaks in our navy" Then he began addressing the remaining recruits, "Anyone else wants to test my resolve? "I didn't think so he said. Then he ordered the MPs to pick up our signed security documents."

Once the recruiter handed me my security forms, he returned to the front of the room and called everyone to attention. As they escorted Scott out of the room the recruiter smiled, "Well at least we got that out of the way. We truly don't have any tolerance for little pipsqueaks in our navy" Then he began addressing the remaining recruits, "Anyone else want to test my resolve?

"I didn't think so he said. Then he ordered the MPs to pick up our signed security documents."

After all the security documents were picked up the recruiter began passing our exams. While he was passing out the exams everyone was quiet until he stood back up at the front of the room and ordered everyone to exchange their exam with the person to their right.

Now that everyone has their proper exam, while you are in this room taking the exam your new name is written on the top of your exam. I suggest you memorize your new name as the recruiter will have one final rollcall using your new names, I looked at my exam and my name was now "Frank Wildwood"

Once the recruiter handed out the test, he barked his final instruction. "You will have an hour to complete each section. There are a total of three sections in the first portion of the exam. Which include knowledge of, History, Math, and English. The final part of your exam is structured around each recruit's mechanical knowledge, computer skills, and reading comprehension.

After completing the first two sections of the exam you need to raise their hand. Then I will pick-up your exam and give you the final portion of the exam, which is tailored toward each recruit chosen rate. Since I was going to be a storekeeper I would be tested in basic accounting, business administration, and finance.

Then he picked up his stopwatch and said, "you may now begin your exam." When exam began you could hear a pin drop. I was finally taking my exam

Three hours later I finished the third section of the exam when the bell rang, and the recruiter stood in front of the room for the final roll call as he ordered us to put our pencil down. When I put my pencil down it felt like my brain had been completely fried.

"Remember Ladies and gentlemen when the appropriate officer calls you to review your exam you will be called by you knew name. As I suggested before you need to memorize your new name and if you have a bad memory.

I suggest you right you name down on a separate sheet of paper as a keepsake before I pick-up your exams. Because this will be you name from this point forward.

Everyone needs to get comfortable and remember there is no moving around or talking until all exams have reviewed. After the exam have been reviewed everyone who passed the exam will be given their assignments" "If you did not pass the exam, don't worry you will still be a part of the Navy but, you will be assigned to a different department for processing. After the recruiter speech s several recruits decided it was time to get lunch, as they started heading toward the door the recruiter stopped them in their tracks. "I am sorry ladies and gentlemen you will have wait until all the exams have reviewed. Once you have been given you assignment you will be able to take a break."

Then the door suddenly flew open, and several high-ranking officers came into the room and started reviewing our exams.

"Everyone needs to get comfortable, and remember, there is no moving around or talking until all the exams have been reviewed. Ladies and gentlemen, the appropriate officer will call you by your new name. Therefore, I suggest before that you memorize your new name, and if you have a bad memory, you need to sign your name on a separate sheet of paper as a keepsake, because this will be your name from this point forward."

Time seemed to stand still as they slowly started handing out exam results. One by one the recruits were silently ushered up to one of the officers' desks and told to sit down. Then each recruit was given their assignment. If they were called up to the chief's desk, they were told they did not pass the exam. One of the MPs would usher them out of the room for further processing.

CHAPTER III

The Naval Exam

When I looked around, there were only seven recruits left. I was growing restless, and it seemed like I had been forgotten. Finally, the MP came over to my desk and ushered me to a seat in front of Commander Johnstone.

The commander looked me square in the eyes. "Please sit down. Frank, son, can you keep a secret?" I nodded. "Yes, sir." Then he ordered the MPs to usher the remaining recruits to another room.

Once he was sure we were the only remaining personnel in the room, he reached over and turned off the recorder.

"Son, what I am about to tell you is highly classified and you cannot tell anyone. Is that understood?" I just nodded my head. "Good. First, I want to congratulate you. I did my research on you and your friend Scott and I found out some interesting information.

While you are the first recruit ever to pass all the sections of the exam with a score over one hundred, I wanted to have you retested because it seemed like you tried to make a fool out of the navy. However, after I reviewed you resume, I felt like you score on the exam were legit."

"It seems like you were the top student in high school. You could have gone to any school you wanted, yet for some reason you decided to join the navy. With your perfect SAT score, you could have easily gone to the naval academy at Annapolis, yet you decided to join the enlisted ranks.

And your leadership skills, administrative skills, computers skills, and accounting skills are off the chart. Plus, you have a photographic memory therefore, you will succeed in whatever profession you choose if you decide to get out of the navy after you four-year contract. Thus, with all your skills, along with your test results I have determined that you will eventually make a great leader and I hope you decide to make the navy your career.

Therefore, I personally stepped out on a limb to vouch for you, making you your unit's commanding officer. And I decided to assign you to one of the most elite units in the military. And I have been given the honor of becoming your commanding officer.

You will be in the navy. However, no one must know that you are a part of NSA, and your NSA code name is Wildwood. Your rank in the navy will be SK3 after you complete you training in Meridian Mississippi. And since you bypassed the naval academy, I have decided to grant you rank of GS-11 in NSA, which is comparable to a Lieutenant in navy

"After you complete you NSA training you must always remember, you cannot tell anyone about your assignment in the NSA."

"I personally matched you with our nation's best assets James, John, who will be part of your team to track down and destroy terrorists that want to harm our great our nation. Your job will be to lead the team to infiltrate and destroy terrorist groups. George," he said as he shook me, "not only did I vouch for your team, but I also put my entire naval career in your hands. After you are trained, your team's first target will be to infiltrate and destroy one of the nation's most notorious terrorist groups, led by Donna Rangel."

Commander Johnstone continued speaking. "You will report to your recruiter tomorrow and it will appear that you have enlisted in the navy." Then the commander stood up and shook my hand. "Welcome to the navy, George. Once you complete boot camp you will be sent to Meridian Mississippi to an elite storekeeper school before you are officially stationed on board the USS Bunker Hill CG-52.

Then he whispered in my ear, "George, you have been given two separate sets of service records. Your NSA records will be under your new name, Frank Wildwood. Your naval records will be under your name George Cantwell. You will be assigned to a secret unit, no one no will know your secret identity as Frank Wildwood except you and your team. This gives you deniability.

You cannot tell anyone that I am assigning you to a covert unit of the NSA. Eventually you will have full command of the mission and everyone else will be filled in on a need-to-know basis. Currently your two new mates, James, and John, have been appraised of the situation. However, they have not been given the full scope of the mission."

The commander hesitated. "There comes a time when you must cut the cord, I know you have concerns about Scott. We were considering him as a member of your team. The reason I am emphasizing Scott's disposition is to let you know your friendship nearly blew our cover story during the exam. We were hoping Scott would be a member of your squad, and he failed! He does not have the necessary qualities, and he is not ready for the sacrifice it will take to bring peace to the world. You need to be prepared. You must not relax around him or anyone else, because very soon people will try to tear down your confidence and you may even want to give up. Don't let it get to you. This is all a part of the process that will only make you stronger."

Your enemies know that once you succeed with your mission the world will be safe from terror. You need to understand you were chosen to lead the team that will ensure the world has peace instead of war. Not only that, but several of the world's top terrorists tried to infiltrate this exam today, wanting to find out who would be the leader of the Peace Task Force or PTF, and they have been watching every recruit who took this exam like a hawk.

"They are frantically trying to determine who we have chosen to lead the PTF. Therefore, it is imperative that you maintain your status as a storekeeper until your true rank and mission is revealed.

Because once that happens, terrorists will search for any weakness that you may have and distort them."

"Currently they do not know that you are part of the NSA, but once they do figure it out, they will try to disrupt your training and destroy your team before it even starts. That's why you must remain strong. George, you must stand firm in your decision, and follow through to the end."

"George, someday the very people you call your friends may wind up being the same people who threaten your existence."

"Scott made his choice when he failed his test. I am asking you to pay attention to your surroundings. The only people who know and understand the complexities of your mission are James and John. You will feel like there is no way the three of you can succeed. The pressure will be unbelievable."

"You will even begin to have doubts regarding joining the navy. Don't worry, just follow the path I have set for your team. You will become one of the United States' most valued military units and I am certain that James and John will be with you every step of the way."

Then he shook me. "George, do you understand the importance of your mission? Should I be concerned? Beware of your friend Scott. Do you understand me, son? I am ordering you to drop Scott like a hot potato, because as the adage goes, lose lips sink ships. I suggest you must move on and let Scott live his own life."

"Eventually, you will be alone, and only you will be in direct communication with me. Other than James and John, the rest of your team will be set up once you report for duty on board the *USS Bunker Hill*. I will let you know who you can give information to and who is on a need-to-know basis. I realize this is an unexpected burden.

I hope you are on board, and I will see you at the Great Lakes Training Center, and then onboard the *USS Bunker Hill* after you have completed your NSA training."

"In all our private communications concerning the NSA I will address you as Frank Wildwood. Whenever I see you in a public setting, I will address you as George Cantwell. Your friends and family must think you are a storekeeper in the USN."

Once he finished addressing me, the commander turned the recorder back on and stood up to shake my hand. "Welcome to the to the navy, Mr. Cantwell." Then he smiled as he told me to go home get some rest.

Before I reached the exit the commander came up behind me and firmly put his hand on my shoulder and whispered in my ear, "Remember, George, you cannot tell anyone that you are part of the NSA. After reporting to your recruiter tomorrow, it will appear that you have enlisted in the navy. To ensure the secrecy of this operation, you must maintain your cover as a navy storekeeper until I deem it necessary to change."

Once he finished addressing me, the commander turned the recorder back on and stood up to shake my hand. "Welcome to the to the navy, Mr. Cantwell." Then he smiled as he told me to go home get some rest.

The commander chuckled. "At ease, George. Relax, go catch up with your friend Scott, get yourself something to eat, and then go home and rest. Tomorrow is your big day, and you must remain sharp. Your recruiter will pick you up at 6:00 AM, and then he will pick up two other members of your team to take you to Spokane, where you will officially enlist in the navy. The last person your recruiter will pick up is Scott. All he knows is that you are supposed to be stationed on the same ship after boot camp."

I smiled at the commander as I quickly made my way to the exit and began my search for Scott. I did not have to look far because Scott was sitting in a bench across the hallway from the door. He had been waiting for me in the hallway for over an hour. When Scott saw me, he jumped to his feet. I could see that he was excited about something.

"There you are, George, I thought you were never coming out. Can you believe it, we are finally going to be able to see the world. I can't wait until tomorrow! Did you they give you a chance to choose your rate yet?"

"Scott, I'm a storekeeper, how about you?"

"They told me I would be boatswain mate for the first six months, and then I will have the option of training to become a signal operator or a navigator. Once we get through boot camp, they will sit down with me and go over my options."

My mind was suddenly shaken back to reality as we made our way home to tell our folks the good news. However, Scott's stomach let out a loud growl that nearly shook the car off the road.

"Scott, I don't know about you, I think it's time to get something to eat."

Scott looked at me and smiled. "I thought you'd never ask," he said as he pulled up into a Denny's parking lot.

While we were eating, Scott looked at me and shook his head. "I sure don't pity you. I can't image how you are going to tell your folks the good news. I know how crazy your folks can be, and they sure ain't going like the fact that you joined the navy."

Scott was right about my folks. We hardly ever agreed completely, and I already knew they disapproved of my decision. However, this time there was nothing they could do. I had already signed the papers. I was going to become an asset to the NSA. Yet I knew I could never tell them what my real job was. The hardest part was that I couldn't even tell my best friend the truth. That's why I was quietly stewing over what I was going to say to my folks.

After we finished eating, we jumped into Scott's car and slowly made our way toward my house. While we were driving from the restaurant to my house, I began rehearsing what I was going to tell my folks. My mind was so focused that I did not even realize Scott had pulled the car next to the curb. When Scott looked at me, he said, "Well, I hope your folks ain't too mad."

I started to go into panic mode. I was trembling inside as I was once again in the middle of my driveway pondering how I was going to explain my decision to my father. When I opened the car door, I turned to Scott, who was smiling. For the first time in my life, I felt alive. Why were my parents so dead set on making my life miserable?

I could not understand why my parents were making it so hard on me. I knew I was not a bad kid, and I had never given them any trouble. When I stepped out of the car, my mind was about to explode as I slowly made my way down the driveway. I heard Scott putting his car in gear, his wheels squealing, vanishing in a puff of smoke, disappearing into the darkness, zooming down the street like a maniac, jarring me back to reality.

I slowly lumbered down the driveway, hoping I could somehow sneak past my dad and deal with the situation later. However, before I could even get to the front door of the house, my dad busted out through the door like a maniac, nearly ripping the door off its hinges.

"George, what is this nonsense about you joining the navy? I just got a call from a Lieutenant Commander Johnstone. He told me that a Master Chief Escondido is picking you up in the morning, and you are supposed to go to Spokane tomorrow to enlist."

My dad's reaction to the commander's phone call shook me to my core. I felt like I needed someone to lean on. That's when I remembered what the commander whispered to me after he told me about my assignment. *"Son, you will feel like you are all alone, because you can tell no one the identity of your mission. Remember, it's too late in the game for you to change your mind, and any your friends and family will turn on you. You will seek to find an ally, but for the moment they have all disappeared into the darkness and all that is left is you standing and bearing the full weight of your choice to defend your integrity and honor."*

"Nice to see you too, Dad," I sarcastically replied. "You should be happy I found a job that allows me to travel the world and get paid."

"I'm not in the mood to play games with you, George. Unless you want me to knock some sense into your head, I suggest you don't get so arrogant with me. This a serious decision, and you didn't even give me a chance to call my friends at the army base. We had talked about you joining the army earlier this year. George, don't you remember how you assured me that you had no intention of going into the military, and that you were going to apply to Tech to start working on your accounting degree? And you applied for a bookkeeper position at my friend Joe's TV shop."

"I am not trying to be disrespectful, sir. I thought you would be happy that I got a job with the bonus of having a place to live, and I will finally be able to take charge of my own destiny. I have listened to your lectures for the last three years about getting out on my own and supporting myself. Matter of fact, last week you told me I was lazy, and that if I did not get a job soon you were going to stick me in the basement until I become a little more responsible.

"Dad, you don't need to worry about me anymore, just let me go and sprout my own wings. Be happy for me, I found a job that allows me to travel the world and get paid.

Chill out, it's only a job. It's not like we are at war. Besides, it's my life, making my own decisions. I will have a place to live, and I will finally be able to take charge of my own destiny.

Sorry, Pops, but you can't help me with this one. My mind's set, and I am going to Spokane to enlist tomorrow. And you don't have to worry anymore. Just let me go and sprout my own wings."

The abruptness of my answer stunned my father. I will never be able to forget the expression on my dad's face as he grabbed my shoulder and shook me. "You know if you go into the navy you'll be gone for quite a while. Are you sure that's what you want? Let me talk to my friends at the army base. They can help you make a more informed decision. I'm asking you not to go off without having a second opinion. It might ensure you are not being duped by a crazy navy recruiter. Those boys in the navy will tell you anything but the truth. Just give my friends a chance to explain all your options before you make a choice you may regret the rest of your life."

"What is wrong with you, Dad? Can't you just be happy for me? This is not a decision I have taken lightly. You have no right to dictate to me where I should or should not be working. No matter how much you huff and puff, it is too late.

"Dad, I have already explored several options for my future, and you don't have to be sad. Hold your head up and realize that you taught me well and set me in the right direction. I know you had to realize my future was in my hands. If I were you, I would stop trying to tear down your son's success and join me to move forward into an exciting future. You must realize it does not matter if you accept my decision or not. it is my life. I would love for you Mom to be on board, but if you are not now, I understand. I believe once you see my reasoning behind joining the navy, you will eventually come around."

Before I could even turn around, my mom was standing behind him, weeping. "Son, you must consider what you're doing. We don't want you making the wrong decision and messing up the rest of your life. You know how Jimmy went into the navy and his parents never saw him again until he was coming home in a box."

"Mom, will you please stop being so dramatic? I know what I'm doing. For the first time in my life, I am free to make my own choice. I am ready for this more than you or Dad will ever know. Besides, I'm not like Jimmy. I already have gotten certain assurance from my recruiter that they will give me all the training necessary to work in my chosen field. So, there is nothing you can do. I have already signed the paperwork and I leave tomorrow at 6:00 AM."

It felt like I had taken an arrow and pierced them in their heart. My mom placed her head on my dad's shoulder and sobbed uncontrollably. The look on their faces was tearing me up inside.

To add more drama to the situation, when I turned around and grabbed the banister to walk up the stairs to my bedroom, someone had forgotten to pull the blinds on the window at the top of the staircase and the sunset was beaming through the window, nearly blinding me. I just covered my eyes and slowly made my way to my bedroom.

The glare from the sun made me realize that I was getting ready to start a whole new chapter of my life. However, nothing seemed to matter because I felt like my parents would never understand my decision, but it was time for me to grow up and move on. My mind was filled with so many questions as I sat on my bed, trying to relax. My body was so tense as I looked around my room and saw the posters of my favorite baseball, football, and basketball players plastered on the walls. The more I stared at the pictures, the tenser my body became.

Suddenly I was beginning to have doubts: He just wouldn't show up tomorrow! They couldn't do anything because he hadn't signed the paper yet and nothing was official until I raised my hand and got on the bus to Great Lakes Training Center.

What was the matter with me? As I shook myself, I could not let my folks stifle my dreams again. My folks had stifled my dreams for too long. My mind was made up, I was ready for a change of pace.

It would be four years, and then if I wanted to get out, I could move on to something else. For the first time in my life, I was going to be a part of something that I could be proud of. I was being given the chance to save lives while becoming an asset. Very few people were granted the opportunity that was handed to me, and I could not let anyone get in my way of my pursuit of happiness.

It was useless as I tossed and turned in my bed and desperately tried to shut my eyes and relax. Why was my mom weeping so hard? I could hear my dad consoling her near the bottom of the stairwell. All I do to shut out the noise was forcefully kicking my door. My room shook as it slammed shut. However, I could still hear Dad consoling Mom in the kitchen. The more I tried to tune it out, the louder it got. Why couldn't my parents understand I had to get out on my own and take control of my own destiny?

The more I heard my mom weeping, the more conflicted I became. I felt like I was being torn into pieces. Yet, in the end, I knew I had made the best decision. I turned on the radio and began to listen to the Beatles. I could hear the words echoing in my mind, *Let it be, let it be."*

Around midnight I dosed off, yet my parents kept coming to my room and standing in my doorway.

"Honey tell him, we didn't mean he had to be so drastic."

My mom was completely losing her mind as she babbled, "You told me you had an excellent job lined up for him! What about Janis? Remember how crazy he said he was about her? I could tell her and let her know he really liked her. Because I don't think he has told her about his true feelings. I know I have issues with Janis, but at least he would still be around."

"Dear, if George joins the navy, we may never see him again. I would rather him be married and having a family. If he is married, I am sure he would go to college and get his degree so he could take care of his family." she said forcefully

"Dear, are you crazy? You know his tongue gets tied every time he is around Janis. We all know how crazy he is about Janis. Remember you told him to beware of her. You told him you were afraid she would steal him away from us. Now you are talking about them getting married. Dear, if he wants to mess up his life, we should just be supportive and ready to console him when things don't work out. He's a smart kid. I told you I already called Ray. I said I'd talk to him in the morning."

That was the final straw. I could not take it anymore as I sat up and pushed my door open and stared at my folks, I said, "Mom, Dad, that's enough. Please go somewhere else, I need to get some rest. How many times do I have to tell you, you can call Ray all you want, it ain't going to change things

I am fine! I know what I am doing! I need to get some rest. I will be leaving with Chief Escondido at 5:00 AM. I know that is earlier than I told you. But I can't wait to get started. I'm going to Spokane, where I will be sworn in after I take my physical and sign my enlistment papers. My mind is made up, and there is nothing that you can say or do that will change it. I am begging you, take your crazy speeches somewhere else. I don't know how many times I need to tell you there is nothing you can do."

It looked like I had wounded my dad as he dropped his head and put his arms around my mom, and they slowly walked away from my door. He turned toward me and was about to say something, but he shook his head and they slowly disappeared down the steps.

I was truly angry as I forcefully kicked by bedroom door shut to stop the noise. *What a relief*, I thought to myself, *now I can get some rest*. I looked at the clock on the other side of my room. It was around midnight when finally, I closed my eyes and tried to relax. It was useless as I tossed and turned in my bed. Why was my mom weeping so hard? I could hear my dad consoling as they slowly walked to their room on the other side of the house.

The more I tried to tune her out, the louder she cried. Her weeping was driving me insane. Yet at the end of the day, I knew I had made the right decision. Finally, her weeping sounds drifted away.

The next thing I knew my alarm was going off and I quickly jumped out of bed and raced to take a shower. After taking a quick shower, I quietly walked down the steps towards the kitchen, hoping not to wake anyone. To my surprise, when I got to the kitchen my entire family was sitting around the table eating. My brother, Billy, didn't seem incredibly happy to be getting up so early in the morning as he retorted, "What's up with you, bonehead? How come you got Moms and Dad so upset? Did you have to just go off half-cocked?"

I replied, "Glad to see you bro. We can finish our tennis match when I get back from boot camp. I forgot! I already beat you."

"You is one crazy dude," my brother said with a smirk.

Suddenly my sister grabbed me and hugged me. "We wanted to see you before you left. Mom and Dad told us last night, said you enlisted in the navy? It's not true, is it? You were planning to leave without saying goodbye."

"Yes, it's true, sis." However, I'm saying goodbye to you right now. It's not like I'll never see you again I'll be back in three months. Then we can talk."

What was it with women? They are so sensitive, suddenly my sister, Sally, was weeping harder than my mother. She was trying to break me down. I had to stay strong. I smiled at her and put my arm on her shoulder to reassure her everything was going to be fine, as she wiped her tears on her T-shirt.

Then she hit me with a whopper. "How come you don't like Mom and Dad anymore?"

"Sis, what are you talking about? I will always love Mom and Dad. Just because I'm joining the navy doesn't mean I am abandoning my family.".

CHAPTER IV

The Warning

She became very distraught and grabbed me. "You'll come home soon? You can't leave me by myself in this crazy house."

"Will everyone please give me a break? It's no different than when you went to that private school for six months. Sally, Mom, and Dad will always be Mom and Dad, but it's time for me to live my life, and see the world."

After I what I had to say, it seemed like an eternity before anyone else spoke. Then Billy said, "Guess I'll see in a few months. Don't be a stranger. We are all going to miss you."

Before I had time to respond to my brother, I heard my recruiter honking his horn. "That's my new boss, I got to go. I'll see you in few months." I looked at my brother. "Man, please try to talk some sense into Mom and Dad and let them know I'll be alright."

He looked at me with his crazy eyes. "Bro, you always were a spoiled brat and had a flair for dramatics. It will be all right, just kick someone's behind for me."

My sister chimed in, "Mom and Dad will get over it, but if you stay away too long, I don't know if I will."

"Thanks, guys. I gotta go. Don't worry, I'll be back before you know it."

When I opened the door, Chief Escondido was yelling at me, "What's wrong with you, boy? Don't you know we are on a tight scheduled? And if I am late, they will give us both extra duties."

"Sir, what are you talking about? We have plenty of time to make it to Spokane before the induction ceremony."

"Son, I suggest you button up that lip of yours and hold on, we have several stops to make before we get to Spokane. I must pick up your two new friends, James, and John, and I also got to pick up some stupid little jerk named Scott."

I was so stunned by the chief's comments, I nearly jumped out of the sedan. However, I realized I was stuck, because unlike Scott, even if I hadn't signed my papers and I was still bound for the next four years of my life. Yet, I truly didn't understand the way he was talking about my best friend Scott. I felt like the chief had no right to talk about Scott any type of way and I wanted to explode, but I knew I had to be smart and hold it in for the time being.

The chiefs comment made me wonder if my dad was right, and I had gotten in over my head. However, I could not let the chief know how I was feeling. Thus, I sat in the backseat contemplating what my next move would be. While I wanted to jump out of the car and go home to beg my parents for forgiveness. I knew I had to take it on the chin because I knew college was not the right choice for me. So, I let the chiefs comments slide and continued my journey to join the navy.

Then the chief pulled the car up at the recruiting station. "George, I want you to stay put. I forgot some important documents. I will be back in a few minutes." Then he slammed the door and went into the recruiting center.

Once the chief disappeared into the darkness the door flew open, and I was face-to-face with a high-ranking navy officer. It was the man from the testing center.

"Mr. Wildwood, my name is Commander Johnstone. I have been assigned as the commanding officer of the PTF. We met at the examination center. I realize this meeting may seem inappropriate, but I needed to re-introduce myself.

"Chief Escondido will be picking up the other two members of your team, James, and John. They will be your shipmates once you complete boot camp and are assigned to the *USS Bunker Hill*. Captain Silverton will be the CO, and I will be the XO.

"I don't have much time to explain the situation, what I need you to understand is that you will soon be the leader of PTF. You already know the examination you took was not a regular naval entrance exam. But what you did not know is that we were looking for candidates to back-up your operation and while Scott was not chosen for the PTF he may still be working with you in a back-up capacity at our secret training center."

You are the only person who knows the examination was not an ordinary naval entrance exam. The few recruits that passed the exam, will not be informed of their task until they reach their duty station.

I understand you were thrown for a loop when I divulged the true intent of the exam to you. I am sure the first thing that popped into your mind was who is this strange man and what is he talking about. We all know that you never intended to be selected for an elite squad in the NSA. I realize you have a million question for me. But you need to be patience, after you complete your training thing will begin to make sense. And once you reach you final duty station and begin to select the final members of you team you will feel a whole lot better. Remember I am counting on you to keep James, and John in line.

"I came to warn you, there are going to be many people who will try to tear down your confidence. They will pull on your heartstrings, which is why I am concerned about your relationship with Scott. You need to understand that your friend Scott is not part of your immediate squad, and he has no idea who will soon become.

"George, your relationship with your friend Scott is a big concern. He failed his test. If you continue to hang around him, your team will be exposed to unnecessary risk.

I have put my entire career at risk by choosing you to lead the PTF and I am not going to go down without a fight. Thus, this is a friendly reminder that you need to be ready mentally for the pressure of leading the PTF.

Thus, you must keep your distant from Scott. I realize that

you joined the navy under the buddy plan, and we need to keep up appearances. That is why I am allowing you to stay connected with him for the moment. But, as I stated before after the exam that if he blinks an eyelash in the wrong direction, I will come down hard on him to make sure the mission is successful. I know this all sounds harsh; you'll understand why your friend Scott is not part of your immediate squad.

Remember, George, there's a time in everyone's life when they must cut the cord and stand on their own two feet. After you complete training you need to understand that things will be different between you and Scott.

"Scott cannot see the simple essence of serving his country. He's too tied up with his own personal agenda to become a man of honor who is willing to endure the ultimate sacrifice and become a member of an elite unit with a higher purpose. I gave him a shot at the exam center, hoping that he could change. I know Scott is a bad person. However, is not ready to take the next step to become a hero."

While he does have many has many good qualities, he is not ready for the sacrifice to bring peace to the world. You must be prepared. It would help if you did not stick around him or anyone else as many of your family and friends will try to disown you. And if you are not careful this will end up destroying your confidence and make you vulnerable. You may even want to give up.

However, you need to stay strong because you are going to lead a team that will ensure the world has peace instead of war. However, several of the world's top terrorists will be watching your every move. They want to know how you fit into the picture. They still don't know the extent of your mission. Therefore, you are in a dangerous situation. If they can figure out a way to disrupt your training and destroy your team before it even starts, they will be able to control the world's destiny. You must remain firm in your decision, following through to the end.

"Scott, your parents, siblings, and teachers have no idea whom you will become. That's the reason I broke protocol and decided to meet with you. It is of the utmost importance that you focus on your mission. By focusing on your mission, everything else will fall into place. Currently everything seems a little crazy. Don't worry. In a few months you will, begin to understand the importance of the secrecy surrounding your team. And when your team finally integrates into the NSA, you will know what it's like to be a hero.

"You've already taken the plunge, have a little faith in the system. Soon you'll have all the answers you need, so stop worrying about Scott and your family. When the time is right, they will appreciate and understand your sacrifices. I have no ill will toward Scott. I want to see him succeed as much as you do. But until he sees the bigger picture, I cannot allow him to control the narrative.

"Sometimes friends must get out of the way and let their those who are close grow to their potential instead of holding them back. It is your time to take your place among the world's greatest leaders. George don't blow your future because of your family and friends. They cannot understand your current situation, but when they see you return as a hero, they will all beg you for forgiveness, not realizing how important your mission is to maintain the balance of peace in the world, by eliminating terrorists such as Donna, who have become a member of those who cannot stand peace.

"Our mission depends upon your undivided attention. Any distractions will be a weakness, and lead to the possible failure of our mission to make the world safe from terror. You are going to lead the team that will ensure the world has peace instead of war.

"You need to keep your head in the game and remember not to be surprised by anything that happens, because it is all mind over matter as you will be evaluated and pushed to your limits, both physically and mentally.

"The only people who know about the true essence of the PTF are you and your new friends, James, and John, who will soon be joining you. Remember, George, someday the very people you call your friends may wind up being the same people who threaten your existence. Scott made his choice when he failed his test."

"You need to Pay attention, you'll quickly learn that the only people who knowledge the complexities of your mission are James and John. I plan to give Scott orders to the USS Carl Vinson CVN-70 in San Diego. This should please his father. Once Scott settles into his new life, he will eventually lose interest in contacting you. That is enough information for now."

"Good luck, my friend. I will be talking to you again. I have inundated with enough information for now. I will be talking to you again soon."

Then before I had time to blink my eyes, the door shut, and the commander disappeared. The weight of what I was being asked to bear was nearly destroying every ounce of my sanity. Everything concerning my enlistment was getting stranger by the moment, and I was beginning to wish I had never taken the exam or signed those blasted papers. It seemed like my values were being challenged. Yet I had not even raised my hand to swear in and join the navy. Currently, all I could do was go with the flow until I get a little clearer understanding of what is going on.

I was freaking out. Where was the chief? Why had he suddenly left me alone in the darkness? Did he know about Commander Johnstone's plan? I hoped that no one would suddenly appear I didn't know if my mind would be able to take any more surprises.

Suddenly Chief Escondido blurted out, "Buckle up, George, we are about to hit the road."

When he started talking, I nearly jumped out of my skin and thought I was going to have a heart attack.

"Where did you come from! What happened to the naval officer to whom I was talking?"

The chief burst out laughing. "I just went inside to get your paperwork. You look like saw a ghost!"

"Sir, did you see that crazy man that was talking to me?

"What man? Are you sure you are not seeing things? I'm the only one here. I'm sure no one is within twenty miles of this place. Are you sure you weren't dreaming? Man, get ahold of yourself. You ain't going loco on me, are you, George?"

The chief's voice jarred my mind back to reality. All I could think about was Scott asking why I had to space out all the time.

"I don't know what happened to you when I went inside to get my paperwork. I suggest you prepare yourself for the next step of your journey. You are about to enlist in the navy, so snap out of it, because I ain't got no time for any monkey business. You need to put aside all these crazy dreams and start acting like a real sailor." He rolled the windows down. "Just look, the city is still dark, everyone is still at home sleeping."

It did not matter how much the chief said I was dreaming. I knew Commander Johnstone was real and he wanted me to be the leader of a special squad. However, as far as I was concerned, I was just supposed to be sailing the seven seas and traveling around the world. I never agreed to become part of an elite military squad.

My dad might have been right, I should have waited to talk to his friends on the army base. But I was slowly beginning to realize it was too late for me to step back. I had already taken the exam, signed a secrecy agreement. I was trapped! The pressure, the expectations were too much. The chief's voice was slowly jarring me back to reality, and I began to focus on what he was saying. He might just reveal some of the secrets of this crazy life that had been dropped on me like a bomb.

"George, from the moment I first laid eyes on you, I realized that it had been a long time since I had met someone with your caliber of honesty and integrity, which exude from your spirit. I finally felt like I had found a decent, respectable recruit with some brains. I have seen many strong recruits. However, before the examination yesterday, many of my colleagues were skeptical. They did not think you had the willpower to stand up and be counted like many of the brave men and women who have served their country before you. However, you proved them all wrong when you faced your parents and refused to back down.

"There are many who say they want to serve their country, but few can make the changes to stand up for what they believe in. I am proud to be your recruiter. Please don't let anyone change your mind.

"George, we are at war, and the navy needs strong recruits like you and Scott. However, there is something special about you. Only a handful of people could make a strong declaration of independence from their family and friends like you have over the past few days. It was quite a change for me, because most of the smart people I have recruited tend to be stuck-up snobs and think they are better than everyone around them. You and Scott were different, and I was beginning to change my mind about smart recruits. That is why I recommend both of you for the special unit."

"When my superiors saw how down-to-earth both of you were, they agreed with my assessment, and it seemed like you were both ready for greatness. Everyone felt like you would both be great sailors. However, during the exam, Scott blew his chance to become part of your special unit when he stood and challenged one of the guards, thus deliberately failing any chance of him being a part of your special unit. His action showed that he was nothing but a stupid little jerk and cared more about himself than your friendship. When my superior saw how his crazy antics nearly blew your cover story, they considered him a security risk, thus refusing to make him a member of your special unit.

"You and Scott may have been friends for years. However, you need to be careful when you are around him because it seems like he cannot fathom that you can succeed without him, and he is trying to sully your image. George, he cannot face the fact that you will become a great leader, thus Scott left when you needed him the most. His actions since you graduated have been very puzzling. It seemed like all the animosity started off when Mr. Peterson spoke with his father and left you to fend for yourself, and it made Scott angry.

"Ever since that moment, he has been festering inside. He did not understand why Mr. Peterson told his father about his plans to join the navy. He felt like he could stand up to his father by himself and has tossed your friendship out the window with his crazy antics at the exam center.

Scott still is a decent bloke. The traditions, the honor that both of you would have brought to the mission would have been grand if he'd dropped his pride and let the examiner do his job. He got crazy and almost started a riot. Scott felt like he had the right to take things in his own hands. He failed to realize you were under scrutiny and the chain of command is stronger than anyone's pride. And what kind of a friend would insist on holding a friend back from true greatness?

Believe me, George, Scott knows you can become one of the greatest leaders the world has ever seen, and he is jealous and he does not have enough strength and courage to take the next step.

"George, you will be a far better sailor than your whiny friend Scott. Don't get me wrong, I think Scott will one day be a great sailor. But your friendship with Scott is pulling you down because the two of you are opposites. There are a lot of strange things concerning your friendship that has you trapped in a bubble. When you took the exam yesterday, you dropped all your smugness and decided to become part of a great tradition.

You made me proud. I am honored to be your recruiter. I'm glad you can discern our enemies. Whatever top-secret operation you are being trained for will bring our country hope again.

"George don't let your friendship with Scott drag you down. I have seen too many good men waste their lives standing up and talking about freedom and justice. In the end, they failed to preserve our country's dignity. Mark my word, after completing boot camp, your eyes will be open to the many deceptions surrounding your life. One day you may join forces with Scott, not this mission. You are better off without him. The experience of boot camp and your induction into the NSA will change your perception of life and give you a wider perspective of what friendship and family truly mean.

"Stop worrying about Scott. He can take care of himself. You need to spread your wings and open to a world full of possibilities for you that will strengthen your friendship and your relationship with your family. Once you enlist in the navy, your life will become organized. It's time to put aside all the craziness of the past year and begin to realize your dreams are within reach. Just kick back and enjoy the ride.

"Enough about the past, George. Soon you will be meeting two men who will become your most trusted allies, and they will drastically change your life as you team up to create your special unit. Together you will fight to make our country safer. James and John might be a little rough and I have already voiced my concerns about some of their actions, they are honorable and trustworthy recruits. They will become your partners and friends; someone you will eventually trust with your life. And no matter how lonely you may feel, I am on your side, the commander is on your side, and your two new friends will be on your side once you get to know them."

I was stunned by the chief's speech. It seemed like he was trying to trap me into admitting I was part of the PTF. Was he one of the terrorists that the commander was talking about. I had to put a stop to his treachery. The commander told me to be careful.

"George, the commander let me know you must not let anyone know you are about to become the leader of a top-secret unit."

"What are you talking about, chief? I am enlisting in the navy, and there is no top-secret unit. James and John are sailors just like me. If you don't stop talking crazy, I am going to get out and find my way back home. If the navy is planning to breach their contract with me, there is no way I am going to Spokane with you."

"George, you can't do that. Please, you gotta listen to me when I tell you this process has destroyed many friendships. The sooner you realize that the better off you will be. You were chosen to uphold a great tradition. Therefore, my friend, it is time for you pull yourself together. I need you to remain sane, and I don't want you giving up your promising career because of someone like Scott."

Suddenly the chief's phone rang. It sounded like someone was incredibly angry at the chief. I heard him say, "Yes, sir," several times before he hung the phone up. After hanging up the phone, the car came to a complete stop on the side of I-5. That's when I realized that the chief was just a small part of the larger picture.

"George, I am sorry for talking about your friend Scott. I have been ordered to turn the car around and take you back home. I did not realize that I had broken protocol and I have been reassigned. If you still want to join the navy, a new recruiter has been assigned to pick you and Scott up tomorrow.

"Whatever the problems you have with your parents, I have been told to apologize to them for the mix-up in the process. Since neither you nor Scott have signed any papers, you have been given the option to continue to Spokane and enlist in the navy today or wait on a new recruiter to take you tomorrow. George, I know that I said some crazy things. I hope you can forgive me, and my comment will not change your mind about enlisting in the navy tomorrow morning. Because the navy needs more men with your strength and courage."

"The world is waiting on men like you to step up to the plate and make our nation honorable again. Whatever top-secret operation you are being groomed for will bring our country hope again, and it has been an honor meeting you."

"Please stop talking. I need to know the truth. Is the navy going to live up to their end of the deal and make sure that Scott and I have the same duty station once we sign the official papers, or has that changed? Were you just lying to me like my dad said, 'them navy recruiters will tell you anything just to sign the papers."

"Sir, if you do not stop talking about my friend Scott, I will call and tell him that joining the navy was the wrong decision. I am not sure where you are getting your information. Scott and I have been friends since I was five, and the only reason I joined the navy is because we were promised that we would be stationed together."

The chief was quiet for a few moments, before he answered, "If that's what you want, I will stop talking about your friend Scott, and I will make sure your original agreement with the navy is still intact."

Then I replied, "As long as you can ensure the navy will live up to its end of the bargain and you stop talking about Scott, I am ready to join the navy."

The chief said, "Give me a minute," then he called Commander Johnstone. "Sir, George, has agreed to continuing to Spokane under the following conditions. One, that the navy agrees to his original contract, and that I stop talking about his friend Scott."

Commander Johnstone chuckled. "Chief, keep up the excellent work. Let George know that you will meet his terms and continue to the rendezvous points to pick up James and John. Hopefully, this will be the last conversation we have concerning George and his friend Scott."

The chief smiled. "We have an agreement, George. I need to turn the car around and get this trip back on track. Soon you will be meeting two men, James, and John, who will change your life drastically. They will become your partners and friends. Regardless of how crazy they act I will need you to stay strong. With your brains and willpower, you can lead your team to higher heights.

I could not listen to the chief anymore, so I closed my mind off to the chief. How could anyone expect me to just roll over and play dead as they insulted the essence of my life? The weight of what I was being asked to bear was nearly destroying every ounce of my sanity.

The car came to a screeching halt, and the chief pushed open the door and yelled, "Johnny boy, get your behind in this car. I called the warden and let him know you tried to escape. Warden Jones does not play games. We got you out of the detention center, now's your chance. Once we get to Spokane, you'll be free. You need put a little pep in your step." Then chief floored it. Somehow John was able to jump in the moving sedan and slam the door.

After he slammed the door, he was suddenly sitting on the seat next to me. The chief looked through the rearview mirror and said, "I suggest you show me and your new friend a little respect."

"Mister, what is wrong with you? They told me you were crazy, but I had no idea you would try to leave me on the side of the road. You know I can't go back to that place again, because they'll lock me up for good. They assured me I would have a fair chance and I was told I'd finally be free from them bums at the center. The only reason I accepted this mission is because I want to bring Donna down. They told me I going to be stepping into a special unit.

CHAPTER V

James and John

This just seems like another broken promise. And from the look of things, they were trying to punk me."

John looked at me and laughed. "Why didn't they tell me my mission was to be a babysitter? Who is this man sitting next to me? I was supposed to meet this Cervantes named George, and he is supposed to be one of the navy's top recruits? It sounds like a babysitting job to me. This guy may have brains, but it sounds like he's just another mommy's who ain't never been away from home."

"Johnny boy, I suggest you mind your manners, because this is your last chance. And if you want to get away from those bums, I suggest you meet your new best friend George," chief blurted out.

"Mister, what is wrong with you? If you expect me to respect this crazy-looking lunatic I'm sitting next to, you got another thing coming. Plus, you just tried to leave me on the side of the road."

The chief did not like the tone in John's voice, so he slowed the car down and turn to John.

"Son, you got a choice, you can either get out or you can shut your whiny little mouth. You have been given a chance to start all over, so I suggest you get with the program. Once we get to Spokane you will be free. But until that time, just sit back and enjoy the ride. If I were you, I would think carefully about what you say next, unless you want me to leave you on the side of the road. I am sure the commander can find us another candidate who will follow orders."

John knew he was in a very tenuous situation, yet he could not let this stranger talk to him like he was a bum. However, before he had a chance to say anything, the chief introduced me.

John stared at me hard for a second, then he stuck his hand out. "Pleased to meet you. I didn't realize I was going to be surrounded by such a pretty boy. I bet you ain't never been anywhere unless your mommy okayed it. I hope you ain't like the last fool they tried to hook me up with. He's the reason I ended up at the farm."

Then I shook John's hand and stated, "Well, at least you have half a brain and you do know two plus two equals four."

I noticed the chief glaring at us through the review mirror seconds before he stomped on brakes again. When he stomped on the breaks, we both flew forward nearly hitting our heads on the back of the seat. What was going on? I thought we were going to Spokane where I would enlist in the navy. Why had the chief stopped the car in the middle of nowhere?

Before either of us could say anything, the chief got out of the car and opened the door next to John and smacked him in the face. The chief did not like the tone in John's voice. Then he pointed to John. "You got a choice, you can either get out or you can shut your whiny little mouth. You have been given a chance to start all over, so I suggest you get with the program.

Just sit back and enjoy the ride. If I were you, I would think carefully about what you say next, unless you want me to leave you on the side of the road. I am sure the commander can find us another candidate who will follow orders."

After he smacked John, he reached across John and smacked me. "George, you need to stop being so uppity the two of you need to play nice while I get James." Then he slammed the door and slowly walked into the cornfields and disappeared.

While we sat in the hot car waiting for the chief to return. All I could hear were the chief's words rattling around in my brain. It was so strange that he kept talking about me being part of a special unit. No one was supposed to know, yet it seemed like the chief knew more than I did.

Were we ever going to make it to Spokane? I tried to open my door, but the chief had locked the doors so that we couldn't get out. "We're trapped," I wanted to scream. Instead of screaming, I sat quietly and stared at John in disbelief. When John stared back at me, I began to feel uncomfortable. I had no idea what the crazy dude was capable of.

After about thirty minutes, he took off his boot and began banging on the window. He did not realize the windows were bulletproof, and his boot bounced off the window and flew across the car, nearly hitting me on my head. I ducked as his boot hit the back of seat, and I bent over and handed the boot back to John.

"John, are you crazy? You could have seriously injured someone. I could have told you that the windows were unbreakable. All you need to do is look at the seams in the window. The curvature in the window lets you know these are not ordinary car windows. Now I suggest we figure out a way to get out of this car before anything else happens. The chief has been gone for over thirty minutes, and we have no idea if he will return. This must be a test. Do you have a knife or something to cut with?"

John looked at me. "George, even if I had a knife, why would I give it to a punk like you? I may look like I'm dumb, but I ain't that dumb."

"Chill out, John, I just wanted to see if we could pop the seat and get out through the trunk."

John just smiled. "Alright, mate, I'll see if I can find the latch to pop the seat."

While he was feeling around the seat to find the latches, we were both suddenly caught off guard as James just appeared in the middle of the darkness, banging on the window like a wild man. He was begging us to let him in the car.

I turned to John in a panic and said, "I don't know about you, but I ain't letting that crazy man in this car."

John looked at me a shook his head as he calmly said, "Dude, that crazy man ain't getting in this car no matter how hard he tries. Cause we can't open the doors even if we wanted to. I just hope that's not the guy we were supposed to pick up. ."

I was going into panic mode and shook John. "You're crazy, man," I said as I went into full panic mode. "It's a trap. Someone might have kidnapped the master chief. Just keep trying to pop the seat and then we can make a run for it."

John brushed my hands off his shoulder. "Dude, "calm down. I'm sure the chief will be here shortly to straighten things out. Plus, if we get out of the car, ain't no telling what that lunatic may do."

"I guess you're right. I just hope the chief is all right, because we need to get out this crazy place as soon as possible."

Suddenly the door flew open, and I nearly fell out of the car. It was the chief, and he was talking to the crazy man. Then he turned to John and ordered him to move over so that James could get into the car. We both looked at the chief like he was out of his mind.

John said, "Sir, I ain't letting that crazy man sit next to me. If you want him in the car, he is going to have to sit up front with you."

I smiled. "Ditto that, chief," then we both slammed the door.

To our surprise, John's door flew open and the chief shoved James into the middle of the seat. Once the chief was sure James was secure, he jumped into the car, and we started speeding down the empty dirt road back toward the main highway.

"Chief, put some pep in your step and let's get out of here before anyone finds out I'm missing."

Both of us were still in a state of shock as James reached out his hand to shake my hand. "Glad to finally meet you. I have heard a lot about you and John. It seems like you're supposed to be the brains behind the whole operation." Then he winked at John. "What you think about the boss man putting this young chump over us?"

"Take it easy, James," the chief said. "Let the boys relax for a minute. Your entrance shook them up. Matter of fact, I am still wondering how they knew I was picking you up tonight. I was told that everything was supposed to be a cakewalk. He just said you might be in a little trouble. It looks like everyone around this blasted place is after you. You were not aware that we were setting a trap for the traitor. Thanks to our intel, I was able to recover some valuable information in our quest to destroy the true traitor.

"You see, James, the one who betrayed you is just a small part of the network of terror that has surrounded our nation for too long. However, he has supplied us with some very integral part of Donna's network of which we were unaware. The commander told me that you were on the run, and you became the bait to bring the enemy out in full force. Your knowledge of Donna and her friends will be a valuable part of bringing her down.

"The commander decided too that you only needed to know specific information about your escape, and now that you are free, he was hoping that you would not flake out and try to run away from your destiny. As far as George and John go, they were top candidates for the team, and they have no secret agendas. John is one of your best allies, and he wants to bring down Donna and her puppet Mr. J far more than you can imagine.

"James," the master chief said sternly, "you need to calm down and count your blessing that you are still alive. Don't worry about what happened. I already know who the traitor is. It is going to take some work to flush them out. And when we do, Donna's entire network will be exposed."

"You need to let the commander know that we have a traitor in our midst. There is no way anyone should have known about the meeting tonight. Yet we barely made it out, and then you tell me I must work with these two jokers? One of them reminds me of my distant cousin John."

"I am sure that the commander will brief you once you get to boot camp. For now, I expect you to behave and get to know the two men that you will become an integral part of, blowing everything wide open. Knowing that in the end the world will be a safer place, and peace will finally overcome all the wars and insecurities that have been the face of terror that has gripped our nation and the world for far too long. I cannot tell the full scope of you mission, but I do know you need to see the bigger picture that the United State will once again become the leader of world peace.

"Just calm down and make friends with George and John and realize that they have been through a lot just to ensure that you could have your freedom."

He just started laughing. "Take it easy, chief, we are going to be fine now that I am in the car with my new partners. I made a few calls to throw them off our scent. No one will ever think to look for us in Spokane, let alone Great Lakes Training Center. Now, if you just keep your pedal to the metal, we got a schedule to keep, and picking up another nerd boy is holding up our progress."

The chief just glared at James through the review mirror. "Son, you'd better be on the right side. Because if your actions harm anyone in the team, you will have to answer to me. I am not planning to disobey my orders to make sure the three of you make it safely to Spokane. If you don't put a lid on it, I am going to pull the car over and make sure you are very secure for the remainder of the trip.

"Son, you're crazy. Your actions are very unprofessional and could put an end to your team before you even get started. Don't you understand? When you disobeyed the commander's orders and contacted your old friends, you have put us all in jeopardy. Several of your old friends have joined Donna's terrorist network. They will not hesitate to give our location away. Give me your cell phone, because I am not going to take the blame for your stupidity."

The chief pulled the car over. "This is the last time I am going to stop until we complete the mission. You three goons need to lighten up and drop your pride. All three of you want the same thing. Everyone needs to buckle up because we're three hours behind schedule and I still must pick up Scott. When we pick up Scott, the three of you need to be on your best behavior. Is that understood?"

Immediately after the chief's speech, James patted the master chief on his left shoulder. "Chill out, chief, I was just messing with you. Just do your job and get us to Spokane so we can join the navy tomorrow. Don't worry about me. I can be very civilized when I need to be. There is no need to slow down anymore until we reach nerd boy's house."

I was laughing to myself. How could this strange commander, whom I had never met before tonight, expect the three of us to become heroes? I was slowly beginning to feel as if I was being isolated from reality. Why was I sitting next to two whack jobs? James smelled like a sewer, and John seemed as if he had a few screws loose upstairs. And the longer the silence, the looser the screws I hear rattling in James's head.

When I started to focus on James's conversation again, he was screaming at the chief, and we all looked at James as if he were a lunatic. "You dudes are making me upset. I'll just have to call the commander to sort things out." Then he pulled out his phone and started pushing the button. The master chief desperately tried to grab the phone from James.

James quickly jerked the phone away from the master chief. "Hey, man, watch the road, and let me take care of my business."

Suddenly a lady picked up and James said, "May, let me speak to Kenny." The lady on the other end of the line said, "You must have the wrong number," and then she hung up.

Seconds later, the chief's phone rang.

"What is going on, chief? I just got a call from James's phone. It seems like he is in trouble. May told me it was urgent that I call. You know we can't afford any screwup. I have already taken a substantial risk by putting George over the team. I am ordering you to make sure James is secure. Do whatever you have to. We cannot let him fall into our enemies' hands. He is too valuable to lose. But if you see he is captured, I am giving you the order to shoot to kill. He must not fall into to the enemy's hands. Is that understood? Just tell me you got everything under control."

The chief meekly replied, "Sorry, sir, it was my mistake. James told me he had to make a call before we got to Spokane. I did not realize he was calling you."

The commander was silent for a moment, then he ordered the chief to hand James the phone. "James, this is the last time I am going to tell you don't call me on this phone again unless it is an emergency. One fatal mistake and everyone's cover will be blown. Then we will have to start all over."

"Sir, it was an emergency," James replied. "Somehow Donna found out where I was hiding, and she sent a team to pick me up. If it had not been for the chief, I would have been a goner. I am going to send you the coordinates to our pickup location so your people can scan the area to make sure that they are not following us. I can't really say much more, because these three goons do not have security clearance yet."

The commander was silent for a moment. "James, are we on speaker phone?"

"Yes, sir."

"Son, you need to turn off the speaker so we can talk."

James quickly muted the phone. Then the commander continued, "James, I am ordering you to play nice. George and John, remember, they are on our side. However, George's friend Scott does not have the slightest idea what is going on. If you start acting crazy, it will blow your cover. Plus, George is new to all of this, and he may get offended if you push his friend too hard. It is a very delicate situation. Do I have your word you'll act civilized for the rest of the trip?"

"Sir, I'm sorry if I overreacted. I've been under a lot of pressure. I wanted to make sure Donna wouldn't attack us."

The commander listened to James and did his best to remain calm. "Don't worry about it. I'm going to throw Donna a few bones. She won't bother you anymore."

James sharply replied, "Sir, yes, sir," as he gave the phone back to the chief.

"Chief," the commander said, "it is in your hands now. I am counting on you to ensure there are no more incidents and that everyone makes it safely to Spokane. Is that understood?"

"Yes, sir," he said, as hung up.

"Get comfortable, gentlemen. We only have one more stop and then we are on the way to Spokane. I hope the three of you can act cordial when our next guest arrives. I do not want to have to talk to the commander again until we are safe in Spokane."

Once the chief hung up, a light went on in James's head and he seemed to calm down, and we all just sat quietly staring out the window as we turned onto the main highway and made our way towards Scott's house.

I was slowly beginning to feel as if I was being isolated from reality. What should have been a joyous occasion had suddenly turned into a nightmare, as a ten-minute ride had turned into a two-hour fiasco.

How could we face off against traitors, terrorists, and the destruction of the planet when it would take a miracle for us to make it through the night without one of us having a major meltdown?

The chief could tell by the look on my face that I was having a tough time grasping the situation, and he broke the silence. "George, I want to introduce you to the third member of your team, James. You need to play nice and introduce yourselves, because your lives are going to depend upon the friendship that you develop from this moment forward. Like I said, I we have one more recruit, Scott, to pick up. I need the three of you to be on your best behavior. All our lives depend upon it."

However, when James reached across John to shake my hand, we nearly passed out. I put my hand on my nose and said, "Look here, mister, I don't know who you are or where you came from, but I suggest you put your grimy hand back in your pocket. Chief, I am not sure where the two of these jokers have been, but I hope both of you take a bath when we get to our destination because I feel like I am in the middle of a biological attack, and none of us may be alive by the time we reach Scott's house.

I ain't planning to get sick before I enlist in the navy. Can someone please roll down you window? That odor is about to takes us out of here and need a fresh breath of air.

When the chief rolled down the window and I could breathe again, he glared at me through the rearview mirror.

However, I knew I was in trouble. "Son, as I told you before, you need to stop acting so snobby. These two men have been through enough, and they don't need another fool trying to judge them."

After the chief rebuked me, I felt like my life was being turned upside down. I smiled and stuck out my hand. "The chief was right; I have been acting a little stuck up. We can start over. My name is George Cantwell, thrilled to be joining the navy tomorrow. I realize I have been a little anxious. Just give me a break, I can be a nice guy."

James quickly replied, "Well, at least we can get the pleasantry out of the way. "Nice to meet you. . My name is James Mathers. I joined the navy to be free from my stepfather's tyranny. Sorry about the scene, but I lost the chief and I didn't know if them goons at the roadhouse were coming." What about you, bub," he said as he turned to John.

"My name is John. I prefer not to state my last name. I joined the navy to honor my family's tradition of proudly serving in the military to protect our great nation from foreign and domestic enemies."

"Glad to see we got one hero in the bunch," James smirked. "I don't know too many people who still believe in honor, country, and duty. Too many people are out to get what they can for themselves. It's an honor to be with royalty. The two of you are like peas in a pod. You both believe there's something grand about serving your country. More power to you! I happen to be a crazy man who is trying to escape his past and start a new life far away from the horrors of yesterday."

John was starting to reply to James when the chief chimed in. "Now that you have all introduced yourself, I need you to be on your best behavior. We are about to pick up George's friend. Can you a least act like normal human beings?"

The chief's speech felt weird. It was like the chief was controlling our minds, and I nearly forgot Scott even existed. I tapped the chief on his shoulder.

"Chief, how do you expect me to react to such glowing insubordination? These guys are a joke, and you said we are supposed to be best friends. You must think I grew up in a dump somewhere."

My life was being turned upside down. As I became preoccupied with my future, I failed to realize that we were approaching Scott's house.

When the car stopped in the yard, I sat motionless for a few minutes. I felt like it was all a dream, and I was trapped. I wanted to pinch myself to see if I was awake. I had this horrible feeling that Scott knew something was going on. What was I going to do? Then the master chief pumped the brakes a few times and I flew into the back of the seat. Why was this crazy man slamming on the brakes? It was as if he had a death wish.

Before I could say anything, he turned around and said, "What's the matter with you, can't you take a little bump on the head," as he patted me on my shoulder. "Time to get Scott. I hope he was worth the trouble. Now, get out of my car before I change my mind and take off without Scott."

The tone of the master chief's voice sent shivers down my spine. I was still in a state of shock from hitting my head. I sat motionless for a few minutes, trying to figure out if this was all just a game or was I about to step out of the car and throw away my friendship. I just wanted someone to pinch me to make sure I was still alive.

James whispered, "It's going be all right, friend. I'm sure we can deal with your friend. If he is as nerdy as you, it will be simple."

"Don't worry about it," John snickered, "by the time we get done with Scott, he will feel like he's a king. He will never suspect that we are setting him up and destroying your friendship."

"Buddy, one day you'll be sorry for those comments. It may not be today, or tomorrow, but you will never destroy my friendship."

I angrily pushed the door open and quickly made my way to the house. At least I would be able to get away from all the noise for a few minutes. I knew Scott. He'd still be packing his gear.

I began to panic when no one answered the doorbell, so I frantically pushed the button so hard that it broke off and crumbled. Then I remembered Scott had busted the doorbell the day we graduated; he was supposed to fix it. However, he forgot when we took the navy exam early.

The chief stuck his neck out of the car. "George, is there a problem? We can leave without Scott and still be fine."

"No problem, man. I forgot the doorbell was broken."

After knocking on the door about five times, Scott's dad, Steve, came to the door. I was relieved to see a familiar face.

"What is wrong with you, George? Do you want to wake up the entire neighborhood?" Then he smiled. "Why don't you just go sit in the den and wait for me because we need to talk."

Then he turned around and yelled, "Scott, son, your ride is here. You need to hurry up. They are waiting for you in car."

Steve looked at me. "George, Scott is not ready. Why don't you come in for a few minutes while you wait for him to get ready." I signaled to the chief that I was going inside, and I would be out in a few minutes. The chief smiled and waved back. "Take your time."

Once we sat down in the den, Steve looked at me and frowned. "I don't know what you and Scott have planned, but if anything happens to Scott I will be coming after you. While I am glad that I asked you to convince him to join the navy. I did not realize it would change his attitude so drastically and I hope you have a good explanation for changing my son's mind about an investment banker."

"Sir, you got it all wrong. Scott wants to travel the world for a couple of years, and then he's planning to get his degree. He told me the navy had offered him a way to travel, and that they would also help him pay for his education. When you told me they had a buddy program and that we could do our time together, it sounded great. I figured Mr. Peterson had explained everything to you.

CHAPTER VI

Spokane

I would have never agreed to joining the navy early if I thought that you had changed your mind about him joining the navy."

Steve's entire complexion changed as he grinned. "Thank you for being honest. I did speak to Mr. Peterson already explained everything. However, I feel better hearing it from you." Then he griped my hand tightly and said, "Please keep an eye on him so he doesn't get in any trouble. Now, that I know the whole story, it is little easier to understand.

Did he tell you where he is planning to go to school?"

"Sir, all I know is he has already checked out some courses at the Washington State University."

When Scott came down the stairs, he saw us talking in the den he poked his head into the den, he looked worried. He knew his dad rarely allowed people into his den.

"What are you two talking about? Dad, I hope you have not asked George to talk me out of joining the navy. It's a little bit too late for that."

Steve smiled as he stood up and whispered to me, "Remember, George, I'm counting on you to make sure that my son does not become a stranger." Then he went over to Scott and gave him a long hug. "Take care of yourself, son."

Then we walked out of the den and made our way to the car. Scott smiled at me. "I don't know what you said to my dad. Whatever it was, it worked. That was the happiest I have seen him in months."

I shook my head. All I knew was that we were finally on our way to Spokane to be enlisted.

When the chief saw us coming, he quickly opened the door. "Scott, you can get in the front. And, George, you can get in the back with James and John."

I was so glad Scott's house was our final stop.

As soon as we hit the freeway, James and John started asking Scott all kinds of questions.

"Why did you join the navy? How did you and this meathead become such good friends? What about your parents, how did they take it when they found out you joined the navy?"

Scott just was lapping up all the attention.

Finally, I could get some rest as I blanked out until we arrived at the recruitment center. I vaguely remember hearing James and John start telling Scott a few things about their own history. That's when he found out James was going to be a mechanical engineer and John wanted to be a cook.

When we reached Spokane, the chief pulled the car in front of our hotel and stopped the car. The he told everyone to get out of the car except me. "Remember, loose lips sink ships. You got to keep Scott out of the loop about your secret assignment, because if he does, it would be a disaster."

What was the chief talking about? I stepped out of the car and was shocked. No one except the immediate team was supposed to know about the mission.

Scott looked at me and jokingly said, "What was that all about? It seems like they put you in charge already and we haven't even enlisted yet."

I just glared at Scott and handed James and John their key cards.

"Well, guys, it looks like they gave us two separate rooms. Chief said to let everyone know to be ready at six sharp tomorrow morning. He said if you change your mind about enlisting, tonight will be your last chance to back out. He wanted me to ensure that everyone rests well tonight, because tomorrow is going to be a busy day. After our physical and induction ceremony, we will be catching a bus to Recruit Training Command at Great Lakes."

John looked me like I was crazy, and said, "Catch you dudes in the morning. I got some partying to do before those goons induct me into the navy tomorrow."

"Ditto that, Johnny Boy, you mind if I tag along?" James said with a big smile.

"Sure, thing man, but I don't know about them other two so-called sailors."

Suddenly James laughed. "Hey, mommy's boy, you think you can hang with some real sailors, or you are going to stay with your goofy friend Scott?"

I shook my head. "Didn't you hear what the chief said?"

John could not hold back his disappointment as he snarled me, "Roger that, George, but we don't take orders from you or any other goon yet. We are still free men until we get on the bus to Great Lakes Training Center. We have the right to party hardy. I just hope you and nerd boy get plenty of rest. Don't want you failing the eye exam in the morning because you stayed up to late playing video games."

"Well, John," I said, "I see why they didn't want you to lead our unit, 'cause all you can think about is yourself. I sure hope that changes once we get to our first duty station."

John snarled, "Guess it's true what they said about you. They said you were strictly by the books."

Then James decided to put his two cents in. "Refreshing to see someone can hardly wait to get to work. Lighten up, Johnny boy, you gotta give the new guy a little breathing room. He'll come around." James looked at me. "You'd better dump Scott, because he is going to ruin us all."

I looked at both men like they had gone insane. If these two jokers don't get themselves under control, they would destroy our entire mission.

My brain felt like it was on fire as I slowly walked back to my room. James and John's conversation was ringing in my brain. What had I gotten himself into? How could I entrust my life to two strangers who had total disregard for authority?

When James made his statement, I began to wonder how much these two pranksters knew about the PTF. Then I focused back on the conversations as he was pleading with me and John not to let things get out of hand.

John looked at me and threw his hands up in the air. "It ain't worth it, man. We can deal with it later. Let's hit the road, James. Time to enjoy our last night of freedom. Just let the nerd boys play their games. It ain't worth the trouble." Then John looked at me and said, "we'll see you in the morning" and they took off toward their room to take their showers.

I was glad that Scott still seemed oblivious to us being part of the PTF. However, on the way to our room, I was going crazy as the anger began festering inside my brain. How could those two jerks nearly blow the mission. The chief told them to take it easy on Scott. Yet, once the chief left it felt like they were out of control. It made me feel like I had made the wrong decision to join the navy and I should have just stayed home and went to college.

However, the anger was so strong, and I just wanted to punch someone. Instead of punching anyone, I turned around and shook the ladder to the stairwell leading to my room.

When I shook the stairwell, Scott nearly fell. "Lighten up, George," he yelled. "You gotta cut the new guys a little slack. I can tell from their actions that they come from a different lifestyle than us. Just give it time, they'll come around."

"Don't be too sure about that, Scott. If those jokers don't get themselves under control, they could ruin everything for us."

"What are you talking about, George? You been acting strange ever since we left home. Is there something you want to tell me? Because you know, whatever is bugging you, we can work it out just like we always have, you me against the world," Scott said as he threw his hand up in the air and high-fived me.

"You're right, Scott. Just give me a minute to apologize to them two goons. I'll be right back."

Scott looked at me strangely as I turned around and made my way toward James and John's room. He was beginning to worry about me. As he turned around and went to our room, he was desperately hoping that I would not do anything crazy. He felt like I was losing my grip on reality. He had never seen me try so hard to have a good relationship with anyone before. Scott was wondering why it was important for his best friend to have a good relationship with a couple of goons.

Scott got impatient waiting for me, and he decided to take matters into his own hand as he followed me to James and John's room to make sure that I didn't make a fool of myself. Because he had a strange feeling about my two cohorts. We had always stuck together through thick and thin. It was his duty as my friend to back me up by running interference to ensure that I didn't get too mad and destroy everything we had worked so hard for. Scott's mind was made up. He was going to break through the rough exterior of James and John and bring them into our fold.

When I finally reached their room, I banged on the door with all my might. I was losing my mind and it seem like nothing mattered anymore. I could not understand why John was trying to undermine me.

As soon as James opened the door, I let him have a piece of my mind. "You know I can't tell Scott about the PTF, and I gotta keep things under control. Johnny boy seems just a little too wild for me right now. I am begging you to back off my friend before I have a meltdown and we all get sent home."

When I looked up, I realized I was screaming at the wrong person. I dropped my head and started to freak out. "I'm so sorry, James, I thought you were John, and I nearly blew our cover again. I ought to call the chief and tell him to forget it. Surely, we ain't going to make it as a team."

Then John stepped out into the light and shook me. "George, you can't do that. This is my last chance. I can't go back to the cell they had me locked up in. I know I may get a little crazy at times, but the PTF is my only hope to pick up the pieces. Please don't bail on me now! Please don't give up on this team! I'll get better, I promise."

Then James stared me straight in the eyes and said, "It's cool, George. I know it's kind of a new thing for you. Try to lighten up a little. John is just as valuable to the team as you. We are like the Three Musketeers, and if one goes down, we all go down."

I just stood still for a moment. It was like I couldn't move.

I was about to say something when Scott suddenly appeared. "Hey, what you doing? Do you think we can have a little fun before tomorrow? I just rented Madden. I thought we could have a little tournament to help us all relax a little. I replied. "Sure thing, Scott. Let's get back to the room. I'm ready to wipe you out again."

"I know the two of you got other plans. However, I could use a partner to take George down. I haven't beaten him in a game of Madden in the last six months. I thought one you might have some type of strategy to help me take him down."

John reached out and shook Scott's hand. "I am sorry for insulting you earlier. You are a cool, but as I stated before, I'm more of the partying type. I haven't played a video game in several years, and I would just keep you from enjoying your last night of freedom." Then he looked at me. "Are we cool now? I hope we can still work together. It would be a shame not to be working with two brilliant men like you and your friend Scott."

Scott smiled. "George, they are not as bad as you thought. I just hope this doesn't change your mind about tomorrow."

I looked at Scott. "Are you crazy? You know I can get a little upset at times, but once I make up my mind there is no turning back. Let's get back to the room. I think I'm ready to whoop your behind one more time before we go to boot camp."

"Don't think I am going let you slide for trying to get James and John to help you out."

Then we both burst out laughing.

"Why don't you go order the pizza? I'm right behind you."

Scott whistled as he raced to the room to order some pizza.

Once Scott had disappeared, the door flew open and nearly hit me in the back of my head as James and John stood there staring at me, shaking their heads. "That's right. We will catch up with you and your nerdy friend tomorrow. Just remember, after we enlist tomorrow, you'd better be prepared to rock and roll. There ain't going to be no more games, and we are going to be your backup to make sure you don't wind up in the hurt locker."

I looked at them both. "This won't happen again. Starting tomorrow I will have my act together. I appreciate both of you for your understanding tonight. I just hope that we haven't bitten off more than we can chew. Once again," I repeated myself, "are we cool? I'm sorry I let things get out hand. You need to be ready 06:00."

I was thankful that James stepped in because if he hadn't, we might have blown our cover. James shook his head. "We will be there, just go enjoy the rest of your evening." Then he closed the door.

"Then," I said to myself, *I'm on my own.* That's when I knew James and John were not coming to bail me out and I would have to endure playing another game of Madden with Scott.

When Scott saw me coming up the stairs, he raced out of the room and grabbed me. "You need to get some food and relax."

Watching Scott plop down on the side of the bed and sit by the TV with the remote control in his hand, I nearly burst out laughing, "You're right, Scott. I gotta learn how to control my temper. I can't go off half-cocked anymore. Things are not always as bad as they seem."

Scott had his game face on, and he retorted, "I don't care about all that right now. Pick a team so I can finally give you the whooping you deserve."

Scott was hoping that all this craziness would give him an extra edge. It had been a while since he'd beaten the socks off me. Tonight, he had a feeling that he would break his streak of losses.

Scott and I sat in front of the TV playing Madden for the next few hours, battling back and forth as the game went into triple overtime. On the final play of the game, I tricked Scott into thinking I was going to pass the ball. However, I called an end around and my guy ran fifty yards for a touchdown

Scott threw his controller on the floor and nearly broke out into tears. "It doesn't matter how upset you get; you always wind up getting lucky. There is no way you should have beat me tonight. Somehow you pulled it off."

Then I smiled at Scott and jumped on my bed. "It's time to hit the hay, see you in the morning."

Life seemed great. Scott was still my best friend. The only thing that bothered me was that he was not going to be a part of my team. Somehow, I had to convince the commander that Scott was fit for the team. I felt like the NSA was not giving Scott a fair chance. Once the commander saw how well Scott and I worked together, I felt like he would reconsider Scott as an official team member. Most of all, the commander did not seem to understand that Scott was the best person to be my backup.

The next morning at six sharp, everyone was waiting for Chief Escondido to take us to the recruiting station. When he did not show up, I called the recruiter's office to find out what was going on. A few minutes later, Alice came spinning around the corner in a Ford van. "Sorry, boys, Master Sargent got called away on a special assignment. He told me to pick you up this morning. I got stuck in traffic."

We immediately jumped into the van and Alice floored it. When she pushed the accelerator, the van sounded like it was gasping for breath as it slowly began to pick up speed, and we made our way through the traffic to the recruitment center. We were about six blocks away when Alice stomped on the brakes and ordered us to get out of the van. "There's too much traffic, so this is the end of the line. Get used to it, boys," Alice chuckled. "When duty calls, you got to go wherever they send you at a moment's notice."

Then Alice tossed us our gear and mumbled, "Chief told me to wish everyone good luck and to let him know when you finish boot camp. But right now, I suggest you double time it because you only got about ten minutes to get to the third floor for your physical and induction ceremony. And you'd better not be late, 'cause I don't want to hear the chief yelling when he finds out you had to wait an extra day to enlist."

John said, "What is wrong with these crazy people? We have not even enlisted yet and they are already barking out orders."

"Look, guys, we can cry about it, or we can just move our behinds. I don't know about you, I ain't planning to wait for an extra day for anyone."

Somehow, I managed to outrun everyone else, and I reached the third floor first. The elevator opened. I looked at the few recruits who were signing in and began to panic.

When the officer at the desk saw me, she laughed. "Son, you're fine but you'd better get yourself in line, because I don't have patience for slackers. I am sure your friends can catch up with you next week."

"Sorry, ma'am," I replied, "I can't go through unless my friends are with me."

The officer just looked at me and said, "Have it your way, son. But you only have three more minutes before I lock the door, and then you will have to wait until next week."

"I'll be back, ma'am." Then I turned around. I knew I had to get the other guys before they shut the door, so I went back to the main lobby. When the elevator door opened, James and John quickly stepped inside. "Are we too late?"

When I saw that Scott was just entering the building, I looked at James and John. "Boys, can you help him out? 'Cause unless we all make it on time none of us make it on time."

James looked at me. "Dude, you must be crazy."

"James, we only have a couple of minutes left, and if we all don't show up our cover will be blown."

James just sneered at me and was about to disobey my order when John shoved him. "James, the man is right. So, get the lead out of your ears and let's help Scott before we all go down in flames."

James and John carried Scott into the elevator.

"I just hope we make it. The last few recruits were entering the center and the chief in charge told me she wasn't going to wait on anyone. Alice said it would be one day if we were late. The chief told one of the recruits that once they shut the door to the center it was being relocated to another floor, and they wouldn't be able to hold any more induction ceremonies for at least a week."

John looked at me. "I hope you're happy. Dude weighs like three hundred pounds, and if we don't make it, it will be his fault."

James chimed in, "He's right, boss."

"You know the rules, John, we can't leave any man behind." I looked at James. "Dude, what's the matter with you? Remember, loose lips sink ships."

He looked at me. "What are you talking about? You weren't going to let these two goons convince you to leave me, were you?"

"You must be delirious. If it hadn't been for these two goons you'd still be waiting on the elevator. You owe them an apology."

Scott wiped the sweet off his face and weakly said, "Sorry, guys. Thanks for your help." Then he turned to me. "George, I'm beginning to wonder if this idea of us joining the navy together is really going to work out, because if you can defend these goons so quickly without even considering how I feel, I think you owe me an explanation."

"Scott, snap out of it. We can't let them see we aren't in shape, or they may not let us through door. As far as James and John go, Scott, we will have time to talk to about them on the way to boot camp. Just remember, it's you and me against the world."

When Scott heard me, he straightened and smiled. "That's more like the George I know."

The first thing I noticed when the elevator door opened was that it looked like the last recruit was walking through the door. The door was slowly closing. However, James managed to race over to the door and prop it open with his knee.

When the chief at the desk saw James blocking the door, she stood up. "Son, what is wrong with you? Don't you know how to tell time? I'm sure that everyone was supposed to be through that door before 7:00 AM."

"Yes, ma'am." James said, "However, if you look at the clock, it is only 6:59 AM. We have one more minute until you shut the door."

As James talked to the chief, we all rushed through the door. The chief laughed. "Glad to see you made it, boys. The three of you had better be glad your friend with the ugly mug went back for you. Most people would have left you behind.

That's the spirit we instill in the navy, and it is an honor for me to ensure that your process today goes off without any hitches. If anyone gives you trouble, you tell them to see me. It was nothing short of a miracle, but you boys made it and you're on way to becoming sailors."

Then she locked the door and mumbled, "I just want to make sure no more of you morons try to slip in on my watch.

You lazy morons need to get your behinds over to the desk and sign my log before I send you back home to Mommy. Make sure you sign in at 7:00 a.m. Now you'd better run down the hall for processing.

When we reached the auditorium, Senior Chief Fristoe had already started his induction speech. When he saw us slip in, he stopped mid speech.

"Who let these boys in? You know I hate repeating myself?"

Then the chief came on stage and whispered something in his ear, and he calmed down. Next thing I knew, we were all being ushered into another room to fill out some paperwork. However, the senior chief put his arm around me and pulled me to the side.

"Pleasure to meet you George. They told me you were one of the top naval candidates. However, if you ever bring your men in late again, I will not hesitate to report you directly to the commander. You better be glad the chief knew who you were because I run a tight ship here and I am not afraid to make you an example. Is that understood?"

"Yes, sir," I said smartly.

"Good, now you just make sure you keep your team in order, because you got a lot of people watching and you just used one of your get-out-of-jail-free cards. I don't know how many more you got."

Then the senior chief turned around and left the room.

After filling out our paperwork, we had our final physical. After our physical, we went to the cafeteria and had lunch.

When Scott saw me, he shoved his way across the cafeteria.

"Sorry for earlier, George, I go a little overexcited. But when are you going to tell me what's up with them two strange dudes?"

I looked at Scott. "I don't know what you are talking about. I was just trying to be friendly, and they did help us make it through the door. And I would rather have them as my friend than my enemy."

Scott laughed, and we started talking about the good old days. How many times had our friendship been pushed to the limits, but we always survived? Scott seemed so happy that he's finally free from his dad's control. All I could do was smile inside as I slowly began to feel like I did make the right choice. Finally, around 1500 hours, we held up our hands for the final ceremony before we were officially inducted into the navy.

The strangest part of the entire process was that after I finished boot camp, I would have to go through the same process again when I joined the NSA. Going to Great Lakes Training Center was the beginning of my journey.

One boot camp for the navy and then a second for the NSA. However, only me, James, and John knew our true destination. I felt sorry for Scott because they had promised that we would be stationed together, and I knew that was the only reason Scott had joined the navy.

CHAPTER VII

Enlistment

After the enlistment ceremony, James, John, and I met secretly with Alice for further orders. Following the meeting, Scott saw me in the hallway and came over to me and slapped me on the back.

"George, where did you disappear to? I can't believe it's finally happening; we are getting ready to sail the seven seas. I thought it was just my imagination at first, but after being sworn in, I realized we are on our way to freedom."

All I could do was just stare blankly at Scott and nod my head as we made our way to our transport, which would take us to the airport. Scott poked me. "What's the matter with you? Cat got your tongue. You have been different since you met them two strangers, James, and John. They sure seem like they were from another planet. They didn't even have the decency to play some Madden with us."

When Scott finished trying to cheer me up, James and John appeared behind us and started messing with Scott's mind.

"My friends, are you two jokers ready for boot camp? You do know the first thing to go is your hair, and I'm guessing you ain't had a haircut in a while," James said as he looked at me and laughed. "The two of you should have come with us last night. We found a nice, sweet-looking barber who chopped our hair off. Then she gave me her address and she invited us to her party.

She told us to bring all our friends. We were going to bring you along, but when we saw the two of you were totally freaking out over playing Madden Football, we decided to roll without you. When we got to the party, our barber was disappointed that the two of you did not show up. She assured us we would have a wonderful time without you. Matter of fact, I feel great this morning. Plus, I got her number, so after boot camp we can hook up," James said sarcastically.

Then John butted in, "I don't understand you two guys. I would have thought you two were ready to mix it up, because we are going to be in Great Lakes Training Center for the next three months doing some hard labor."

Scott could not take it anymore, and he abruptly cut John off. "You two dudes are crazy. I am honored to be going to boot camp. This is my life you are talking about, and I don't have time to waste partying and playing around like a lunatic. I want to be a part of something bigger than me, and if I hang around with you two goons my life will be destroyed. Don't you realize that we will soon be sailing the seven seas and be visiting ports we never even dreamed of? And I am not going to throw away my chance for happiness."

"Good for you, Scott," John said, "I'm glad to see someone with goals in their life. What you are misinterpreting is that you will be sailing the seas and basking on beaches all over the world. The word I heard is that once you get on a ship, you are lucky if you see land once every couple of months. And when you do see land, you only have a few days to relax before you are back sailing the seas for another couple of months. You need your head examined if you believe everything Chief Escondido told you. As the saying goes, NAVY means 'Never Again Volunteer Yourself,' because you will learn how to work all night long, and you will get used to seeing the steel decks for months at a time.

If you are lucky, you might have a few nice-looking 'Waves' on your ship. But you'd better watch out, 'cause most of the Waves have one thing in mind, and that is to make your life miserable. Because they want to sit in the captain's seat, and if you ain't got any bars on your collar, you might as well forget about having any fun."

Before James could open his mouth and make the situation worse., I realized I had to take charge knowing I could not allow his insubordination to ruin our cover story. So, I jumped up in James's face and angrily spit at him, "if you don't back-off I'll make sure you are removed and checked out of the navy before you even get started. Because you two lunatics have completely lost your mind? Remember Scott is part of our cover and regardless of your opinion you need to back-off and leave my Scott alone. Or I'll be forced to call the OIC. I'm sure he wouldn't mind getting rid of the trash before boot camp.

When John saw I was serious, he looked at me and Scott. "Sorry, I did not know I was overstepping my bounds. Someday we'll be able to make it up to you."

James just stood there like a crazy man and shook his head in agreement. "We just thought we might be able to enlighten your friend to the reality of what is about to happen once we get to Great Lakes Training Center. But you already got it covered, boss man. Just remember, if you need anything, we will be in the back of the line waiting to catch you and your friend when life's reality truly hits the fan."

Once James and John disappeared, Scott turned to me. "Thanks, George, I appreciate you looking out for me. But if you continue to hang around them two goons, you and I are through. Don't worry about me anymore, George, I can take care of myself. I know you think I am unstable at times, but this is one decision that I am sure off." Then he lightly shoved me away. "Please just buzz off and let me find a seat by myself to cool off. I guess we can talk later at boot camp."

Scott's reaction stunned me, and my new partners had left me high and dry. Once again, I was seriously beginning to think I might have made the wrong decision. I drifted around and finally found an empty seat at the back of the bus.

Meanwhile, George's Dad Toby set-up a meeting with the

Commandant of the Marine Corp. General Armstrong while he was visiting Fort Madigan. The purpose of the meeting was to have George transferred to his old army unit at Fort Madigan.

When the general met with Toby, he was able to convince him George's enlistment in the navy was more important.

"Toby, your son will hate you for the rest of his life if he finds out you interfered with his mission."

The more the general talked the angrier Toby got. Finally, he threw up his hands and agreed to stay out of it. However, he stipulated that if anything happened to George during his enlistment, he would hold the general responsible. He told him he would have no mercy and would come after the navy full throttle.

The general laughed as he talked to Toby. "Now, I know why you never made rank, because in my book you were one of the most qualified sergeants that I served with in Afghanistan. If it had not been for you, I would have never made it out of the desert alive. I told all my superior officers about you and tried to get you promoted to warrant officer, but they told me you turned down the job because you were getting out after your final tour in Afghanistan.

"Toby, there were many people who wanted you to continue your career, and I even put in word for you to my superior officer. However, when they told me you turned down the job, I was stunned. I blamed myself for you not accepting your commission. I had worked so hard to show my appreciation to you for saving my life, and you were one of the few men I knew I could trust. I was angry you bailed on me, giving up everything because you didn't want to do another tour in Afghanistan or Iraq. Whether you knew it or not, there were several high-ranking officers that blamed me for you not re-enlisting.

"I regretted not doing more, and it took years until I felt like I was free from the burden of ever seeing your ugly mug again. Then several months ago, I was asked to put together a special unit.

When I looked over all the current active-duty personnel, I came up one man short for the assignment. That's when I considered calling you back to duty for this new operation we were about to start.

"I realized you have been out of the service for quite some time now, and I wasn't certain if you would accept the position. You're still a young man, and I was positive you were still in shape. Thus, against my better judgment, I submitted your name. I was told they would give you a meritorious promotion to chief warrant officer.

"I started to pat myself on the back. I felt like you were finally getting a fair chance." Then he paused for a moment. "I laughed to myself, because if you would have accepted your commission back in Afghanistan, you would have been in my position. Everything was looking promising, and I hoped that I would be able to repay you for saving my life.

"It would be a terrific way for us rekindle our old relationship. And everything was in the final stages when I asked my sectary to get your files for my final review. After reviewing your records, I thought I would be ready to present my plan to the joint chiefs of staff, and you would become an officer in the army.

"While I was reviewing your files, I stumbled upon a footnote in your records regarding Frank Wildwood. I immediately asked my sectary to bring me the file regarding Frank Wildwood. Where I learned about Frank's death in Afghanistan. I had forgotten you assaulted General Starlow and blamed him for Frank's death. The army made you retire after you assaulted General Starlow. Many of my fellow officers wanted to press charges and throw you to wolves. General Starlow refused to press charges.

He stated that it was all a misunderstanding, and if you retired, he would have your records regarding the incident be marked as top secret and that you would be able to retire with your head held up high. But if you ever breathe a word of what took place during the war, he will make sure you were locked up in prison for life.

"For years I was in the dark about why you did not accept your commission. It was a relief when I understood why you didn't accept your commission. After finding out about Frank's death, I did a little research of my own. Come to find out it was General Starlow's fault that Frank was murdered. It seems like Frank had uncovered an illegal operation the general was controlling. General Starlow used your attack on him to deflect his guilt.

"I never thought that I would find out the circumstances surrounding Frank's death. When I finally understood why you had to retire, it broke my heart." The general turned his head as he didn't want my father to see the anguish he was in, and he continued. "Toby, we lost a lot of good people during the war. I am so sorry I didn't clear this issue up a long time ago.

When I presented my plan to the CNO to make you a part of my new unit, he felt like we should include a letter that would absolve you of all guilt regarding your attack on General Starlow, and retroactively grant you your commission. Regardless of what you decide, you will be given back pay since the time of your retirement.

"Toby, I hope you consider this new assignment, but if you don't, I understand. I just wanted to let you know personally that neither you nor Frank are forgotten. Toby, do you see the picture of our old unit on my desk?" he said as he pointed to the picture on the corner of his desk. "I keep it there to always remind me of what it was like to serve with such great men."

Then the general took the picture of their old unit from his desk and placed it in Toby's hand. "I know you think you are too old to make a return to your former duties, but before you completely disannul the request and make any rash decisions, I want you to look at this picture and tell me what you see. I see a group of the bravest men I know ready to take on the world. I am asking you, are you ready to stand tall again and defend your country with the same honor and integrity that you had back then?"

Toby sat down and started weeping when he saw the picture of his old unit. "Sir, I don't want you thinking that your gesture is not appreciated.

You must know that I have been out of the army far too long, and I am not fit for the assignment. Therefore, I regretfully must turn down your request to return to active duty." Then he stood up and wiped the tears from his face. "However, I will always be in your debt, my friend, and I will be able to sleep peacefully tonight knowing that General Starlow was caught and prosecuted."

Toby's emotions got the best of him. "Sir, I know things have changed since we served together. I am sure you remember the troubles we had when we came back from the war. You know the burden of the secrets we hold. I just don't want my son to suffer like we did. I want to make sure that he is not tied up in an operation that would endanger his life. I don't care about the changes, and I don't care if he is in the navy, army, or air force. My only concern is that my son is going to be safe.

Then he slammed his fist on the general's desk. The force of his fist hitting the general's desk echoed throughout the building. Seconds later, a red light started flashing and Toby heard "Code one, secure the badger." And before he even had time to take his hand off the general's desk, several MPs were standing in the middle of the general's doorway.

"Sir, I suggest you back away from the general's desk and put your hands in the air," an MP stated as he forcefully shoved him into the chair next to the general's desk and pulled out his gun and his handcuffs, ready to take Toby into custody.

Then he turned to one of the other MPs. "Sammy, you guard the door and shoot him if he moves." Then the senior MP slowly moved toward Toby, who had his hands in the air.

General Armstrong said, "Solider, stand down. I will take it from here. You can guard my office until I am done. It was just an accident. I'm fine."

"Sir, yes, sir," the MP shouted as he ordered Sammy to move to the end of the hallway until further notice.

General Armstrong looked at the MP as he stood in the doorway. "Son, I will be fine. Now just close the door and wait outside until I finish my business with my friend."

"Respectfully, sir, I cannot leave my post until your friend is either in custody or walks out on his own free will. I have been ordered to protect you from all harm."

When the general saw that the MP would not leave his post, he picked up the phone and called the head of security. "This is General Armstrong. I'm secure, call off the MPs."

Immediately after the general hung up, a green light started flashing. "The badger is safe. All MPs return to your stations."

The MP stood at attention, saluted the general, and stood by the door as he ordered Sammy go back to his original post before the incident.

He refused to shut the door because he still did not feel like the general was safe. General Armstrong looked at the MP as he stood in the doorway. "Son, I will be fine. Please close the door and wait outside until I finish my business with my friend."

"Sir, yes, sir," he hollered as he quietly shut the door.

"Toby," he continued, "you know I will always have your back. And as far as this business with your son and his best friend Scott enlisting in the navy, I cannot change anything." As he put his arm around Toby's shoulder he said, "You must remember when we were young and we thought we could take on the world, and we thought we could bring honor back to a wounded nation.

Toby, I am telling you when your son team succeeds, the world will be a much safer place. He will restore our nations honor and help bring peace to the world. I don't have to tell you the risk involved. But" the general said, "That is why it is an honor to make sure your son is taken care of. However, there is one condition. You need to cut George some slack about joining the navy.

"To ease you mind I am about to tell is above your pay grade. I received a call from my friend Captain Silverton. He told me they had found the final piece to the puzzle of who could help get the peace initiative off the ground."

"Captain Silverton let me know that he was the perfect candidate to run the PTF, and all we had to do was make sure he and his friend stayed together until after boot camp. He explained to me that he had already run everything up the chain of command."

"When I asked him who was the candidate, he hesitated for a moment before he told me it was George Cantwell. I choked, and I did my best to keep anyone from suspecting that George was your son."

"After receiving the call from Captain Silverton, all the old memories started flooding back, and I dreaded the moment you would come walking through my door and ask me to change George's mind regarding his enlistment in the navy."

I have been ordered to tell you to back down. The navy needs your son. You should know that both Captain Silverton and Commander Johnstone personally handpicked your son to lead a secret unit known as the PTF. I cannot tell them they have made the wrong choice. Their recommendation and the captains explicit explanation about George's enlistment in the navy were without reproach.

"Captain Silverton and Commander Johnstone are two of the most decorated officers in the navy, and after their next tour the captain will become the new CNO, and the commander will be promoted to captain and take commander of Georges Ship the *USS Bunker Hill*. They both firmly believe your son is going to be one of the nation's greatest military leaders. When they chose your son for his position, to ensure everyone understood that they were serious about George's abilities as leader they put their careers on the line. That is how strongly he felt about your son's capabilities."

"After reviewing your son's test scores, which were off the chart, I agreed with Captain Silverton, your son is going to be one of our nation most trusted assets once he completes his training. While you are not able to join my special task force, I am glad that your son will be under my wing.

The reason I was so remorseful was because I knew it would be impossible for you to forget the past. Yet I knew that would be too much to ask for, so I was expecting your call because I knew that your son enlisting with his best friend Scott brought back a lot of bad memories about your best friend Frank Wildwood.

"It was hard for me to keep quiet, but I knew if anyone found out about your son they would know about our relationship. That's why they have put pressure on me to have you silenced about what happened years ago in the desert.

Toby, you saved my life and the lives of countless others, and then you just dropped out of sight. You refused your commission and you let us all hang out to dry. And everyone felt like you were disloyal to our country because you didn't want to fight anymore.

However, I straightened them all out. They were not the ones who had to fight in the desert. They did not understand how it felt to be laughed at, scoffed at, and later forgotten; their service to a nation that did not understand why we were at war.

"The rest of the nation wanted to put it all behind us, but we were a constant reminder of a failed policy. Most of our friends were either killed in battle or left to suffer from the scars of war. You and I were luckier than most and were able to continue with our lives. Not a day goes by without me remembering and honoring our friends' valor.

Toby, I am telling you your son has already made a difference. I don't have to tell you the risk involved. But you know that I will do everything in my power to make sure he is safe from harm.

"I have already developed a plan to ensure your son will be safe. Now you are standing here in my office with a reasonable request from a father who has his son's best interest at heart. I must tell you with a heavy heart that your son's enlistment in the navy is out of my hands, and I cannot undo what has been done.

"Toby, your secret is safe with me. And I can assure you that your son is safe. He is about to become one of our nation's top assets. He will be the leader that you were never given the opportunity to be, as he leads a top-secret unit called the PTF.

Toby, you think what we did during our time in Afghanistan is a secret. I am telling you that whatever your son is involved in goes far beyond what we did. Your son is protected at the highest levels of the government, and if his secret gets out before the proper time, our whole operation will be blown.

"You cannot tell anyone, including George, that you are aware that he is going to part of the PTF. I certain that with George, the plan for the PTF has only grown stronger. Once I found out the extent of your son's knowledge and his linage I was honored that he decided to join the navy and serve his country.

Not only will he have the protection that I have already set up, but he will be protected at the highest level for national security And after we are done with our conversation today, I will contact Captain Silverton to ensure he doubles your son's security at boot camp.

"Since I have made you fully aware of the circumstances regarding your son's enlistment, I am sure you understand what would become of your son if word of the NSA's secret task force gets out before the proper time. He would be toast! My friend, this is way beyond both of our pay grades.

The navy needs your son I'll speak to Captain Silverton, and he will order Commander Johnstone, who is the commanding officer at the base in Recruit Training Command at Great Lakes, to place him in Master Chief Walters' squad. Master Chief Walters served with me during the war, and he is the top naval instructor currently in Recruit Training Command at Great Lakes.

"You must be ready for me to call you back to duty if things get out of hand. We have also been keeping watch on Steve and Scott. Thus, if anything happens to Steve or Scott, I will need to put you and your family in our secret location for your protection. If that happens, you will have no contact with the outside world, and you will automatically be reenlisted as part of the base command structure."

Then the general smiled. "Now I am trusting you to keep our secret. Toby, the only reason I divulged this information is I wanted your mind to be at ease. However, our conversation must remain between you and me.

That is why I turned off my recorder to ensure our conversation was private. Toby, that is as far as I can go. Your son's assignment after boot camp is top secret.

Then he leaned over and whispered, "Toby, I am about to turn my recorder back on. "You know the drill. If I don't turn my recorder back on soon, we will both be in hot water. I will keep you informed about your son's progress, but it must remain between us. Because if you or anyone else disrupts his training, his life will be in jeopardy.

Toby after our meeting today, you cannot contact me anymore regarding your son's enlistment. If there is any additional information you need to know, I will send it to you via my private courier."

He sat silently for a minute before he looked at the general and replied, "You have my word that I will not bother you or anyone else regarding my son. However, if you or anyone puts my son's life in danger, they will regret their actions. Because if I ever tell the world what really happened during the war, everyone involved will be hung out to dry. The reason I have kept our relationship a secret for such a long time is that I am a soldier, not a traitor. I know if our relationship were to be brought to the forefront there would be too many questions that would have to be answered.

For now, our secret is safe, but you had better pray that no one puts two and two together and makes our relationship public. Trying to explain why my son enlisted in the navy would be the least of your problems. I reiterate, if anything happens to my son that endangers his life, our secret will become public."

Then the general reached across his desk to turn the tape recorder back on, "Toby all you need to do is follow my lead when I turn my tape recorder back on." Then the general turned his recorder back on as he thanked Toby. "I appreciate your concerns, Toby. You must understand that I am the commandant of the Marine Corps, and I cannot allow any parent to dictate how we train our recruits. I'm sorry for being so abrupt. I'm going to have to transfer your request to the personnel department. his sounds like an issue that they can oversee. Must I remind you of the oath you took when you joined the army. And if you want everything to remain calm, you need to believe me when I tell you not worry about your son's naval career. He will be compensated for his service.

CHAPTER VIII

General Armstrong

"Your son will officially be a sailor in twelve weeks. If you need any further assistance, I would be breaking protocol and giving you classified information that is above your pay grade."

It was your son's choice to join the navy, and I cannot change the-'s enlistment in the navy, and you have my word of honor, my commitment to make sure that your son is safe."

"Before you leave, I hope that we have a clear understanding. I am asking you a favor; can I count on your support?"

Toby quickly said, "Sir, yes, sir. Whatever you need from me or my son, I will support 100 percent." Then Toby stood and saluted General Armstrong before he left his office. While he was not able to get George out of the navy he was satisfied with his meeting with General Armstrong.

The only thing Toby had left to do was to go home and explain to his wife that while George was still in the navy he would be protected, and she needed to trust the process. While they may not agree with Georges choice the best thing they could do was love and support him. While he was talking to his wife Lucy, he asked her to remember he had a big fight with his dad, and it was years before they talked again. He said hopefully they had learned from the incident and would not drive George away.

Toby knew it would not be easy, but they had to do their best to support him because he did not want to lose his relationship with his son like he had lost his relationship with his father for twenty years.

He still remembered how his father told him he regretted being so harsh on him when he joined the army. And he told him that if he ever has children that he should let them live their lives and be there to support them through the good times and the tough times.

The next morning at 3:00 A.M. we finally we arrived in Recruit Training Command at Great Lakes. I went back to the front of the bust to see if Scott had calmed down.

It was like he had lost his mind. When I tapped him on the shoulder and looked in his eyes. He quickly brushed me off. I could tell something had happened to him.

"George, you ain't nothing but a chump. Ever since we left home, you have been hanging around with them two goons. I thought this was supposed to be our time to bond. I didn't expect you to turn on me so quickly."

"Scott, what are you squealing about? I stayed with you at the hotel. We had some pizza, played a few games of Madden, and watched a movie. I hardly even know those two goons. You know you are my best friend."

Scott just kept looking at me strangely. "If we are such good friends, how come you left me in the front with this buffoon Ricky? He's got to be the craziest person I ever met. Just when I thought I was over his craziness, he started letting out some ghastly sounds. I thought the engine was about to explode. I haven't slept all night, and I am going to have to take a long shower just get his stench from this fools deadly gas attack."

Ricky stood up. "Are you talking about me? You know, you are a moron, and you ain't got no room to talk. All you did was cry like a little baby all night. I would say *boy*, but them sounds you was making were like some little baby girl and that is just a condensed version of the story.

'Cause there ain't a person who should be making them kinda sounds." And suddenly I am the crazy one. Son you have insulted my integrity and now I am going to show how truly crazy I am.

Then he balled up his fist and hit Scott so hard it knocked him into the window. "I suggest you move, mama's boy, unless you want me to teach you a lesson too."

Scott looked at me" George, let me take control of the situation. You ain't got to act like my dad. I can take care of myself"

Then Ricky laughed. "You're the one this bug calls 'George.' Man, I ain't never heard someone talk about another man so much."

"Please, George, don't go crazy. I don't need a bad mark on my record. Just let the big oaf go."

Then Ricky turned around and acted like he was going to hit Scott again. "Little dude, you ain't helping any, 'cause the two of you is about to get squashed if you don't shut that trap."

Then I looked at Ricky and said, "Hey, Ricky before I get really angry are you sure you name ain't Tubby Malone."

"Ricky face turn red as his voice cracked several windows on the bus when he replied, ain't no one been crazy enough to talk to me like your friend since Jasper. You should remember Jasper. He was one of them recruiting dudes who called me a tub of lard. I showed him what a tub of lard can do, and he's still in the medical facilities in Spokane." Then he jumped up and tried to squash me.

I was too quick for him, and when he hit the floor, it gave way and his huge behind hit the pavement. Everyone immediately started laughing as I slapped him around like a basketball. The more I hit Ricky the angrier he became the force of his voice cracked several more windows and blew me into the wall.

Somehow Ricky managed to wiggle himself free and stood up as he started moving towards me, I knew I was doomed. Because if Ricky smashed me into the wall, I would not survive. Suddenly I heard two voices from behind.

"Just stay down, we got it from here."

Then James and John flattened Ricky like a pancake.

The force of Ricky weight hitting the floor caused the front tires of the bus to burst like bubbles. Then the bus began to teeter with only the middle tires remaining to hold up the bus. The scariest part of the incident was that when Ricky's head hit the floor he put a big dent in the floor as he laid motionless for several minutes. We all began to panic as we thought we might have killed him. Suddenly Ricky let out several loud groans and slowly sat up.

That's when I yelled, "You two better get lost. I can't afford you getting into trouble; I'll take the rap. I'm sure they will have a little more mercy on me."

James and John quickly disappeared into the line of recruits who were desperately trying to get off the bus. When Ricky finally opened his eyes, he shook his head and looked at me. Then he finally stood up and started to wabble towards me. It was a miracle that everyone except for me and Scott had cleared the bus.

Ricky was shaking his head. "You got a wicked hook. I never been knocked down before. You're small, but you got a wallop."

When Ricky was about to apologize to me for overreacting as he reached out his hand to shake mine. However, several MP's had entered through the back door and snuck up behind him and immediately yanked his arms behind his back and handcuffed him. Then they handcuffed me and Scott.

"All right, gentlemen, that's enough of this nonsense," the chief said. "I suggest you explain to me who caused this ruckus."

Ricky was about to say something, but before anyone could open their mouth, Scott blurted out, "It was George and those two goons he's been hanging around. Ricky and I were having a friendly conversation and they tried to separate us. I don't know what has happened to my friend, but George is jealous of my newfound friendship." Scott grabbed his left arm. "See, one of them crazy goons threw me into the window and nearly broke my arm. Sir, George, and his crazy friends provoked Ricky. They were making fun of him because of his size. I tried to call for help, but no one heard me because of all the panic."

The chief looked at Ricky. "Is that what really happened?" the chief said as he growled in Ricky's face. Ricky just looked at me and weakly nodded his head as he mumbled "sir yes, sir"

Chief Langer frowned at Scott and uncuffed him. "Scott, I suggest you just mosey along on to the clinic and get your arm looked at. Once they fix you up, you need to report to the barracks. As far as Ricky is concerned, we are going to have to take him to the office for disciplinary action. Scott don't worry about George. I will take care of this little boy personally and question him to see what happened to the two goons that helped him perpetrate this fraud."

I was utterly shocked by what happened next. After Ricky and Scott were gone, Chief Langer could hardly contain his laughter as he bent down and whispered to me, "Way to go, champ. You just fixed one of our biggest recruiting problems we have had in the past twenty years. None of us knew how we were going to handle Ricky. He's got to be one the biggest recruits we ever had come through this place, and you broke him down in less than five minutes."

I looked at the chief and said, "What just happened? I thought you were getting ready to take me to the brig." The chief snickered again. "Not me, George. The navy owes you and your friends a huge debt of gratitude. Ricky's afraid we are going kick him to the curb, so he ain't going to be any problem. Sorry about the handcuffs. I had to make it you were being disciplined.

Don't worry about Scott's lies. Everyone knows that Ricky was the one who started the fight, therefore Ricky will be locked up in the brig for a few days. As for your fate, you will have to go to the administration office to be disciplined and warned about your actions. Then we plan to send you back to join the rest of the recruits. But if I were you, I would avoid Scott because he's got it in for you."

Tears began swelling up in my eyes and as I started to have a mental breakdown. "Don't worry about me, sir. Scott deeply wounded me suddenly acting so strange toward me!" I said as I felt like I had been betrayed.

When James and John saw the tears in my eyes, John quickly jumped on the bus and began screaming, "Sir, what are our next orders? Everyone wants to get to safety. I think some of us are going to have a nervous breakdown if we don't get away from all this craziness. I thought I was joining the navy, but it looks like I have joined the WWF. Can you please help us find our barracks?"

John's diversion worked, as the chief turned his attention.

James came up behind me and smacked me in the side of my head as he whispered, "George, you need to get you act together! Dry up them tears and start acting like a real man! Remember, around here tears will get you and the rest of us in a lot of trouble."

That's when I finally understood I was not on my own. It was time for me to stand up tall and take whatever was dished out. It didn't matter who I used to be. Today was a new beginning, and I had to command the respect of my friends and foes.

By the time the chief turned back around James had disappeared back into the crowd. The chief looked at me strangely. "Son, I don't know what you are up to, but I suggest you chill out a little. I know the commanding officer is not thrilled by your action. He nearly tore my head off when he heard about the incident."

I smartly saluted the chief. "You won't have any more trouble out me. I don't need to hang around scum like Scott. I have a whole new group of friends whose got my back. I do not believe Scott's pack of lies. I beg you to forgive me for any trouble that I have caused."

The chief just smirked. "You're beginning to understand, son. However, Commander Johnstone ordered me to bring you to his office. It seems like the commander has taken a special interest in your case, and he wants to ensure this is your last incident. You'd better show him some respect because I don't want to have to explain to him how I allowed one of our most promising recruits to wash out before they even started boot camp."

When we arrived at the commander's office, I could hear Ricky being taken down the hall to the brig. "Please, don't send me back home. I'll act right, I'll watch my temper, and I'll do whatever it takes. Please don't send me back home."

"Son," the chief said, "I hope you have a good explanation for the incident with Ricky. If it were up to me, I would give you an award.

But it's not up to me. You gotta convince the commander. He will be coming around to see you after he talks to that wacko Ricky."

Now I suggest you stay silent while we wait for the commander. The less you say the better it will be for both of us. You can explain you situation to him behind closed doors. Hopefully he will see the navy owe you a debt of gratitude for taming Ricky. Then the chief looked at me and just shook his head.

I could see the worry written all over the chief face as drops of sweat from his brow were soaking the seat next to me. I wanted to tell him it was going to be all right, but it was quite frightening sitting outside the commander office not knowing what to expect next.

We were both unaware that someone informed General Armstrong about the incident with Ricky and the General had called Captain Silverton to make sure George was safe.

When Captain Silverton picked up the phone the General sounded shouted. "How could you allow George to nearly get snuffed out by Ricky. Don't you know who George's father is? He is Sergeant Toby Cantwell.

Captain jaw almost hit the ground. "Sir, I never dreamed that Sergeant Cantwell was George's father. If I am not mistaken Sargent Catwell retired after you returned from you last tour of duty. When I saw the last name I did not make the connection. And I did not realize the two of you had served together."

General Armstrong continued "We not only served together during the war, but Sargent Catwell saved my life more than once. I have known Sergeant Cantwell, for a long time. He can be a hothead. This afternoon he came into my office and demanded that I have George transferred to an army unit close to where he lives."

"I thought long and hard before I called you. and I know this conversation may be a little out of order because I am not used to being in this kind of fire. The only way I could calm my friend Sergeant Cantwell down was to assure him that George will be safe in boot camp and there would be no incidents with his son's training."

"I told him that you and Commander Johnstone had all your

ducks in a row. Thus, he gave me his word that he would drop his pursuit of trying to get George out of the navy.

I am so glad Sargent Catwell had already left my office I got the call about the incident on the bus today. My sources told me about the incident between Ricky and George, it did not sound very good. That is why I am ordering you to put him in my friend Master Chief Walters's unit, because if anything happens to George, I will hold you personally responsible. If you follow my orders and put him in Master Chief Walters's company, I know he will be safe."

"You may think I am being paranoid, but if the word about this incident with Ricky gets to Sargent Catwell we will all be in trouble.

"I will cover todays incident on my end. But you must promise this is the last incident with George. I must know that he is protected. I have been with you from the start, now that you know whom you are dealing with, I expect you and Commander Johnstone to make sure George finishes boot camp without any more incidents because if George steps outline one more time, you can kiss the PTF goodbye."

After the General hung up, the first Captain Silverton did was call Commander Johnstone and ordered him to have George transferred to Master Chief Walter's squad.

"Commander, we were right when we chose George to lead the PTF. Yet I find myself treading on thin water. Did you know George's father was Sergeant Cantwell? Sergeant Cantwell saved General Armstrong's life serval times while they were serving together in covert ops during the war."

The commander was silent for a moment then the captain broke through the silence and stated, "The bigger issue is we have a security leak, someone told General Armstrong about the incident on the bus. When he heard that George was almost snuffed out by Ricky, he was not too happy. The general ordered me to make sure that when you speak to George you stress to him that he needs to stay under the radar there can be no more incidents, or we will all be toast. Use your power of persuasion to calm George down. Now, that General Armstrong is completely on our side with the PTF. We need to keep it that way."

May came into the commander office. Sir" you know George and the chief are waiting outside to see you. However, I thought you told me you wanted to see Ricky first. You want me to cause a distraction so you can deal with Ricky. Because I am sure I can persuade the chief to run down the street and to Starbucks and get them a cup of coffee while I sit down and interview George. In my office. Once I close the door you will be able to clearly visit Ricky in the brig.

May, the commander said, "Please leave me be for a few minute I have to think about what my next step is going to be. When I am ready I'll call you. Now get out of here before someone began to think there is something fishy going on."

Once May left the commander slumped in his chair for a while wondering what he was going to say to George. Then he suddenly jumped out of his seat and pushed his door open. and we could hear the commander yelling at some lady. "May, hold all my calls while I go deal with these two crazy recruits. I knew Ricky might be a problem. But I never expected George to be so stupid."

When the commander turned around, I nearly went into a state of shock. It was the strange man who approached me in the car the night I left for Spokane to enlist.

Commander Johnstone did not want me to be overwhelmed by meeting him again, so he distracted me as he turned to the Chief Langer, "Chief, you need to get with the senior chief and resolve the situation with Ricky. I need to deal with Mr. Cantwell."

The chief saluted the commander quickly and made his way to meet with the senior chief and deal with Ricky.

Then the commander yelled to May, "May hold all my called while I speak with George."

Then he ushered me into his office and slammed the door. "Mr. Wildwood, you haven't even started boot camp and you are already becoming a liability. Do you realize how close you came to blowing your cover?"

"You must remember what I told you at the examination center. I tried to warn you about your friendship with Scott. If you would have listened to me, you could have avoided the entire situation with

Ricky. I thought Chief Escondido made it perfectly clear that the only two people you can trust to keep your secret is James and John. I hope you understand the seriousness of the situation."

I just stared at the commander. He was a lunatic. I did not want to become the brains of the PTF. All I wanted to do was sail the seven seas. How did he even know if I was cut out for this task?

My dad was right, I should have let him introduce him to his buddies in the army. I am sure my dad's friend Ray would have never hatched such a crazy plan.

The more the commander talked, the more I zoned out. I did not want to become an integral part of our national security.

Yet there was a wee voice down inside of me that took over and kept me from completely zoning out, because I was slowly beginning to realize I had less freedom now than when I was arguing with my parents about joining the navy.

Suddenly the commander shook me, "George, are you listening it is time for you to your ducks in a row."

"You should be thankful that I am in the position where I am able to let my actions slide"

He continued, "I have granted me a full reprieve. However. your actions have forced me to give me one demerit. If you get anymore demerit, you will not be unable to join the NSA. That'll destroy the fabric of our mission. Mr. Wildwood, your actions are unacceptable and from this point forward you must stick to the script."

"I need you to understand that your squad comes first, and if anyone gets in the way of you executing your duties, they must be moved out of the way. I have been considering a special assignment for Scott ever since he failed the NSA exam. He has been a thorn in my side, and now I am going to have to follow through with his transfer orders. Your actions today had forced my hand, and I am going to have Scott stationed on a ship in Philadelphia. Scott will be assigned to an elite group of recruits that we have to keep under lock and key to ensure the underbelly of our current security operations are not destroyed," the commander said.

"I need you to promise me you will buckle down and turn things around. Remember you are joining the navy and will be stationed on board the USS Bunker Hill CG 52 upon completion of boot camp and Storekeeper Class A school."

"Sir," I retorted. "I mean no disrespect, but you are making a huge mistake if you are trying to keep our mission secret. Everyone must still think Scott and I are going to be stationed together."

I know that Scott is a problem, but how will I be able to explain to everyone that Scott and I are being split up? Steve and my family would know something is going on, and Steve might try to sue the navy for breaking their contract with me and Scott."

After my outburst, there was an eerie silence in the room, and it seemed like the commander was upset with me. He took a deep breath, as if he were taken aback by my words. Commander Johnstone ordered me to be quiet as he threw up his hands.

"Mr. Wildwood, you have answered all my doubts about your assignment when I watched you calmly defuse the situation with Scott and Ricky. I stand firmly behind my choice. I believe you will become one of the greatest leaders the NSA has ever known. You need to stop babbling and start realizing your actions will determine the greatness of your team."

Then the commander blatantly stated, "After today's incident, I became incredibly angry and nearly made a very grave error, but thanks to your quick evaluation of the situation, I have decided to transfer Scott to the *USS Carl Vinson CVN 70* instead of transferring him to a ship in Philadelphia.

Your story will not change. As far as everyone is concerned, you and Scott will be stationed on the same ship, yet immediately after boot camp Scott will be assigned to detail in Adak, Alaska, on a top-secret mission while he is waiting on the *Carl Vinson*. Scott will not be allowed outside contact until he has officially boarded the *USS Carl Vinson CVN 70* in Adak before they finish the first phase of their mission in the Philippines."

"While Scott is in Adak, you will be sent to Storekeeper A School in Meridian, Mississippi. After A School you will be sent to the *USS Bunker Hill CG-52*. It is not uncommon for orders to change upon completion of an A school. The reason behind the switch will be that you made rank faster than was anticipated and there were no slots on board the *USS Carl Vinson* for SK3s. All of this will be explained in a letter to your parents, stating that the navy did everything possible to ensure assigning you and Scott to the same ship.

"While you will not be assigned to the same ship, your ships will both be stationed in San Diego and all your deployments and training exercises with be joint. Technically the navy lived up to its end of the bargain. And there is a stipulation in your assignment that if either one of you decides to apply for a transfer your transfer will be approved once the slot for your rate is available.

"George, understand that once Captain Silverton and I agreed you would be a perfect fit to become the leader of the PTF, both of us put our career on the line. Please don't make us regret our decision, because Captain Silverton does not like to be proven wrong."

"The last time he was proven wrong about a recruit was when Bill Clinton was president, and that recruit wound up with a discharge from the military for dereliction of duty. And is now considered an enemy of the state."

I looked at the commander. "Sir, you need to stop calling me Mr. Wildwood. My name is George Cantwell and by continuing to call me by another man's name it's confusing."

"I am sure that you do not want to add to the confusion when someone starts snooping around to find out who Mr. Wildwood is. Thus, I suggest you get your names straight and remember I am in boot camp. I am sure that the naval command structure has never heard of Mr. Wildwood, nor do they know your plans. If they did, they would certainly have a heart attack trying to figure out who Mr. Wildwood is. Therefore, sir, while I am at a naval facility, you must promise never to call me by that name again."

CHAPTER IX

George's First Demerit

I could see the fury in the commander's eyes as he stared at me for several minutes without saying a word. Finally, he said, "Son, I will not tolerate any more insubordinate acts. I hope our discussion today has enlightened you. Your mission is quite simple. Complete boot camp and report to your first duty station without any more demerits. Is that understood? George, I expect nothing less than an exemplary performance of your duties from here on out."

Is that understood, recruit?"

I replied, "Sir, yes, sir."

Then the commander called Chief Langer. "Chief you need to drop everything and return to my office to pick-up George for processing. Make sure the senior chief Dean understands that George is not to be messed with. To ensure there will be no more incidents with George all he needs to do is safely to turn George over to master chief Walter company for training."

Chief Langer replied. "Aye, sir," as he immediately dropped everything and made his way to the commanders office.

Several minute later the chief smiled at me as he returned to the commander office to get me ready to meet master chief Walters. "I guess it's time for you to get back to work. Remember you need to be careful from here on out. I have been ordered to take you to the processing office, where you will meet with Senior Chief Dean, who will ensure that you are assigned to the proper barracks. Take heed to the commander advice and everything will be fine."

Suddenly Senior Chief Dean came barreling down the hallway and stopped Chief Jones in his tracks. "Hey, Joe, where is this dimwit recruit. I wanted to see what all the fuss was about." When Joe pointed to me, Senior Chief Dean burst out laughing. "Are you kidding me? This little pipsqueak he look like he should still be in high school. Are you sure he's the one who took down that big oaf Ricky?

You ain't got to go any further. I am relieving you of your duties," he said as he grabbed me and took me to his office.

As soon as Chief Langer turned around, Senior Chief Dean came up to me and slapped me in the face. "Son let's get one thing straight. I am the OIC of all the recruits in their squad for the next twelve weeks. Remember, son, you belong to me now. And if you so much as blink an eye I am going stomp on you and personally throw you in the brig. You got that, recruit?" Then he looked at me and mumbled, "I'm not sure why they want to give you a chance, but orders are orders. If I were you, I'd keep my head low for the rest of your time here."

I shouted, "Sir, yes, sir."

Once I was in his office, the senior chief threw some paperwork on the desk regarding the incident on the bus and ordered me to sit down and review the report and sign it. Then he disappeared down the hallway to make sure that Ricky was secure in the brig.

It took me a few minutes to read the incident report. Everything was in order. The report stated I was not responsible for the incident and that Ricky had attacked me. They said I acted in self-defense, trying to protect Scott and myself. After signing the document, Senior Chief Dean was supposed to transfer me to Master Chief Walter's squad. Yet I had to wait until Ricky was secured in the brig.

While I was waiting for the senior chief to return, I blanked out for a second. Then I started reading the rest of the documents he placed on the table. It seemed as if my father had contacted General Armstrong the commandant of the Marine Corps, General

Armstrong, and tried to get me transferred out of the navy completely or transferred to an army unit closer to my home because he knew I would never be stationed near my hometown while I was in the navy.

What stunned me the most was that my father had served with General Armstrong and had saved the general's life. Why had my father kept his relationship with General Armstrong a secret from my entire family? I had no idea the two men had such a close relationship.

Because of his relationship with the General he felt like he would be able bogart General Armstrong and convince him to change my orders to an army base that was less than two clicks from my house. My father felt like it would be the perfect solution for everyone.

General Armstrong refused to have me transferred. Then he called Captain Silverton to request that the Master Chief was my company commander. I was so glad the chain of command did not break and allow my father to change my orders. My dad's plan failed; I was going to become a sailor. And I was glad when Captain Silverton stepped in because I didn't want to explain to Commander Johnstone why my dad had tried to change my enlistment and have me released me from the navy.

Yet. it seemed like the most important aspect of this whole thing was that the senior chief should be thanking me for solving a big problem when I took Ricky down. It seemed like the chief was too proud to admit that there was ever a problem. Immediately after I finished reading the document about the senior chief, I shook my head, as I was still having a tough time wrapping my mind around why Commander Johnstone was watching out for my welfare. It was nice to have someone on my side. It felt weird that a high-ranking officer like the commander would take a keen interest in my welfare, and the possibility of my dad knowing General Armstrong was awesome.

I sat in my chair and patiently waited for my final orders to release me from Senior Chief Dean into the hands of Master Chief Walters's, and my mind was going into overdrive, And I was slowly beginning to get used to the idea that my father and General Armstrong were friends. However, the more I pondered my present situation, the more stressed I became.

The clock on the wall above the exit door was driving me crazy. It seemed like every time the second hand moved it exploded, and the ticking of the clock was freaking me out and I was so glad I was about to be released into the hands of Chief Walters

Suddenly Senior Chief Dean suddenly burst through the door and grabbed me. He started yanking me by the collar. "Did you finish reading the document that I left for you to sign?"

"Sir, yes, sir," I quickly responded.

"At ease, recruit. It's going to be about another ten minutes before everything is processed, so don't go nowhere," He said as he chuckled. "One more screwup and no one will be able to protect you. That's when you'll be all mine.

You'd best be glad it wasn't up to me, because I would have put you in the brig next to your friend Ricky. I never would never let you roam free as a bird. However, I found out you are one of those pretty boys.

"It seems like your father has some pull with General Armstrong, and he ordered the Captain Silverton to make sure that you were placed in Chief Walters's company. Master chief is one of General Armstrong's friends. Don't think for a minute I won't have my eye on you."

Son, if you want to survive, you'd better listen to Chief Walters and watch out for me, because you've already got one strike and I don't want to see you making any more stupid choices. You better hope that I don't find the two goons who helped you perpetrate the attack on poor little Ricky. Because if I do, all three you will be gone in a heartbeat."

The senior chief was still barking at me as I blanked out.

"However, if you see either of those two weasels that helped you attack poor Ricky contact you. You'd better immediately inform Master Chief Walters so we can put a close to the incident regarding how the three of you attacked an innocent man like Ricky and made it seem like he was dishonorable. However, the truth of the matter is the three of you are destroying the fabric of the military. You'd better sleep with one eye open because I am coming for you. If you make one wrong step, it'll be the last step you make in my navy."

He threw a few more documents on the table and angrily said, "Just sign these papers so I can turn you over to Master Chief Walters." He continued looking at me like he was disgusted as he said, "Punks like you make me vomit, but for some reason you are different from all the other recruits. Everywhere you turn someone is looking out for you."

I wanted to laugh at the senior chief's idiotic words. It was hilarious how things were working out, and all I could do was just stand there and smile at the master chief. Not only was I back with James and John, but I would be able to do some recon while we were in boot camp everyone was oblivious to the fact, I would be a part of the NSA.

It seemed liked me being a part of the PTF was all that mattered to them. The more information that was revealed to the crazier it made me. The PTF was now becoming like a poison in my veins and until I understood more I was like an orphan without a family. I only hoped that once the PTF was worth it and that we would be able to bring peace to the world by destroying those terrorists who have been trying to destroy the world for too long.

I was so glad when Master Chief Walters walked through the door and looked at Senior Chief Dean

Suddenly I felt like I was safe, and my journey was just beginning as he looked at Senior Chief Dean "Joe, what are you trying to do scaring one of my recruits?"

"Honestly, you need to get over it."

"He made a mistake that made your job easier. I know the entire base was trying to figure out a way to deal with Ricky after he somehow got around injuring the admission chief who was accused of calling him a tubby boy who had no business becoming a sailor until he lost at least one hundred and fifty pounds. Ricky went off on him and accused him of harassment, saying that he was told by his recruiter that he would be able to lose enough weight in boot camp to fit his height and weight standards. At first, they were going to place Ricky under arrest for assault charges. However, when Ricky's father hired a lawyer to defend Ricky, the military was forced into a settlement. It seems like Ricky was justified in getting angry, and his harassment suit would have left a scar on the navy's public relations."

"However, when Ricky enlisted, it stated that if he had any more outbursts within the first twelve months of his enlistment he would immediately be discharged. Senior Chief, hold on to your ideals and thank my recruit for taking care of Ricky. While you say you are not willing to give George another chance, remember how that turned out with Ricky. And we don't need to burn down that bridge again. Therefore, you owe my recruit an apology."

Senior Chief Dean snarled at me. "Boy, I don't know what kind of friends you have. Just remember I will let it ride this time, and I'll give you a pass.

"However, one more mistake and you are all mine. Master Chief Walters just make you sure you keep George on a leash. I ain't the only one around here who can't stand arrogant recruits who think they can change the rules."

Then the master chief looked at Senior Chief Dean and smugly taunted him, "Boy, you may oversee the divisional training because of rotation, but don't you ever try to threaten me or my recruits again 'cause I will have your hide. George don't listen to that blowhard. He's a jealous young man who thinks he has special authority because they put him over all the other chiefs."

Once I was safely in the hands of Master Chief Walters, Senior Chief Dean reluctantly ordered him to take me to the barracks. As we started walking toward the barracks, I turned toward Master Chief Walter and whispered, "sir, you won't have any problems with me or my two friends. I am glad that I am finally with someone who is sane."

"I know I am not supposed to say anything, but Senior Chief Dean is a complete moron who has no idea how to be a chief."

Master Chief Walter looked at me seriously, "Son, the next few days, keep your mouth shut and stay under the radar. Trust me, it's the best for all concerned. It will also give me time to make a strategy that will keep you safe from any more scrutiny while you are in boot camp. Right now, my job is to take you to the barracks without any more incidents. Do you think you can keep your thoughts to yourself at least until we get you situated in the barracks. Because I don't want you getting in any more trouble before you even get started with training."

I just smiled at the master chief and walked with him silently toward the barracks. When we arrived in the barracks, he whispered to me, "Son, for the next few days, you just keep your mouth shut and stay under the radar I have already assigned me a bunk, and he did not want any of the other recruit snooping into our business. Trust me, that'll be the best for all concerned. It will also give me time to make a strategy that will keep you safe from any more scrutiny while you are in boot camp."

I was just thankful that I would finally be able to get some rest.

When I finally shut eye, and I began to dream about the absurd conversation with Senior Chief Dean. None of it made sense. However, I slowly beginning to forget all the craziness of the past few days. My asleep was suddenly over when some fool started banging garbage can lids, jarring everyone from their sleep. When I looked at my watch it said it was 4:00 AM.

It was Senior Chief Dean, and he was screaming like a maniac, ordering everyone to stand at attention, then he began assigning us to our companies.

"Since there are a total of twelve companies, I am going to start off with the first recruit," he said as he pointed at Dean. Then he went down the aisle and counted off the first twelve recruits. He stated that the first twelve recruits would be each company's squad leader. Then he proceeded to order the next twelve recruits to line up behind their leaders as he numbered the rest of the recruits off from one to twelve. He continued walking down the aisle until every recruit was standing in line behind their squad leader.

I could not believe it when I realized that Scott was going to be in a different company and James and John were both assigned to my company. There had to be a mistake because it was my understanding that Scott and I would be together through the entire process. I started to raise my hand.

When James saw me raising my hand, he quickly slapped it down and whispered in my ear, "George, you should have listened to that recruiter. He tried to tell you that you and Scott might be separated in boot camp. You refused to listen and did not realize that it was against naval regulations to ensure that Scott and you would be in the same company in boot camp. When you signed your final enlistment paper, you failed to have a statement added stating that you would be in the same company during boot camp.

"Most of all, you already have one mark against you. And if you complained, it would interrupt your training process and you and Scott will be forced to stay in boot camp for several extra weeks until they can sort out what happened. Thus, blowing your cover in the PTF. And you will lose your friend Scott for good. He will never forgive you for causing a ruckus before you even started boot camp. I realize that it may not have sunk in yet, but you are going to have to learn to trust me and John. We may have our rough edges, yet we are loyal to the cause. You'd better become organized, especially since you are going to be our leader."

I remained speechless after James's rebuke as the OIC introduced each company to their commander. I was assigned to Chief Walters's company. Chief Walters noticed the look of despair on my face. He leaned a back to whisper to me, "Remember, I told you not to do anything stupid if you and Scott are assigned to different companies. Your friend just saved you and my company some embarrassment. We're all counting on you."

Yet, I did not take heed of the master chief's warning, and I went over to Scott and stuck out my hand. Scott looked at me and went crazy. Scott shouted at the OIC, "Sir, please do something. This crazy man thinks we are friends. I am no longer a part of his pity program."

Senior Chief Dean went berserk when he saw me trying to shake Scott's hand. He immediately slapped my hand down.

"What is wrong with you, mister? You're in boot camp, and for the next twelve weeks the only friends you have are in your company. All other companies are your foes and if you don't learn quickly, you will be sent back to your mama where you belong. Gentlemen, I am only going to tell you this once. From the moment you got off the bus, you belonged to me. I am the one you should be worried about.

"I am the officer in charge, OIC. There will be twelve companies. All issues must be addressed to you company's commander.

"However, I am the OIC, and they all answer to me. Before you go to chow, I want you to take your last look at the recruit next to you and understand that every one of you little crybabies have come to the point of no return. The man standing on your right and on your left is not your friend, nor is he a member of your squad. When you line up in your squads, I want you to take a good look at each member of your squad carefully. For the next twelve weeks, they will be your friends. Everyone else is considered your enemy.

"You will be competing against each other to see which squad will be carrying the brigade flag at your graduation ceremony." Senior Chief Dean stared at me and continued, "As I mentioned to one of the ugliest recruits I have ever seen come through this joint, if he does not understand the concept of being in a squad, then he can return to his mama and let her ease his pain. He's an idiot if he thinks he has the power to change navy protocol."

Then he went down the aisle and looked at all the squad leaders square in the eyes. "You have been chosen to lead your squads. If you cannot keep the idiots in line, you will be demoted. This will be everyone's last warning. If I catch any of you fraternizing with anyone other than those in your own company and they decide they want to cross the line; you will truly regret, it. I will ensure that your company commander gives you the honor of doing a little extra work each night while everyone else is asleep."

Finally, he called all the squad to attention and ordered our company commanders to line their squads up for chow. A few minutes later we were all marching to the mess hall. One by one, each squad did an about-face and we marched to the mess hall. My squad was the last squad to enter the mess hall. It seemed like the OIC was playing games with the master chief and punishing him for my indiscretion. The master chief looked irritated by the OIC's childish gesture, as he growled at the company when we finally got to the chow hall.

"Alright, you turkeys, you have exactly thirty minutes to eat. I suggest you skip the small talk and eat."

As we slowly advanced through the chow line, everyone was asked how they wanted their eggs except me. When I placed my tray on the line, the cook just slopped some eggs and meat on my plate and laughed. "Hopefully, you won't try anything else stupid today."

All I could do was put my head down and silently sit down next to James and John. Before I was even able to take a bite, Senior Chief Dean came over to our table and sternly scolded me.

"Son, you must not have heard me last night. I am the OIC of all the companies, and I saw you trying to fraternize with someone from another company. You are making a big mistake. Don't let me see you get out of pocket again or you're going end up like Ricky. Understood?"

"Sir, yes," I shouted back.

Then the senior chief stunned everyone as he picked up my food and threw it on the floor.

"What's the matter with you, son? Didn't your mama teach you how to eat? I suggest you clean up that mess and get back to the barracks before muster.

I was about to say something back until I heard the senior chief yell again, "Son, you must need to get the cotton out of your ears. Didn't I tell you to move? If you don't move, I will have to let you join your friend Ricky."

As I was bending down to clean up the mess, the OIC went over to Master Chief Walters and looked him square in the eyes. "I don't know what you are trying pull, but if one of you recruits does not follow my orders your whole squad will suffer. Is that clear?"

Then the master chief quickly replied, "Whoa, son, you need to calm down. You may be the OIC, but I outrank you. Before you mess with my company you must come through me. I will play your games for the moment, but if you ever touch one of my recruits again without my permission you will truly regret it!"

"Fine, Master Chief, I am letting you know it is time for your squad to return to your barracks for some much-needed discipline. Because if any of your recruits step over the line, they are mine and your rank does not matter, because I am technically responsible for the training of all the recruits on this base. You may outrank me, but my position trumps your rank. I want you to understand that if you complain to our superiors, I will turn in my report on the disciplinary actions required for your recruits to remain at this facility. They will rule in my favor. And then grant you the honor of transferring to another duty station where you can quietly retire."

The master chief silently laughed as he stared down the barrel of the senior chief eyes and whispered, "Dean, I have more friends than you think, and I will never quietly let a punk like you destroy the very fabric of the navy that I have served and honored for years. Take your best shot, we will see who ends up in the junkyard."

After the master chief's comment, the OIC's entire face changed color as he quickly called our squad to order. "After George cleans up his mess, I have ordered Master Chief Walters to discipline anyone who thinks they are greater than the tradition of the navy." He smiled and turned the squad back over to Master Chief Walters.

As we marched back to the barracks, I thought to myself why the commander had already fixed my spot in Chief Walters's squad. Then Chief Walters looked at me strangely and whispered, "Son, don't worry about Master Chief Dean. While he can be a pain, he is usually a reasonable man. I am sure he will cool off in a couple of weeks if you stop agitating him."

I felt like it was my fault master chief's reputation was under attack, and I was tired of feeling like the master chief was my babysitter. I was just in awe of his strength as he remained loyal to the cause, and he felt like Commander Johnstone would never put his career in jeopardy unless he had a good reason.

Meanwhile, the master chief had turned his focus back to the squad and yelled, "Double time march," and we nearly ran the rest of the way to the barracks. However, just before we reached the barracks, I noticed that he approached both James and John and whispered something to them. John quickly switched places with the man directly behind me and whispered to me, "Just be careful Master Chief Walters seems like a good man, but if you cross him, he will show you no mercy if you continue to act like an idiot."

"I am almost certain he will start giving you some slack once you start fulfilling your end of the bargain. For the moment, you need to play along and get rest when you can. I suggest you let me and James handle things for the next few days. I'm sure once you get integrated into the squad Chief Walters will slack off a little."

Once we were inside the barracks, the master chief called everyone to attention. "Men, I want to introduce you to George, the newest member of our squad. I know many of you may have heard stories about how he is nothing but a troublemaker. I assure you he has learned his lesson and is ready to become your brother."

"So, if anyone has any issues, they better be straightforward right now, as I am granting you time to voice your concerns or issues regarding Mr. Catwell's placement in my squad. I suggest you stand tall while I am giving you the chance, or you will regret it later. After today I will not tolerate any insubordination."

Once he finished his speech, he left the recruits standing alone in the barracks. to give them time air out any grievance they might have. I could see the sweat pouring down everyone's faces as they went back to their bunks.

CHAPTER X

Boot Camp Begins

Everyone remained silent until John stepped up and blurted out, "What is wrong with you people? I can hear your mumbling. Why don't you just step forward and say how you really feel aloud so we can get this issue behind us and start acting like a real navy team.?"

Then Mathew turned around. "Who is this dude and why did he call him Mr. Cantwell? Because according to what I have heard, only officers are called by their last name. So why is he so special, Joe chimed. "First, we are forced to integrate this man into our company, and now the master chief is disrespecting everyone else. It's like we don't matter." They requested that the master chief call George by his first name just like the rest of the recruits; they felt like he was giving George an honor he did not deserve.

While they were debating what to do with George, James quietly slipped away and went to the master chief's office.

When he knocked on the door, the master chief did not respond at first. So, he began to knock on the door a second time.

He was shocked when the master chief opened the door, and he ended up knocking on the master chief's chest instead of the door.

"James, what is wrong with you? You know I can't be seen associating with any of the recruits unless I initiate the request."

"Boss, we have an issue that needs to be addressed. I don't think you understand how close you came to blowing our entire mission when you called George 'Mr. Cantwell."

The master chief looked at James. "What are you talking about? I would never do something that stupid." Then he put his hand over his mouth. "James, thank you for correcting me. It will never happen again. Now I suggest you get back to the squad before they find out that you are missing."

A few minutes later, the master chief returned to the barracks and demanded someone tell him about their grievance against Seaman Recruit George, everyone remained silent, as they began to wonder how the master chief knew their major grievance regarding George.

When the squad remained silent, the master chief yelled out, "I am glad everyone came to their senses because it is now official, Seaman recruit George is a member of the company." Then he barked, "James and John, front and center. I am ordering you to make sure that George is seamlessly integrated into the squad." Then he screamed, "At ease, men, you can go back to what you were doing.

Immediately after our discussion regarding George, the master chief told everyone to wait by their bunks until he returned. When he returned Ten minutes later, we began our march to the barber to get our heads shaved. Then we went to the uniform shop, and we were issued all our uniforms and gear. After the last person received their gear, the chief lined us back up and we marched back to the barracks to stow our gear before lunch.

While the rest of the squad was focusing on stowing their gear, the master chief ordered James to escort me to his office. James knocked on the master chief's door, and we waited patiently for several minutes. I could hear the master chief arguing with someone, and then he angrily slammed the phone.

"Is that you, James?"

"Yes, sir," he smartly replied.

Then the door slowly flew open. "I have a request from the top brass that you return to the barracks and make sure George's gear is properly stowed. You need to be discreet, because I don't want it to seem like I am giving George special treatment.

Now, if you don't mind leaving me and George alone for a few minutes, I need to make sure he understands his position in the squad."

When the master chief slammed the door and James plopped down into the chair outside the master chief's office.

"George, now that we are alone, I need to explain your current situation. It is my job to make sure you make it through boot camp. The commander told me you were the most gifted recruit that he has ever encountered, your computer skill, you mathematical skill, your accounting skills, and are photographic memory were all evident when you passed you exam with a score of over hundred on every section of you exam. No recruit has ever scored that high on the exam. And your leadership skills were exceptional, especially the way you dealt with James, John, and Scott during you enlistment in Spokane. The chief reported that if it had not been for you perseverance all four of would not have made to the enlistment office on time. Then when you handle the situation with Ricky with great finesse you made me a believer. I am honored to have you in my squad.

"Therefore, the commander has authorized each squad to have a member of their squad remain in the barracks studying for the exams while the rest of the squad is out on the grinder preparing for inspection. Thus, I felt like the best way to keep you out of trouble is for you to remain in the barracks while the rest of the squad is out on the grinder training."

"What I am trying to tell you is that you will become our education liaison. I have put a lot of stock in what the commander told me, and I am sure that with your brains the squad will score close to a hundred percent on the educational portion of boot camp."

The more he talked, the more befuddled he looked. It was as if he felt like it was unfair to put such a high emphasis on the education portion of our training. I could tell he felt like he was denying me one of the most valuable lessons in boot camp which was the drills.

"George, don't mention our conversation to anyone. I do not want the OIC and others to suspect that I have an ace in the hole. The naval exam has become a huge part of every squad's evaluation. But the commander has put his faith in us working together and with your brains and my expertise as a drill instructor we will become a legend."

"Your actions in the next twelve weeks will define the "rest of your life and once we succeed, it will strengthen the commander's choices. Thus, showing that you have the capability of being a great leader. It may look like the weight of the world is on your shoulder, but you must consider how your decisions from this point forward will not only affect your life but will also affect the lives of all those who have put their faith in you.

"You will be watched like a hawk, and every action you take will seem like you are living be under a microscope. Remember, whatever the problem is I will be here for you. The first time you run into trouble like when the OIC threw your plate on the floor, you must tell me so I can protect you and ensure that no damage has been done."

When the squad returned from drills each afternoon, I expect to see if I had made any progress. After you have shown me the basic information, I expect a detailed summary of what has been learned during the week. Then on Monday morning, I will give you a list of all information I expect to you research during the week."

Then by the third week you will begin training the rest of the squad to pass our final examination.

George I am begging you to vigilant and never lower your guard to anyone. You need to let me protect you from the naysayers. Because, son, once you finish boot camp you will be on your own. I will not be around to pull your feet out of the fire. I am asking you to use you head and stay calm for the next twelve weeks. Use your time wisely and learn as much as you can about your responsibilities to the navy and your new friends James and John. Because they are going to be by your side for the rest of your naval career.

"George," he stressed, "You must learn how to pick your battles before you jump in with all your might. I know all of this may seem strange to you right now, but you will understand, in the future, the importance of building relationships that are stable and will not bend under pressure. Remember, son, we are all counting on you to rise to the occasion and become a great leader."

Then the master chief paused for a moment. "George, I was skeptical at first and I did not fully buy into the action of my superiors. But when I saw how they were willing to put their careers on the line for a small glimpse of peace and strongly believed in their cause, I had no other choice but to get on board. I just hope our faith in you does not destroy the very fabric of the navy. Thus, I am leaving my door is open to you. Any sign of trouble, I need you to inform me immediately and I will stop the charade before it goes too far.

"I need you to return to the barracks and act like you have sense. And remember to let James and John handle things for the next few days. I'm sure once you get integrated into the squad things will get easier." Then he turned me and said, "Before you leave my office, I need to know that you have a clear understanding of what you are getting yourself into."

I dropped my head and nodded yes.

The master chief looked at me sternly. "Son, you better get this right. You are now in the navy and that is not a proper response. Now, I am going to ask you one more time, do we have a clear understanding?"

I quickly lifted my head and shouted "Sir, yes, sir."

The master chief smiled, "Good, now get back to barracks and make sure your gear is stowed properly."

Wow! I thought about what I was going to tell James. The master chief was one intense man, and he truly scared me. My mind was running a hundred miles an hour, I was finally starting to get a clearer picture of the burden that the commander had put on the master chief. I decided to roll with the punches and focus myself on not letting him down.

I realize the commander went out on a limb to have me assigned to his squad, and I must earn the safety net he has granted me. However, in the back of my mind, I felt like it was a trick to see if I could stand alone.

Was I going insane or was this just the beginning of my training?

It seemed so unfair because I still did not know the answer to why I was chosen to lead the PTF. I had to dig deep to fulfill my part of the bargain without giving away my secret identity.

I bumped into James as I turned the corner.

"George, what took you so long? The rest of the squad is beginning to grumble about having you in the squad, and they don't know if your addition is a curse or a blessing. Plus, I must make it look like you stowed you gear. You heard what the master chief said, we need to be discreet. John and I have been running interference, but you are going to have to play your part by keeping your mouth shut."

"I got it, James, the master chief made sure of that. That man is completely off the hook, and he is coming unglued. George, you must help me stay low-key until we can figure out why he's on edge."

James tried to assure me that this was just part of process in boot camp. However, his assurance didn't seem to help as I continued my downward spiral into the dark abyss. Was I ever going to have a normal life again? My thoughts nearly drove me crazy until John interrupted our conversation.

"Snap out of it George. Stop worrying about your surroundings. If you don't, the PTF will become outdated." John shook me. "You'd better be ready. Everyone is depending on you to lead and now is your chance to show what you are made of, regardless of the odds. George, you started at a disadvantage because of the incident with Ricky. If we succeed, all that will be water under the bridge."

You must make some hard choices before the master chief returns. Whatever doubts you have, you need to find a way to express them without disrupting the flow of your secret identity. George, you gotta snap out of your funk, because the master chief is a wise man, and he catches on quickly. He will know if you are real or just playing games. And if he sees one hair on your head out of place, he will inform his superiors and they will have to decide whether to continue with their plans for the PTF."

I was about to give John a piece of my mind when the master chief suddenly appeared and called everyone to attention.

"Recruits, before I begin my first inspection of your bunks, I have some information for the squad. I don't take screwups lightly. And since I already have one named George, I suggest everyone pay close attention to what I am going to say next. It is imperative that this squad ensure that George does not screw up anymore. George was sent to our squad for a specific reason, and I can tell you right now it sure wasn't his muscles. I was told he can help our squad in the educational portion of our training."

Several members of the squad started to laugh.

"What's so funny, gentlemen? If you had any brains, you would be very worried right now, because if we don't harness this man's brain waves our squad is doomed. I suggest you keep your snarly faces to yourself. You do not want to make me your enemy. I just hope you're still laughing when I get done. Because anyone who just laughed better hope that they have squared away their gear and I can see my quarter bounce off your bed into my hand."

Suddenly the laughs turned into fearful looks. No one wanted to answer to the master chief as he swiftly made his rounds, inspecting each recruit's gear. I felt sorry for the first recruit as the master chief turned over his bunk and threw all his gear on the floor.

"Son, you think this is a laughing matter. My three-year-old daughter can make her bunk better than yours. And the way you placed your gear in the wrong order is simply disgusting. It looks like you ain't nothing but a little mama's boy. Bet you don't even know what two plus two is. I suggest you get busy, 'cause the next time you mess up I am going to send you to night school."

Then he went on to the next recruit and smiled because he had stowed his gear properly, when the quarter bounced back into his hand. He said, "Now this is more like finally someone did their homework."

The inspection seemed to last forever. All he could do was shake his head. The master chief finished the inspection and called the squad to attention.

"Not bad for the first inspection. Next time I want to see perfection from every member of the squad. All those who failed, take a moment to contemplate what you did wrong. And if you're not sure why you did not pass, ask one of your fellow shipmates to help you. If passed this time, don't get complacent but help your brothers to ensure our squad is perfect."

Then the master chief ordered everyone to stand at attention in front of their bunks. "All right, gentlemen, let me see how well you follow instructions." Then he started at the far end of the barracks and inspected each recruit to make sure their shoes were shined, and they had on the proper attire.

When he was about halfway through the inspection he paused, "Gentlemen, I have a little surprise for you. After chow, all the squad will be meeting on the grinder. The OIC has scheduled a meeting with Commander Johnstone for all the squads, and I expect everyone to be on their best behavior.

He will introduce you to the staff on base and give a brief introduction to what to expect while you are in boot camp for the next twelve weeks. After meeting with the commander, we will go to the infirmary, where everyone will have their shot records updated. Once we are done at the infirmary, we will march to the chow hall for dinner. Today will be a long day.

I do not expect to return to the barracks until after dinner. Once we return to the barracks everyone will have time to finish storing their gear and get ready for lights out at 22:00 hours. In the morning, I will reinspect everyone's gear and their bunks. Anyone who is not prepared will get a demerit. Three demerits and you will be sent back two weeks. I suggest you work as a team to ensure that everyone is prepared for the inspection."

It felt like all the air had been sucked out of the room when we learned we were meeting the commander, and the sweat came pouring out. I knew this was important, and no one in the squad wanted to have a bad rep before meeting with the commander.

When John heard the news, he whispered, "George, be prepared for the me to give you a signal about future meetings."

When the master chief saw John whispering to me, he stopped in front of us. "John, do you have something to say to the company because I do not take kindly to recruits playing games with me?"

John froze for a moment, then he replied, "Sir, no, sir."

The master chief smiled. "Good, because normally the base commander does not meet with the recruits until the second or third week of boot camp. However, the OIC decided to shake things up a little this year. I want everyone to make sure that you understand who oversees this squad. There will be no more whispering or playing while you are at attention. This is my final warning. The next person who steps out of line will be sent home.

After lunch we marched to the grinder where would wait for the commander. When we arrived at 13:30 the OIC came over to the master chief. Why is you company always late. I sent an email changing the time 13:00, I wanted to ensure we were ready. Now I will have to trust that you are prepared for your company to meet with the commander in a few minutes. The commander was running a little late and did not arrive on the grinder until 14:15. When he arrived, the OIC called the squad to attention, and the commander briefly inspect the companies before beginning his speech.

"For the next three months, you belong to me and the United States Navy. When you meet the commander, his main objective is to introduce all the recruits to key personnel on the base, and he will give everyone a brief intro to what to expect while you are in boot camp. He will also discuss the pitfalls that have caused many recruits to fail in the last few years.

This year will be the turning point in the navy's retention. The commander wants to ensure that every recruit feels like they have a place in the navy long-term. In the past few years, we have lost 30 percent of our force due to retirement, and those recruits who reenlisted are now getting out of the navy after four years.

.

I realize that a lot of this may not make sense to you now, but our country's future is in your hands. Commander Johnstone wants to let every recruit know that he is a valuable part of keeping hope alive.

"While there may not be any major wars, the United States is under constant threat from terrorists all over the world, and the navy is part of this country's first line of defense. That is why sometimes it feels like we are hard on recruits. The truth of the matter is we know how important each recruit is to our nation's success."

After meeting with the commander, the squad marched to the base infirmary, where each recruit had .to be weighed; their blood pressure read;' give three tubes of blood; finally get four shots one in each shoulder, and one in each thigh.

Senior chief Dean was still playing games with Master Chief Walters as he made sure our squad was the last squad to enter the infirmary. When the corpsmen saw our squad enter the infirmary at 16:00 they were angry.

Normally they were done with shots by 16:00. When James received his shot, the corpsman looked at him. "Stand still, cause if you move it will hurt a lot more." Then the corpsman stuck James in both of his shoulders, and both of his thighs.

As James was limping away the corpsman laughed. "Where is George, I got something special for him. I heard he is the reason you goons were late reaching the infirmary. Thus, Senior Chief Dean told me to specifically handle George."

James looked at her like she was crazy. "I don't know whom you are talking about we don't have anyone in our squad called George in our squad." Then he turned and signaled John to get George into another line before the crazy lady gave George his shots.

However, it did not matter, when the corpsman saw George's name he smiled. "Welcome to navy George," After sticking George several times he could not find George's veins, so he had to stick him in his knuckle to draw his blood. Then he forcefully jabbed him below his shoulders, and right above each kneecap. Whoops, my hand cramped up, guess I am more tried than I thought.

That's life friend, I hope the rest of your day is great. I need you to move on so, we can all get some chow.

After the last recruit received his shot the OIC of the infirmary turned the lights out and began locking the doors as he told the Master Chief his squad would have to use the exit on the far side of the building because the corpsman did not want to miss chow.

The Master Chief was very angry as he lined up the squad and told us to double time it until we reached the mess hall. It was 17:45 when we stepped through the doors at the mess hall. We quietly made our through the serving line. and the mess cooks started flinging our food on our trays.

Then the chief Culinary Specialist hollered, men you got fifteen minutes to eat before I call the MPs to clear the room.

The master chief went up to the chief and called him to the side. “I don’t know who you are, but if you try and funny business with my squad, you’d better be prepared to face the consequences of your actions.

He laughed at the master chief, “I don’t care if you are a master chief, the OIC Senior Chief Dean ordered me to shut down the mess by 18:00. I’ll give your squad an extra fifteen minutes. But that is the best I can do because I got to get everything cleanup for an early inspection in the morning”

I suggest next time you get you squad to the mess hall a little earlier. I heard you held up all medics for an extra hour while you squad was getting shots. That’s what you get for giving recruits like George special treatment. No disrespect master chief, but I must follow the chain of command, Senior Chief Dean is the OIC, and his rank is currently higher than you because he is over all the company commanders for the next twelve weeks.

What the master chief did next surprised everyone. He grabbed the chief Culinary Specialist by the throat. “No disrespect son, but you can tell Senior Chief Dean if he continues to mess with me or my squad, he will become part of Operation Deep Freeze in the Artic where the only thing he will oversee is the polar bears shoveling snow.

When the master chief let go of the chief culinary specialist his face had turned red and he immediately went out the back door to get some air. Then the master chief hollered, attention recruits you have ten minutes to finish you chow. So, whoever is already done I want you to stack you trays neatly and stand outside in line until the rest of the recruit’s finish eating.

Once we return to the barracks everyone will have time to finish storing their gear and get ready for lights out at 22:00. In the morning, I will reinspect everyone's gear and their bunks. Anyone who is not prepared will get a demerit. Three demerits and you will be sent back two weeks. I suggest you work as a team to ensure that everyone is prepared for the inspection."

Immediately after dinner, John came over to my bunk. "George, I realize we have not had much time to talk since we arrived. I spoke with the commander last night and he said it would be good if I explained some the background on the Peace Task Force, PTF. I am not sure where to begin.

"Tonight, I will be brief, and each night after dinner we will sit down with you and give you more background about the PTF and your part in the scheme of things. During the day you can study for the exam and do any additional research you need. Hopefully, if you have a question regarding my info the research that I will do will be able to give you a better picture of what your future in the PFT entails. At the end of our twelve-week training, the commander has assured me he will meet with you to fill in the gaps regarding our mission."

Before John began cramming info into my thick skull regarding the PTF. I already knew it would be over five months before I went to my NSA training, because after boot camp I had been granted two weeks of R&R. "Then I would attend SK A school for two months in Meridian Mississippi. Once I have completed my naval training then I would begin my NSA boot camp for three months. Upon completion of all my training, I would be assigned to my first duty station the *USS Bunker Hill* where I would be expected to lead the PTF.

I understand that you and Scott are not on good terms right now. The PTF will take priority over my friendship with Scott. Eventually, I would understand how Scott fits into the program. But for the moment I needed to concentrate on fulfilling my duties."

When John began telling his version of the story. I stopped him. "John, what are you talking about? Take it slow I never knew you and James existed before Chief Escondido picked you up on the way to Spokane.

CHAPTER XI

Peace Task Force

None of this makes sense to me and I have no idea who this lady Donna is? It's like I am in an insane asylum and I'm just waking up for the first time. You mean to tell me my life has been a lie. And now you are asking me to collaborate with you to take down some mythical lady named Donna."

John began laughing. "George, you were always a part of the equation. Donna has been setting you up for years. She started before you were even born. She was close friends with Steve, and she was there when your mother left Portland and moved to Tacoma. It nearly broke Steve's heart."

I stopped John again. "What are you talking about? Steve and my mother were just childhood friends. I know my mother, and she would have never been mixed up with someone like Steve. And even if what you are saying is true, I am sure there is more to the story than what you are telling me. I know my mother, and she would never intentionally hurt anyone."

"Slow your roll," John said. "I'm not trying to make your mother look bad, I'm explaining the connection between Donna, Steve, and your family. If you want to know more about her relationship with Steve, you must talk to her. All I know is that after your mother moved Donna stepped in and comforted Steve. It all seemed innocent as Donna introduced Steve to his wife. However, Donna was only using Steve's relationship with your mother to start messing with your family before you were born. Because of Steve's relationship with your mother, she was able to gain Steve's trust."

"This was the beginning of Donna's primary plan. Because she knew that Steve was loyal to her, she slowly made Steve the leader of her special forces. He is a very integral part to her plan to destroy the NSA and take down our government. All you must do is think back to how your family met Scott and you became friends. It was all a setup Scott's dad, Steve, is part of Donna's special forces."

"The first stage of her plan started when she arranged for Steve to bump into your mother and rekindle their friendship. While it seemed like Steve had moved on with his life, Donna knew that Steve was still in love with your mother. Thus, she was able to use Steve's relationship with your mother to drive a wedge between Steve and his wife. The first time you met Scott was when you were in preschool. Steve's wife became jealous of all the attention Steve was paying to your mother, so she insisted that Steve take a job in Alaska."

"For three years, they worked at salvaging their marriage. One day Steve came home from work and his wife was gone. She had packed up all her belongings while Steve was at work and Scott was at school. Suddenly, his phone rang. It was Scott's school asking when someone was going to pick Scott up from school. He was informed that if he did not have someone pick up Scott before he left the facility, they would have no choice but to call the authorities."

"After picking up Scott, Steve nearly went crazy trying to find his wife and get some answers. So, he called Donna, and she gladly came to his rescue. However, she was playing him and setting him up to become her main recruit, and she convinced Steve to move back to Washington and rekindle his friendship with your parents.

So Steve contacted your parents and told them that his wife had abandoned him and that he just wanted to move somewhere and get a fresh start. Your parents encouraged him to move back to Washington. They told him that with his skill as a carpenter and electrician he would not have any problems getting a job. Your father even got him an interview with one of the local construction companies. And a few weeks later, Steve was hired.

Steve was glad to be around your parents, and he contacted Donna to thank her for her help. That's when Donna pounced and started filling Steve's head with lies and deceit, and she finally convinced him to help her take down the NSA."

"When you met Scott, you instantly became friends, and you've been inseparable ever since. Thus, Steve and Scott would become part of your parents' inner circle of friends. And that's when Donna recruited Steve to keep an eye on you. Thus, making your friendship with Scott part of her plan to infiltrate the NSA"

"When you look back over your life, everything has been centered on your friendship with Scott, which was based on lies and deception. You know I am telling the truth. You met Janis at Scott's house. Your family took trips together. And Scott became like another brother. The most impressive part was that both of you were nerds, and together you aced all your classes until you started high school."

"Looking back at when you started high school, I'm sure you noticed the change and wondered how Scott was slowly becoming a chump and the other students began picking on him. That's when Scott developed a complex, and he began having lapses of memory and mood swings. At first, it was funny, but by your junior year, Scott's emotions took over. He started acting very strange. Suddenly he went from a straight A student to a total meathead."

"Everyone could see how Scott started acting strange. That's when Donna had ordered Steve to implant false memories into Scott's mind. Steve used his relationship with you to control Scott. He made sure the change took place over time and most people thought it was just part of a normal teenager's mindset. It seemed like no matter how he changed, you stuck by him. You stuck with Scott through it all. You never left his side, and you became very protective. That's when you started defending Scott from bullies. Steve used Scott's relationship with you to control the situation. Because of the changes in his life, Scott started viewing you as the only person whom he could trust. Thus, making your friendship stronger."

John looked at me. "George, because you and Scott were such good friends; you didn't even question the fact that Scott had changed when you convinced him to join the navy. You didn't even question the fact that Scott did a 180-degree turn after you convinced him to join the navy. Suddenly Scott knew all the answers in his classes and his grades started to go up. By the end of the year, he had straight A's. Matter of fact, he impressed your recruiter so much that when you approached him and told him that you would not enlist unless you and Scott had the same duty station, he immediately contacted the NSA and told them that he was sure Scott would make an excellent addition to your team."

"When Steve found out that you would be stationed together, he was elated. His plan to help Donna infiltrate the NSA had worked, and he was able to use your relationship with Scott as you planted the idea in Scott's mind that the two of you should join the navy. Scott never considered you were breaking your promise to your father."

"Just think about it. If Scott were such a great friend, he would have never let you entice him to join the navy, knowing that you wanted to be an accountant. Remember how you felt when you first approached him with the idea, he totally blew you off. The more you talked about all the benefits and how you would be able to travel the world together under the buddy plan Scott finally realized how serious you were. That's when Scott began to feel like you would be invincible and there is no way your parents would stand in your way once they found out the two of you would be together.

He felt like your parents would be happy that you had a job. He explained to you that after Mr. Peterson spoke to his father that he was ecstatic. He was almost certain your parent would be overjoyed when they found out that would allow you to travel the world and enjoy life before settling down to the grind of going to a traditional college."

I turned to John and said, "So, that's why Scott started acting strange when he found out that I was joining the navy? I would have never encouraged Scott to join the navy. It was Steve's idea, as he convinced me that it would help Scott get back to his normal self. However, following the incident with Mr. Peterson, I started having doubts. The only reason I agreed with Steve to push Scott to join the navy was to help Scott. That is when I began to question Steve's motives leading up to your enlistment."

"Why had Mr. Peterson just talked to Steve and not my parents.? When I spoke with my parents it seemed like the worst day of my life. They did not understand why I decided to join the navy." Suddenly my parents made me feel like I was the biggest jerk on the planet, and they vowed to never talk to me again unless I reconsider my plans to join the navy. I broke your sister's heart, and my brother suddenly hated me. However, when I started feeling the freedom to control my own life, I became too stubborn to look at all the facts. Because if I would have been paying attention, I would have noticed that Steve had been pushing me to help his son join the navy was all just a lie. What was the real reason for his deception?"

John threw up his hands, "George that is the second time you have interrupted me you need to calm down and listen before you jump to conclusions. There will be plenty of time for you to ask questions later. But if you don't stop interrupting me, I will not be able to show you the picture of what it means to be honored to become part of the PTF."

"There is a lot more to the story, however if you keep jumping in, I will never be able to finish telling the story. That is not good for any of us because you don't need to sum up things until we are finished giving all the pertinent information about why you were chosen to lead the PTF. Thus, if you want to continue you must stop interrupting me."

"Sorry, John I promise not to interrupt anymore, I just get a little over-excited at times. So, I will do my best to hold in my question until the appropriate time."

"Good now just sit back and relax."

"You made Steve's day when you changed your mind, He was elated. He realized that Donna's plan was about to become reality.

He saw it as an opportunity to push his son in the same direction of hopefully becoming a part of the NSA's secret mission. The fact that you would be stationed together was a caveat to this plan to help Donna infiltrate the NSA, and it nearly worked when Scott's mind did a 180-degree turn right before you graduated."

"We still have not figured out what caused Scott erratic behavior and very few people cared as Scott slowly turned back to his nerdy self and he knew all the answers in his classes. His grades were even better than yours in certain subjects. By the end of the year, he had straight A's. It was like Scott had been reborn when you told him you were going to join the navy with him."

"Around this time is when the commander had gotten the authorization to tap Steve's phones and place videos in various rooms throughout his house because someone had secretly informed Captain Silverton that Steve was one of Donna's main contacts before you and Scott enlisted in the navy. They were explicit with the request to put a tap and place videos in Steve's den. Thus, they were able to hear most of his private conversation. They were hoping to see if they could tap into his conversation with Donna and find the mole inside the NSA. Therefore. Only a few people knew about the taps in Steve's house. One of the main persons with access to the taps and videos was the commander assistant May."

All this may be surprising because at the time you couldn't see the deception when you talked to Steve the day you picked up Scott. When he told you he would never forgive if you did not look out for Scott, Steve has been playing games with you all along. He never was worried about Scott, because the night before you left for Spokane, he gave Scott an injection he claimed would help Scott with his allergies while he was in boot camp. He was hoping that the dose would last until Scott came home from boot camp."

John paused for a moment, "Steve also gave Scott some pills for allergies and told him to take two a week. No one knew what the injection and pills were for. Therefore, between the shot and the extra pills, Steve felt like he could control Scott just like he had during high school. While no one knew how the medicine affected Scott they knew Scott would not be able to take the medicine while in boot camp unless they knew what it was.

However, Steve was confident he had given Scott enough medicine to control him until he finished boot camp. Soon Steve would be on top and he would have proved his worth to Donna once the two of you were on board the *Carl Vinson CVN-70* he felt like Scott induction into the NSA was the next step."

"While Scott was acting normal the first day after you were sworn in, the second dose and the pills he had taken were part of the reason Scott started acting so crazy on the bus, and when the senior chief put you in separate companies. The issue was that he has always been jealous of you. He felt like his father liked you better than him. He went off when he saw you in the den talking to Steve. He had only seen Steve invite your mother into the den, and the rest of the time he either had it locked up or would come outside of the den to talk and deal with him and any of his other friends."

"When Scott saw him allow your mother into the den, he felt like Steve had an agenda. It felt like he was having an affair with your mother. Scott never mentioned it to you because he did not want to create any issues with you or your family. Yet, he had never seen his father happier than when he and your mom were together in the den having their weekly conversations about life. While he could tell your mother was not interested it seemed like Steve was laying down the red carpet for your mother hoping he could stir up something from their past relationship."

"However, when Scott saw you in the den it freaked him out. What was his dad doing? Was he trying to replace him with you? Scott felt like he always did speak higher of you and Janis than he did of him and Cindy. He could not remember the last time he had heard his father give him credit for anything but acting like a meathead when he lost his mind during sophomore and his junior years. However, Steve nearly blew his cover when became overly happy that the two of you were getting ready to enlist in the navy."

"What impressed Steve was when he went to see your recruiter and talked to him about his son's enlistment. Your recruiter told him not to worry about Scott or George because George requested that they put in writing that they were to be stationed together after boot camp."

It nearly blew Steve's mind, as he called Donna with the news. "Donna, you should have seen George in action today, the way he stuck it to the naval system and made them go outside their normal protocol so that he and Scott would be placed in the navy's buddy program, which means that George and Scott would be stationed together for the next four years. And if the navy broke their contract with George, he and Scott would be free and clear to be honorably discharged from the navy."

"Finally, you have your way back into the NSA. Not only were you about to be promoted to the PTF, but the commander also issued the order to have Scott reevaluated after boot camp, then Scott would become a part team."

Donna laughed at Steve. 'Son, that' old news. My contact told me several days ago that when George approached him, he was very staunch in defending his friendship with Scott. My contact immediately called me, and I put my plan in motion to make sure Scott would become a member of the PTF"

"Donna's plan was working as the commander was seriously thinking about adding Scott as a member of our team because your recruiter was so excited about you and Scott, he called the commander. That's when the commander started watching both of you more closely. He was about to agree with the recruiter's assessment of you and Scott. The commander knew you would be a great leader, and it looked like both you and Scott would be a welcome addition to PTF."

"However, before Commander Johnstone turned in his final report that would have cleared both you and Scott. His assistant, May, discovered several strange financial transactions in Steve's bank account that were tied to Donna's. And she warned the commander that you needed to be separated from Scott or there would be total chaos in the ranks. While the commander really felt bad because he wanted to bring Scott into the fold, he knew it would be too risky."

"Therefore, it was decided that you need to forget Scott until

Scott's mind is right. Then the commander will reconsider him for a role in our PTF. The commander realized the level of Steve's involvement with Donna if it had not been for Mays due May's due diligence and hard work."

Thus, he would not consider Scott for any specific role in the PTF until May completed her research."

"After reviewing May's report, the commander began to see a pattern of information that Steve was somehow passing on to Donna. The commander became worried that there was a mole in the NSA."

"The fact that Steve found out the two of you would be stationed together before Mr. Peterson told him Scott and you were joining the navy was a disturbing thing. How long had Steve been putting you and your family in jeopardy?"

"Thus, the commander told May to continue her investigation of Steve financial records. She immediately noticed several large cash transfers from one of Donna's secret accounts to Steve's account.

"The first transaction was written several years ago. It became evident that somehow you and James were tied together. The commander told May to continue to follow the discrepancies in Steve's financial history to ensure that there were no issues."

That's when things started to get weird. May had tracked down the discrepancies and reported back to the commander. May had tracked down several large deposits that were made around the time of James's father's death. She noted that deposit came from the account of Mr. J, James's stepfather, several weeks after Donna, James's mother, married Mr. J.

"When Mr. J was informed that all the money going into; Donna Steve's account had come from a special account that Donna had set up for the maintenance of several of Donna's old properties. Mr. J sent several Emails to Donna asking her about the deposit, Donna replied that she had paid a contractor to do some work on her vacation home in Florida.

However, the notation on the account said seemed to confirm the funds were for a repair contract on Donna's vacation home in Florida. And Mr. J had no reason to disbelieve her story.

May had a hunch that led to the real purpose of the money for Scott's father. It seems like Steve played a key role in the death of James's father, and the money that Donna had sent him was used to tie up all the loose ends surrounding James's father's death. Because it was the exact same amount given to the PI who had warned the NSA that Mr. J, Jacque, was responsible for James's father's death."

Plus, May reports, uncovered several additional discrepancies in Steve's finances. It seemed like 50 percent of the deposit into Donna's account were going into a special trust fund set up by Steve.

"The main concern was regarding the information about James father's death. For years, the NSA had fallen into Donna's trap. And Mr. J was the chief suspect in the murder case, and Donna was a woman in distress, desperately trying to escape Mr. J's clutches. It was a brilliant plan, as Mr. J would have been blamed for the murder of James's father and Donna would come out smelling like a rose."

"At first everyone fell into Donna's trap, and Mr. J was the chief suspect in the murder case.

"However, the case against Mr. J. began to fall apart when Donna had James sent away to boarding school in Europe. Because the friends she had paid to take care of James were caught in a sting operation by the NSA and they confessed that Donna had set up Mr.

"Although they could not provide any hard evidence of their accusations against Donna until May uncovered several phony transactions to the PI who had warned the NSA about Mr. J being responsible for James's father's death.

"As May continued to follow her money she discovered there were also transactions transferring funds to a company called Keller Contracting Services for repair on her home near LA about two days before the Emmys. Yet it was all a ruse to create a diversion that would tie Mr. J to the chaos and murder. Donna knew if Mr. J sent her to LA to try and reason with James, everyone would think that she was trying to warn him of the danger of returning to New Jersey."

"The real scope of her plans was to get rid of the rest of her enemies and take over Mr. J's corporation. She wanted James to be by her side, but when she found out, he had a weak spot for his father, Victor she knew she was going to have to take him out of the picture."

"Although Donna knew her husband would be in prison for the rest of his life, she decided it was best to silence him for good and that is why she had him killed."

That's when I chimed in, "That was the reason James was acting so crazy when you first met him. He did not want to be captured. He finally realized that Mr. J had been telling the truth, and now the NSA had given him an opportunity to clear himself and start a new life once Donna is defeated"

"George, I am glad you are beginning to understand the situation, but can you please stop interrupting and let me finish so we can get some sleep."

I nodded my head as John continued.

"May refused to stop investigating as she contacted Keller's Contracting Services. Finally, she discovered the private contractor whom Donna claimed did the repairs did not work on her vacation home in Florida. Since the contractor only worked on her commercial properties she was given the number to the company's headquarters in New York. Where she would be able find out the name of the subcontractor who did the work on Donna's vacation home in Florida.

The contact in New York no longer existed, when she recalled the original contractor, the operator who picked up, the phone stated that they had never heard of the company she was trying to contact."

"May was stumped. So, she decided to make one last call to the company in New York and she used Donna's name. The operator immediately transferred her back to the New Jersey office and after several minutes of silence someone asked her for some additional information regarding her properties in Florida and then they gave her a list of several contractors they may have used for the repairs. "However, due to recent upgrades in their accounting software and a fire in their warehouse, all their records related to repairs on Florida properties had been destroyed."

"May checked the names against a list of prior repairs done on Donna's vacation home. The name matched with a contractor who had done some work on her home over the past several years. When she called the contractor, she was stunned when Steve picked up the phone in his Den. Since the NSA had bugged the den the conversation was recorded "Keller's Contracting Services, how may I help you?' May apologized and told Steve that she had dialed the wrong number."

"After the phone call, she immediately looked back through the records of repairs done on any real estate that Donna owned. The name Keller's Contracting Services showed up several times, and all the payments eventually wound up in Steve's account. Keller Contracting was a dummy corporation set up by Donna so she could funnel funds to Scott's father whenever she needed his services."

"With the new evidence May found tying Steve to Donna it looked like the NSA had the enough evidence against Donna. Finally, NSA had evidence against Donna. By following the money trail, the commander found out that Steve had been working behind the scenes for Donna for over twenty years. The commander was overjoyed by the information that May had uncovered. Therefore, he made her a permeant member of the PTF.

Upon the completion of the investigation, Commander Johnstone felt like it was time to turn in his final report that would have cleared Scott's father of any wrongdoing, but he informed everyone that it was uncertain if he would allow Scott to continue as a recruit for the NSA because Scott started questioning the recruiter during the examination, several red flags went up.

That's when we found out about Steve controlling Scott's mind the night before the exam. The commander finally understood your friendship with Scott and your enlistment was a sham that Donna used to infiltrate the NSA. She felt like your strong bond of friendship would slowly bring all of us crumbling to our knees.

Yet, the commander realized that your strong friendship would be Donna downfall as he decided to use Scott induction into the NSA as an avenue to trap Donna. "Due to the discrepancies, the commander felt like he would be able to pass on information to Donna without anyone suspecting he was the culprit. Because he knew that you and

Scott could not keep secrets from each other, and at the end of day you both trusted him, and he would be able to suppress any issues that might come up."

During the meeting, the commander informed the board that he was thinking about adding Scott as a member of the PTF, but he would be under surveillance until he proved himself fit to be a member of the NSA. Then he turned in his final report that seemed to clear Scott's father of any wrongdoing. And the commander made it seem like he was going to reunite you and Scott after Scott's secret mission to Alaska. Thus, your naval orders currently showed you and Scott would join the PTF after you finished A school and your NSA training."

"The commander reiterated the importance of you and Scott were working together onboard the Carl Vison CVN -70. Then he stopped and looked around the room. Does anyone have any questions regarding George and Scott's status? I realize that many of you think I jumped the gun by making George the leader of the PTF. And now I am asking you to take a leap of faith regarding Scott's induction into the NSA. It's important that everyone gets on board and welcomes Scott and George to the PTF"

"After the meeting the commander was all smiles, he felt like he would finally be able to find the mole and have enough information to trick Donna into revealing herself. "Plus, with Steve's house under surveillance, along with the additional bugs on the cell phone of all the PFT committee members and placing extra agents to spy on specific members of the committee who had recently shown suspicious activity. The commander had all bases covered."

"Once the meeting was over the commander had one of the agents leak the information hoping to find to Scott's father's contact at the NSA. The Commander hoped he would find the mole inside the NSA. At first, the commander did not think his plan had worked, but around midnight the commander's patience paid off and one of the agents contacted Steve with the information regarding Scott's induction into the NSA"

CHAPTER XII

The Plot Thickens

"Suddenly the commander's plan seemed to be working worked perfectly, and the commander had discovered the mole. "As Steve fell for the commander's trap. He became paranoid, and he went to see your recruiter. He told him as a concerned parent that he wanted to ensure that the navy lived up to their part of the deal. Steve told your recruiter that if you and Scott were separated, Scott would be in danger because you and Scott were like brothers and had protected each other since the day you met in grade school. He told the recruiter he was worried, and he felt that it would be a grave injustice if the navy separated them."

He told your recruiter that if you and Scott were separated Scott would be in danger because you and Scott were like brothers and had protected each other since you met in grade school. Steve told the recruiter it would be a grave injustice if the navy did anything to cause a separation between you and Scott.

The recruiter reassured Steve that the navy had every intention of placing you and Scott onboard the same ship. Before Steve left, the recruiter stopped him and said, 'Sir, I know I am not supposed to show you this, but I also have a son and I understand your concerns."

"The recruiter went over to his safe and pulled out several

documents. On the documents were yours and Scott's orders to your first duty station. When Steve saw the order, his face lit up. However, what he didn't know was that those were your true naval orders, not your NSA orders. As far as the navy is concerned, you and Scott were to be stationed on the same ship."

"Thank you so much for looking out for my son, I don't know how to repay your kindness." The recruiter shook Scott's father's hand whispered, "Just don't tell anyone I showed you your son's orders, because I could get court-martialed if anyone found out."

After Scott's father visited your recruiter, he contacted Donna and told her that everything was still on schedule and that once the two of you completed boot camp, they would have their foot in the door at the NSA."

"When Steve contacted Donna, the commander knew it was only a matter of time before we would be able to take her down. That is why he only told his most trusted associates his plan. Because he knew that we only had three months to infiltrate Donna's organization, and this was not the first time the NSA felt like they had her cornered."

"The agent who discovered the mole became very unsettled, and he informed the commander that he was going to have to go off the books, and he started worrying that Janis and your family might be in danger. He also felt like Steve had done something to Scott mind lapses while he was in high school. He did not know yet, but he told the commander that he had to go deep undercover this time to ensure everyone was safe."

The commander was sure he had tracked down the link between Steve, Donna, and the mole, Collin was a member of the British Secret Service. Knowing if the agents intuition was on target this was only beginning to a complex issue that the commander hoped would end Donna's reign of terror. When the commander realized that a British agent he secretly met with his counterparts in the British Secret Service."

"This new information about Donna's team sent a wave of disbelief throughout the NSA. For too many years, Donna had gone unchecked, and now everyone realized that her reach was deeper than they had originally thought."

"When the commander presented this new information to the committee they were scrambling to figure out how they could justify May final report. The commander assured the committee that he had everything under control. And while the commander made it seem like May had submitted her final report he was reluctant to tell the committer that he had secretly ordered May to track down any additional discrepancies and report back to him."

Therefore, he told everyone on the committee they needed to be more alert to what was going to happen next since they found the mole. Were they going to continue down the rabbit hole and disregard and the new information that had been recently discovered or were they finally going to join him in creating a plan to wipe out Donna and he worldwide network of terrorist.

One by one the committee members voted to work on taking down Donna and that they no longer had any perceived concepts about who to trust. At the end of the meeting, they all agreed to bond together and create a more united front. They also threw their full support behind the commander and the PTF. They were all angry that Donna had deceived them for so long.

"Now that the commander had the full support of the NSA he reached out to May. Since, you are member of the PTF, we have the NSA full support to search for any more surprises regarding Donna and her group of terrorists. I need you to stay diligent and remember that we must keep in mind that the PTF is not fully in motion until George completes his training and is on board the *USS Bunker Hill.*

Also, once Scott is cleared he will be you backup support at a secret location. Eventually, Janis and Georges family will be sent there for their safety. This will be the last time I mention Scotts name. Everyone must think Scott is still station on board the *Carl Vinson.* If you mention this conversation to anyone I will deny it and you will immediately be removed as a member of the PTF is that understood"

May was quiet for a few seconds and then she replied sharply "Sir yes sir you can count on me."

Then Mays interjected. “Sir, I have some important information for you, Steve was only a small part of the bigger plan, and it seemed like Keller Contracting Services was a worldwide engineering firm that Donna hired to take care of her real estate projects all over the world. And Steve’s financial records are very shocking, there were several unusual purchases. It seemed like Steve had been purchasing some unusual mind-control drugs from an experimental drug company in Dallas. The conclusion was that these drugs were used on Scott, and May traced the purchases to the time when Scott nearly failed his first two classes during tenth grade. Not only was Scott failing his classes, and he was also almost suspended from school due to his erratic behavior toward teachers and students.”

“Then several months later Steve made his second purchase of drugs and Scott miraculously started getting straight A’s. And because of his attitude change, his teachers dropped their request to suspend Scott. However, for the next two years Scott had several episodes, and each time it was attributed to the drugs that Steve had given Scott.”

“The commander double checked all of May’s information because he could not believe that Donna and Steve were that evil. After rechecking the data and correlations to the changes in Scott’s behavior, there was a 99 percent chance Scott was under the influence of some type of mind control when he joined the navy.”

‘Several weeks before you joined the navy, Donna sent Steve a commission for some additional work on her house in Florida. Yet we know that Steve did not use the funds for any repairs. It seemed like he purchased several more doses of the mind-control drug, and he transferred the rest of the funds into a special trust for Scott. However, it seemed like Steve was worried about his son, and he asked Donna for extra funds so that he could take care of Scott if he went insane due to the continual usage of mind-control drugs.”

“Thus, he evaluated you and Scott to make sure that both of you were clean and prepared to become part of the NSA. The commander assessed both of you during the entrance exam, then he made his final decision regarding both of you becoming members of the PTF.

The reason he pushed you so hard was that he needed to make sure that Steve had not gotten to you. The commander was also aware of the friction between you and your parents, and he wanted to ensure that you would be mentally prepared to continue your transformation into the leader of the PTF. Both you and Scott passed the first test. However, Scott failed the second test when Scott started questioning the recruiter at the examination center."

"During the final selection process, the CNO contacted Commander Johnstone and ordered him to investigate Scott's family history. The commander told the CNO that he had already done his recon and that he had everything under control. However, the conversation left the commander skeptical about your resolve to join the NSA once you found out that Scott was not going to be your partner. Therefore, it was important that everyone played their part until you reached Spokane, and everyone was enlisted."

"What the commander failed to realize was the extent the mind-control drugs had on Scott. When you were separated during the entrance exam, Scott nearly blew his cool. However, your conversation with Scott after the examination seemed to calm him down and we were able to proceed with our plans to induct you into the PTF. Everything was back on track until you picked up Scott. When Scott saw you in the den talking with Steve, he flipped out."

"He could not understand why Steve called you into the den. He knew that Steve had never invited him into the den. Why would he bring you into the and leave his son on the outside." He felt like his father was trying to replace him and that he was going to break both of your families apart. You were his best friend. He did not need a brother. The fact that you and your mother had suddenly become cozy with his father was driving him insane. Then he jumped into the sedan and saw how cozy you were with strangers. He began to wonder if you were still his friend and would truly protect him."

"While the four of us were in the dark and were unaware of Scott's condition, the trap was being set. The commander was not certain how potent the drugs that Steve had given Scott were. However, when he saw how Scott reacted to you on the bus, it seemed like Steve may have given Scott an extra dose. And it made Scott paranoid. He tried to hide it from everyone, but he could no longer hide his true feelings.

"Steve had pushed him too hard. "And Scott went crazy. There was nothing the commander could do. Thus, he left us to fend for ourselves, hoping that we would be able to control Scott until the commander was able to reverse the drugs' effect after he got to boot camp. The incident should have made you realize how dangerous Scott is right now. Hopefully, you can understand the commander is only trying to protect you by making sure you were not attached to anyone who could affect our mission."

The commander was so glad that the three of us were in the dark. The good news is that by the time Scott completes boot camp the drugs will have worn off."

I turned to John and said, "So that's why Scott has been acting so strange. And when Steve told me he felt like Scott and I were making a wise decision, it was all a ruse to gain my trust." Then I stopped John for a moment. It was hard for me to grasp that someone could be so devious, but everything was starting to make sense.

Although Scott was being controlled, he was the one who made me face my parents and tell them that I was going to enlist. He made me close my parent off, which I had never done before. I had always respected their advice. I looked at John and told him to continue, although inside I was about to burst. *How could Steve drug his son and destroy our friendship?*

However, I realized how the commander had played his part in breaking up my friendship with Scott with his grand scheme to take down Donna. I looked at John and was about to ask him to stop explaining the mission, but I knew I was no longer in control of my own destiny. And for the first time in my life, I suddenly felt like I was unable to control the narrative. I stuffed the anger within myself and continued to listen to John expound on the benefits of their mission.

Then John said, "George, now that we are in boot camp, you must decide. Are you going to let Scott's father control the situation, or are you going to collaborate and work with us to take down Donna?"

Then I looked at John, "That's enough, for now. Please stop explaining their mission." That's when I understood I was no longer in control of my own destiny, and for the first time in my life, I suddenly felt like I was unable to control the narrative."

I was angry when I realized how the commander had broken apart my friendship with Scott and wanted me to be a part of his grand scheme to take down James's mother.

John laughed. "George, you need to control your emotions. The commander has already figured out a way to keep you in the good graces of your family. The moment your family sees the cruelty of Steve toward his son, they will understand how much you cared for Scott's well-being. All they will do is ask you how any man could use his own son as a pawn in such a sinister plot. George, the bottom line is that power can be true or imagined, yet in the end, it does not matter because it is the choices, we make with our perceived power that define who we are. Right now, at this very moment, you must decide how to use your power. Will it be for the greater good, or will it lead you down the path of destruction?"

"When you look at men like Steve, who feel like they hold all the power, you must make a choice. Will you become like them and destroy your life and the life of all those who trust you, thus telling the world that you are beyond help? Will you make a wise choice and push past your friendship with Scott, which will allow us to work as a team to destroy our common enemies?

Knowing that we did everything to use our power to unite and take down people like Scott's father who are bent on destroying the world. We all have lived with regrets, but when you are presented with the opportunity to change those regrets and create a better future, you should grab hold of the moment. Remember, we are not the ones responsible for the chaos that exists in the world today."

"Once you get that through your head, we will be able to move beyond the tricks and deception that has been surrounding us for far too many years. I know you are being asked to make one of the most important decisions you have made in your entire life, and it will not be easy. You will feel conflicted whatever your decision is. I remember when I first met James. He had just found out his mother was a traitor, and he was very confused. He had so many doubts about whether he had the courage to turn on his mother. The more he learned about the depths of her betrayal, the easier it got. Today, James finally has some purpose in his life. He has grasped the reality of what his mother did and is working with the NSA to help bring her to justice."

"Donna has become my example of what a waste your life will be if you are always trying to destroy someone else for your own gain. She has gotten to a point when she now has no conscience. She has left so many people hopeless and just laughs at their calamity. The team we will be creating will ensure the world is a better place by putting people like Donna and Scott's father behind bars, where they belong. I cannot decide for you. But from my experience, I have learned to go with the flow and trust that one day everything will work out."

"I am hoping that our team can work to create a better world by putting away people like Donna and Scott's father. I beg you to think long and hard before you make your choice of having a life of freedom from oppression or a life where you can truly help others escape oppression."

"One of the benefits of leading the PTF is that you will have a chance to strike back at Donna and fix your relationship with Scott and your family. Yet this opportunity is greater than just fixing your relationships. You will become part of an elite unit that will be keeping the world safe from Donna's reign of terror.

The more John spoke, the more I felt like I was slowly dying inside. It's as if your past did not exist anymore, but now you have been given a chance to become productive members of society. Get some rest, 'cause you're going need it.

"George, you can't blame Scott, because he was just a pawn like you. No one expected the mind-control drugs would have an adverse effect on Scott. The more Steve pushed Scott to betray your friendship, the crazier Scott became.

Every time he pushed Scott to get closer to you, he felt like his father favored you more than him. Which is what slowly started driving a wedge in your relationship. However, when as we picked him up on our way to Spokane Scott greeted you as if your friendship was still going strong. Thus, Steve felt like were still on good terms until after boot camp. Thus, when Scott returned home for R&R, Steve would restart Scott on the full dosage of his mind-control drugs"

"However, the commander threw a monkey wrench in Steve's plans after the incident on the bus, when he ordered the medics to confiscate any prescriptions Scott had. Then he had them dump all of Scotts old prescription drugs and issued him new drugs. And the commander as able to hide the fact that Scott was slowly being weaned off the mind control drugs. Even Scott did not know that his prescriptions have been changed. Once the medics determine the dosage of the drugs that had been prescribed to Scott they were able to estimate that it would take at least eight weeks for the effects to wear off and before Scotts mind would be normal again

However, for the next eight weeks Scott was a burden as he tried to falsify reports regarding the incident on the bus to make it seem as if you had started the fight with Ricky. That is why you must not let your guard down, because Steve is still in the mix, and we must be careful. There is no way of knowing how the drugs will affect Scott.

However, as long Donna is unaware that Scott's father failed to give Scott the proper dosage of mind-control drugs. By allowing Scotts false report to circulate the commander was able to keep Donna and Steve at bay, while being able to flush out the spies in the ranks..

Once the commander found out who the spies were he made sure the report that you signed was the truth behind the incident on the bus. Also, his decision to send Scott on a secret mission to Alaska right after boot camp was to protect him. He hope that the medics would be able to find something to counteract the mind drugs Steve been giving to Scott. With the extra 90 days he was almost certain his team of medics would be able to reverse the effect of the drugs completely. Thus, keeping Scott safe if Steve tried to drug him some more once he arrived on his duty station the *USS Carl Vinson* upon the completion of his mission to Alaska."

"It is very important that you make Steve feel like you would never turn your back on Scott regardless of the circumstances. It will become difficult for you to keep up appearances with Steve when he finds out that Scott is being sent to Alaska for 90 days.

The last statement that John made my mind cringed, for my life was being so profoundly thrown into disarray. All I could think about was how would I be able to face my family and tell them that Scott and I were suddenly enemies?

"John, you are crazy, you know about me or my relationship with my family. They will begin to question when they do not see Scott. They will want to know why I was not sent to sent to Alaska with Scott. You know I have not spoken with him since the incident on the bus and we are now enemies"

"George, slow down the less say, the better off they will be. Just stick to the story. Once the navy send your parents the letter after you leave for your training in Mississippi stating that you will be station on two different ships it may cause a problem with Steve. But you father will understand the situation because he was in the military. My family may be more understanding then Steve due to my father military service. But Steve is another whole story."

"When Steve picks me up once, it will be hard for me to even look him in the face knowing what he has done to his son. You make it seem so simple as if I can just smile and say Scott would be on a special assignment to Alaska, and I will be going to SKA school. Then we will both report to two different ships. Instead of the same ship which the navy guaranteed us at the time of enlistment. This will cause Steve to contact the navy and immediately fix the situation between me and his son.

That is why you must make Steve feels comfortable with the situation. Make Steve feel like you and Scott will be living together in San Diego after you return from you first tour. Let him know by the time you return you will be able to be station on the *USS Carl Vison.* Because by that time you will have made rank as second-class storekeeper and you have been assured that there will be a slot available for you rank on board the *USS Carl Vinson.*

Thus, Steve will still think that both of you are a part of the PTF. The commander knows he is asking a lot of you, but it is necessary to keep up appearances."

"What you are asking me to do is impossible. How can I convince anyone my relationship with Scott is still rock solid when I know the truth. Steve and Donna are trying to kill me and my family. They have destroyed Scotts mind and I have been left in a broken field to lick my wounds."

John smirked at me when he said "What do you want me to say George, you wanted answers. You got them. I told you if you keep digging you might not like the answer you find."

"I agree with you, it is criminal how Donna and Steve have messed with Scott's mind. The two of you were destined to be best friends for life. Your decision to join the navy put a bubble in your friendship."

Suddenly John stopped. "George, that's enough for now. I will be setting up a meeting with the commander. I'm sure he will answer any further questions you may have. After meeting with the commander, you will have all the pertinent information you need to make an informed decision on whether you want to become a part of his special unit or if you want to just serve your time and get out."

"I know what I told you tonight might be hard to bear, but just think, you will be leading a team that will wipe out terrorists like Donna and help bring peace to the world. There are so many people like Donna who feel like they can control the narrative. It is not only our choice to control the narrative, but it is our right to stand up and fight for a peaceful narrative. Too many good people are suffering because of the action of a few rotten apples"

"It is time for those of us who care about what happens to our future to bond together and create a force that has never been seen before to bring a blanket of peace to the world and stop the terror and deception of people like Donna. It is a horrible thing to lose a friend, but in the end, when we stand up and fight, we not only save our friendships, but we create a stable environment for those we love."

"Remember this is only part of the story. I can stop any time you want. But you wanted answers that is what I am here for. I know right now the story may not be to your liking. That is why the commander decided to create the PTF. He wanted to give us the chance to redeem ourselves by taking down those responsible for ruining our lives.

Scott may still be your friend, but you need to stay clear of him until the mind-control drugs wear off. You know he will only become more conflicted each day. Thus for all of our safety I am begging you to stay away from Scott for the remainder of our time in boot camp."

I could tell John was trying to calm me down as he kept trying to tell me how concerned the commander was about breaking up my friendship with Scott and if I tried to engage with him, it may push him over the edge, and his mind may never come back from the deep abyss into which it had fallen.

I looked at John and shook my head as if I agreed with his assessment of the current situation. There was no use fighting the commander because right now he had the upper hand, he knew how important my friendship with Scott was, and John kept stressing that the commander would eventually make Scott a member of the PTF.

"Righteous, brother, for the time being we will keep the illusion that Scott is part of the NSA. Now it's time to get some sleep," John said as we walked toward his bunk. "I just hope you can learn to let off some steam without blowing up the engine, 'cause we all have our own problems, and a good leader tries to keep everyone else calm. I'll see you in the morning, friend."

After John's speech, I realized that I had a lot of information I needed to process. And no speech was going to take away my burden. Everything was not fine and dandy. Because I had never realized how despicable people could be, and it made me sick to my stomach.

CHAPTER XIII

George Doubts

I am not a hero, and I am not someone to cling to courage or honor. All I want to do is get my life back to some sort of normality. I had been told that I can trust James and John, that they were the best at what they did. But that could not help me sleep as mulled over the information that had me shoved into my mind.

I finally went over to John and shook him. When John opened his he looked at me like I was crazy.

"George, I told you to get some sleep, can't this wait for until revile. I can't sleep I just need to ask you one question then I will leave you alone. Did you make the right choice, when you joined the PTF and are you 100 percent with the program?"

"You have told me some of the stories surrounding the PTF, but why did you join the PTF, and what was the decisive moment when you knew your service would truly matter? Also, I need to know if you are going to follow my orders once I officially become the leader of the PTF. Ddo you feel like everyone else around this place? They say I am too young, and I have no experience."

"Are you going to walk the first time you think I am making a mistake or are you going to work with me to resolve the issue? Whatever you say will not change my decision, I just need to know with whom I am working. because I am assessing all my options before I jump to any conclusion. And if I decide to put my life in someone else's hands, the commander will be the first to know."

John replied sheepishly, "One day you will learn the truth about my connection to the NSA. There is a reason I stopped where I stopped. I was ordered not to overload you with too much info. Today is not the day for us to banter over who is right or wrong, but it is time to reflect and understand that our brains can only analyze so much information at any given time."

All I could do was smile, knowing John had shown his true colors. I knew it would not make any sense to pursue the truth about John, because it was becoming evident that John was an agency man, he would never break. I had to be discreet from this point forward. Knowing he would only draw farther away if I continued to bug him.

Suddenly John began to repeat himself. "George, I think I have inundated you with enough for one night. We have twelve long weeks ahead of us. You need to get some rest. I will give you more info later. With my data and your research, you'll be prepared to lead PTF."

"I am sure the commander will fill in the blanks before graduation. After a couple of weeks of R&R, you'll be ready to go to Meridian, Mississippi, for your final naval training.

Then once you have completed your naval training, you will begin the hard work of joining the NSA. It will be like and additional twelve weeks of boot camp."

What John did next threw me for a loop as he stood at attention and saluted me. "Is there anything else I can help you with before you let me get some sleep? Remember, it's your move, George. Just make sure you make the right choices to keep our mission from failing."

He stood there at attention until I said, "At ease." Then he looked at me as he jumped on his bunk "You need to lie down and get some rest, or we all go crazy." Then John plopped down on his bunk and instantly fell asleep.

John was right, my mind was in overdrive, and I needed to calm down and get some rest. I came to the realization that only one person could fill in the blanks. That person was Commander Johnstone. I did not understand how the commander expected me to lead a team when I didn't even know the specifics of the mission. Hopefully, John would set up my meeting with the commander before I went crazy. Surely, I would have a clearer picture of why the three of us were chosen for this secret mission. It did not matter how painful it was, I had made up my mind that I had to forget Scott and focus on my main objective: leading a team to take on the enemies of the NSA.

I was glad that the chief had picked me to stay in the barrack while the rest of the company was on the grinder. This would allow me to use my skills to gather information regarding the members of the team. While John and James might fill in some of the gaps, I knew nothing about their background. Who was commander Johnstone, Captain Silverton, and General Armstrong? They seemed to be the ones running the show.

For years I had been honing my computer skills, and I had even figured out how to program several types of software languages to enhance my ability to search for people on the internet. The reason I scored so high on the Naval exam is that I had hacked into the Naval Academies Database and was able to figure out the probabilities of what question I would be asked on my exam. Once I figured out the probabilities of what question would be asked my photographic memory kicked in and I was able to ace the exam.

While I scored high on the exam, I did not want to make it seem like I had cheated. Therefore, I answered certain questions incorrectly. It was like a game Scott, and I used to play before he was drugged by his father. We used to challenge each other to see who could find out the most information on a different subject. That is why we were consistently on the honor roll in high school.

I also worked with my father's friend Bernie who showed me how to build and repair computers from the ground up. He also taught me how to write computer programs that allowed me to bypass computer protocols. Eventually, I was one of his top techs. Thus, it would be easy for me to train the rest of my squad on how to take the naval exam. Most exams are based on probabilities. Thus, all I had to do was figure out the scheme used for each exam. I had always been drawn to accounting, my dad's friend taught me about investments, banking, and marketing. Thus, I had a well-rounded skill-set.

Very few of my friends or family knew the skill I had. Because I kept myself under the radar. My father had not realized that his friend Bernie was a technological genius. He was one of the first people to figure out differential math, Boolean expressions, and various other computer theories.

Therefore, with my knowledge of business statics and probability granted me an advantage. And there weren't many areas that I did not know about computers. Therefore, with the time I had I would be able to access the computers in the barracks. I knew I would find the answers to many of my questions. And though I was not sure when I would meet with the commander, I had to make sure that I used all my available time and assets to help me make an informed decision.

I still remember when I was ten how I accessed a major bank and deposited money in my dad's account. To this day the bank has not figured out how the funds were transferred into my dad's account. Nor could they figure out whose account the funds were transferred from. Thus, my dad did not have to return the funds. The bank considered it a bank error. That is when I learned to keep myself anchored. Because if anyone figure out the various tricks, I had played I would be sent to a maximum-security facility.

While the computers in the barrack were not the most sophisticated machines I knew they were connected to the government's mainframe and I would be able to use the computer to hack into the NSA mainframe since they were part of the military's system. I was sure they would have plenty information in the NSA database regarding, Donna, Steve, James, and John. In time, I would be able to find out the true nature of my squad's mission. I knew I had to work fast because I only had twelve weeks before I would take some R&R and then head to Mississippi for my additional training.

Suddenly James came up behind me and pounded me on the back. "How is it going, George? Has John gotten to your mind yet? He has a way with words. We've got a few minutes before lights out. How 'bout you and I play a friendly game of chess? I packed me one of them travel-sized games just for a moment like this."

I threw up my hand. "What the heck, let's have a friendly game of checkers. I guess it can't hurt."

James quickly threw his set on the table, and we went at it. It was hard for me to concentrate. The first game, He whooped me badly.

"You ain't no fun, George. You play like my grandma. I thought you were the big boss and could give a little challenge."

"All right, the best three out five and then we hit the hay."

James laughed. "Are you sure you're up for it?"

I stared at James and said, "Just set up the board, man, I don't feel like talking."

For the next few minutes, I was king of the hill as I beat James and we were about to start our third and final game. It looked like I was going to win again, but James tricked me as he pulled out a picture of his sister.

"What you think, George? You can write her for me and tell her all the good things about how you're my new best friend and you hope to meet her after we get out of boot camp. You know, she's twenty-five and she's been looking for a good man for a couple of years. But I had to chase away too many of them dingbats. Most men don't even know how to address a lady. They all start acting crazy when they see how beautiful my sister is. What you think, think you can you help me out?"

"James, you're a lunatic. Play the game so we can finish before the lights go out. Are you saying my sister ain't good enough for you? Just take another look. You ain't going to find anyone sweeter who knows how to take care of a man."

"James, stop with all the questions. It ain't about your sister. I'm sure she's nice, but you don't know anything about me. I have a fiancée; we are supposed to get married once I get out of boot camp."

"Good for you, George. Do you have a sister? Because I could use a good woman in my life. You have her picture, can you put in a good word for me."

"It's your move, man, just keep my sister out of it. She is already spoken for. Plus, you're not her type. You're a little too rough around the edges. I don't think she needs anyone like that in her life right now."

Suddenly James stood up and started to walk across the room. "George, you know, you can say some harsh things. I may not come from your cut, but I ain't no bad man. All I want to do is meet your sister and talk if she doesn't like me, then that's fine."

"James, get back over here so we can finish the game?"

"George, you need to apologize and tell me you're sorry. And can you at least show me a picture of your sister?"

"I don't have a picture of my sister. If you ever visit me, I'll introduce you, okay?"

James smiled. "Sounds good to me." Then he calmly stated checkmate. He chuckled. "You gotta keep your mind focused, man. You get distracted too easily. Guess we will have to finish the match tomorrow," he said as he packed up his game when the master chief came through the door and shut off the lights.

How was I going to be able to get some rest? I knew we would soon have a rude awakening. My mind was going into overdrive with all the revelations running around in my head as I closed my eyes and desperately tried to sleep. I kept pondering how I could find out the true story behind John's obsession with the NSA. There were just too many thoughts rolling around in my head. I was not used to going into things blindly. I needed some more answers now. I wanted to throw the towel and let Commander Johnstone know that he had picked the wrong person for the mission.

Maybe if I asked John a few more questions I would be able to get some sleep. However, when I leaned over to his bunk to ask John one final question, John was already in a deep sleep and my faint whisper had no effect. I wanted to speak louder, but if I did, I would wake up the entire squad.

I could not understand how John could be so at ease. It didn't seem fair that John could be sleeping so peacefully. How was I going to be able to get some rest? I knew we would soon have a rude awakening.. I needed to be prepared for the onslaught of training that would begin around 4:00 AM. With the recent revelations, my mind was very perplexed, and I tossed and turned in my bunk for the next thirty minutes.

Suddenly John let out a few snorts and busted out snoring. The sound of his snoring shook my bunk. Out of desperation, I reached down and smacked John on the forehead. "John, you gotta give me a break please, turn over and put a muzzle on it."

John opened his eyes and just shook his head. When he turned over on his side, his snoring subsided. What a relief. Finally, I had some peace a quiet.

Several minutes later, two maniacs flipped on the lights and were running around the room banging on garbage can lids.

"Boys, it's time to get up. You got thirty minutes to muster outside on the grinder. Anybody who's late will have some special duty this evening while everyone else is sleeping, so I suggest you all get ready for a glorious day."

Bang, bang the garbage can lid rang. This morning we had a special surprise and reveille was played out of the loudspeakers, and the master chief burst through the door smiling.

"Rise and shine, it's time to live that adventure. Remember the old saying 'it's not just a job, it's an adventure.' Where else can you start your day off with such a beautiful tune?"

"Good to see you too, sunshine. You got one more day and then I expect you to start educating the rest of my recruits. Just remember, my friend, one more day and it's time to rock and roll."

Then Chief Walters ordered everyone to line up as we marched to the mess hall. While we were eating breakfast, Chief Walters came over to me.

"Son, after you eat breakfast, you and Jimmy are to return to the barracks. Jimmy is your security and the security of our berthing space.

All I want you to do is study for the next exam. With your answers and knowledge of the educational portion of boot camp, our squad will be able to be on top of all the competitions. So, you'd better get your brains in gear while the rest of the squad is on the grinder. Once the company returns from drills, I expect you to be prepared to sit down with each member of the squad for ten minutes."

I was glad there were several computers in the barracks. Now I knew that I would be able to research the Peace Task Force, before heading to a secure location for my NSA training.

Since I had access to several computers, I figured out a way to spend about an hour every day doing research into the PTF and an hour working on the educational components for the remaining exams.

After giving my report to the master chief I would try my best to get some rest. Before I sat down with John, and he gave more information about the PTF.

"George," he said, "it's time for you to learn the importance and value of our team and how it fits into our national security. I am not sure how come everyone is so worried about you. Because regardless of what you decide to do, the PTF will continue. However, I promise you that I would ask the commander to answer some of your questions. He told me he did not have much time, but he would be glad to meet with you sometime within the next few days. You better be prepared to ask your questions. The commander is a busy man, and he does not have time to waste with a chump like you."

I could not understand why John was offended that the commander wanted to meet with me. I asked John why he was so angry. John looked at me like I was crazy.

"Mister, I am not upset with the commander. I am tired and need to get some rest, so I suggest you just leave me alone."

I yelled at John before he closed his eyes, "John, I thought you could tell me why you joined this special unit. You told me all about Scott and James. I want to know how you got tangled up with the NSA because you just don't fit the bill for an agency man."

John looked at me and laughed. "If you haven't figured out my story by now, you are not as smart as they said you were. You've got a lot of nerve questioning me. I don't care what they say about your skills, your indecision proves my point that you are a novice. There is no way you are ready to hear the whole scope of the mission. The recklessness of the commander choosing you over me made me truly angry. I was about to hand in my resignation this morning. before I could make a decision that would change my life forever."

"George, you need to understand that I should be leading the squad, I am the one who has all the experience. I suggest you stuff your self-righteous opinions back in the hole they came out of.

John if you have a problem with the commander choosing me over you, you need to sit down with him face-to-face and discuss the matter. I have no problem marching you right over to his office now and tearing apart this entire façade. After you have done that, I hope you will be ready for me to hand in my resignation from the NSA, then the commander will let you lead."

"Do you want me to track down the commander myself and tell him that his most experienced agent is a phony? I have not even been shown the scope of the mission, and you are already denying my ability to lead. So, until you have that conversation with the commander regarding his decision to make me the leader of the PTF. I am suggesting that you shut your mouth and get in line with the program. To me, you are already considered a traitor to the cause because you are denying my ability and suggesting that the commander did not know what he was doing when he picked me to lead the PTF."

"Have you gone bonkers? A few minutes ago, you were singing the commander's praises. How can I decide to join a team when the members of the squad don't even know how to take orders? If I had my druthers, I would have you taken out back and given the boot you deserve. If you cannot answer my question with dignity, I suggest you get out of my way. Your actions today could destroy the cohesion of our squad before it even starts. I suggest you line up with the commander or direct me to the people who are in line with the purpose of the mission."

"I did not question your loyalty for a moment. When you told me everyone's story, when you refused to tell me why you joined the mission, I was intrigued to find out what you were hiding. Since you feel like you should be the leader of the squad, I assure you that a leader cannot make a sound decision until he has the pertinent info."

"All I am asking is for you to be real with me so I can protect the special unit from falling into a trap."

"The first step in that trap is when we begin to question things without having all the facts. You assume to know what I am all about, yet you are hiding some of the most valuable information needed to ensure a smooth transition. I am sorry if the commander chose me over you. If you disagree with the commander, the best way to resolve the issue is to show your side of the story and make the commander understand why you should be the leader of the unit instead of me."

"You're right about my ability, and you may be a better leader than I am. I don't know the answer to that question. However, if you don't bring your disagreement out in the open and put all the facts on the table, you are either a traitor or a coward."

"For the time being, the commander feels like I am the leader of the unit. You need to fall in line or move on to greener pastures where you can be the leader of your team."

"I have not decided if I want to put my life in someone else's hands, but the commander told me that you and James were the best at what you do and that I could trust you to make the right choices. The decisive moment is here, John, are you going to follow orders or are you going to walk? Whatever you do will not change my decision, because I am assessing all my options before I jump to any conclusion."

John looked at me and smiled. "Don't get so worked up. You'll find out my story soon enough. My story is quite simple, and one day you will learn the truth about my connection to the NSA. However, today is not that day. I'm not sure when the commander will allow me to reveal the entire scope of our mission. I'm not sure you're ready for the whole truth. I have my reasons for stopping where I stopped. I was ordered not to overload you with too much info. I'm almost certain that you will make the right choice when the time comes."

Before my mind went completely off, John turned his head and said, "I hope that you decide to lead this team, because I am sure you will make a fine leader. Whatever grievance I have will not affect my support for our mission."

"The commander has always treated all of us with the utmost respect. I have no doubt he has his reason for making you the leader of our unit. I will always support and defend his decisions. I just hope that your evaluation puts you on the right side of history. We need a strong leader, and I can see many good qualities in you. However, you need to learn to chill out and have a little faith in the system."

"The captain and the commander know what they are doing, and they have developed one of the greatest covert units ever assembled to protect them from the backlash of those who would rather fight a war than peacefully resolve our problems."

"Don't worry about me. I will talk with the commander about our conversation. I will relay your concerns to him."

John laughed, "George if you only knew how James and I felt when the commander said you would be our leader. We were shocked that they would put a novice as the leader of the PTF. However, the commander was right to choose you because we are too close to the situation, and we would have never asked some of the questions that you are asking. You may be raw and need some more training."

"However, I believed eventually, you will be a great leader. While you are not completely on the outside of the situation, you are much more subjective than either one of us will ever be. I am sure we both have a slight edge. The truth is we are both tired of hearing how Donna can't be stopped and that her reign of terror will only increase. That's why we are putting our trust in you, George, you have shown the ability to comprehend the situation and have learned how to improvise, adapt, and overcome."

"I know the commander is asking a lot of you, but once you see the entire picture you will understand why you are a valuable part of the equation. The doubts that I had about your leadership were erased when I saw you deal with Ricky and the OIC. That's when I understood why you were the right choice to be the leader of the PTF. Just try and relax and stay cool. I will continue to update you on the PTF and what will be expected of all of us. Hopefully, you will be able to make some type of sense out of the information and learn how to mold it into the info you already know."

"I have already told you the major details of the PTF. I only have a few more minor details and then I will begin to show you how James and I fit into the picture. And when you finally put everything together, I am sure you will be glad to join us in our quest to take down Donna and rid the world of her terrorist network."

"Remember, George, the commander has already heard my side of the story and he still decided you were the best person to lead the team. But if I were you, I would make sure you don't do anything crazy. Because if you do, I will be the first one to take you down. George, I am bound to our mission. I will do everything in my power to ensure our mission succeeds. The commander will not stand for insubordination. So, if you feel I am not good for the PTF, take it up with the commander. He will fairly assess both sides of the issue and do what is best for the integrity of the team."

"John I'm just trying to understand the scope of the PTF. I need answers. I don't care what you think. I am not some kind of chump, and I feel like you think I am nothing but a snotty-nosed petty punk who assumes to know what he's doing, Yet you cower behind your insecurities and that will not lead to a smooth transition today, tomorrow, and in the future."

"Before you open your trap again, I suggest you consider that you might be destroying whatever cohesion we had built up to this point. John, I need to know I can trust the people that I am going to be working with. I will continue to ask you that question until I am sure that we have a bond of trust that will allow us to overcome any enemy. It's not about personalities it's about actions. I have seen how you are loyal to the cause, and you have impressed me with your skills."

CHAPTER XIV

The Barracks

I appreciate your support in dealing with Ricky. Most of all I thank you for giving me a glimpse of the PTF."

I turned away from him because I could hardly contain the anger that I was feeling inside and mumbled, "John, I hope you have taken the cotton out of your ears and are ready to line up with the commander. Because if you are not ready, just point me in the direction of someone sane enough to answer a few important questions that could decide the fate of the PTF and the nation."

"John, I will never doubt or disrespect you unless you give me a reason to. However, if you think I am going to continue to listen to you destroy my friend without having any questions, you are totally off your rocker. You have put a damper on my entire life. And when I start asking questions to find out why you and James joined the PTF, you start acting like I am a criminal. It just adds more fuel to the fire and makes me more intrigued to find out what you are hiding.

"All I am asking is for you to put your feet in my shoes for one minute before you proclaim that I am unfit to be the leader of the PTF. Now, I am doing my best to protect the members of the PTF from falling into enemy hands and you have already breached the first protocols of our team's secrecy by questioning your superior's order without having the knowledge to prove that their orders were incorrect. Regardless of how I feel, I must continue to have an open mind, because some of the burdens that will be dropped on me will not be easy to hold."

After my harsh words, John completely zone out on me, as he put his head down and turned away from me for a moment. Johns mind began drifting back to how he was asked to become a member of the PTF. The images were still clear in his mind. One day two men in black suits appeared at his job and told him that he had a chance to become part of a secret government agency. Then they shoved some papers in front of him.

"Just read it and sign on the dotted line."

Once he signed the paper, they quickly picked it up a placed it in a briefcase which a PTF monogram stamped on it. "Thank you, you will not regret your action today." Then the other man said, "We will you contact when you are needed, I suggest you go back to work and act as if nothing happened."

Several months later, they appeared at his apartment in New Jersey late one night.

He was coming home from work, and they ambushed him as he was opening the front door to his apartment. "John," they said as they came up behind him, "hurry up and open the door. We don't have all night. And we certainly don't want any of your neighbors getting any crazy ideas."

Once the door was open, they quickly shoved him inside and slammed the door. Then one of the men looked around his house and spoke. "Go to your room and turn on your lights. Then go to the front room and turn on the TV."

He was beginning to freak out. Who were these crazy men and what did they want? He returned to the hallway. Then they shoved him into the kitchen.

"John, we have a sealed envelope containing your orders. You must respond to your orders within two hours. If you do not respond, we will be forced to terminate your services. You won't hear from us again. Do not open the envelope until after we have left."

Then the two men got up and turned the lights off. After they left, it took him several minutes to muster up the courage to turn the lights back on. Then he grabbed a pair of scissors and cut the top of the envelope. Inside the envelope, there was a letter and a silver phone. The letter asked him to join the PTF. It stated that they had contacted several other people and were putting together an unofficial military unit to track down terrorists. Due to the security risks involved, they had to use unusual methods to contact the three main members of the task force. If he wanted to join the special task force, all he had to do was pick up the phone and enter the code "PTF."

He sat in the middle of his kitchen for about ten minutes and wondered if this was a game. However, he was curious to find out why they had picked him out for such an important job. So, he decided to play along with the game, and he entered the code into the phone. Several minutes later, he received a phone call. It was from a Lieutenant Commander Johnstone.

He told him he was glad that he had decided to join his task force. There was not a lot of information he could give him because he was the first member of the team he had contacted, and the process may take a couple of years to complete. He told John he would provide him with all the pertinent information regarding the team.

The next few years of his life were out of control. It seemed like everywhere he turned he was getting into trouble. One day he walked into his job and his boss called him into his office. He told him that the company had recently experienced a string of robberies. And due to the robberies, he was going to have to fire John. His boss informed him that there were rumors that he was the leader of the gang that had been robbing local stores.

The store manager told him they had installed a security system to catch the robbers, and last night during your shift the camera showed you letting the robbers in through the rear entrance. He said the video was fuzzy and they could not hear the audio, but he was almost certain John participated in the robberies. He said he did not want to cause any trouble for John because he had been such a good employee. That was why he decided to fire him instead of turning him over to the police.

After losing his job, John felt like his life was going completely down the tubes because no one would hire him. He had used up all his savings and was about to lose his apartment. When he got a call from the commander, he asked John if he was ready to join the PTF. The commander told John that he could start in the morning. All he had to do was take one exam and he was in.

The next morning, he found himself sitting at a civil service center taking the exam. After he passed the exam, the commander called him and told him he was going to be his commanding officer once he completed his training at a secret site in Arizona.

The rest was history. After he got to his first duty station, he was given his first assignment as a covert operative at one of the local detention centers. About a month before George enlisted, while he was on an undercover assignment. The commander planned his escape and he wound up enlisting in the navy. John did not fully understand how he became a member of some secret military task force, yet he did not question the commander's motive. It felt like the commander was protecting him and had his best interests at heart.

George shook John when he realized that John had zoned out on him. "John have you heard anything I have said in the last ten minutes."

John shoved George and asked him to stop talking. "George it's all just too much for me right now. I need to focus on getting some rest. We've got a long day ahead of us tomorrow. Remember, George, the commander will be meeting with you soon. I will do my best to start telling you my story tomorrow. I will try to integrate it with the rest of the info I still need to give you."

I responded to John by nodding ok because I truly did not want to make any more enemies. With the information I had about James and John, I would have enough info regarding the PTF.

It felt like I had put enough pressure on John, and hopefully, he would live up to the end of his bargain. Finally, I was beginning to feel like things were gelling, and I would be honored to serve alongside James and John.

Although I must admit James and John had a crazy side when it came down to business, I had a feeling that we all had one thing in common: we wanted to destroy those who wanted to harm our country. We wanted to be free from tyranny. The only thing left was to meet with the commander face-to-face.

Hopefully, the next time I saw the commander I would have an answer regarding my leadership ability, and if I felt like I would be able to lead the PTF in heart of Donna's terrorist organization.

However, it was driving me insane not knowing what my future held until after I spoke with the commander. And the decision would change my life forever. Once I received my orders, there would be no turning back. Currently, against my better judgment, I was leaning toward becoming the leader of the PTF.

I was certain the commander would be overjoyed with my decision. It felt like the opportunity far outweighed the sacrifice that I might have to make.

However, I still needed more detailed information on the purpose of the PTF. My main concern was how could such a small group execute any plan to create peace and eradicate a terrorist groups like Donna and her network.

Knowing that we would lack the resource and strength needed to destroy the hold on the world without some radical changes. Before I seal the deal I had make sure we would have the leeway to make those changes even if it meant we were traveling at supersonic speed and had to stop on a dime.

Because I knew the element of surprise would shock the terrorist into revealing themselves thus allowing us to swoop in and take them down without any drama. Once we took them down then the peace process would have a chance.

However, our strategy had to be precise, and place them in a point where they had no choice but to surrender.

That is why I knew I had to get creative with the time I had left and figure out a way to spend about an hour every day researching the members of my new team and an hour working on the educational components of the remaining exams. The next few weeks went by so fast, and I still had little current information concerning the NSA.

I felt like I was getting a lot of information on the personnel and the story behind the creation of the PTF. As far as what was expected of me, I was still in the dark. Why had they chosen me as the leader of the team instead of James or John?

After we mustered, we marched to breakfast, then back to the barracks. Then it was off to the grinder for the rest of the company while I did my research, back for lunch, and off to the mess hall. Then off to the obstacle course. Four laps around the track, push-ups, pull-ups. Back to the mess hall, back to the barracks. John would tell me about the PTF, I would play three games of chess with James, then lights went out.

Most of the info regarding John, James, and Donna was top secret, and three-quarters of the documents I found were redacted.

Yet my research, helped me find out that John had been in the NSA for about five years and that there were several missions that he had completed. Yet when I tried to find out information about the mission, none of them seemed to exist.

Maybe I was looking at everything from the wrong perspective. I decided to go back to the beginning when I was approached to join the navy and my recruiter had promised he had something life-changing to offer me if I joined the navy. I was excited when I found out I would be able to travel the world and sail the seven seas, I was sure it would be a great opportunity for me.

A big red flag popped up during my research. I saw a letter from the naval academy requesting my records. They were considering me as an officer candidate. But the more I thought about it, the more I wondered why my recruiter hid the information about the naval academy from me. I knew I was one of the smartest students at my school, and I had been offered scholarships to some of the most prestigious schools. When I questioned my recruiter and asked him why the regular navy trumped all the offers for my future, he told me I could become an officer if I wanted, but it was better for me to join the enlisted ranks and work my way up to chief warrant officer to gain the respect of my shipmates.

At first, all this made sense, but the more I thought about it, the more I began to doubt my recruiter's reasoning. However, against my better judgment, I listened to my recruiter and enlisted in the navy. The more I researched my enlistment, the more I began to understand the deception. My recruiter was afraid that they would lose me if I joined the naval academy, and he could not have another bad mark on his record like when he tried to recruit John. John nearly refused to enlist in the navy when they had offered him a naval commission if he joined the team. But John had turned them down because of his father. John's father was a famous naval officer who had mysteriously disappeared.

That was why they hid the offer from the naval academy. However, I still was unsure if I wanted to help clear the name of a traitor. John's father's disappearance still bugged me. And the more I investigated, the more I felt like Captain Silverton had helped him disappear. I hope my research would be useful as I was considering embarking on my first mission of my NSA career.

I knew I was supposed to pose as a storekeeper onboard the USS *Bunker Hill.* But I could not figure out how James and John fit into the picture. What was the true story behind John's obsession with the NSA? The more info I dug up, the more holes I had to fill. It was getting harder for me to keep my cover because I needed some answers. It seemed like everything was a dead end and the only one who had the key to the mystery was Commander Johnstone. He was the only person who could fill in the blanks. I begged John to set up my meeting with the commander before I went crazy. However, John informed me that I had to wait to see the commander, if I talked with the commander every day, people would start asking questions.

Yet I knew that if I panicked it would be the end of my naval career. The commander told me if I failed it would cause a major storm in the ranks of the naval hierarchy.

Every night I tossed and turned as I desperately tried to sleep. My mind had gone into overdrive as I pondered how I could find out the true story behind John's obsession with the NSA. There were just too many thoughts rolling around in my head. I was not used to going into things blindly. I needed some more answers, or I would have to let Commander Johnstone know that he had picked the wrong person for the mission. Maybe if he asked John a few more questions I would be able to get some sleep.

Surely John could give me a clearer picture of why the three of us were chosen for this secret mission. When I shook him he just continued to snore. When he did not respond it became painfully clear that I had to forget Scott and focus on my main objective, leading a team to take on the enemies of the NSA.

The next morning all of the info I found regarding the PTF only a repeat of the info John had already told me.

There were a few discrepancies, but none of them threw up a red flag. I was beginning to wonder if I'd ever find out the true story behind why John was such an important part of national security until I met with Commander Johnstone.

Between my research and our talks every evening, for the past six weeks I have had a lot to think about just dealing with my situation with Scott. I still didn't know how James's father fit into our task to save the world. Most of all, why would Donna hire Steve to plot his assassination? It is hard for me to see Steve hurting anyone.

That's why every morning I would sit down at the computer, wondering if I would find out the essence of my true mission and I was running out of patient. The suspense was slowly killing me inside.

Yet, when I thought about the how our enemies were breaking down Scott. I was warming up to the idea that I would finally be able to protect him from the horrible acts of treason that his father had committed Therefore, my drive was only becoming stronger as I began to dig in even harder.

Although the image of Donna's treachery was becoming clearer with each passing day. I still didn't know how she was entangled with my family. I still had a lot more questions for the commander. However, my frustration was beginning to boil over when I felt I would not be prepared to ask the commander any intelligent questions. Plus, I was not sure the meeting would take place before I graduated from boot camp. Thus, I needed to ensure used the waning moments of boot camp to determine whom I could trust to be my assets. As, I hacked into the NSA mainframe daily searching for info on the NSA, Donna, Scott's father, James, and John. I was able secure some interesting info about John's father. His father mysteriously disappearance had triggered a life altering change because he had be the face of the NSA for over twenty years, and his disappearance threatening to expose the NSA and congress was considered disbanding the NSA.

Yet what was more interesting than that John's father had also abandoned John's sister who was only five years old at the time. On top of that, his mother was Candice happened to be Donna's sister. For some reason, Donna and Candice had a falling out after her husband's disappearance. Not long after John's father disappear it seemed like Candice had taken James's father daughter and went into to hiding.

What stuck with me even more, was the fact that Donna was James's mother. Thus, James and John were related. However, due to the bad blood between Candice and Donna, they had never met before they enlisted in the NSA.

The reason Candice fell out with her sister was because she believed Donna had extorted husband into having an affair with her, and that had been a major factor in John's father's disappearance. When Candice found out that her husband was having an affair with her sister, she went berserk. It did not matter how much Donna kept trying to tell Candice that she would never have an affair with her husband. Candice continued to fight the rumors about her husband's affair until the day she faked her death. Before she faked her death, she told John to ignore the rumors about his father.

"Son, I know you have many questions about your father, and I am sure they will be answered in time. I want you to know your father was a good man and loved you very much. Many people have tried to destroy his legacy and make him look like a traitor. But, son, I have the proof that he is a hero."

Then she handed him a key to her safety deposit box. "I am giving you this key. Guard it with your life. You must not open it until you meet Captain Silverton. The commander assured me that your father will be given a fair trial once he is captured and questioned.

Remember not to open the box until you are sure the evidence has been placed in the right people's hands. Captain Silverton and Commander Johnstone are the only men I trust. You will know what to do when the time comes. Hopefully, your father will be able to return once you are able to show the evidence of his innocence."

However, don't be surprised if you are reunited with your adopted sister. Currently she is being protected. Your father assured me at the proper time he would reunite with her and train her.

You may not recognize her but, she will become a vital part of taking down Donna and Commander Revile. Then she smiled and said, "Son, be strong, and know that I will always be with you."

Several days later, his mother fell into a fake coma. Suddenly John was all alone. After his mother's fake death, he tried to understand why his mother never talked about his father. There was so much that John did not know about his father because he had disappeared when he was young. John was in a state of disarray until he came across a picture of Donna. On the back of the picture, his mother had inscribed "My sister and best friend Donna, why have you gone astray?" Next to the picture he, found his mom's diary.

Inside the diary was a series of numbers. The numbers were navigational coordinates to where the evidence was to clear his father. John was shocked when his mother mentioned an alleged affair between her sister, Donna, and his father. When he turned the page, in bold letters, his mother had written:

LIES, DECEIT FROM THE ONES I LOVED
IS WHY MY LOVE HAS BEEN SHOVED
NOW HE IS GONE INTO HIDING
NOW HE IS NO LONGER ABIDING
REMEMBER TO PROVE ALL THINGS
BEFORE YOU LET YOUR MOUTH SING
THE TRUTH WILL BE IN SUN'S LIGHT
LOVE WILL PROTECT WITH ALL ITS MIGHT

THEN MY LOVE WILL BE SET FREE
THEN THE WORLD WILL SEE
IT WAS ALL A TRICK OF A FRIEND
WHO DID BETRAY ALL IN THE END
BECOMING AN ENEMY SO VAIN
PLEASE NEVER LET HER REIGN

John understood why his mother had never mentioned her sister because she felt betrayed and never forgave Donna. Instead, she was warning him to be careful whom he trusted. John never knew that his father had been an integral part of the NSA. After his father's disappearance the NSA got wind of him having an affair with Donna, Due to Donna's reputation there were many bitter people within the NSA and it nearly tore the NSA apart.

Many people inside the NSA felt like Donna was somehow behind his disappearance. Although there was never any proof, the accusation was taken very seriously. And when his father disappeared, they refused to give Candice any benefits from the NSA or the navy until they found out the truth behind his disappearance. When NSA got wind of that Candice had died of a broken heart, several high-ranking NSA officer wanted John's father tried for treason..

John's heart was broken because of the way the military had treated his mother after his father's disappearance. That is why he joined the PTF to prove his father's innocence. Yet the more he tried to prove his innocence, the guiltier John's father looked. John was unaware of the fact that his father might be a traitor and was working with some type of terrorist group. Thus, he held on to what Candice had told him.

Candice had warned John that the only person he could trust was Captain Silverton. She begged him not to show what was on the disk to anyone else because he would understand the evidence and he would not stop working until he was sure John's father was safe.

She hoped their friend captain Silverton could use the data to prove that Donna had extorted John's father. Candice tried to change the narrative on James father and frame him as a hero. Because she knew his only reason for disappearing was to save the NSA, from Donna's deception.

John wondered what was on the disk, but he refused to open it until he met with Captain Silverton he finally, he opened the disk and then he understood why Candice was so afraid. Because while the evidence proved that James's father was not a terrorist, he was still a traitor. He had allowed Donna to extort him, and he knew he had to disappear, or his family's lives would be in jeopardy. Therefore, John decided to join the PTF. He felt like it was his best shot at clearing his father's name.

Yet, when he disappeared, he had taken an integral part of the plans for Project Light Shield. He thought he was doing the right thing. But he failed to destroy the all the copies of the *Light Shield* and his partner, Commander Revile, found the remaining plans.

However, the key component to make the *Light Shield* operational was locked up in James Father's head. And if Donna or Commander Revile found him, the world would be in danger.

When Captain Silverton saw the evidence, he was confounded, because he could not understand why his friend did not bring him in on his plans before he disappeared. While they were reviewing the information on the disk, John noted something was off with Captain Silverton. He could not put his finger on it, but he trusted Candice, so he let it ride.

I mumbled to himself *That's why he was being so secretive.*

The more research I did, the more I began to wonder what I had gotten myself involved in. I was supposed to be leading a special team that was going to bring peace to the world. Yet from everything I had seen, it looked like I was just a patsy. We were supposed to be fighting terrorists, and yet it seemed like the terrorists we were fighting were related to James and John. It seemed like both wanted to prove their parents were innocent of all wrongdoing. And now I wanted to find out what my parents knew about Donna and Steve.

I know the commander, told me not to trust anyone but the close group that he was knitting together to take on the world. However, I still had doubts about both James and John.

CHAPTER XV

Jimmy

Suddenly I was beginning to wonder if Janis was John's missing sister and by her, I would be related to John. Thus, that make Donna and Candice my Aunts. All this data was too much for my delicate mind and it was knocking me for a loop.

However, when I stumbled upon an email in the trash on Captain Silverton's computer. I was shocked he had not deleted the email. I knew I had to act fast, so I encrypted the email and sent it to my email, and deleted traces of it from the captain's computer. Then I saved it on a flash drive that I had snatched it from the desk in the master chief's office.

I was feeling great, and I felt like I had made great strides in the past few days to finally be able to understand why the PTF was so important When I opened the email there was information regarding a top- secret project called *Project Light Shield.* Now I had proof that John's father had taken *the Light Shield 's* research and hidden it.

This one action had put the NSA in a serious state of disarray. To date, the NSA, CIA, and FBI were still trying to find John's father. They nearly caught him in New Jersey, but he somehow avoided them and changed his name. That's when I knew if I found John's father, I would have all the answers.

The email also tied John's father to Captain Silverton. What surprised me the most was that the email was sent to the captain several days before John's father disappeared. However, Captain Silverton did not open the email until after John's father disappeared.

In the email, he was begging his friend to bring down Donna's terrorist network. It did not seem like he had betrayed his country but that he was trying to save the country from destroying itself. He tried to explain what he had done, and why he had to hide.

"The Email seemed like a warning to Captain Silverton."

My friend I know I have not communicated much lately. I will not be seeing much after this email as I must go into hiding.. Everything has been very chaotic with the elections and all the terrorist attacks. I realize that I will be blamed for some of the attacks and branded as a traitor because I tried to destroy the plans for a top-secret project. While I did manage to stop the production of the project, I was unsuccessful in destroying the plans.

I only hope that you are ready to jump into the frying pan with every ounce of fight that you have left so that we can end the games that Donna and the commander Revile have been playing with all the world's top agencies. I am suggesting that you start a small team of covert operatives to disrupt Donna's plans with Commander Revile. I will send you a list of three top candidates for the core of the team.

It is of the utmost importance that we find Commander Revile before he has a chance to build the Light Shield and use its full power. Because if he can harness the power of the light shield. I am certain the world will be constantly terrorized, and he will try everything in his power to put a damper on the peace process.

"One of the most important things I have learned these past few months is that you must never underestimate the resolve of your enemy. They will have no mercy, and they will seek to destroy you at your weakest point when you least expect it. With the help of your good friend Commander Johnstone, I am sure Donna and Commander Revile will be destroyed. My only concern is that your team will be able to destroy the enemy before too much damage has been done.

I hope that you will be able to forgive me one day and realize my intention are to keep the world safe. My friend I assure when the time is right I will come out of hiding and produce the evidence to prove that I not a traitor and I am innocent of all the slander, that is being spread around. I am begging you to work with commander Johnstone to immediately set up your secret task forces."

With much respect CG

PS: 1-GA:2.- CS:3. CJ-: 4. SC: 5.- JR-:6. JM: 7-. STB/SCB

That's why the Captain decided to put a special squad together to protect our national security. The captain was using the PTF to throw everyone off while he was secretly working with some of the greatest minds in the United States' history to track down his old friend and prove that he was not a traitor.

Yet even with the clues, and it would be hard to track down John's father. Because he was the NSA's top covert officer and when he went off the grid it was impossible to track him. My only hope is the captain was not being set up thus endangering all our lives.

Suddenly, Jimmy came up behind me and grabbed my shoulder, and shook me. "What are you doing over here, George? I thought I saw something strange on the computer. The master chief told me to keep an eye on you to make sure you are not playing around. I have been watching you the past several days and something smells. You need to step away from the computers and let me have a look at what you are working on."

"Jimmy, you need to calm down a little. I need the computer to do my research for the exams." I quickly changed the screen on the computer and turned the screen around, so Jimmy was looking at the naval exam center test site.

Jimmy squinted at the screen and said, "I'll give you a break this time. I overreacted."

"That's all right, Jimmy. However, if you want to help me, you can join in."

He looked at me like I was crazy. "You can help yourself. I ain't no computer geek. Just remember, I am keeping an eye on you. And if I find out you are messing around, I am going to take you out back and rattle your cage."

Better yet if you don't keep up your end of the bargain I am sure you will like my knuckle sandwich."

I looked at Jimmy and laughed. "Easy, man, I don't want any trouble. I've already had enough since I arrived at this crazy place. All you need to do is make sure I am safe. And I will make sure you are going to be the smartest recruit ever to come through this joint. It's going to take a few days, but once I find out how they work on their test, the exam will be easy to pass."

He grabbed my shoulder.

"Man, can you relax? You're hurting me. I'm sure you don't want to explain to the master chief how I dislocated my shoulder."

Jimmy gasped. "Sorry, George, I guess I don't know my own strength sometimes."

Then he turned around and walked off so he could finish his sweep of the barracks. I could hardly contain my laughter. This guy was the king of idiots. Jimmy was all muscles and no brains. I was grateful that the master chief had left me with Jimmy because no one would dare try to raid our barracks while Jimmy was on watch.

I waited until I knew Jimmy was gone before I turned the computer back to my research. And with each new discovery made my brain numb, as I began to go completely insane.

After a couple more hours of research, I was completely exhausted as I put my head down next to the computer, waiting for the squad to return from their drills. I finally got to a point where I realized that the commander held the key to the operation and there were too many questions that only he could answer.

While I believed John when he told me I would be meeting with the commander soon, I was beginning to get nervous and did not know how much longer I could play games with Jimmy. Jimmy was just an innocent pawn, and it was crazy to think that they would have me watched by someone who wouldn't harm a fly.

Each day, once Jimmy left the room to make his rounds, I quickly flipped back to my research on the PTF. However, for the next couple of weeks, I was careful because I did not what Jimmy to grab me again. His iron-like grip had nearly dislocated my shoulder.

As time dragged on, I began to miss my best friend, Scott. It had gotten to the point where I felt like I was just wasting my time, and I knew the only person who could lift me out of my funk was Scott. Scott always had the answer that I could not see. We had not been separated since I was in grade school. I was becoming so conflicted because I knew that if I wanted to become a part of the NSA I had to start getting used to being separated from Scott.

It just seems so unfair to me. How was I supposed to be the leader of two of the most hardcore recruits in navy history?

I was beginning to feel isolated with each passing day. My depression was affecting my job performance. There was a spot for James, John, and even Jimmy. Why couldn't they find a spot for Scott?

I knew if I'm not careful, all this info about the PTF is going to be my downfall. If that happens, the commander will have to find someone else to be the leader of the PTF. Plus, I have not even touched the surface of why James joined the PTF. While it seemed like someone close to John killed his father. It seems like James and John had more invested in capturing Donna than I did."

It felt like I was struck by lightning once I learned the importance of my decision and how it would affect me for the rest of my life. The reality is I was nothing but a patsy when I took everyone at their word.

When I lost my best friend Scott, suddenly I was beginning to doubt if I would even ask Janis to marry me. Was I expected to become a loner for the rest of my life I did not want to get anyone else tied up in my life. My life was messed up enough.

And all I could hear was the commander ringing the back of my mind as he told me not to trust anyone but the close group that he was knitting together to take on the world. However, it was hard for me to overcome my doubts about both you and James.

Then when I found out that you were related and if I married Janis, I would be marrying John's sister he had not seen since she was eight- or nine years old I really began to trip because that meant that Donna would become my Aunt and I would be related to both James and John.

However, I was beginning to miss by best friend Scott, and I was being forced to choose between destroying my friendship or joining the NSA to track down some crazy terrorist who had altered the path of my life forever. I did not realize that my actions were affecting the squad as the grueling task of training everyone to take the exams was becoming more unbearable every day.

I was holding on by a small thread, hoping that when our enemies are taken down Scott would be held blameless for the horrible acts of treason that his father has committed. Also, Steve's actions have affected my relationship with Janis because I don't know if he messed with her mind.

Could I trust Janis? Did I still want to marry her? How will Steve's action affect my family? It all seemed so confusing right now, and you want me to act like everything is normal. There ain't nothing normal about the current situation I find myself in.

John knew something would have to give; thus, he interrupted my train of thought and began talking. "George, if you are going to let your friendship with Scott keep you from doing your duty, then you may as well pack up your bags and go home now. James and I are not your enemies! Scott is not your enemy! You are your own worst enemy! You must stop feeling sorry for yourself, pull yourself together, and become the leader that we all know you can be. Your poor decision will destroy all the work everyone has put into making sure that the PTF is successful just because you are having a few doubts about the mission."

I know you are getting anxious and have a lot of questions for the commander. But I have been telling you that before we complete our training you will see the commander again. The commander will answer all your questions about what is going to take place after boot camp. Once you have talked with him you will have a clearer understanding of the team's main objectives and why you were chosen to lead the team."

"You are worried about Scott because you found out about his father's secret double life collaborating with Donna.

Donna is one of the most notorious terrorists in the history of the United States. Yet things are not always as they seem. I can see you are holding on to a small thread, hoping that when our enemies are taken down Scott will be held blameless for the horrible acts of treason that his father has committed. My friend, sometimes you have no control over your destiny. It is time for you to try and relax. Because if you don't find some way to center yourself, your only destiny will be a trip back home. I am warning you, George, if you don't become organized you are going to sink the ship. Then he walked off and told me to get some rest."

While he was walking away I stopped him in his tracks. "John don't worry about me I will be all right. It's just that everyone wants me to act like I don't care about my friends. Ever since I found out about Scott's father's secret double life collaborating with Donna. I worry about the uncertainty surrounding Scott and Janis. But I can assure you I keep my end of the bargain. We all know Donna is one of the most notorious terrorists in the history of the United States. Yet things are not always as they seem. I am holding on to a small thread, hoping that when our enemies are taken down Scott will be held blameless for the horrible acts of treason that his father has committed.

Once I decide to join the PTF it will be based on the facts. That is why I have been taking my time and not rushing to any conclusion. And right now, there are still quite a few important points missing. Which is bogging my mind down because I did not join the navy for all this cloak-and-dagger stuff. All I wanted to do is to travel the world in peace." Once I find out that everything is on the legit I am all in."

John snickered, "George, sometimes you have no control over your destiny. It is time for you to try and relax. Because if you don't find some way to center yourself, your only destiny will be a trip back home. I am warning you, George, if you don't become organized you are going to sink the ship. The commander chose you to lead the team for a reason. I suggest you think more clearly about getting through these next few days by helping the squad ace the exams. Sometimes you must improvise, and this is one of those times. What are you going to do to correct the situation with the master chief"

John, if I'm not careful, all this info about the PTF is going to drive me crazy. If that happens, the commander will have to find someone else to be the leader of the PTF. Plus, you have not even touched the surface of why James joined the PTF. All I know is someone tried to kill his father. It seems like the two of you have more invested in capturing Donna than I do."

John turned around and smiled at me, "George, you need to stop taking things at face value and consider what is best for you and your country. Do you want to continue walking around in the dark or do you want to do something about it and protect those that you love while destroying the present evil that surrounds you.?

I know that it is a hard choice to make, but I am sure once you understand the facts surrounding our mission you will make the right decision. Remember it does not matter what you think about me, James, or anyone else. You must make a choice to deny your present situation to establish and better future for all those you love.

In the end, it is up to you if you want to live in terror or if you want to join the battle and fight for the future of our country.

I put my head down and slowly turned and walked away from John. I could not take the pressure, so I decided to take walk around outside the barracks in the cold dark night. What was I going to do? I could not relax. Did I want to pursue freedom from terror, or did I want to live a normal life with Janis and have a house with a white picket fence and three kids?

The more I thought about it, the more realistic it sounded, because I knew if I continued down this path my life would be nothing but heartache and frustration. It seems like no one I knew had any brains upstairs, and I was beginning to think I was at the top of that list. However, I still had to wait until I spoke with the commander.

I did not want to just be reckless and make my decision based on incomplete information. Yet the more I researched, the closer I was getting to the truth. And that is what scared me the most.

Knowing that there were people like Donna running around, spreading terror, and clogging up all possibilities of peace, I did not feel like I was holding to the values I had been raised with. I was constantly thinking about my dad. He had always done his best to steer me in the right direction. And if he knew General Armstrong like the documents I read stated, then my dad was a true hero of democracy.

While he had never talked about his service, I knew he had done many valiant things, and saving the general's life several times was at the top of the list. General Armstrong was one of the most trusted military men on the face of the earth. And the more I found out about Captain Silverton and the PTF, the more honored I felt to be considered a member of the PTF. Yet in the back of my mind, I did not feel worthy of such a task. The world had been fighting so many battles for so many years. How was a person like me, without any experience, going to help solve the key issues that my country faced?

Working with James, John, and May seemed like an impossible task due to our different personality traits. Yet the more I discovered about each of my new partner's valor and loyalty the easier my decision became. I knew I could not fail to honor my father as I continued his legacy to create peace in the world

Therefore, for the time being, I was going to quash my doubts and put my full attention on becoming the best leader of the PTF I could be. Knowing that in a few weeks, I would be making a decision that would affect the rest of my life. And the closer I got to the deadline, the more it looked like I was going to put my hat in the ring and help create one of the world's greatest teams to destroy the reign of terror created by terrorists like Donna and Commander Revile.

John replied. "There're times we have no control over our destiny. Yet things are not always as they seem. You need to find some way to center yourself, or your only destiny will be a trip back home. I am warning you, George, if you don't become organized you are going to sink the ship. Stop worrying about your friendship with Scott. It is keeping you from doing your duty."

When will you realize James and I are not your enemy? Scott is not your enemy! You are your own worst enemy! You must stop feeling sorry for yourself, pull yourself together, and become the leader that we all know you can be.

Remember the commander chose you to lead the team for a reason. I suggest you think more clearly about getting through these next few days and start doing your job. Once you start doing your job it will help you learn that there are times you must improvise, which is one of those times. Because if you don't come out of your funk might as well just pack up your bags and go home.

Then John left me to ponder what I was going to do next as I laid in my bunk and drifted off to sleep. What I did not realize was that the commander had called John to his office to talk about my situation

When he returned several hours later, and John sat down in the bunk next to me. "George, we need to talk. I know this might not be the might not the best time for a conversation. At first, I was not sure if I was dreaming or if I was having a conversation with John.

"George, you need to stop playing and start focusing on getting this squad ready for the exam. Your position in this squad is becoming increasingly volatile every day.

He shook me, "your actions are, unacceptable. You're supposed to be the leader of the PTF, it is time for you to pull yourself out of whatever funk you are in and begin to lead. The Master Chief is slowly becoming our enemy and if you don't do something soon, we are all doomed."

"The master chief called me into to his office and informed me he was getting ready to demote you in the morning. He said that he didn't believe you were going to help the squad. And he was beginning to feel like the only reason the commander put you in his squad was to take him down. That is when he informed me, he was getting ready to demote you. Upon hearing that you were being demoted, I begged the master chief to allow me to work with you. I explained to him that you're homesick, but you would come out of it."

When he looked at me and said "Shut your trap John, I don't want to hear any excuses. Either he is going to do his job, or I am going to have to get rid of him. However, since you seem certain you can fix the problem, I am going to give George one final chance, but if he does not have anything concrete for me in the next three days, he may find himself in the brig next to Ricky."

"It has been over eight weeks, they have kept Ricky in the brig, and he will not be released until after everyone else has completed boot camp. They could have let him go weeks ago but they want to make sure he feels the effect of his actions."

Then the master chief was silent for several minutes before he grabbed me and started shaking me. "John, you need to make sure that George understands the importance of his job. Without his help I will be forced to retire, it seems like the Navy is getting away from the old school. Thus, if he does not deliver the goods, I will be considered a failure. These young punks have been gunning for me since the moment I accepted the responsibility of protecting George."

Then the master chief nearly broke down in tears as he began to tell me the true reason, he wanted to demote you.

"John, he said, "several of the other squad leaders approached me yesterday and they were making fun of our squad. They said we were the weakest bunch of recruits they had ever seen."

One of the punks turned to me, "don't you have that crazy recruit George in your squad." They'd heard it through the grapevine "he must be connected with the top brass, and they only stuck him in my squad, because they hoped you could whip him into shape."

"When they mentioned George's name, I became a little nervous and I was ready to fight. When one of them young punks stuck his nose up in the air and started laughing at me. The punk just took things a little bit too far when he said that that joker George had gotten the better of me, and now the top brass is saying it's time to get rid of old dudes and turn things over to the new generation of leaders." Then he nudged his friend, telling him they should get out of there because they didn't want any of this dude's old rusty ways to rub off on them."

"John, I had no pity for the young punk as I slowly looked him in the eyes and told him I was training recruits before they were even in diapers. And if the top brass wanted to take me down, they were going to have to try a little bit harder. Let me tell you punk, once they turn this place over to snot-nosed little babies like you, the navy is in trouble and me ain't going to be a part of the Navy anymore."

"Get your squads ready for some competition because I am coming after you with all my barrels blazing, and I don't intend to take any prisoners. I hope you have a white flag, 'cause the two of you will be remembered as the most overhyped chiefs ever seen.

I Replied "The brass will have to rewrite their entire strategy on training to return to the strengths of the old while protecting the wisdom and integrity of the navy's true recruits. But he just said that the top brass was saying it is time to get rid of old dudes and turn things over to the new generation of leaders, because at least they weren't always running their mouths, like they have any inclination of what the navy was all about. It ain't about having muscles, it's about having brains, which they seemed to lack.'"

Oh, you may need a therapist to put your arm back in place, because it seems like you don't know the slightest thing about being fit for duty."

Then the Master Chief wiped his tears and slammed his fist on the desk next to me. "John all this nonsense with George has made me furious. I am tired of defending him."

"One of the chiefs turned and spit at me. "Old man the top brass has been waiting to get rid of dinosaurs like you. They are ready for the next generation of leaders. You crazy old dudes are always running your mouths, like they know what the best for the Navy. It is no longer about having muscles, it's about having brains, which you seemed to lack. Then I grabbed the punk slammed him the ground"

"You sure are crazy, old man. You are going to wish you never would put your hands on me. Your days are over, and you can no longer intimidate me. Because I have friends in high places too and I am going to take you and the rest of your squad down."

The master chief said I heard his friend whispering, "Frankie, I told you not to be stuck up. The old dudes are out of their minds, and they are not afraid to show it. Next time, he might let us out alive."

"Don't worry about him, Ray. It's the last time he will disrespect us because his unit will never pass the exam. I have made sure of that."

"What are you saying, Frankie? We can't change the exam.!"

The Master Chief stated he was angry when Frankie start laughing. "Ray, you are funny. I don't have to change the exam.

Then Frankie started laughing. "Ray, you are funny. I don't have to change the exam.

All I need to do is make it seem like the master chief is conspiring with the examiner and they will reassign him and bring in Master Chief Gurley to ensure the exam is legitimate. Master Chief Gurley and Master Chief Walters haven't agreed on any subject in over twenty years."

"George, I could not take any more as I looked at the Master Chief and stated, "Sir, those punks are wrong about you and this squad. I will straighten George out and they will never disrespect you again. And as far as the top brass is concerned, when they see how you turned the squad around, they will deeply appreciate the strength and wisdom of someone who is a true warrior.

Chief, I happen to believe that they put George in our squad as a show of force to take them young punks who fail to realize that the old ways need to merge with the new ways to allow a smooth transition into a bright future for the navy."

Master Chief Walters looked at John and smiled. "Son, how did you become so wise? If the rest of the squad is like you, the young punks don't stand a chance. I am going to allow you a couple of days to get George back on track. Remember, he must make sure our squad is prepared for the exam. Because if we do badly on this exam my career is in jeopardy, and the young punks will slowly take over the navy. So, Johnny boy, failure is not an option.

CHAPTER XVI

The Final Exam

You had better not fail to get George back on track, I'll personally make sure both of you are sent back to wherever you came from. Is that understood?"

"Sir, yes, sir," John promptly replied, then he immediately got his gear together and went over to my bunk.

"George," he shook me, "have you been listening to me"

I looked at John and let out a snorted. "Have you gone completely nuts? Don't you see what time it is? We've got to muster in less than three hours, and I am trying to rest."

John whispered, "No problem, kid. If you don't listen to me in a few days, Chief Walters is going to send you home. I just hope you have a more open mind in the morning."

Good thinking John I'll talk to in the morning, and I rolled over and went back to snoring.

The next morning, when the lights came on, I rolled out of my bunk and was stunned to see John in the bunk below me.

"What's going on, John? I thought I was dreaming last night when you woke me up with some crazy notion that the master chief is going to send me home."

John smartly replied, "Sorry to tell you, buddy, it ain't no crazy notion. I did tell you last night, the Master Chief was preparing to demote you today. I begged him to let me collaborate with you. I explained how you were homesick, but you would come out of it. At first, the chief told me that he didn't believe you were going to help the squad and that the only reason you were put in his squad was to take him down. I was able to convince him that would have something to show him in the next few days."

Then I stated calmly, "What is the chief doing messing with me? You know he could be blowing our cover just by choosing you to help me out. I thought we were supposed to keep our distance until after we finish boot camp and go into the next phase of our training."

John looked at me like I was out of my mind. "Straighten up George or your only destiny will be a trip back home."

"John, it seems like the master chief's playing games with you. He knows the value of experience, and he would never go against the commander. I am in complete control. I am about to put everything in place within the next couple of days. Don't worry, my friend, this unit will set the example for all future exams. You know he could be blowing our cover just by choosing you to help me out. I thought we were supposed to keep our distance until after we finish boot camp and go into the next phase of our training."

"I'm sure you're right, George! But I'm letting you know right now; you'd better be glad I stepped in because if I hadn't you would have been gone last night. "George, I am glad I decided to step up. We are going to have to work together to rectify the situation. You need to push everything else to the side because the chief only gave me a few days to get you back on track.

I just shook my head as we made our way to the mess hall and John changed spots with the guy next to me and whispered The commander chose you to lead the team for a reason. I suggest you think more clearly about getting through these next few days by helping the squad ace the exams. Whether you like it or not, sometimes you must improvise, and this is one of those times. What are you going to do to correct the situation with the master chief?"

2 "John, what do I need to do to get through the next few days."

John retorted, "The first test is next week, and if we don't ace the exam, you and I are history."

I shook my head. "John, you should have just left me in the brig to rot with Ricky. If I would have known how crazy the people would get over a simple exam, I would have never agreed to become a part of this squad. The commander told me he was looking out for me, but I thought it was going to be something a little more challenging."

"You don't get it. Your dad's request was not the only reason the master chief was ordered to have you in his squad. When the commander told him that your brains could resolve his squad's educational component, he was offended.

The master chief is old school, and he used to be all about the brawn, but he could never understand why they put emphasis on the educational part of boot camp. He feels like he is on his last leg because of all these young chiefs who feel like his methods of training are outdated.

They even told the base CO that the master chief is resistant to change and that without changes the navy will not be able to compete in the new global warfare. It seems like every country is phasing out the old system of combat and training for a better, more sophisticated military that uses their brains instead of brute force."

I chuckled. "John, that's the problem with everybody. All they think about is push-ups and running three miles. They forget to exercise the muscle in their brain. The pressure on the brain is what makes this experience almost unbearable. John, these goons don't even know two plus two is four, let alone military strategy."

John replied, "I'm aware of that, but you are the only one who can help this squad achieve their educational requirement. So, I suggest you get busy before we take our first exam. Because if you fail training, our squad fails. The master chief will have to retire, and the NSA will be in complete chaos."

"What are you talking about? The master chief is the most highly decorated soldier on the base. They can't just kick him to the curb without giving him a fighting chance."

"You are right, George. Unbelievably, you are the one who is going to instill that educational determination into this squad. And we only have a few days before the first exam, what are you going to do? Are you going to sit on your behind in the barracks and soak in your own tears, or are you going to rise and help this squad pass the exam?"

"Whatever you have been showing the squad does not seem to be working. And we both feel like we are going to fail the exam. I suggest you stop being such a snob. Just because you have it all figured out does not mean the rest of the squad does."

Then I grinned. "John, I'm game. Are you? I am about to show the master chief a side of me that neither one of you knew existed. While the rest of the squad is off playing games on the grinder, I will get my presentation together that will blow the top of the master chief's head off."

I looked at John and smiled. "John, I know you just met me, but one thing I always stand by is that failure is not an option. It does not matter what type of test we run into in life, we must rise above our fears and conquer them."

"That's the spirit," John said as he high fived me. Then I proceeded to bark at him with a list of tasks the squad needed to complete every day.

"John, if the squad works together there is no way anyone will fail the exam, because I have already taken a practice exam last week and discovered a pattern in the test. It should be a breeze for the rest of the squad. Matter of fact, I have already given each member of the squad the patterns for the exam."

Then I whispered to John, "Here is what I need you to do for the next few days. You do your part, I will do mine, and we'll all ace the exam. Once we pull this off, you've got to get me another partner besides Jimmy."

I know that I am supposed to be the brains of the squad, but I am still working on the basic format of the exam. And if I am stuck with Jimmy there is no way that will happen. I know Jimmy is not a bad guy, but I would like to feel like I am part of the squad."

John agreed to get me a new partner as long I came through on my end of the bargain.

The next morning upon returning to the barracks, I immediately started researching the naval education database. After determining which questions, they would use on the exams, it was easy. It took me about three hours, but I managed to devise a way for the squad to ace the exam. It did not matter how they changed the questions up; they always maintain a certain pattern in their testing. Thus, I was able to train the squad how to decipher the test questions. Now all I had to do was put my plan into action.

I was certain the squad was going to pass the exam without a hitch. However, the master chief was still on me like a wild lion ready to devour his prey.

The master chief had learned from past experiences that you have to put your money where your mouth is. John and the master chief both felt like I had a big mouth, but I had not yet proved myself. The chief could not stand people like me who thought they had all the answers. Too many times he had been disappointed and left out to dry because the brains of the outfit did not consider the simple things.

However, everyone had to pass the test for the master chief to be successful. He felt like I had not been paying attention to Jimmy since Jimmy was the one person who could throw the entire squad into chaos. The chief finally got upset with my strategy and called me out in front of the entire squad.

"Gentlemen, we have less than twenty hours before we take the exam. I am confident you will pass with excellence. However, that is not good enough. Everyone must pass the test, or we fail. George, you have done an excellent job with the squad, but Jimmy still seems to be a little hazy about the test. Let's ask him a few questions to see if he is prepared for the exam."

The chief asked everyone the same ten questions, then he told me to grade everyone's answers. When I finished grading the answers, I gave the chief the results.

"Sir, everyone answered your questions correctly except for Jimmy. Jimmy missed six of the answers."

Then he looked at me sternly. "You need to spend the next twenty-four hours with Jimmy, I told you before, everyone must pass this exam with a score of 90 percent or higher."

The squad with the highest total scores thus far was company A. Their overall score was 94.9 percent without any failures. This was unfamiliar ground to the master chief; however, his experience led him to believe if he didn't push me, his squad would fail the exam. Knowing if that happened, he would have to retire or face charges of insubordination.

On the day of the exam, the master chief woke me up several hours before the rest of the squad and ordered me to take an extra thirty minutes with the entire squad to review for the exam. After they completed the review, the master chief lined the squad and we marched to the mess hall for breakfast.

While we were eating breakfast, several members of the squad whispered in my ear, "George, you know if we don't do good on this exam the master chief is going to hang you out to dry, so I suggest you start praying 'cause you're going to need all the help you can get. We are not worried about most of the squad, but that idiot Jimmy could sink everyone. We sure hope the two of you have worked out a plan that will ensure he doesn't fail.

Matter of fact, the master chief was thinking about leaving Jimmy at the barrack while we all took the test. But several of the other squad's leaders took it up with the base commander and he was informed that every recruit had to take all the exams."

I nodded my head, asking everyone to chill out. "Don't worry about Jimmy. He'll do fine. If Jimmy did what I told him, I know he would have the squad's highest score on the exam."

John could tell by my smugness was upsetting most of the squad. Therefore, he had to mellow me out a little or the master chief was going to have me on the grinder after everyone else was asleep.

Suddenly I had the Master Chief's attention, and I was nervous. He grabbed me and started shaking me, then blurted out, "I cannot have any failures in my squad. In less than ten minutes, the squad will be here. I want you to go over any last-minute instructions you have. Then I have ten minutes to get the squad over to the testing center."

The first member of the squad I saw was John.

"George, are you ready? The chief is really bugging out."

When the final member of the squad stepped into the barracks, the chief called everyone to attention. "Men, this is your final opportunity to ask George any questions regarding the exam."

When everyone was silent, I took that as my cue and handed each member a piece of paper.

"All you need to do is memorize the patterns on the paper I have just handed you. The navy only uses three patterns in the exam. Once you have memorized the patterns, I want everyone to throw the sheet of paper in the garbage can on the way out."

Then I called Jimmy to the front. "Jimmy, all you need to do is remember what we have been going over every day for the past three weeks and you will be fine. Don't worry about anything. Just keep your mind clear and look for the pattern I showed you. I hope you understand that your test score could very well determine if our squad passes or fails the exam today. Therefore, I want you to close your eyes for a minute and relax."

Finally chief called the squad back to attention and we slowly started our march toward the exam center. John made sure everyone threw their paper in the trash cans on the way out of the barracks. Once I was sure everyone had thrown their paper in the trash, I lit the can on fire. John looked at me.

"Are you crazy, George? You might set off the alarm."

He looked sternly into the eyes of each member of the squad and told them he would not allow any failures. Then he lined the squad up and they marched to the testing center. I was relieved because I knew that all the agony would soon be over. However, I could tell that the chief was nervous. He could not allow any failures in his squad.

3 Once we were in the head, we dumped the ashes into the toilet and flushed them down into the sewer.

"Now, we need to double time to catch up with the chief and the rest of the squad. Before we joined the squad, John came over to me and whispered. "Are you sure you got this covered'

." I was sure they would ask questions if we don't all enter the exam center at the same time. I looked John square in the eyes and said, "Calm down, John, I got it under control. Just help me take this can into the head

When we finally reached the testing center, all the agony was about to be over. As soon as our squad stepped in, the chief examiner ordered everyone to take their seat. When the squad took their seats in unison, the director of the center was impressed. He complimented the master chief on his team discipline and wished him the best. I could see that the master chief was sweating, but I was not worried because I already knew what the chief examiner had planned.

Thus, no one knew what was on the other recruits' exams. However, I had already prepared the squad for the deception, and I had put the squad in sequential order so that each member of the squad would receive the extract exam I had trained them for.

The examiner was trying to throw the squad off by giving them four different exams. What the chief examiner was unaware of was that I had managed to figure out every combination that the examiner would use, and I knew that he would give Jimmy the hardest exam.

I knew I had done my job and prepared each member of the squad for any disruption of the testing process. Everyone knew exactly which exam the other had by the numerical division of the squad.

They gave Jimmy the hardest exam, and it really ticked me off. Even if I had prepared Jimmy for the exam, it was unfair how they were picking on him just because Jimmy seemed like a big oaf. Jimmy was my friend and I hated to see him being used. That's why I had trained Jimmy to take the hardest test, and I knew that Jimmy was going to surprise everyone.

However, I noticed there was something strange going on when I handed out the test. Dean and Simon's tests were different from the rest of the squad. It looked like they had cut a deal with the OIC to keep the squad from passing the test. I immediately made a mental note of each traitor and would report the incident up the chain of command to ensure that those who were responsible would reap what they sowed.

I was not worried if the squad failed because of their test scores. I had all the evidence I needed to have their scores thrown out. Not only would their score be thrown out, but the OIC would be investigated for tampering with the test scores.

When I handed them their exam, I gave Dean and Simon a chance to redeem themselves. I knew I had them dead to rights, so I put a note on the top of their exam. The note read: "I know that you are working with the OIC to ensure that our squad fails. There will be consequences for you and the OIC if that happens. I have prepared notes and have proof of your treachery. The choice is yours to pass the test or go to the brig."

I secretly kept an eye on both men to see how they would react to my note. Dean raised his hand. The OIC quickly came over to his desk. "Son, this is unusual. I have never had someone ask for my help during an exam before."

"Sir," he whispered, just loud enough for me to hear. "I have two questions for you. One, can I get a new exam, it is hot in this room and my sweat has smeared several of the questions to the point where they are unreadable. And the second question is may I use the head?"

When the Master Chief saw me being called up by the OIC. He began to panic. What was going on? Had someone in his squad tried to cheat? Then when he saw Dean get up and leave the testing center, he became even more worried. Was this the end of his career?

The OIC smiled and told Dean to go use the head and then he motioned for me to come over to Dean's desk he seemed relieved.

"George, it seems like there is a problem with Dean's exam and need you to pick up Dean's exam and bring it my desk in the front. Once I review the exam I will give you Dean's new exam and you will throw the old exam in the trash and place the new one on his desk. When he returns from the head I have given him an extra ten minutes to complete his exam due to the circumstances."

"George the rules state that I am unable to take the exam directly from a recruit once the examination process has started.

"I explained to Dean that he will have an extra ten minutes to take his exam. Thus, I am counting on you as my witness that I followed the testing procedures to the T. I cannot allow any snafus on my watch is that understood son.

Before I went to pick up Dean's old I stood at attention and smartly saluted the OIC. "Sir, yes sir. Then I turned around a went to Dean desk to pick-up his old exam. When I picked up old test I noticed a note that Dean had written with his sweat: *"Simon and I are on your side."*

I knew if I tried to use an eraser the questions the OIC might catch me. Therefore, use my palm of my hand to smudge and erase the message while also making it seem like Dean's sweat had smudged several of the answers to the exam.

After reviewing the exam, the OIC ordered me to throw the exam in the trash and he gave me the new exam to place on Dean's desk. Then I returned to my seat in the rear of the room.

Shortly after I sat down Dean returned from the head and began taking his exam. When Dean returned and sat down to take his exam the master chief began to breathe a little bit easier.

Everything seemed to be going according to plan as most of the squad finished the exam with time to spare. However, when I looked up, I saw that Dean, Simon, and Jimmy were the last three to finish their exam Simon and Dean were sweating like pigs. I could tell they were nervous. They were acting like they still had something to hide. Because I knew they should have been the first ones to finish the exam and the fate of the squad and the fate of their time in the navy would be based on how they scored on the exam.

When the bell went off, the OIC came over to Simon and Jimmy. "Gentlemen, you must turn your exam in." Then he looked at Dean, "Son, you have less than ten minutes to finish your exam."

Then Dean looked at the OIC. "That's fine, sir, I don't need the extra time," and handed him his test. I was still uncertain if Dean and Simon had kept true to their word or if they had deceived me. All I could do was sit quietly until the OIC had finished grading all the exams, then I would know the extent of their deceit

Suddenly the master chief stood up and was about to call his squad to attention to march to the mess hall. When the OIC saw the master chief, he stood up and said, "Master Chief, I am ordering you to stand down. The base commander ordered me to ensure all the squads remain at the testing center until I have completed grading their exam. There have been incidents of cheating reported to the base commander, and he has added extra security to make sure there are no more problems with the exams."

This angered the master chief. He approached the examiner officer and had a few words for him. "I don't know whom you think you are, but if you are not done grading the exam within the next ten minutes, I am going to march my squad straight to the commander's office and lodge a formal complaint. The mess hall closes at 2:00, and they stop allowing recruits through the door at 1:45."

The OIC just laughed at the master chief and calmly said, "Chill out, big man, your squad will be at the mess way before then. I am grading the last two exams, and I am sure you have been waiting to hear the results. Once I have completed grading the exam, I will send the results in a secret email that only you and the base commander can access. The results will be available after your squad has eaten chow.

Then the master chief put his head down and slowly made his way back to his seat in the rear of the classroom. You could tell the master chief was not happy that the snotty-nosed examination officer was so flippant with him. The master chief hated the young punks who thought they could change the way the military was run. If the master chief had his choice, we wouldn't even be taking these silly exams. He realized that to keep his job he had to play the game.

Several minutes later the OIC stood up and you could hear a pin drop. "Master Chief, you may take your squad to the mess hall. Remember, the results of your exam will be available to go over with your squad after they eat lunch."

I was truly worried that Simon and Dean had tried to fix the result so that our squad would not be in front of the pack. To everyone's surprise, the OIC saluted the master chief while we were lining up to march toward the mess hall. "Congratulations, Chief. I am not sure how you prepared your squad for this examination, but I am certain you will be happy with the results."

Then the master chief was relieved as he called the squad to order, and we proceeded to march to the mess hall. However, I could see the panic on the rest of the squads face as they anxiously waited to hear the test scores. Thus, everyone quickly scarfed down their food and we marched back to the barracks, where he would tell us how we did on the exam.

"Gentlemen," the master chief said, "I am about to tell you how we did on the exam. However, before I read the results, I want everyone to know that this squad has been one of the best squads I have ever had the opportunity to command."

When he opened the email the chief's eyes lit up as he began to read. "This is a letter from Commander Johnstone, your base commander. 'It is an honor for me to write this letter. There has been much discussion regarding the old guard in my command over the past few months. I am pleased to announce that Chief Walters has proven that there will always be a place for their experience in the navy. Many of the younger leaders have laughed at the old guard, but in hindsight, they have failed to understand that there will always be a place for the old guard's wisdom and experience in the navy.'"

Commander Johnstone was careful to ensure that George's name was left out of the conversation as he continued to congratulate the master chief. "I have ordered all the other squad leaders to find out the secret to how your squad was so well prepared for the exam. Because Chief Walters has proved that all our drills and examinations are needful for our recruits to continue to be the best naval force in the world. You should be proud of your squad because I was informed by the chief examiner that you just recorded the highest scores since the beginning of this process five years ago.

"Beyond your squad's test scores, he asked me to single out Seaman Recruit Jimmy Durbin. Congratulation, son, you were given one of the hardest exams this center has ever given to a recruit, and you only missed one question. But after reviewing the question, it was ruled invalid as we realized that there was an error in the wording.'"

After the master chief read the results to the squad, he allowed the squad to take the rest of the afternoon off. Then John approached the master chief and said, "I told you if you gave me a chance to speak with George he would come through, and it was so good to see them young punks eat crow."

Then the master chief shook John's hand and said, "I'm grateful for your help, and I will never forget that the old and the new can work together to create a stronger navy."

Once the word got out that our squad had aced the first exam, we became celebrities. Everywhere we turned, recruits were trying to infiltrate our squad so they could find out how we passed the exam. Matter of fact, the other squad leaders asked the master chief if he would help them to line up their recruits for the final phase of the examinations would be the week before we graduated from boot camp.

Before the master chief allowed any members of his squad to collaborate with another squad, he made them swear that they would not mention George's name. Because he knew that if the other chiefs found out that I had participated in training his squad they would cry foul. Thus, he protected the integrity of the training program and ensured each chief respected and valued the new process. I can still hear the master chief laughing at the young chiefs for not having the hindsight to train their squads for every drill or test in the same manner, thereby creating a stronger and more efficient navy that had brains and brawn.

CHAPTER XVII

Final Days of Boot Camp

Chief Walters was very conservative when he helped the other leaders. He broke our squad into several units and each unit was given a specific squad leader to help..

However, the master chief kept Jimmy and me specifically to train his squad. I was so glad that I had passed my first test and now I could finally relax. It seemed like my rocky beginning was outdated as I became a hidden legend in boot camp. I had helped Chief Walters create a record that would take decades to break. Not only had the master chief taken a broken-down squad and passed all the physical aspects of training, but his squad was also the smartest class in the history of the Great Lakes naval training center.

John congratulated me and let me know that even though I could not be given credit for my training program that he was proud of me, and he felt it was time for me to spend my remaining time in boot camp getting prepared for the P TF.

"George," he said, "it is time for you learn the importance and value of our team and how it fits into our national security. Once I have filled you in, the commander will meet with you to give you the final details of your position at the PTF. After we have laid out the team's organization and structure, you are going to have to make a choice. Do you want to run home to your mom like a baby or are you going to become a man and rise to grab hold of your true destiny, which is to lead PTF under the auspices of Commander Johnstone."

I still did not understand the scope of what was expected of me, but I was no longer worried. From the various information James and John had explained about the NSA, I was slowly summing up all the facts surrounding the squad. I could hardly wait to meet with the commander and let him know what I final decision was.

Three days before graduation I was summoned to Commander Johnstone's office. I realized this was now the decisive moment, and I would have to decide if I want to continue my naval career and join the NSA. It seemed like becoming the leader of the PTF was the chance of a lifetime, and it could become a blessing in disguise. Yet when I walked into the commander's office, I was very uncertain how I would approach the situation.

"How are you, George? John told me you had questions concerning the background of your fellow shipmates and the true purpose of your assignment to the NSA. John also informed me that you had been digging up some unauthorized information on me and his father. I don't know if I should have you shot or congratulated. It seemed like you have found more information than I had expected. It was easy to enlist James and John because they both have something at stake in the success of the mission. However, you are wondering how you are tied to the mission and why I choose you to lead the team."

"Sir, how did you know I was researching the mission? I thought I was careful in covering my tracks."

The commander said, "George, you may be a master with a computer, but you lack the skills to know when you are being watched. I thought you would catch on during the examination. Simon and Dean told me they thought you were on to them when they were taking the exam. I know you wondered why they scored lower than Jimmy and half of your squad.

When you let them go, they backed off just enough so that you would feel secure. That's when they caught their first break and saw you downloading several top-secret files.

"Once they were able to get a copy of the info, they reported directly to me. I was about to shut you down but then I realized you might be able to help me finally get some type of resolution behind John's father's disappearance. You might think I had something to do with it, but you are off base. If I knew where he was, I would have arrested him for treason. What you failed to realize, George is that no matter how close I was to John's dad, he had betrayed me. I would have never let him slip away; I'd have had him stand trial to get down to the bottom line of what really happened to Project Light Shield.

"To me there was no excuse for John's father to steal and hide the plans to Project Light Shield, because Project Light Shield was one of the most important security programs this nation had. Once it was completed, we would have been light years ahead of the rest of the world. When he disappeared, it was like a personal attack on our friendship. I thought he trusted me with his life, yet he did not even have the decency to let me know what had happened.

"I know this may sound crazy, but when you have known someone all your life, you come to expect a certain type of respect from your friends. And when a friend steps outside the boundaries without as much as a simple explanation, it tends to create animosity between you and destroys your friendship. Even though I still maintain that he is innocent, our friendship will never be the same anymore. All I want to know is what had caused him to betray our friendship. That's why I understand how you feel regarding the loss of your friend."

"Sir," I said, "please don't bring Scott into this discussion, because he is innocent. I don't blame you for what has happened, but I do blame all the awful deceit that he has been surrounded by for so many years.

Please don't ever try to justify your guilt to me. Your friendship with John's father it is nothing like my friendship with Scott. I know at the present time Scott hates me, but in the end, he will understand the choices I make, because that is what friends do. They forgive each other and move on. However, if I never regain my friendship, at least I know he is safe from the mess you want me to become a part of."

"George, I hope you are right, but we have a duty to protect the safety of our nation, and I don't think the team is complete without your wholehearted participation. Only you can decide if you want this nation to rise or fall. I think you will make the right choice. That is why I made you the leader of this special squad. I'm sure James and John have been keeping you busy during boot camp, but there is so much more that you need to learn.

Here is the final scoop, son. Your orders have been cut. You have been granted two weeks of R&R before you start your training. After your R&R, you will be sent to SKA school in Meridian, Mississippi, for six weeks. From there you will be sent to an undisclosed location for an additional fourteen weeks in the NSA. During those fourteen weeks, you will learn the entire scope of your mission and how important it is to our nation's security. That is what is known as your second boot camp.

"James and John will have already completed their training and will be sent to the USS *Bunker Hill* before you. We have already selected several members of the crew to complete your team. James and John will integrate them into the mission. By the time you have completed your training, your squad should be prepared and ready for action. If you need additional personnel, May and Christy will help you find those who are qualified.

After you have reviewed the members of the team if you require any additional members they must be vetted by Christy and May. I have complete trust in their decisions. However, Christy is not a full-fledged member of the squad. She reports directly to May. And until May feels like she is ready, Christy will not have the full scope of the squad's mission.

"During your R&R we have devised a plan to ensure that Scott's father is thrown off track. He must believe that you and Scott are still stationed on the same ship. We made sure that Scott will not be able to contact his father for the next three months. He has been placed on a temporary assignment in Adak, Alaska, where he will be awaiting the arrival of the *USS Carl Vinson.*

While he's stationed in Adak, he has been given strict orders not to contact anyone. Scott has been told that he is on a secret mission to determine the extent of Russian troop movement before the *USS Carl Vinson* arrives. He has been assigned to the communication center, and Chief Bernie Jenkins has been assigned to watch over him. So, when you see Scott's father, you can let him know that his son is on a secret mission."

"Once you leave home, it will be the last time you will be able to communicate with your family until after we return from Australia. I realize this is a lot to take in, but with your ability to infiltrate almost any computer system I'm sure you will eventually put all the pieces together and understand the importance of our mission. The only thing I cannot tell you is what we will be doing when we get to Australia. That information is top secret, and there are very few people who know the true nature of why we will be going to Australia. George, I hope you see past all the deceit and look at the bigger picture. What we are about to do is going to either make or break the security of our nation for the next one hundred years."

The commander looked at me standing at attention as I smartly saluted him. "Sir, I support you, while it may take me a little while to adjust to your methods, I want to see the world at peace. And if there is anything that I can do to help, I am up to the task. I have considered my friendship with Scott. Currently, it is a distraction to the mission.

However, I will never give up trying to make sure he is safe. And I hope that when this is over, he and I will remain friends." Then I turned around and walked out of the commander's office and went back to the barracks.

The commander was stunned that I left so quickly. He was sure that I would be asking more questions concerning the goal of the squad. Even though I had agreed to lead the squad, he felt like my mind was preoccupied with something else. The commander knew he was putting himself out on a limb, and he had to make sure I didn't crack up before the mission even started. Therefore, he told John to keep an eye on me to ensure that I didn't make any detours.

Thus, the first person I met upon returning to the barracks was John. As he slammed his hand on the table in front of me. "I see you finally meet with the commander. I know you have a lot to think about, but I am honored to be on your team." I quickly replied to John, "I don't really know how much you know, John, but you and I are a lot closer to finding out the truth behind all this chaos.

Then James came up behind me and patted me on the back. "I guess it's official. You are going to be my boss. I just hope you know what you're doing. Because I ain't 'bout to submit to any of them old jokers who think they have all the answers.

When the commander assured me, you were the best person for the job, I had my doubts. But, during our time in boot camp I have slowly begun to trust your judgment. Yet, I don't want you to think John and I are going to be easy on you. Because if you do anything to try and destroy our mission, I will make you regret your decision to join the navy."

John looked at me and quietly said, "Don't worry about him, George, he just gets psyched sometime. But he really is just all talk and no action."

"What are you talking about, John? I can't let a yellow belly coward run around in the PTF thinking that he can get psyched any time he wants without paying the consequences for his stupidity."

Then I threw a pair of my socks across the barracks and hit James in the back of his head. John could not believe what I did, and he just shook his head.

"I guess I gotta get used to having a couple of whacko teammates. I guess I'm going to have to play the part. "James laughed at me. "I guess you gotta be ready for anything when you're in this crazy joint. I don't know who you are, but I think it's time for us to move to the next chapter of our relationship. 'Cause I'm about to show you how crazy I can get, you little pipsqueak.

The next time you throw one of your temper tantrums in front of me it will be your last, and I hear your mama calling her crybaby into the back room because he needs a spanking from his mama."

"Remember, Duffus, I was made the leader of this team for a reason. Now I understand! The big picture is that you ain't got no manners, and you certainly ain't got no respect for authority. Today

I'll make sure the next time you lose your temper around me won't forget the lesson I am about to teach you. Understand, little boy?"

Suddenly, James raced across the room like a wild bull, and I moved out of his way and stuck out my foot, tripping James, who ran smack into the table and hit his head.

While James was rubbing his head, I pinned him down and started twisting his arm behind his back and whispered in his ear, Who's your uncle, man? To whom are you going to be nice?"

James just growled as I twisted his arm tighter.

"You can get up now. I'm just asking you for a little respect.

The longer I held him down, the angrier he became. It got so bad that his face was turning blue.

When Chief Walters saw us, he rushed over and forcefully pushed me against the table. "That's enough, George. If I see you bother any other member of this squad that will be the last thing you do before I throw you into the brig for good. Just because you helped the squad pass the exam does not give you any special privileges. Is that understood?

Sir, yes, sir," I hollered. When Chief Walters heard my reply, he burst out laughing. "George, you really are insane. Just remember you only have a couple of days left until you are gone for good, so just take advantage of my final warning, because I would hate to have to train you all over."

Then he looked at James. "Son, it's time for you to wake up and stop making yourself look like a lost puppy. We ain't trained you to act like little girls. And if you let this dork, get the best of you, you ain't nothing but a chump."

Then the chief turned around and stormed out of the barracks. When the chief was gone, I looked at James. "Are you ready for another round, or are going to fall in line and stop acting like the end of the world just came?" Then I started dancing around and chanting in a strange language. "You boys ain't seen nothing. Where's my knife?"

James burst out laughing. "I thought I was crazy, but you got to be the craziest man I ever met. You ain't going to have any more problems out of me."

Then John looked at both of us and threw his hands up in the air. "The commander told me that I was collaborating with lunatics, but the two of you take the cake. I knew what James was capable of, but he didn't tell me you were crazier than James."

James looked at John. "Bro, you need to stop talking about our boss and get on board because we got a lot more issues to deal with. And if you think we are crazy, you'd better reexamine your definition of crazy. I heard what you did when you found out what Donna had done to your family. It took a stint at the nuthouse to calm you down."

John just looked at us and said, "Alright, you got me. Let's just forget about the past. It's time to take down those who have been deceiving us for years. And I am willing to overlook a little craziness if you forget about my moment of insanity."

Then I looked at James. "What you think, bro? Should we give him a chance, or should I dig a little further?"

"I don't think you want to have John as an enemy. I think we can give him a little break this time. But if he goes too far, we always have something to fall back on."

Before James could answer my question, John angrily stated, "James, why you gotta let this goon get into your head? As I told you before, that it was all a game the commander was playing to get into my mind. They had to let me go after twenty-four hours when they figured out that I was sane."

I laughed. "Thanks, friend. You gave me the last piece of info that I needed to figure you out."

James just stared at me. "Sure, you dig all you want. But you'd better not dig too hard because you may find out some things you'd rather not know. All three of us have a sordid past, and there are secrets we would rather leave buried. Be my guest, George. You are the team leader. And if you feel like you need to figure everything out on your own, we will sit back and let you fry."

John said, "I heard that your friend Scott ain't going home either. You are truly on your own for a few months. I hope you're prepared when you get onboard the USS *Bunker Hill.* The commander will even be there before you. He told me earlier today that he just received his orders last night.

We are all going to be one happy family now. Remember, George, you are part of the NSA. You need to watch out who you hang with, 'cause the next few months are going to determine our destiny as a team, and if anyone of us steps out of line we will be toast."

"Don't worry about it, John. I know what I must do. But I don't think you will understand it. That's why we need to get ready for graduation."

The next day we marched in front of the commanding officer, and turned the corner, and it was over with. We had completed boot camp and were ready for the next stage of our lives to begin.

I went over to Scott and shook his hand. "Scott, I know that you don't understand what's going on right now but give it time and you will. I'm sure we will meet again in the future under better circumstances. I just hope that we can get past all the craziness of the past few months. I understand why you reacted towards me the way you did, but now that we are getting ready to head home for a couple of weeks, I was wondering if we could patch things up. I'm willing to do whatever I need to, because you are my best friend and I deeply miss our friendship."

Scott was shocked and hesitant to respond to me. He could not understand why I would even talk to him because of the way he had been treating me in the past few weeks. But when we shook hands, something changed, and I could see that old smile on Scott's face. "No problem, man. I know it has been strange ever since we left home."

"I just got my orders, and I found out we are going to be separated for a while. They gave me two weeks of R&R and then I am going to SKA school in Meridian, Mississippi."

Scott was speechless. "George, I thought you were going to be with me in Adak. That's where I am supposed to meet the *USS Carl Vinson.*"

"What the heck are you talking about, Scott?"

"When I spoke with the master chief this morning and showed him my orders, he assured me that our orders would be to the *USS Carl Vinson* were in place."

Scott leaned over to me and whispered, "I know I am not supposed to tell anyone, but they told me I was on a secret mission, spying on the Russians until the *Carl Vinson* arrives. They only needed one person for the job. Don't worry about it, George. When I speak with my dad, I'll tell him I won't be able to take the trip home with you. I just told him that I am on a special assignment and that I could not tell anyone where I would be for the next three months. He seemed to understand."

I was so glad that Scott said his dad was relieved to hear that we were both stationed on the *Carl Vinson*, and he understood that we both had special assignments to prepare us for our jobs once we got on board the *Carl Vinson*.

"I just hope they don't decide to change your orders while you are at A school."

I looked at Scott and said, "Don't worry about it, buddy. We will be shipmates once I'm done with my school."

Then I let Scott know that I had to get ready because I knew his father would be looking for me soon.

When we turned and went our separate ways, I was thankful that the commander's plan was working out, and Scott's father did not suspect the truth about me being part of the NSA.

Once they were sure that Scott was gone, James and John rushed over to me. John exploded, "Why would you get so cozy with Scott? You blew our entire mission." They were both going berserk.

James said, "George, don't you know that we are being watched and your friendship with Scott may blow our cover?"

"You two need to calm down because you two are off base. If you haven't learned by now, we are going to be fine. Don't you realize that if I had not shaken Scott's hand his father would have known something was off. I was doing my recon so that I could be prepared to answer any question Scott's father might have. But now I know that everything is fine, and I don't have to worry about Steve digging into the reason Scott and I are being sent to separate duty stations."

Immediately after I spoke with James and John, I met with Scott's father. I was really looking forward to being home for a while. When Scott's father saw me, he gave me a big hug. I felt very tense because I knew I had to keep everything concealed from Scott's father. And If I made one mistake, he would know I was hiding something.

"George, I just spoke with Scott. They have him on a special assignment for a couple of months before you meet up on the *Carl Vinson,* I am glad that the navy kept its promise because I know how close you and Scott are. Scott really would go crazy without having his best friend by his side. Matter of fact, I talked to Sam at the recruiting center several weeks ago, and he assured me that the two of you would be stationed together throughout your naval career. Sam told me that he appreciated my concern about you and Scott, and he was glad that everything had worked out."

The commander's plan was working. I sighed, "Sir," I said to Scott's father, "I need to go back to the barracks and pack my gear. If you could just give me about thirty minutes, I'll meet you at the exchange."

Scott's father replied, "Take your time. I'm not in a rush. Plus, it will give me time to talk to Scott before he heads out. You don't need to call me "sir," please call me Steve. I think we should be on a first-name basis after all that we have been through."

I just smiled at him and made my way back to my barracks and to packed up all my gear.

It was a relief knowing that Steve was beginning to trust me. While I was packing, all I could think about was how great it was going to be to see my family. I wanted to tell them about being in the NSA. However, I knew that I could not tell them the truth. Knowing that I could not tell them about my true duty station.

It was going to be hard deceiving them. However, that was the least of my concerns. As I finished packing my gear, I had to make my way see the commander. I had to go the back route because I knew if anyone spotted me with the commander my cover would be blown.

My mind was going a thousand miles a minute while I made my way through the old tunnels at the rear of the barracks. I was beginning to doubt if I could pull it off. My parents were good at detecting lies. The last time I tried to lie to them, they stood back and let me fry. Then they finally told me they knew what I was doing the whole time. It was hard to get around the fact that everyone in town knew my folks.

Yet this was different. This time they had no spies watching me. I was all alone, and even my best friend didn't know what was going on. I guess if I could fool Scott and his father, I could fool anyone. However, the pressure was beginning to eat me up inside and I was starting to freak out.

When I finally reached the commander's office, I noticed that the commander was talking with a high-ranking naval officer. Therefore, I had to wait several minutes before the commander noticed that I was standing outside his office waiting for his final orders. About five minutes later, the commander stepped out into the waiting area and motioned for me to come into his office.

"How are you, George? I see you finished boot camp. Are you ready for the next chapter of your life?"

I saluted the commander and smartly said, "Yes, sir. I just got my orders today and it seems like everything is going as expected."

The commander just looked at me and laughed. "Son, you don't have to be so formal all the time. You do understand that we will be working together for a while, and I prefer that my partners don't feel like they must be so formal. Plus, I have a major surprise for you. Captain Silverton just informed me that he will be our commanding officer on the USS *Bunker Hill*, and the captain is looking forward to meeting the team, so you showed up just in time."

Captain Silverton stuck his hand out. "How are you, George? I have heard a lot about you, and I am honored to meet you. I was telling the commander that I had a major surprise for one of the members of his squad.

CHAPTER XVIII

R&R Begins

I was supposed to wait until after you complete your NSA training, but since you are here today, I wanted to congratulate you."

What was the captain talking about? I was not expecting anything special from the NSA. All I wanted to do was do my job and ensure that I did my best to protect the security of the United States. It was an honor to even be in the company of such great men as Commander Johnstone and Captain Silverton. I did not desire any special awards or recognition, I had not even finished my training.

"Don't look so shocked, George. After you decided to get on board with our special squad the SECNAV reviewed your records and saw how much you were willing to give up. So, the SECNAV decided he wanted to give you a little incentive. I have been authorized to give you a special promotion. You will become the first sailor to receive a commission without going through the naval academy. The SECNAV informed me that you would have been invited to the naval academy if you had not decided to join our special squad. Therefore, I have been allowed the honor of presenting you with your commission as a lieutenant in the navy."

Then the captain handed me the lieutenant bars. When the captain handed me the lieutenant bars I could see the big smile that came over the commander's face. While you are in training at the NSA they will give you all you proper uniforms. I will have them stowed in my cabin on board the ship in case you need to wear them. But, most likely you will not need to wear them until we complete our mission in Australia.

"I told you, son, you ain't got to salute me, because you are now one of us."

After the completion of the ceremony, I stood there in a state of shock. "Sir, I am not sure why I deserve this honor, but I won't let you down." Then I saluted the captain.

Once he was done with the ceremony, the captain turned to me. "George, you realize that you cannot tell anyone about this until the appropriate time. Because as far as everyone else is concerned, you are still only a sailor.

As far as your pay goes, you will get your regular pay like any other service member. However, the navy has set up a secret account for your excess pay. Only you and the appropriate people will know about the account. It will be set up under alias Frank Wildwood and will be tax free.

Once you have completed training, you will be given access to Frank Wildwoods account. However, you will not be able to access the account without prior authorization until we have completed our mission. Once the mission is complete, the SECNAV will determine the proper time to reveal your commission and then you will have full access to all the funds in Frank Wildwoods account.

George, I think it's time for you to get back to Scott's father. I hope you have a wonderful time with your family, I look forward to seeing you on board the *Bunker Hill* after you've completed training."

The captain turned to the commander "You picked a good one this time, and I think we can finally move forward with our plans."

Then I saluted the captain and the commander one more time.

The commander looked at me and said, "Get lost, kid, you need to enjoy yourself for a couple of weeks. I'll see you after training."

As I walked out of the commander's office, I did not notice that his sectary May was smiling at me.

"Hey, mister, I realize you may not remember me. But I am the Lady who summoned you into the commander's office after the incident with Ricky. Also, he told you Christy and I would be working with you once you get on board the *USS Bunker Hill*. Maybe when you get back from your R&R you can take me out on a date?"

I turned around and looked at May like she was crazy. "I can't. I'm getting ready to go home before I go to my next duty station. And I probably won't see you again."

May said, "Don't be so sure about that, you silly man. 'Cause if you're going to be collaborating with the commander, you will definitely see me again."

"I understand, but I'm not sure that's a promising idea. I don't think I should fraternize with the people I work with."

"Handsome, do you think I'm worried about you and your fraternization? It's only one date. But if you turn me down, you'll be sorry."

"Look, lady, I'll agree to take you on a date, but you gotta chill out some."

May just laughed. "Are you sure I'm the one who needs to chill out? It seems like you're the one who's getting hot under the collar, and if I do say, your collar is looking fine."

Then May came over to me and pecked me on the cheek. "You don't know what you're missing. I'm sure we can discuss it all on our first date next time I see you."

My face turned very bright red after her comment, and I was about to say something until the commander stuck his head out of his office. "George don't let May get to you. She does that to everyone. And if you let her get you messed up, I'm not sure you're ready for the mission. Now, I'm ordering you to get out of here."

"Sir, yes, sir," I replied and turned around and started making my way to the entrance in double time.

When the commander and May saw me running toward the elevator, they burst out laughing. Then the commander turned to May. "You gotta stop messing with my recruits. I'm not sure they can take all the pressure."

"All right, sir, this will be the last time. 'Cause this time I found my mate."

The commander bust out laughing. "I think this one is out of your league. But if George takes you out, I'll pay for the date."

May shook the commander's hands and said, "It's a deal, I think you are wrong about me and George."

All I could think about as I made my way to meet Steve was how crazy May was. Why would she play games with my mind? She knew I had to focus on my mission. But before I could think another thought, my thoughts were interrupted when I got to the barracks to pick up my gear. To my surprise, the master chief was waiting for me.

"George, where did you disappear to so quickly? I wanted to talk to you before you went on R&R. I always give my men one last speech before they go off into the wild blue yonder. In your case, I am at a loss for words. I am not sure how you ended up in my squad when you should have been sent to the naval academy.

You showed great perseverance. I was lucky to have such a great man like you on my squad. From all your actions in boot camp, I can tell you are one of the first recruits I have had the honor of training who I believe will have an influence in how the navy operates. When you get to your command, don't forget to drop me a note occasionally, to let me know how you are doing. You know I will be retiring soon, and it would mean a lot to me if you kept me up to date with your progress. Because if the navy makes too many changes, I will have to unretire and whoop up some new recruits' behind."

Then he shook my hand. "It has been an honor to be your company commander, and I wish you the best of luck in whatever your endeavors are. Just don't ever forget where you came from, because there are a lot of people counting on you succeeding." Then he turned around and ordered me to get out of his sight before he did something he would regret.

As I saluted him, I saw the tears welling up in his eyes. He was an extremely hard man, yet I had broken him down. For a moment it felt like I was back home listening to one of my father's lectures.

However, when the chief finally stopped talking, I felt encouraged for the first time in a long time.

I knew I was late for Steve. Right now, I did not have time for empathy. I had to run all the way from the barracks to the exchange. All I could think about was the fact that all these crazy meetings were going to ruin my vacation.

When I arrived at the exchange, Steve was pacing back and forth. "George, I began to think you weren't coming."

"No way, Steve, I wouldn't miss this trip for anything. I'm glad to be able to take a break."

I could tell my tardiness agitated Steve, so I turned to him and assured him that I was glad to be on my way home. "I know I was late, Steve, but my company commander, Chief Walters, trapped me in the barracks and he was trying to tell me how he would miss our squad.

Then he started lecturing me about getting back into civilian life. I kept telling him I had someone waiting on me, but the more I tried to get away the more he talked.

Then Steve just lowered his head and said, "I'm sorry. I guess I'm just on edge today. You see, I promised your mother I would have you home in time for dinner, and you know how your mother likes to be on time."

"Don't worry, Steve. I'm sorry for the disruption of your plans. We can make up the time once we get on the road. I know several shortcuts that I can Google that should take at least thirty minutes off our time."

Steve smiled as he loaded my bag into the back of the car, and we took off.

Minutes later we were on the road. Steve was talking nonstop, and my head was beginning to hurt so much that I had to close my eyes and relax. It was crazy though. I could not relax because my mind continued to play tricks on me and all I could think about was May's smile. I could not understand why she would be playing games with me. Yet I could not deny my attraction to her. For some reason, when she asked me out it was like a dart stuck me in the heart. Then the commander's comment kept playing in my head. Was this just part of a trick to see if I was true to the mission? Or was it just a game she and the commander played with all the new recruits?

I thought to myself all that did not matter, I was on my way and hopefully, there would be no more distractions. For right now, all I could do was try to forget May's crazy request, because I am sure once I see Janis, May would be a faint memory. I knew it was only a trick because I loved Janis, and I could hardly wait to see her. Since the moment I met her when I was fourteen, I had dreamed of being married to her. I was almost certain the subject would come up when while I was on R&R.

It was crazy because before May had asked me out, I was sure that I would be walking down the aisle with Janis. Now, what would have been the easiest decision of my life was in limbo. Why was I beginning to have second thoughts about Janis? I could not get rid of the queasy feeling in the pit of my stomach after May kissed me. I knew I had never felt this way about Janis. I realized I had better get her out of my mind or it could mess up my life with Janis. That's when I decided that my feelings for May were not true. She was just a bump in the road to my true happiness with Janis. It was all a trick or mirage because I didn't want to lose Janis on a humbug. Therefore, I decided to do my best to act like I was still crazy about Janis.

It seemed harder to shake the fact that I had never felt these strong feelings with Janis. Yet I knew that if I didn't act like I was still crazy about Janis. she would sense something was wrong, and the whole mission would be in trouble. I did not want Janis snooping around, because Janis would not stop until she got answers, if I was going to keep my mission a secret, I must act as if nothing had changed.

Eventually, I was able to calm my mind down and get a few hours of sleep as I shut off Steve's nonstop talking.. Suddenly a couple of bumps and Steve shook me.

"George, you're home. We made it with minutes to spare. I must take off, so I hope you will come by, and we can talk some more tomorrow. Just let your parents know that I won't be able to make it for dinner tonight."

"Steve, I'll come by tomorrow. I gotta pick up Janis in the afternoon. I hope you don't mind if I bring her along."

When I mentioned Janis, Steve's face lit up. "Sure, I am so glad the two of you are together. You know how sometimes after people graduate from high school they drift apart."

"Steve, that's one thing about me and Janis. We are crazy about each other, and we want to work things out. That's part of the reason I was so glad I got a little time off before I report to my duty station."

"Thanks again for the lift. I'm sorry that Scott couldn't get some time off, but I'm sure he'll be back before you know it."

Steve just smiled at me and said, "Remember to tell your mom I had some business to take care of." Then he quickly pulled out of the driveway and took off down the street.

When my mom heard Steve's car pulling off, she burst through the front door and nearly knocked me over. "Son, I am so glad to see you. I made your favorite meal. Plus, I got a massive surprise for you. Before I open the door, I wanted to let you know something. Son, I am so proud of you. I know it seemed like your father and I were upset when you left.

"However, we will always be proud of you. I was being selfish because I felt like I was losing you. Can you ever forgive me for overreacting? The navy was the right choice for you to get your life together before you head back to school. The past few months, your father and I decided it was time for change and we have rekindled a flame that I thought was lost. I'm just giving you a heads-up, so you are not shocked by the changes we made to the house."

I stood in the driveway with a blank expression. I became nervous when my mom was talking about changes. I began to wonder if my parents were going through mid-life crisis. Yet I knew I had to act like everything was hunky-dory. I smiled and played along with my mom. As my mind went into overdrive trying to figure out how I was going to conceal the fact that I was joining a top-secret unit.

Would I be able to hide the fact that I was going to be in the PTF? Or would I fall apart knowing that if I told them the truth it might put my family's life in danger?

While the commander had assured me if I stuck to the script everything would be fine. He told me with progress taking down Steve and Donna if everything went according to plan it would all be over soon. Meanwhile, the NSA would keep my family protected and if they were in danger, they would be sent to a safe location.

Yet I was still nervous because if Steve's found out that I knew he was working with Donna things could get out of control quickly. It was like I was walking a tightrope and any small mistake, and we would all be dead. Thus, I had to be extra careful about how I approached the situation with my parents.

All I had to do was keep my act together and let the NSA do its job. They were already gathering information on Steve and planned to raid Steve's apartment two days after I left for Mississippi.

That way Steve would never suspect my involvement in his capture. However, I would not feel safe until I knew that Steve was in custody. I also knew that once Steve is in custody, Donna would try to track down whoever captured Steve.

That was why it was important that I got as much information on Steve as I could while I'm visiting my parents. I was supposed to find out how much they knew about Steve and Scott. Their information was a valuable part of setting the trap for Donna.

My mother snapped at me. "You seem distant. What did they do to you at boot camp? Your father and I have been patient with you, but if they did anything to you in boot camp, I'll personally contact my senator and find out what the military is doing to our children. I know that the military is a good place to learn about life, yet they are known to take it too far. Thus, many of our children come home disconnected from reality. It does not matter how they travel the world and fight to protect our nation's security, many parents are concerned about the methods used to train our children," she said as she shook me.

"I want assurance from your bosses that they will take care of you and Scott. I heard how they sent him to Adak on a special mission and that they are sending you to some type of school before you both get to your new duty station. However, I am uncertain if they will honor their agreement with you and Scott."

"Mom, what are you talking about? Scott and I are fine. Please don't stir anything up because it would only make our situation even worse. We will be on the same ship, and we will be stationed together for four years. After that time, we will have the chance to either get out or spend another four years in the navy. I don't know what Scott is planning, but I am not planning on re-enlisting.

I just wanted to travel and see the world. The next four years of my life. But I am not planning to make the navy my career. I want to be an accountant. The navy will help me pay for my schooling. So, Mom, you can ease your mind. It's only for four years."

I was starting to get angry with my mother. I had already discussed my decision with my parents before I went to boot camp, and I thought they were fine with the decision. Suddenly I began to feel strange around my mother. Something was amiss. She was talking about a surprise. Could this be a trap? I would never forgive myself if I had endangered my family.

I noticed my mom seemed to be very anxious about the surprise. What could it be? My mind was filled with terror, hoping that Steve had not gotten to my family. My mind was running a hundred miles a minute. I nearly forgot I was with my mom, and she was about to surprise me.

My mind snapped back to reality when the door opened and Janis suddenly jumped out and grabbed me and hugged me as she yelled, "Surprise! Your mom told me you would be here today. I know you were told to pick me up tomorrow, I could not wait to see you."

Janis gave me another huge hug and planted a nice, juicy kiss on my lips.

"Whoa, Janis, slow down a little. Don't you see my mom is standing right in front of us?"

My mom burst out laughing. "Don't worry about it, son. I'm sure you a Janis need to have a private discussion about your life together when you return from your first assignment. I made reservations for you at Sam's Grotto, so you and Janis better get going." She threw me her car keys and handed Janis enough money to take care of our dinner and a movie. "I suggest you get rolling, son. We will see you when you get home. I'm sure you and Janis need to catch up on your love life before you return to ship in the two weeks."

What was going on? Had Steve been using Janis to get to me, or had my mother finally made peace with the fact that I was in love with Janis? I could remember the big argument Janis and my mother had the day before I left for boot camp. She had told Janis to get her grubby hands off her son, or she would make sure that I knew about her secret relationship with someone named Betsy. I gulped. This was my worst nightmare was Janis be John's sister? Had she been collaborating with Donna all along? Was that why John's father disappeared? Something did not add up. I had to find the underlying cause of all this treachery

Since I was going to be a part of the PTF, I could not leave any stone unturned. And if Betsy had adopted Janis, how did she really fit into Donna's plan? Had she been collaborating with Donna to take me out of the equation? I had to get all the facts. I guess the best way to find out was to ask the source. How was I going to ask Janis about her stepmother, Betsy, without blowing my cover? If Steve or Donna suspected anything it would all be over.

That's why I was staring at Janis so hard. Finally, I could not take it anymore. "Janis, do you know why my mom has been acting so strange about our relationship? The last thing I remember my mother was against us being together. You gotta tell me how you made up with my mom because our future depends upon it."

Janis was shocked when I started questioning her. "Can't you just be happy, that we are not at odds anymore? George, you are a piece of work."

"About a week after you left, your mom paid me a visit and started questioning me about Betsy my stepmom. She told me that Betsy reminded her of someone from her past. She told me that if Betsy was the person, she thought she was, she would make sure you knew about my past with a crazy lady named Donna.

For some reason, your mom thought Betsy was someone named

Candice. Once I assured her that I did not know who Donna or Candice was, I told her I would set up a time when she could meet with Betsy.

Several days later I arranged for her to meet with your mom at my grandparents' house. Your mother was shocked when she met Betsy. Because she did not resemble the person she thought. When Betsy explained how she had married my father when I was about wo years old. And adopted me when I was about four years old. Your mother's mind toward me slowly began to change when Betsy revealed she had a son who was ten years older than me.

Everything was going fine until my father suddenly disappeared several months after I was adopted. Thus, she became my legal guardian after my father disappeared.

Janis continued Betsy explained to my mother that my father was not a nice person. He left me feeling like I was all alone. That's when I had a mental breakdown and shut myself off from the world. Betsy did everything she could to take care of me like I was her own daughter after my father disappeared. But when her son enlisted in the navy it was too much for her to handle.

However, Betsy loved me like a daughter, and she was the main reason that I was able to deal with my father's disappearance. Since she knew my father's disappearance affected me. She remembered how we would visit my grandparent every chance my father had. Thus, she decided to contact my grandparents and asked them to become my legal guardian. She told them she would support them in any way she could. But she felt like I was better off with them. Plus, with her son's enlistment in the navy, she was really going through, and she felt like I needed a more stable environment to grow up in."

"My grandparents gladly agreed to become my legal guardian. Betsy was relieved, while she would miss me, she knew my grandparents would love and care for me.

"After helping me settle in with my grandparents I slowly started to recover from the abandonment issues that I felt when my father disappeared. I know I did not discuss Betsy with you or your family because sometimes she reminds me of the hurt and abandonment issue I still feel after my father's disappearance. However, I am grateful to still have her as part of my life as Betsy often visits to make sure I am all right. She contacted my grandparents and introduced me to Steve and Scott. Thanks to her, I was able to be in a stable environment and I met Steve and then I met the love of my life. The rest is history.

"After meeting with Betsy, your mom begged me for forgiveness. She broke down and told me how she felt like she had lost you. Your mother told me you were mad with her because of how she had treated me. Now that I understand the circumstances of why she was so hard on me, I broke down and apologized to her. I thought she didn't like me because she felt like I was going to take you away from her. Once I assured her that I had no intention of destroying your relationship with her, she lit up like a Christmas tree, and we have been friends ever since.

"When your mother saw how much I genuinely cared for you, she started treating me like I was part of your family. Your mom and I are now close, and both of us want to make sure you succeed at what you decide to do. If the navy is your career, we will both wholeheartedly support you. Don't leave me or your mother out in the dark anymore. When you left town in such a hurry, it sent shockwaves through your entire family. Your sister was heartbroken, and your brother has been in a downward spiral ever since you left. Last week he got his third speeding ticket, and he and his wife are about to get a divorce."

I stopped Janis in her tracks. "My brother ain't married. What kind of game are you trying to pull on me? I want the truth because if I hear any more lies you and I are through."

CHAPTER XIX

Janis Surprise

Janis pulled into the parking lot of Sam's Grotto and burst out crying. "You didn't get the letters I wrote you. I explained everything in the letters."

Janis knew I couldn't take her crying because I loved her and would never harm her. "Janis," I said, "we did not get our mail until late yesterday. I put all the letters in my bag because I was in a rush to get home to see you. I am not sure why they held on to our letters for so long, but it is part of the process. They did not want us to have any outside contact during our training."

"I know your brother wasn't married when you left. About a week after you left, he went to the courthouse and married his girlfriend, Lilly Lang. After he got married, he moved out and your mom and dad did not speak to him for weeks. When I saw the tension between them, I did everything I could to bring them back together. But it didn't matter. Your brother said your parents were treating him like a baby, and he would never talk to them again unless they realized he was a grown man.

"George, it seems like when you joined the navy it triggered a revolt in your family. After Billy went away, Sally went crazy. She would lock herself in her room for hours, and she stopped talking to everyone except me. She told me that she felt like I was the only one who could bring her family back together. She asked me to write you and tell you what was going on. She told me you need to let her know you would protect her and that you still loved your mom and dad.

"It seems like she was right. When your mom gave us the news you would be coming home in a few days. Sally stopped locking herself in her room, and she called Billy and told him to make up with your parents or she would never talk to him again.

Billy came over to the house and he sat down with your parents, and they talked for about three hours. Billy went to Sally's room and told her that everything would be all right. He had spoken with your parents, and they had worked it out. It did not matter if his marriage was on the rocks or not, Billy realized he needed the family more than he ever thought. This morning Lily met your mom and dad for the first time, and everything seemed honky-dory."

"We all want the best for you, George. I'll put my life on hold and wait for you if that's what you want. I'm in love with you, and I see a future with you."

"Hold on a second, Janis. We have never spoken about our future together. I don't know what tomorrow will bring. How do you expect me to ask you to put your life on hold for me?"

"George, I thought you loved me, and that someday you were going to come around and ask me to marry you."

My face turned red, "Janis, what are you talking about? You know how I feel. I love you and want to be your husband. Right now, I have other commitments. That's why I have never truly discussed our future together. I knew when I joined the navy that it might put a damper on our relationship, but this is all a complete shock to me. I thought we were going to put a hold on our relationship until after I got out of the navy. And if everything were still on track, we could take it from there."

"I am still trying to get my feet on solid ground. I need to have all my ducks in a row before we take the next step. Are you sure you want to wait on me?"

Once I know what is expected of me, I will find the right time and the right place to keep my promise to you. I remember when we first met, and I told you that you were the most beautiful person I had ever known. You laughed at me when I told that one day you would be all mine. However, I figured if you didn't want to wait, I'll let you go because I love you too much to make you wait on dorky like me. If you want to date or see someone else, I understand. You will still be the most beautiful woman in the world to me.. You deserve the best."

"Shut up, you big turkey. Let's have an enjoyable time. We got two weeks to talk about our future. I'm glad to see you're happy."

"That sounds good to me, I don't suppose you and my mom started talking about us having kids and how happy she would be to be a grandmother."

Janis blushed. "Well, that is part of the package. It would be nice to have at least three or four kids."

I looked and Janis and began squirming. "Janis," I stammered, "you know I'm crazy about you, but I got to make a lot of decisions in the next few weeks and I'm not sure you are going to like the decisions I make. I may have to be away for at least two years."

"George, you must be hard of hearing. I told you I would wait for you, I ain't going out with anyone you are the only one that I want. Then she began crying. "When you left for boot camp I was I was going crazy until Steve encouraged me. He told me not to worry about it. He said you'd come around in time. He told me to remember how you and I had met at Scott's twelfth birthday party and how you were afraid to even talk to me. He said you told him you had never seen someone as beautiful as me, and that you And you wanted to ask me to be your girlfriend, but you were afraid I would reject you and that I would laugh in your face if you tried to talk to me."

"What you did not know was that before we met Scott and Cindy asked me if I liked you. That's why Scott invited me over to his house so I could get to know you a little better. I was waiting for you to get up the nerve to talk to me because I had always thought you were cute in a dorky way. When you ran off and tried to hide in the pool room, I was about to leave until Steve came over to me and said, if you like George, I suggest you approach him and ask him to play a game of pool."

"I can still see the silly smile on your face when I asked you to play a game of pool. You nearly choked as you tried desperately to tell me yes. If Scott hadn't stepped in and racked pool balls, we may have never played a game. I was laughing inside when I saw your stick shaking as you tried to take your first shot. Remember how you knocked the ball off the table and nearly hit Cindy? Scott and Cindy burst out laughing. Then Scott said, "Calm down George, Janis ain't going to bite you, she likes you. If you don't stop spacing out, she may never talk to you again. Since you hardly said a word, I decided to make the first move as I leaned over and pecked you on the cheek. Like Cindy and Scott said, I ain't going to bite you I just want to get to know you a little better."

However, I did not expect you to turn around and trip. When you tripped you hit your head on the side of the pool table so hard that you passed out for ten minutes.

When I saw the blood dripping down the side of your head I began to panic. I was crying because I thought I had killed you.

When you opened your eyes and said "Wow, Scott, did you see that I just got kissed by the prettiest girl in the world?"

Then you tried to kiss me again. By that time, my tears had dried, and I reached down and smacked you on the side of the head. 'What is wrong with you, boy? You nearly gave us a heart attack."

After I smacked you, you seemed to really go off the deep end

"Janis, do you think you and I could go to a movie I would be honored to have you as my girlfriend.' Then you puckered up your lips like you were going to kiss me again.

Scott and Cindy looked at you like you were a complete lunatic. Scott said, 'Slow down. Do you even know if she likes you."

Cindy said, 'Janis, I think you must have really done something to that boy, 'cause I ain't never seen him act like this before."

"What do you think? Are you going to give him a chance?"

My face turned red. I did not know if it was from the anger or the embarrassment, as I threw my pool stick down and was about to leave the room. Then you stood up and said, 'Janis, please forgive me. I truly am sorry if I offended you, but I can't help it. You are the prettiest girl I have ever seen.

I'm crazy about you, and I'm asking for a chance to get to know you. If you would come back and finish our game of pool, I would really be grateful. I promise you I won't do anything crazy."

"I turned around and looked at you square in the eyes and said, 'All right, I'll give you a chance, but you gotta stop acting so dorky. I still remember the smile on your face and the spark in your eyes when I turned around and picked up my cue stick. Not only that, but I also saw the relief on Scott's and Cindy's faces as I took the next shot."

"From that moment until now, you and I have become inseparable. All I am asking you is to stop playing all these games with me. If you have forgotten all the fun we have had and the relationship we created together, please let me down gently?"

"What are you saying, Janis? I am so glad to hear your voice. It is so soothing and relaxing. I really have missed you."

"Very funny, George. I know when you are trying to play games with me. It's like the day you told me you were going to join the navy. It seemed like you were more worried about Scott than you were about me. All you talked about is Scott being your friend for years, and the navy told you, you would be stationed together."

Well, mister, I did a little digging. I found out that you and Scott will be separated for a while. I spoke with Cindy yesterday and she told me that Scott was going to Adak, Alaska, for a while before he meets up with his ship. And it seems like you are going to a special school before you get to your first duty station. It seems to me like the navy has been playing games with you and Scott, and that the two of you are not going to be together on the same ship. Why else would they let you come home for two weeks and send Scott to Alaska?"

"Then Cindy told me she felt like Scott was trying to blow her off. Suddenly it was all about him. He no longer mention your name in their conversations. It seemed like the duty station were a permanent separation. She felt like the navy had somehow broken your spirits and was destroying your lives.".

Before you left for boot camp she said whenever she talked to Scott, he always had something to say about you, But the last time she talked to him was the day you graduated from boot camp and for some reason, he kept talking about getting to his ship and all the beautiful ports he was going to see. He even told her that could not wait to see she her that as a soon as he got a chance, he was going to send for her. It did not matter where he was. If they would not let him fly home to see her he would fly her to wherever he was."

"That's when did some more digging to find out what was going on between you and Scott. I went to see Scott's father. He chuckled and told me that Cindy had it all wrong. He had been assured that Scott and you would be stationed together on board the *USS Carl Vinson* but that there had been an issue with your training.

Once you completed your storekeeper training, you would be sent to the *Carl Vinson CVN-70* in the Philippines, and you will be assigned to work as a storekeeper. And since Scott did not have a trade yet, he was sent to Adak to await the arrival of the *USS Carl Vinson* where he will be assigned as a boatswain's mate.

However, he did not have a guarantee regarding his rank when he signed his enlistment papers. Therefore, he would have to work his way up to becoming a mechanical engineer. Steve told me it would take Scott at least six months before they would send him to his special training course. And they told him that once he was sent to his training, he would have two weeks off to visit his family."

"Why are you lying to me? Whatever they have done to you since you left is breaking my heart. Don't you understand George I love you. "But it is torture not knowing if you feel the same way I do. I want to walk down the aisle with your hand in mine forever. And if you don't want to be with me, let me know now, because I'm beginning to think there is more to joining the navy than meets the eye. Matter of fact, you and Scott are trying to make a clean break for Baker City. I remember how you once told me that you wanted to travel the world and get away from this place, yet you promised me that Scott would always be by your side when you traveled."

"However, ever since you have been back, I have not heard you mention Scott's name in your plans. It seems like the navy has taken your mind and made you forget where you came from and who you really are. I am think the navy somehow got to you. I knew something was wrong when you came home, and Scott was stuck somewhere in Alaska. And now here I am sitting with you and all you can do is act like I am an obstacle to your happiness."

"Are you and Scott are in cahoots?"

Did you plan it so that you could get away from Baker City and see the world without any strings attached?"

At least Scott still acts like he is in love with Cindy."

"Why are so distant?"

"Did you find another girl while you were in boot camp."

"How is that possible, but that's the way I feel. Either that or you are more in love with the navy than you are with me."

"It does not matter if you are on the same ship with Scott if the two of you are not even friends anymore. It seems like boot camp did a lot more than mess with your head, it made you a complete idiot. If you can't see how much you have changed, then I have already lost the battle and I might as well let you find another woman. Because I am not going to be a part of any plan that would destroy my two best friends' relationship."

"You got a choice, buster. Either come clean with me or I am gone. Don't worry, I'm not going to tell anyone your secret that you have chosen the navy over everything else. I'll go home. You don't have to break your parents' hearts like you are breaking mine. It is too late for Scott; you already left him in the dust. I hope you figure it out before it's too late, but you do have people who care about you."

"They are even willing to fight for you if you would tell them the truth. Not only has the navy separated you and Scott because of your various trades, but they have also taken away the man that I loved. My final question for you is are you going to continue to be a dork and let your new life in the navy destroy our relationship, or are we going to get married and have a couple of kids before you turn thirty? Is that still true or have been playing games with me."

All I could do was sit for several minutes with my mouth wide open. Janis had broken me down, and I was about to tell her everything because she was the love of my life, and I did not want anything to stand between us."

However, Janis couldn't take it anymore. "George, say something don't sit there like you didn't know this was coming. Ever since you left, I have been feeling like a stranger. If it had not been for your mom assuring me that you were going through a phase, I would have totally lost my sanity."

"I TOLD YOU I LOVE YOU! What more do you want from me? I TOLD YOU I'D WAIT ON YOU! I'm willing to give up everything to be with you. Please let me know how you feel before I make a complete fool of myself."

"Mister, you owe me more than sitting in your chair and staring out into space like I'm not even here. I want an answer because I don't want to waste the rest of my life pining away for some idiot who cannot see love when it is staring him in the face. Just be honest with me because it is evident that you don't care about me as much as I care about you."

I looked into Janis's weeping eyes and whispered, "Honey, I am afraid I don't know what to say. I don't want to hurt you, but I am not sure if our relationship will be able to withstand the pressures of the next few years. I love you with all my heart and I want you by my side, but I am not certain if I am worthy of having someone completely dependent on me. Right now, I am a wreck, and I don't even know if I am going to make it through these next couple of weeks. The stress of becoming a navy man is almost unbearable because I will be leaving you behind, sailing the seven seas, and I am not sure if that is the type of life that you want."

Before I was able to say any more, Janis got up from the table and looked at me. ". Please don't try to put words in my mouth. If you don't stop playing games, I am going to walk out the door and you don't have to ever worry about me again."

"Janis, please sit down. I did not say that I didn't want you in my life. I am trying to be realistic about our situation. I know I will be gone for the next eighteen months, and I can hardly bear the thought of not seeing you. And even when my tour is over, I am not sure how long I will have before they ship me out again. My life is tied to the navy for the next four years. All I'm asking is if we can chill out tonight and have some fun. Over the next two weeks, we will sit down and work everything out."

"I want you to be my wife and I want to hold you in my arms forever. I may not always know how to express myself because when I am with you, I lose my mind sometimes. I cannot believe that someone as beautiful as you would even consider being with someone as dorky as me. The is no one else, and there never will be. The thought of living my life without you is unbearable."

"The answer to your question is that I love you and only you. Yet, because of my doubts and my insecurities, I did not think you would want to wait on me. I know I should be stronger but how can I expect an angel like you to wait on someone like me.?"

"I am asking you just like I asked you when I first met you, can you give me another chance hopefully we can come up with a solution and you can help me overcome my dorkiness before I return to duty. Janis looked at me and quietly sat back down. "Sure thing, George. Let's enjoy the rest of the night because I did really have a surprise for you after the movie tonight. I know you don't like surprises, but I am certain you will like this one."

For the rest of the evening, we talked about our past and how much we had been through together. It was as if we were finally reaching an understanding of each other that would last forever. After we ate dinner and went to a movie, I took Janis home. I could tell she wanted me to stay, however, I had to get home and talk to my mother.

Once I dropped Janis off, I began to doubt myself. How was I going to be able to keep my secret when I had never been able to keep anything from Janis? Whenever she looked at me with her sweet eyes, my heart would melt. The thought of getting married right now terrified me. How was I going to maintain my cover and have a life as a member of a secret NSA unit?

I was very perplexed. I knew that if I told Janis my secret she would tell Cindy, who would tell Scott. And before you know it,

Steve would figure out it was a trap. How was I going to keep the situation at bay without hurting the ones that I loved? I wanted Janis to come with me to San Diego, but if she did then it would no longer be a secret that Scott and I were not stationed on the same ship, and it would put everyone in danger.

However, I was concerned about the relationship that Janis and my mother had built since I left for boot camp. Something didn't feel right. That is why I needed to talk to my mother. I want to find out why she had suddenly become friends with Janis, and why was Janis suddenly putting so much pressure on me to marry her. I knew we had discussed marriage and we had agreed to let it ride until after she went to school, and I finished my tour in the navy.

I was beginning to panic. Had Steve somehow gotten to Janis like he had Scott? Was she part of the setup? It seemed very feasible that Janis was a part of Steve's plan to take me down. I knew Steve had used Scott to gain my friendship. If he could do something that evil, surely, he could easily work over Janis. The more I thought about how I had met Janis, the more I realized someone like Janis would not fall in love with a nerd like me. I was slowly beginning to cut through the deception that had surrounded my life.

The biggest part of the deception was understanding Steve's control over his family and friends.

After my conversation with Janis, I realized that my whole life had been centered around my friendship with Scott. Even when I met Janis, Steve and Scott were there. Everything Scott did was directed by Steve and required his approval.

When I returned home, my mother was surprised. "I thought you and Janis were going to spend some time together."

"Mom, I had to see you and talk about my future. It seems like everything is getting hazy right now, and I wanted to make sure I was making the right decision."

"Son, Tell me what's going on, what's got you so troubled?"

Where was, I going to begin? "Mom, the first thing I wanted to ask you is how long have you known Scott's father? Did you know him before he moved to Baker City? There are many things I am trying to figure out right now and some of my memories are hazy. I know Scott and I have been friends for a long time, but it seems like we have known each other longer than when I first met him in grade school."

When I asked my mom the question, she burst out into tears. "Son, I have been waiting for years for you to ask me about my relationship with Scott and his father. I don't know where to begin but let me try to go back to when I was growing up in New Jersey."

She explained, "I grew up in a tough neighborhood. I was always being picked on by the local boys, and I was in bad shape. It felt like my father had disowned me because when I was sixteen, I met Steve and we fell in love. Steve asked my father if he could marry me. My father was a stubborn man, and he told him that he would not allow us to get married until I turned eighteen. Steve agreed to wait until I turned eighteen. However, one night, after my seventeenth birthday, we snuck off and I wound up getting pregnant.

When Steve found out, I told him we had to tell my parents and that they would agree to let us get married. But when my father found out, he blew a gasket and told me I could never see Steve again if I wanted to stay in his house.

"Once Steve found out that my dad would not let us get married, he went crazy and told me that we should elope and that we could start our family in another city.

However, because of the shame I was feeling, I told Steve it would be better if we never saw each other again. Once my son was born, I gave him up for adoption and moved on with my life.

However, my father never forgave me, and he was ashamed of me until the day that he died. When I turned eighteen I went to college and left home. That is where I met your dad. The first time I saw him standing in the hallway next to Professor Morgan's door I was in love.

"When he asked me to marry him six months later, I told him that I would not let my past ruin my life, so we picked up and moved to Baker City. A few years later your brother was born, then your sister, and finally you came along. Your father and I had started a whole new life together and we were happy. I had left my old life behind and I was happy until Scott's father showed up in town three years after you were born.

At first, I did not realize who he was, but after seeing him at the local coffee shop a few times I thought he looked familiar. So, I approached him, and we began to talk. That's when I realized it was Steve, the father of your brother. When I finally had enough nerve to ask him about your brother, he told me that a lady named Donna had adopted your brother and she found Steve and told him he could be a part of his son's life. Steve was overjoyed.

However, due to complications when your brother was seven, he had gotten sick and died from pneumonia. That's when he told me he had married my friend Rosy and they had a kid.

"Several years after they got married, they were having marital problems, so they moved to Alaska hoping to fix their marriage. However, while they were in Alaska Rosy left Steve for another man. That's when he decided to move to Baker City and start over.

Then Steve introduced me to his son Scott who was your age. I told him that he was welcome to come over anytime. After telling your father the story he agreed to meet with Steve and Scott. After the meeting we became good friends. While Steve is not your real father, he felt close to you due to our past relationship, and we asked him to be your godfather. I know I've kept this from you since you were small, but I knew someday you might ask me about our relationship. I am so glad to finally get it off my chest."

Wow, I thought to myself. *Not only had Steve played his own son, but he had also played my parents. He had gained their trust and now he was like their brother.*

CHAPTER XX

Mothers Affair

My mom could not stop weeping after she told me the story. "I'm so sorry, son, for keeping this from you for so long. Can you ever forgive me? Please don't think bad about me or Steve. It was a part of life that I must live with, and every day I wish you could have met your brother."

I put my arm around my mom and said, "Mom, don't worry about it. Do Sally and Billy know about our brother?"

My mom began to weep again. "Son, you are the first one to ask. I know it is because of your closeness to Scott and Janis. I am not sure your siblings will ever forgive me if they found out. I should have a family meeting and your dad, and I can talk to everyone together."

I looked at her. "Mom, when you are ready, you can bring it up. But I will never say a word to either Sally or Billy because it is your decision, not mine. I know it was hard on you, but you did what you thought was best for your family. I will always love you. Mom, I do have one more question for you. I want to know what you really think about Janis because we had an interesting discussion tonight and I am seriously thinking about marrying her.

How come you are so cozy with Janis? I remember before I went to boot camp you said you did not want me to marry Janis. I love

Janis, and I was thinking about proposing to her. That's why I'm asking your opinion because it seems like you are best friends now."

When my mom heard that I was considering marrying Janis, she freaked out. "Son, I knew you liked her, but I didn't think it was that serious."

"That is not all I have hidden from you, son. You asked me why I didn't like Janis. You wanted to know what she had done to me. Well, son, when you and Janis first met, I was happy for you, until one day I heard her and Steve talking to someone from my past. Steve did not realize that I had heard him and Janis talking with Donna about your relationship with Janis."

Several days later, Janis approached me and told me that she was in love with you, and she hoped that she and I would become good friends. When I told her that I would never let her get her claws into you like Donna had gotten her claws into Steve Janis became angry with me, and she blurted out.

"Who is Donna? And why were you spying on us? All I know is that this crazy lady was trying to tell me that you and Steve were together at one time and that you had a son. I did not know who the crazy lady on the other end of the line was."

That was the first time I talked to her, and I hoped it would be the last time. I told her I didn't believe that you and Steve had a relationship because you were in love with Georges father, Toby, and you would never do anything despicable like that"

"Steve was upset with me and told me that was no way for me to disrespect his friend Donna. After we got off the phone, Steve told me that if I ever mentioned this conversation to you, it would ruin our friendship."

"She asked me to tell her the truth. Did Steve and I have a relationship? Did I have another son? At first, I was reluctant to tell her anything because I did not know if she knew Donna. However, after asking her a few questions about Donna, I realized that Steve had tricked her. I do not believe she is part of Donna's plan to destroy my life. When she told me Steve asked her about her father. She had mentioned that Betsy had married her father and adopted her before her father disappeared."

"I was skeptical about Janis's story because I thought that Betsy was someone from my past. And that is part of the reason I did not trust Janis. Plus, she was now living with her grandparents why had would her stepmom abandoned her?"

"Janis was furious when she found out that I thought she would try to hurt you. That is why she agreed to set up a meeting with Betsy."

"When I met Betsy, I found out that she had nothing to do with Donna or Steve. And that she had done everything she could to help Janis when her father disappeared. When I heard Janis's heartbreaking story, I was mad at myself for assuming the worst."

My Mom paused, "George, I am sure I am repeating the same story Janis told you if you asked her about why our relationship has changed. Son all I can tell you is Janis is a remarkable woman and if you love her, you better treat her with the respect she deserves.

"Steve may have tried to influence Janis, but she wouldn't fall for his tricks because she loves you and does not want to see anyone in your family hurt, and if I am right Steve tried to introduce Janis to Donna. Thus, I will never trust Steve again. Janis is a good person, and I am so glad that I was able to truly see how much she loves you. That's why we are closer now and if you choose to marry Janis, I will not stand in the way."

My mom smiled. "Remember, I love you no matter whom you decide to marry, I trust your judgment. And if you think she really loves you, I will respect that. However, I hope that you are careful when you are around Steve. He has tried to influence Janis and use her as a pawn to get to me. But his plan backfired, and Janis has totally fallen for your dorky charm."

"Also, I don't want you to end your friendship with Scott because of Donna and Steve. You must learn how to look beyond the hypocrisy of Steve and Donna. Because Janis and Scott are your friends for life and would never try to harm you."

"However, Donna is one we should be watching out for. Donna

befriended Steve and adopted our son, and she has used that as leverage to force Steve to do her dirty work. When Steve and I were young he was the nicest, warmest person I had ever met. But once Donna came into the picture he changed."

"While I was optimistic when I first saw Steve in Baker City. Those hopes have dwindled. I have seen how Donna gets when she feels as if someone has caused her pain. Once Steve fell into her trap, he lost all my respect. I would hate to see either one of you with a broken heart

Therefore, if you are uncertain of anything about Janis's love for you, you need to break it off now before both of you are heartbroken and tormented for the rest of your lives. Son, it is your decision because you are the only one who knows if Janis is the woman you want to be with for the rest of your life.

"George, I have learned you must keep an open line of communication, or your relationship is doomed to fail. And when you keep secrets from the ones you love you may only end up damaging your relationship. That is why it is good to be as upfront and honest with Janis. And you need to make sure you are ready to deal with the fire from Donna's wrath. But if you love Janis as much as I suspect you do, I will support you and do whatever I can to protect both of you from the backlash.

Remember, son, you want to get it right the first time. But if it does not work, you must never harbor hatred toward the other person. It will only lead to heartbreak and loneliness.

"But you are the only one who knows if she is the woman you want to be with for the rest of your life. Take your time and think it through. And at the end of the day, if it feels right, go for it."

My mom dried up her tears and said, "You need to get some rest son. I just hope you know that we are all so, glad you'll be home for two weeks before you sail off into the wild blue yonder."

I hugged my mother and whispered "Don't worry mom I have not made any decision regarding Janis. However, I am still contemplating marrying her when I get back from my first tour. Then I walked up the steps and went to my room, fell on my bed, and instantly fell into a deep sleep.

I woke up early the next morning and I used my secure line and contacted the commander's office. When May picked up the phone, I was shocked.

May chuckled, "I bet you thought you'd never hear from me again. The commander ordered me to assist you. He wants you to give me all the juicy details. Thus, you need to start talking Bro because I ain't got all day." I was reluctant to give her the information. "May this information is for the commander only. He told me to be careful about whom I talked to. Don't take it personally lady, but I don't know you, and I would rather talk to the commander.

Then she got silent, and I heard the phone click. I was relieved when I heard the commander's voice as he interrupted our conversation. "Boy, stop whining like a little baby. Stand up and be a man and give the woman the info. I trust her and she is a valuable member of the team. If you don't hear from me, May is the only other person you should give info to unless I direct you to someone else."

"The captain or the general will not call you directly unless it is an emergency. Anyone outside of May or myself must use the code *69 Myth*. If anyone fails to give you the code, you will reply this is *59 Charlie*, and you will be transferred to the appropriate contact. Then they will transfer them to the voice-operated system at headquarters, which will put the call on hold until they hang up. If they stay on the phone for longer than thirty seconds, the number will be automatically traced thus, pinpointing their location."

"It is important for you to remember the code. There will be outsiders who want to infiltrate NSA by getting you to spill secret information. Whenever someone does not give you the proper code and wants you to communicate with them directly, I am ordering you to steer them in the wrong direction by texting code *59 Charlie* while you try to keep them on the line for thirty seconds. Then either hang up on them of change the subject of the conversation."

"May will be contacted once they have traced the number and

she will let me know the situation. And if there is any further actions needed May or I will contact you.

Right now, I am on my to the *USS Bunker Hill* to meet with the captain so the two of us can iron out the last-minute details of your little excursion. If there is anything you need to know, May is on top of it. She will give you any special instructions." Then the commander hung up.

May immediately called me back, "Well, I guess I'll take it from here, honey."

"First thing May, or whatever your name is. If you don't stop calling me 'honey, this conversation is ended. The only honey I have is Janis, and I am hoping to marry her as soon as I sort through a few things. Did you know that Steve had a relationship with my mother, and she did have a child out of wedlock?

While my mother could have eloped with Steve, she chose to try and repair her relationship with her father. Thus, she placed my brother up for adoption. When Steve found out it broke his heart."

Because of the situation with Steve, my grandfather never forgave my mom for getting pregnant. And it destroyed their relationship. My mother told me she tried to contact my grandfather and begged him to meet her family. But he refused and he died not knowing his grandchildren."

"It was not until Steve came back into her life that she found out that Donna had adopted my brother. When my brother was about six years old, he caught pneumonia and died. Donna blamed my mother for my brother's death."

That is why Donna was instrumental in setting up the meeting between Steve and my mother in Baker City. Donna had somehow convinced Steve that he could make my dad jealous and that my mom would eventually get back together with him. However, instead of my parents getting a divorce they became friends with Steve and made him my Godfather.

When I heard about how Steve was meeting with my mother in his den it seemed like Steve is trying to break up my parents. My mother said since I left for boot camp she and my father had been going through some changes.

Yet, I could not see my mother ever leaving my dad for Steve. She told me Steve had changed drastically since he meet Donna and she had given up hope that he had changed."

Also, it seems like Steve had introduced Janis to Donna. However, she denies she knows who Donna is. And I believe her. Thus, I am planning on purposing to her, and we will get married when I get back from my first tour."

I thought to myself *there was no way I could phantom my parent getting divorced and Steve becoming my father. Especially after the horrors, Steve had put Scott through. It seems like there was no end to what he might do to gain my mother's approval. However, he seems to care for Janis like a daughter, and he has tried to keep her out of Donna's hands because he has only introduced Janis to Donna a couple of times.*

May stopped me. "George, there are a few details you need to know before you marry Janis. Not long after your brother's death, Steve got married and Scott was born a few years before you met. It was no accident It was no accident that right after he moved to Baker Steve met your mother and they rekindled their old relationship. Thus, introducing you to Scott and you have been best friends ever since.

Then when Janis's father disappeared, it seemed like her father had a falling out with Donna and around that same time, Janis's grandparents met Steve. When they found out that he had a son they introduced Janis to Scott and the rest is history. As Janis and Scott became inseparable.

"Meanwhile, Steve and Janis's relationship grew, and she now considers Steve like an adopted father.

While she claims not to know Donna, she has been subject to Donna's plot since she was introduced to Steve. I am sure she loves you but before you marry let me do a little digging to make sure she is not a part of Donna's organization."

"George, you know your mother said she felt like Betsy knew

Donna and was hiding the true reason she decided to let Janis's grandparents become her legal guardians. If I am correct about who Betsy is, we may have found our link to Captain Golden, she is either working with Donna or she is protecting Janis's father, who changed his name to Captain Golden."

"While Captain Golden thought his parents would take Janis in, he was clearly mistaken, as it took six months before they were able to adopt Janis because her father was branded a traitor, and the government had to run a thorough check on her grandparents. During the time her grandparents were being checked out, Janis remained living with Betsy in a witness protection program in case someone tried to contact harm her."

"All this was a trying time for Janis and nearly broke her. When you met her at Steve's house, she was just getting her feet on the ground. She felt like she could trust Steve, and she was finally living with her grandparents. While Betsy is no longer in the picture, Janis still had a strong friendship with her, and they still stay in touch."

"I know you had mentioned you wanted to marry Janis, but you must find out why she is putting so much pressure on you to get married before you finish your first tour. Although you told me she said she loves you unconditionally and is willing to wait on you. I am begging you to let me dig into her relationship with Betsy. She may have convinced your mother Janis is innocent, but before you marry Janis, we need to make sure it is not a trap. I believe we will find the answer when we find out what is the real reason Betsy is trying to make Janis forget her father's disappearance."

"Is it because Janis's father had been collaborating with Donna, or is it because he tried to fake his own death?"

"Maybe Betsy was afraid of Donna's wrath when she found out that Janis's father had disappeared and then faked his death.

Because that is when Donna flipped out and has been chasing after Captain Golden ghost. It seems like he had hidden the plans for a top-secret project called *Project Light Shield.*

Even though, the NSA, CIA, and FBI tried to verify his death found they never found Captain Goldens' body. Therefore, Donna felt like she could no longer be a part of an organization she no longer believed had our nation's best interest at heart. That is when Donna joined forces with Commander Revile to hunt down Captain Golden and find the missing plans for *the light shield*."

To this date, no one knows exactly what *Project Light Shield* is, yet there were two people working for Donna, Commander Revile, and Captain Golden who is Janis's father and a good friend of Captain Silverton. It seems like Captain Golden sent Captain Silverton a coded message describing where he had hidden the plans to Light Shield. And he insisted he was not a traitor. But he felt like his disappearance would be the only way to ensure that Donna and Commander Revile did not get the hands on the plans for *Project Light Shield.* The strangest thing about the message is it was received three days after the captain's Goldens death.

"Thus, the Email you discovered contained a coded message describing where he had hidden the plans to *Project Light Shield.* When the email to Captain Silverton was uncovered many members of the NSA thought wanted to know what captain Silverton was hiding. Thus, they wanted to put the captain under surveillance hoping he would lead them to Captain Golden. Many felt like Captain Silverton is the one who helped his friend Captain Golden disappear.

After Captain Golden faked his death Captain Silverton and Commander Johnstone desperately worked to their friend's name. However, until they can figure out why Captain Golden was working with Donna and Commander Revile they had no choice but to join forces with the FBI, CIA, and NSA to hunt down Captain Golden.

However, Captain Silverton was remained adamant his friend was innocent thus, he secretly formed the PTF. Because he knew Captain Golden wanted to make sure Donna and Commander Revile did not get the plans to the light shield.

"George, one of the main the reason Captain Silverton formed the PTF was that he needed to have a team that would be under the radar and help to find the plans to *Light Shield* while restoring peace to the world and taking down terrorist organizations like Donna's. Thus, he chose you, James, and because the three of you have ties to Donna.

Donna is James's mother, John is James's cousin, and your mother and Steve had an affair thus tying you to the equation. However, do you really know who Janis is. What if I told you she was Captain Golden lost daughter and that if you marry her you might wind up being related to James and John.

I was silent for a minute. Then May chuckled, don't worry about it George, James and John don't know about Janis yet. Because they don't need to know until everything is verified.

Now do you understand why you must keep the PTF a secret and focus on saving the world? Because the existence of the *light shield*, is a threat to the entire world and the only to keep the world safe is for the three of you to work together and find the plans to the *light shield* before Donna's does. Then the world will finally be at peace"

I stopped May in her tracks. "All this time you knew about Janis, Steve, Donna, and my mom. Why didn't the commander tell me these things while I was in boot camp? Because I am freaking out and do not know if I want to belong to his team or help him complete his mission. I can no longer lie to Janis and the ones I love.

Why did the commander let me take a vacation knowing that it would have been better to process all this information once I was on board the USS *Bunker Hill*? I am skeptical and do not know whom I can trust because it seems like I have enemies on all sides and those that are supposed to be the closest to me have hidden secrets and told me lies since the day I was born. I love Janis, and I must decide on whether I want to be married in less than two weeks."

May blurted out, "Hold on, sweetie pie, the general, captain, commander, and your father have not struggled for all these years for you to become insensitive and not look beyond their faults to find the truth. All you are seeing is the surface. What is the important aspect? Chump, you can change the world's concept of war and help to bring peace. That's why it's called the Peace Task Force.

Some things can be pardoned, some may not be. You must keep your head about yourself. Remember, you are part of the solution for peace, not a part of Donna's evil. That is why the commander chose you to lead the PTF because you see through the darkness, and you can see hope for tomorrow. It looks like your life has been turned upside down, but you have people who love you and will go to the mat for you. That's how you know whom to trust."

"Yes, the commander may not give you all the information while you were in boot camp.. But you need to remember how you felt in boot camp about Scott? The commander knew that you were already grieving the loss of your friendship with Scott. And he did not want to overload you with sorrow. That is why he waited until you were able to take some R&R."

He felt you would rather hear your mom and Janis tell there story's then to bog you down more than you already were at boot camp. Now that you know what Janis and your Mom have been through the commander was hoping you would have a better perspective on things. And he hoped you would be able to absorb the chaos and take some time to surround yourself by those that you love before you move on to your next assignment.

The good news is that Scott is no longer under Steve's grasp, and soon he will be a member of the PTF. He may not be on your task force, but he will be the head of a valuable team."

"The commander wanted to show you and Scott that you can be apart and still be friends. Like the commander said, Scott will become one of your most trusted allies soon. It will happen when you least expect it."

When the two of you finally hook up again, your wives will be safe and able to live in peace. "George, it pains me to say but Janis loves you, don't ever forget that. She did not betray you. It is Donna and he evil plan that is causing all the pain. So why not work to bring down Donna and keep those you love safe."

"May it take years before you are able to be together, or it may only take a few months. I will marry Janis. because Janis deserves to be happy. And I know we will be happy together"

"Whatever happens, sweetie pie, don't doubt that Scott and Janis are your friends and always will be. That is why your mother begged you not to give up on them. Also, you now have new friends James,

John, and me, who will battle with you until we see the world free from Donna's terror."

"May, I get it, but please stop calling me baby, honey, sweetie pie. Because if Janis still loves me after all this is over, she is the only one who has the right to call me those names. You need to take it down a notch because I have already found my soulmate. Whatever you think is going happen between you and me ain't" Janis got me all tangled up and all I can see is how beautiful she is. However, it's because of you that I have decided not to run away for the PTF."

I think beneath all that craziness is a woman with a heart of gold. Someday you will find the right person for you. And when you do, I wish you the best, but it ain't going to be me because my love is already spoken for. And all these crazy accusations will never break my love for Janis. Thus, you can let the commander know Janis and I will be engaged before I leave.

May sniffled and blew my mind as she said, "You sure know how to break a woman's heart. They told me you didn't know how to speak to women, but you demonstrated your virility with me, tiger. Now all you got to do is talk to Janis the same way. She will drop at your feet when she sees how confident you have become."

"I wish you the best, my friend. I know it's not easy keeping secrets from the ones you love, and it's not good to start a relationship with a secret like yours. If you can endure hearing your mom's secret and not freak out, Janis will be able to endure your secret when the time comes to let it out. Just stick in there."

"Thanks for the advice, May. Let me know what you find out. I'll call you back in a couple of days. One final thing, we need to get straight. I feel like you might have been a little harsh on the commander. You said the commander did not know what he was doing, look in the mirror and you will see the commander was 100 percent right in choosing you to lead the PTF. After you finish your schooling and the NSA training, you will be ready to serve your nation as a warrior."

CHAPTER XXI

The Argument

"The world needs more men like you who are on fire and can keep a level head. George, can you stop overthinking things and start looking for the best possible solution for everyone? Because you do not belong to yourself anymore. You will be a soldier and you need to consider others. Because you know there are too many innocent people who would prefer peace over war."

After hanging up the phone, I made my way downstairs to eat breakfast. To my surprise, my brother and sister were waiting for me.

"Hey, bro, it's good to see you again. You look cool with that buzz."

My sister chimed in, "I still bet you can't beat me in a tennis match, so I set up a practice session for us tomorrow. I heard you and Janis are going to be playing footsie today, and I sure don't think I can take that image for too long."

What is wrong with you lunatics can't you see I am trying to relax, as I sat down on the couch and tried to eat a bowl of cereal." I said as I pointed at Billy and Sally.

When they heard me call them lunatics, they both jumped up from the table and jumped on me. The couch could not take all our weight, and it shattered into pieces.

Sally looked at Billy and said, "Dude, are you crazy? Don't you know how much Mom loves this old thing? I remember how she used to rock us to sleep every night before your head got too big."

We all panicked as we quickly tried to put the couch back together hoping that my parents would not notice the couch was broken. Suddenly my dad came in the front room. "What is wrong with you kids, your mom and I were trying to relax a little bit then I heard you talking and screaming so loudly.. I just had to come out here to find out what you were doing."

Before my dad sat on the couch he bent down and whispered in my ear. "Well, son, I'm glad you're home. I heard you and your mom had a good talk last night. I hope you don't feel any different about your parents' choices."

The plopped down on the couch, as I smiled and said "Dad you and mom are the best parents a guy could hope for."

Before he could respond the legs on the couch gave way and dad was lying on the floor.

Billy and I rushed over to my dad and helped him up. However, the noise from the couch shook the house and my mom came running into the living room.

When my mother saw the couch, She was so mad it looked like the fire in her eyes was going to burn the house down. The more Sally and Billy talked, the angrier she became. There was no telling what she might do to my lunatic brother and sister.

That's when I used some of my training and threw them both on the floor. I grabbed their collars and made them stand up next to our mother. I hollered out, "Mama, here are the two culprits who broke your couch. You want me to take them out back and put them in the doghouse until they straighten up, or should I make them apologize for not having a brain?"

When Mom saw Billy and Sally standing in front of her looking like lost puppies, she didn't know whether to cry or yell. That's when she let out a scream that nearly shook the entire house. "WHAT IS WRONG WITH YOU? That was a gift from my mom, and it's been in this family for the past fifty years. There is no way it can be replaced."

I could not believe what my crazy brother did next. He laughed. "I think you ought to thank us for trashing the couch. You know Dad's been wanting to get some modern furniture since before I was born."

"Son," my mom said as she smacked Billy, "there is no way to put a value on what you destroyed. You took away one of the few things I had to remind me of my parents."

My mother burst out laughing. "You kids are crazy. Come on over here and let me give you a hug. You know I can't stay mad at you for too long. I'm glad to have such great kids, but most of all, I got one of the best husbands on the planet and I am going to let him deal out the punishment for your insubordination."

My dad could not take it anymore as stood next to the busted couch and looked at all of us. "You are all a bunch of nitwits. To think I thought I could raise a family in this crazy place. You should be ashamed of yourselves. Don't you see how much you broke your mom's heart when you broke her precious couch?"

"It doesn't matter how old and ragged it is. That couch was one of this family's greatest treasures. Yes, I may have thought about getting rid of it, but when I found out it was worth less than a dollar, it became a permeant fixture in our lives. Even the junkyard told me I had to pay them $100 to get rid of it. Why don't you give your mom a break? She hasn't had any style since we got married, and that's why I fell in love with her. You kids will learn about it once you start your own family. If you love someone, it doesn't matter what they do, you still love them. Now that you have finally destroyed that old couch, it will be easier for us to put it in the trash tonight."

"Honey, I am sorry. I think it's time for us to move on and get a few new things in our life. This is the best way to get started. I'm sure that George will make you a souvenir from your mom's couch that will be a permanent reminder of how much your parents loved you. But I think it's time to finally brighten up this place and let me show you, my style."

When Mom heard Dad, she looked at him and said, "This is all your fault, sons fault if he hadn't left to join the navy, the rest of the family would not have gone completely wacko." She turned to my father and said, "Dear, that doghouse George was talking about for the kids is going to be where you are sleeping for the next few days while I figure out if I am ever going to talk to you again."

"That's fine, honey. I've been thinking about it for a while. I think you and I may be through. And I ain't sleeping in no doghouse, I'm going to the Hilton to celebrate with my friends. They told me I should try to contact my true self. Well, honey pie, you are about to see some moves on this old man that you never knew, because I am tired of you taking advantage of me and thinking that I'm a prop that you can push around."

Then he turned around and walked out of the room. About a minute later, we heard his car screeching down the street as he flew out of sight. What had happened? I thought to myself. I was supposed to be having an enjoyable time. First Janis was pressing me to marry her, then his joker sister and brother ruined Mom's favorite couch, and now my parents were about to break up.

I looked at everyone and said, "I got to go. I am supposed to pick up Janis. And don't wait up, because I will be staying at her place for the rest of my R&R. If you want to see me, you know where I'll be, because I sure don't need any more of this craziness."

Before I could reach the door, Sally grabbed me. "I know you've seen enough for one day, George, you gotta forgive me and give Billy a chance. We didn't mean any harm. George don't leave me all alone, not while Mom and Dad are about to split. It's not fair. You got Janis. Even Billy got a wife though he acts like she doesn't exist."

"I haven't had a meaningful relationship in years, and it doesn't seem like I never will. George, you are the only one I can trust to help bring Mom and Dad back together. I know we can get crazy sometimes, but this family is all I got. I love you. Please don't leave us in chaos."

I looked at my sister and gently pushed her away. "Sis don't worry about it. I got to get away for a little while. Come over to Janis's house tomorrow and we will figure everything out. Mom and Dad will be fine, and Billy is going to be Billy, but he loves you as much as I do. You are going to have to start leaning on him.

"Billy, you need to go over to your house and grovel at your wife's feet until she lets you in. Then sit down, calmly talk to her, and let her know that you love her. The next time I come to this house and see you, she better be by your side, or I am going to give you a knuckle sandwich.

"Sally, you need to sit down with Mom and comfort her, let her know that everything is going to be all right and that you are there for her and Dad. Most of all, you are going to have to be the glue that keeps this family together while I am away. I have some things that I must do in the next few years, so you must promise me that you will keep this family together."

Billy looked at me like I was half crazy, then he slumped his head down and said, "Sorry for all the chaos, man. It's been crazy since you left. I will get Lily, and she is going to be overjoyed to meet you, George. Once Lily and I are back together, I'm sure that will soothe Mom some.

"You are so right about Lily. She is the love of my life and I have been a complete moron. How are things with you and Janis?"

I just growled at Billy, "It would be a little better if there wasn't so much drama all the time. I think Janis would enjoy being here with the family, but sometimes you twits don't know how to act. It's crazy that you think I should be so mature when both of you are older than me. I appreciate the vote of confidence, but I see how both of you work.

It's crazy, I am the youngest, yet you feel like I have the most wisdom and treat me like I should be so mature. I appreciate the vote of confidence. Sally you need to learn how to relax. You could have any guy you want, but sometimes you're too emotional."

"Guys like a woman who does not freak out at every little thing. Look at Dad. He feels like he's been playing second fiddle for years. Mom and Dad will be fine, everyone needs to give it a rest for a few days."

I need to fix things with Janis first. Then I will talk with Dad.

Everything will be okay. You'll see, now get out of here, Billy. Get your wife. And, Sally, calm down, you'll be fine. Because you are one of the strongest women I know. Go find Mom let her know that I will talk with Dad, and he will be back some time tomorrow. Tell her she needs to understand the pressure that he has been under ever since Steve showed up."

"She needs to reassure Dad that he is love of his life. And I will tell Dad he needs to stop living in the past. Things happen but with their strong love for each other they can easily overcome any mountain that may get in their way."

"I know they love each other and that it would be a shame for them to waste away without being by each other's side. I will make sure that Dad comes back so they can work things out. When Dad returns we all need to give them some space. I think it would be best if you and Billy come to stay with me and Janis for a few days. I am sure she won't mind. My only request is that you allow me and Janis some time together so we can work out our future together."

After Billy left to go apologize to his wife I turned to Sally. "Sally, I am counting on you. That is why you are the first one I am telling, if everything works out I plan to propose to Janis before I return to the navy. We may not get married until I return from my first tour. However, I was thinking that she would stay with the family until I return. However, everyone needs to get on board."

"Billy needs to reestablish his relationship with Lily, Mom, and Dad need to communicate and get past their issues. And you must be the strong one"

"I know you will welcome Janis, but you need to let me know if anyone disrespects you. I will give you my address, email, and phone number so we can keep in touch."

"Don't worry if it takes me a few days to return your messages. But I know everything will be fine while I am gone. What do you think? Do you think you can handle Janis being around for a little while?"

Sally was in a state of shock when I told her about Janis. She grabbed me and hugged me. "It's about time you told Janis how you really feel. She is like a sister to me, and I will make sure she feels like part of the family."

"I got it George get out of here Don't all this conflict affect things with Janis. None of this was Mom's or Dads fault, hopefully they will open up stop bringing all this negative energy to the family. It does not matter what they have done they are meant to be together. And our love and support they will be fine.

Then she pushed me toward the front door. "Don't worry about Mom crying I will do our best to comfort her."

"Just don't forget to bring Dad home tomorrow."

While I was making my way to meet Janis I began to think about how my father had taken on a boatload of troubles over the years covering up the lies and keeping the family strong. Therefore, I now understood why I had to accept my responsibility to lead the PTF and take down Donna and any other terrorist who wants to keep the world in chaos.

I knew once left and Steve was removed from the situation that my dad would be fine. However, I realized Janis was the key to taking Steve down, if he felt like we were going to get married, he would back off.

Yet, I had to tread very carefully because I still did not know if Janis was part of his evil plan. I was still waiting on May to call me back, before I would be a free man. While I loved Janis I was becoming more skeptical, and I began wondering how deep was Janis's deception. Because realized that someone as beautiful as Janis would never fall for someone like me.

The more I ponder marrying Janis the more concerned I was that it was a trap. Could I trust Janis, or would she break my heart? As it became hard for me to believe that once we got married, she would not throw me to my enemies Donna and Steve. Thus, allowing them to destroy my world forever."

However, I had fallen for Janis's sweetness, and it seemed like she had placed a spell on me. But after our conversation last night, I realized there was another side to her sweetness, and I was not planning on being caught in her web anymore. Before I made any rash decisions, I had to get the information from May.

My gut told me there was no way Janis was working with someone like Steve. She didn't fit the bill. I had to be overreacting and that our marriage would be a symbol of defiance against Donna and her evil threats against my family.

The more I thought about all the chaos and trouble of the last few days the more I was reminded of what James and John told me about digging into the PTF. *The more you find out about our mission, the more anguish you will feel.*

They were right I was being destroyed by all the deceit surrounding my life. While the truth was setting me free it did not feel good. However, when I considered the burden my parents had hiding Mom's relationship with Steve it made me angry.

I knew my father was a good man for loving my mom and taking the back seat for so many years. After my conversation with my mom, I realized my father had been playing second fiddle for years and he got tired of it.

What bothered me the most was that my mom was unable to convince my dad that she was over Steve. I could tell by my earlier conversation that there was no spark in her eyes for Steve. Somehow, Steve had done something to make my dad jealous. It had something to do with my brother.

I could not prove it, but deep inside I felt like there was more to my brother's death than Steve was telling everyone. He might not be dead, and that's why he feels like he can push my mom around. If he is still alive and Steve had convinced my father that he would bring him to Baker, it would make my dad a little wary, because he had to keep the secret But if he also showed my mom the samc pictures my mother and she fell into Steve trap I would know that she had been part of the plan from the beginning, and that somehow Donna was behind pulling the strings to reunited Steve and my mother.

Immediately after leaving the chaos. that had erupted in my house my phone rang. Janis was sobbing on the other end of the line. "George, I am afraid I am feeling like you don't love me anymore and I can't phantom losing you. Therefore, I am about to call Steve. I think if we talk to Steve together, he can help us out. That is where we met, and hopefully, the memories will bring you back to me."

Janis phone call was just what I needed to set the trap for Steve. And at the same time, I would be able to see if Janis was trying to play me or if I could trust her. Because if she did not know Steve's relationship with my mother I would be able to set a trap for Steve. All Janis had to do was ask Steve if he had a relationship with my mom and then mention to Steve that my mom and dad are going through a rough spot when she called him to asks for advice to help her save her relationship with me.

While I was almost certain Steve would agree to meet with us and help us in our relationship. The news that he had finally gotten to my dad and made him jealous would make him wait to meet with us. Because he would try to contact my mom first and try to make a move on my mom before I had time to reunite my parents.

Steve would feel like it was perfect time to make a move on my mother because he feel like my mom was in a vulnerable state.

However, I was slowly beginning to feel like I was on the top of the world. Because I was about to flip the script when I proposed to Janis. Knowing that if she said yes there would be no reason for us to talk to Steve about our relationship. And I finally had the opportunity to destroy my enemy. Because I believed my mom would finally shut Steve down. Knowing my mom was not a coward who ran from danger, but she was a fighter who picked my dad over Steve.

She would prove her love for my dad was stronger than Steve's blackmail. Even if my brother is still alive, she would never leave my father. Thus, Steve would never bother my family again

Yet, the situation was very tricky, and if my Mom faltered and was unable to prove to my dad that she did not love Steve. Because her heart was broken by the fact that my brother might still be alive. Steve would be able to take advantage of the situation and destroy my parents marriage. Because Steve would be relentless and might never leave my Mom alone again.

And if she fell for Steve's trick, I would disown my Mom because

I would never agree to Steve to becoming my stepfather. Thus, I hoped that the news of my proposal to Janis would change the situation between Steve and my mother as well as bring my family back together.

Before I went to Janis house, I went to the local florist to get a couple of dozen roses; I went to *See's Candies* and brought a pound of Janis's favorite fudge. Then on my way to her house, I called a friend and asked him if he could hook me up with our favorite song. I wanted to make sure Janis was in the mood when I popped the question before she called Steve.

Although I was prepared to propose, and I felt like Janis was innocent I had to play the game to ensure that no one suspected I was on to Donna's plot to overthrow the NSA. Thus, I was nervous hoping Donna, would be fooled and she would not suspect that I might be using Janis.

However, my biggest problem was that May had not called me back. Thus, I had to wing it until I heard back from the commander. Once asked Janis to marry me it might be my undoing. Because asking Janis to marry me looked like I was falling in line with Donna's plans.

And I knew there would be many questions on why I did not wait to propose to Janis. Yet, right now, seemed like the most logical time to show Janis my undying love and devotion. And if I waited, I might lose my edge. Knowing that Steve would be elated that I Janis would stop deny that I love her.

The caveat of my plan was that I would be drawing Steve out into the open exposing him for the ruthless low-down moron he was. Because while he said he was happy for me and Janis he would have t explain to Janis why he was trying to destroy my parents' marriage.

When I pulled up to the curb, I watched Janis's face light up as the florist handed her a dozen roses. Then my friends band came around the corner playing one of our favorite songs as I got down on my knees and grabbed her hand. And started singing the Beatles song *I Want to Hold Your Hand a*s handed her the box of candy.

She had a huge smile on her face as she stood still and could not believe how it seemed like everything had stopped and the entire neighborhood had its eyes on us.

Before I could even pop the question Janis bent down and gave me a big hug. "Honey, I am glad to see you. I thought after last night that I would never see you again. I am sorry for putting so much pressure on you. I want you to be happy, and I am willing to wait on you no matter how long it takes. Can we forget last night and have fun while you're home?"

"You have no need to apologize," I said as I melted into Janis's beautiful eyes and began stammering. "*De-de-ar*, I am so so-*sor-r-r-y,* I have *al-wa-wa-ys lo-o-o-ved* you, and I can't im-ag-ag-ine a life without *yo-oo-u.* Please forgive me. I know Steve is waiting for us, and he's excited about seeing the both of us. But hopefully, this will show how much you mean to me," I said as I grabbed her hand and slid an engagement ring onto her finge.r

When we stood up and started dancing to the final song, the entire neighbor was clapping and yelling "Girl tell the man yes, can't you see how much he loves you." When the music stopped, my friend turned to me, "Dude you don't owe me anything That was the sweetest thing I have ever seen. I wish you est of luck, but I got another gig. I'll catch up with you later, George."

It seemed like everything was flowing so smoothly as we kissed, and the neighbors continued to clap.

Suddenly Janis's phone rang. "Janis, this is Sally. My parents just had a big argument. Is George with you? I need him to find my dad because I think he's going out of his mind."

When Janis heard about my parents, she was shocked. "George, what happened? It seemed like their relationship was rock solid. I truly hope they can work things out because they have always been my example."

Janis smiled at me. "George, I hope we have the same strong relationship as theirs one day. This is horrible. We must talk to Steve. I know he is their best friend, and he would hate to hear that your parents are having trouble."

Then Janis called Steve and told him about my parents' argument.

When Janis hung up the phone. “Steve said he would check in on your mom. He told me to help you find you your father.”

Wow! What had Janis done? It looked like she had read my mind. I was almost certain she did not know about Steve and my mom’s relationship. Because her call to Steve felt like she was honestly concerned about my parents.

“Janis, can we go sit down for a few minutes before we go chasing down my dad?”

Janis smiled. “Whatever you want, dear.”

As we sat on the porch swing, Janis started rubbing her fingers through my hair.

For the next few minutes, everything was silent as I pondered my next move.

What was I worried about, I thought to myself, *this is life*. I just wanted to sit on the seat, look at the stars, and hold Janis forever. Then I looked in Janis eyes and said, “How about we forget about my parents for the moment. Cause I want to know how you feel about us getting hitched.”

Although everything seemed to be going as planned I did not want to start looking for my dad until Janis said yes to my proposal.

Janis was about to answer me with I received a call from my dad. He was crying and talking hysterically as he told me, “Your mom’s been hurt. You need to get to the house right away.”

I looked at Janis and said, “There’s been a change of plans. Something happened to my mom, I must go to my house right now.”

It seemed like Steve had played his part too well.

CHAPTER XXII

The Accident

Suddenly the phone went dead. I desperately tried to call my dad back and when Sally picked up the phone she was freaking out. "You need to get home right now. Mom's had an accident, and it does not look like she going to make it to the hospital. Dad's going crazy, and Billy is acting like a complete idiot.

Walking around looking for a weapon so he can chase after Steve and make him accountable for hurting Mom."

"Calm down and tell me what happened I said as I tried to get Sally to talk a little slower so I could understand her.

"I don't know. Billy and I walked in the door and Mom was lying on the floor with a big gash on her head. Dad was trying to stop the bleeding and he was weeping so hard. Now all he is doing is mumbling and you can't understand a word he says."

All I know is it had something to do with Steve and Mom. Please get home now," then Sally hung up.

Janis looked at me like she was wounded when I jumped and said, "Something happened to my mother. I go to my house right away. After everything tonight, you want to run away again. Remember, we were supposed to meet with Steve. Can't it wait until later?"

I turned to Janis and shook her. "Sally called and said my mom was in an accident and she has been injured. She may not make it to the hospital."

Janis's mouth flew open as she said "I am sorry, I didn't know it was serious."

I put my arm on Janis's shoulder and then there was an eerie silence between us as I jumped into my car. "Here is some money. Can you catch a cab to the emergency room? After everything calms down, I will take you someplace where we can discuss our future." Then I slammed the door and zoomed down the street toward my house.

Janis stood on the front porch and started weeping. Something strange was going on with George's family. She could not put her finger on it. Therefore, she shook herself and went to the emergency waiting room at the hospital.

When she got to the desk, she asked the nurse if she would visit George's mom. The nurse told her to sign the log and sit down and wait. It would be a while before anyone can see her as she was still on her way to the hospital. Thus, Janis sat down and lowered her head as she began to silently weep as she waited for me and the rest of my family to arrive.

She was hoping my mom was all right, but most of all she was feeling lonely because it seemed like she was an outsider. She had to get me to understand how much my mother meant to her. Once they had cleared up the issue of Betsy, Sally and my mom had become her best friends.

Meanwhile, I was panicking. Was this the start of Donna's plan? Whom was she going to attack next? As my mind was beginning to explode, all I could think about was my mother's safety. For the moment, nothing else mattered. Unless May gave me some good news, Janis and I were through. If Janis could not respect the fact that my Mom was in danger, how could I think she would ever love me? Her actions when I told her about my Mom was being attacked were far from what he expected from someone I was supposed to live the rest of his life with. The current situation made it look like she might be part of Donna's plan.

Once again, I found myself overreacting. Thus, my future did not matter now, because if I lost my Mom because of my stupidity, I would never forgive myself. Why had I pressed my mom about Steve? It was tearing me up inside, knowing that if I had left well enough alone my parents would have never been in an argument and Steve would have never tried to make a move on my Mom.

That's when I started doubting why I had joined the NSA. It was too much for my brain, considering all the trouble that had befallen my family due to my decision to secretly join the PTF.

When I arrived at my house, they were placing my Mom on a stretcher and slowly carrying her toward the ambulance. What was I going to do? Seeing my dad walking around with a blank expression on his face was horrible.

My dad came over to me sobbing. "Son I don't know what came over me when I walked into the house to talk to your mom Steve hugging her. And it felt like Steve was trying to make a move on your mother, so I jumped Steve.

Steve just laughed. "You always were a crazy man. If you think you can get in my way again, forget it. Your wife and I are going to be together, this time without any interference."

"The next thing he knew, Steve had jumped over the busted couch and started punching him. Your mom could not take Steve punching me, so she raced across the room and slapped Steve."

She started screaming, "Mister, you need to get out of my house. I'm never going to be with you again in this lifetime, or any other time. You let that evil woman Donna know that if she thinks she can destroy my life it will never work. To think I would ever want to be with you again is crazy. I thought you had changed, but now I know you are still the same jerk I knew when we first meet."

After your mom slapped Steve, he went crazy and threw her against the wall. She hit her head on the corner of the fireplace and her limp body fell to the floor.

My father took a deep breath and then he continued. "Steve stood over your mom's limp body and turned toward me. "Toby, you can have her. I never did like her that much. I just wanted to have a little fun. She was always too serious for me anyway. You can have her my friend," Steve said as he pushed me out of the way, and he raced out the front door."

"Then I crawled over to help my mom, but she was in bad shape, so I called 911. While I was waiting for the ambulance, Billy and Sally came in.

"When Billy and Sally walked through the door and saw your mom lying on the floor with a big gash on her head Billy yelled at me "Dad, what's wrong with Mom?"

I turned to him and said, "Son, Steve, did this, he threw your mom and she hit her head on the fireplace. Then he left her to die."

Then ambulance driver came over to my dad and asked him if he wanted to ride with my wife to the hospital. My father calmly said, "George, you can follow the ambulance to the hospital. I'm going to ride with your Mom. Make sure you take care of Sally and Billy for me until we know exactly how bad your Moms injuries are."

Before I had a chance to talk to them, Sally and Billy jumped into Billy's car and raced after the ambulance to the hospital.

When I finally got to the emergency room the first person I saw was Janis. She had been waiting all by herself when I came in. Her face lit up when she saw me. She rushed over to me, hugged me so hard I could barely breathe. The next thing I knew, she planted a big kiss on my left cheek.

I just stood there blankly staring at Janis, trying to decide if she would be the perfect one to unload my secret on, I knew if I told her the truth I would know if she was part of the deception or if she was just another piece of the puzzle.

I needed to feel like I was unraveling the deception to have some peace in my mind. Yes, I knew it was a substantial risk.

Because I did not know how she would react.

Would she keep the secret, or would I wind up in Donna's trap? My mind was fried, and I knew I could no longer hide behind the mask of deception that surrounded my heart. I desperately wanted to tell someone the truth about what was going on or I would burst. Yet I was not sure whom I could trust anymore.

It was crazy, but the only person I trusted right now was May and I had no way to contact her because of all the chaos. I knew if I told Mom the truth about my mission, she would freak out, and it might make her condition worse. If I told my dad he would go ballistic and try to contract General Armstrong again. Which would blow apart the entire mission. Telling my brother Billy was not an option because he never could keep a secret. Finally, if I told Sally, she would go completely bonkers and wind up in the crazy house.

However, the more I looked at Janis's s face and watched the tears rolling down her cheeks. The more assured I felt about telling her the truth. I could no longer hide behind the mask of deception that surrounded my heart.

Could I tell Janis?

Was she part of Donna's plan?

Or did any of that really matter?

The more I thought about my relationship with Janis the more I felt obligated to tell her the truth. I had to trust the unction in my gut which was telling me that such a sweet woman would never betray me.

"George, please, come sit down. I have been waiting an hour and they still have not told me anything about your mom."

"Janis." I said as sat in the chair next to her, staring blankly at the floor. "I have something very important to tell you but, right now I can hardly think straight. Can you give me a little time to absorb the situation with my mother.

She whispered in my ear "Honey I hope your mom is all right, is there anything I can do to help. Whatever you need to tell me can wait until after you see you mom."

When I heard Janis's silky voice whispering in my ear all my were slowly melting away. As my knees buckled and I nearly became a traitor and disclosed the truth that I was in a covert unit called the PTF which was part of the NSA. While I was posing as a storekeeper on the *USS Bunker Hill.* Scott would be stationed on the *USS Carl Vinson*. However, my real rank was Lieutenant.

I wanted to be with Janis until death do us part. However, if she was conspiring with Steve and Donna, then I would have to move on to greener pastures, knowing I could never be married to any woman who was a part of Donna's evil plan.

Looking deep into Janis's blue eyes, which were continually blinking, I went into total panic mode. My mouth was frozen, nothing came out. I put my head down and started trembling.

When Janis saw me trembling, she started giggling and said, "George, you know how to make a girl feel. And whatever you have to say, it can't be that bad. I have known you all my life. Yet sometimes you seem to go overboard.

I'm certain that whatever you want to tell me will be all right. You just need to calm down." She playfully made a cat paw and acted like she was going to claw me.

When she reached over and hugged me, she started purring like a baby kitten, and she pecked me on the cheek, "I ain't going anywhere and when you are ready to talk I am ready to listen."

Why was she acting so calm?

Her demeanor was making the situation worse.

Suddenly I felt like I was slipping into a black hole, and I was about to cross the line of no return. Knowing that I needed to tell Janis how I felt. Yet, if I said the wrong thing and Steve found out that I was on to him, he might try to kill both of us like he tried to kill my mom.

At this point, I was so blinded by Janis's love, that I did not care anymore. However, before I blew my cover Billy and Sally came bursting through the door. He pushed the door so hard that it nearly pinned against the wall.

"Janis," Billy said, "have you seen my meathead brother?" Then he the closed he paused for a moment. "Oh, there you are.

What are you doing hiding behind the door?

Then he sat down next to Janis and yelled "Sally they are over here as she plopped down next to them.

Janis burst out laughing. "Don't you think you are being too nosy about me and your brother?

He told me he could smell a rat like you, especially when you point your nose in our direction."

He was rubbing his bright red nose as Billy turned to face me. Thinking that I would be angry with him, he started to run. To his surprise, I snatched him with one hand and gave him a bear hug. I was glad Billy interrupted me before I blew my cover.

Billy looked at Janis and bowed down as if he was paying homage to Janis. He stood back up and said, "Girl, I don't know what you did to my brother, but you must have put a big hex on him. You can let me in on the trick so he will stop bashing my head."

Janis's face turned three shades of red as she was speechless.

Playfully putting his hand on my shoulder, Billy said, "Sorry, bro, I didn't mean to cause you and your lady any trouble."

"Billy," I said, "you were fine until you opened your mouth. I'm begging, please think before speaking. Before you say something, you can't take back. You should be thankful that I understand you. But next time you might not get off as easy, and someone might stuff a sock in your mouth."

Billy quickly changed the subject and got serious as he glared into Janis's eyes. "Girl, if you break my brother's heart I will come after you, 'cause all he ever talks about is Janis this and Janis that. Sometimes I want to stuff a pillow in his mouth.

Remember that girl. 'Cause I don't take kindly to people moving in on my brother unless they are serious." I quickly grabbed my brother's head and put him in a hammerlock. "Fooled you, bro," and threw Billy on the floor. I started yelling, "Who's your uncle, little boy? Tell me, who's your uncle?"

Billy gasped for breath and squeaked out, "You're the man." I immediately jumped up and said, "Now what's this all about with Pops? Can't I have a few minutes with my fine woman without you spoiling the party?"

Then Sally came over to us and broke us apart. She started wiping her tears. "George, and Billy you need to go find the cafeteria and get something to eat. Hopefully, a sandwich and a cup of coffee will take our mind off everything. Plus, I got something I want to show

Janis." She grabbed her hand and held it tightly as she pulled her toward the door.

You guys go ahead "Janis, and I will meet you there. Just get us a sandwich some chips. If you get a coffee Janis like hers black and I want two cream and two sugars."

Then I turned to Sally and Girl can't you and Janis talk some other time. I really need her by side at the moment for support. Cause Billy is a lunatic, and I might actually hurt him this time without Janis calming me down. I suggest we all go to the cafeteria together and hopefully we can blow off some steam while get away from the emergency room while. You need to walk with Billy and try to make sure he keeps his mouth shut."

"Janis, and I will be right behind you. Once I checked in at the desk to see when we can see mom. If you don't see us in about fifteen minutes call me and maybe you can bring the us some food a warm drink, coffee, tea, cocoa it don't matter. I said as I pulled my card out and gave it to Sally to cover everything."

Sally rudely interrupted my chain of thought. "All you can do is think about and your missy. Don't you know mom is dying?"

"Worst case scenario is that she is in a coma?"

We will just find some vending machines and bring you something back. 'cause I ain't staying away any longer the I need to."

"Mom needs all our support!"

"Dad is going completely belly up. George, you gotta talk to him. You know, if something happens to Mom, it will push him over the edge."

Then she looked at Janis, please, use you magic on George, and make his see it's ain't time to be play footsies." Then Sally shocked everyone and began slapping me. "I'm begging you to work your to wake up 'cause unless you stop making them lovey dovey eyes at Janis we are all doom."

I quickly grabbed her hands. "Take it easy, sis. I ain't no punching bag." I gave her a bear hug and whispered, "Sally I'll loosen my grip in a minute, but you gotta stop slapping me. It looks strange when a little girl like you is slapping a big man like me. I'll give you a chance to calm down before I loosen my grip." She nodded her head that she understood.

My sister was barely able to talk. She looked at me and started sobbing "George, I'm so sorry for slapping you, but I couldn't hit Billy because he wouldn't have understood that I had to hit something, or they might have to lock me up at the crazy house. Are you all, right? I didn't leave any permanent scars?"

"Sis, you're right, I do understand. But if you try to slap anyone again, I will personally put the straitjacket on you."

When I looked at Sally. I could tell she had already lost her mind as she nodded her head, and I loosened my grip and I whispered, "Sis, don't worry. Mom and Dad will be fine. I don't know what to do about you and Billy, because the two of you are driving me bonkers."

Billy, I am only going to say this one mor time you and Sally need to bring us back some food. I am almost certain the cafeteria is closed, so you can just find the nearest vending machines and bring us back something to eat. Billy nodded his head and grabbed Sally's hand and they went to search for some food.

Once I was sure Billy and Sally were gone we went up to the receptionist's desk and I asked if my mom could have any visitors. At first, she would not give me any information. She paused for a moment. "Sir, I know I ain't supposed to let anybody in to see your mom, but if you would like, I will let you wait in your mother's room with your dad until she's transferred."

I smiled at her and said, "That's all right. I'll wait until siblings come back with some food. Then I sat back down with Janis and called Billy and told him to bring the food to the waiting room. It seem like it was going to be at a few hours before we would be able to see dad or mom.

When I sat down next to Janis she was crying, Billy and Sally must hate me. Can't they see I am in love with you and want the best for your family just as much they do?"

I sat quietly next to Janis as she laid her head on my shoulder. And I did everything I could to calm her down. She was right about my family, but she did not know the other side. They could be very sweet and kind. Yet right now everyone was focused on my mom, and they had made some harsh statements.

I only hope when they returned with some food things would calm down a little. The silence was unbearable, and my mind was becoming more conflicted by the moment.

How could I have been so stupid. I had nearly put my whole family in jeopardy if Billy had not come through the door when he did.

Janis I said, let's move to the other side of the room. Cause I don't feel like hiding any more. I don't care what my family says I love you and once we have a few minutes I will be able to show you my love. Plus, you still did not answer me when I asked you to marry me. When we have some private time I am sure we can get past all the other chaos that is going on.

"Just give my family a small break right now. They are anxious because of the situation with my mother. Once we see her and know that she is all right I am sure they will warm up to you. Cause if they don't I may have to give them a couple more of my famous knuckle sandwiches."

Janis smile, "Thanks for understanding, cause I am nervous to. I think you mom is great and I don't want to see her hurt.

Then Billy burst through the door again. When he did not see me and Janis he was about to say something before Sally said, "Bro they moved next to the table on the other side of the waiting room."

Then Sally placed our sandwiches and coffee on the table next to us. She looked and Janis and said. "I am sorry for what I said earlier because you are like a sister to me and if you make George happy, I am happy.

Then I whispered to Sally. "Sally right before all this chaos I asked Janis to marry me, and I am still waiting for her answer. Her face lit up and she was about to spill the beans when I put my hand on her mouth and whispered, "not now Sally I will let everyone else know when it's official."

After we finished eating our sandwiches everyone looked at me and told me I should go see what was taking so long. My dad said he would meet us, but he was still in the room with my mom.

They assured me they would remain in the waiting room until one of us came to get them. After the buzzer rang, I slowly opened the door and walked toward my mother's unit.

My dad was shocked when he saw me. "George why are you here I told the nurse not to let anyone in to see your Mom. She is in a coma. I need everyone to be calm for your mom's sake. Please go back to the waiting room and wait for me. I will be out in a minute to explain everything to Billy, Sally, and Janis.

The he grabbed my hand, son I need your strength. Please make sure everyone is safe until you mom comes out of her comma."

Get out of here 'cause I ain't about to break down in front of you. I'll bring everyone the news soon. Several minutes later my dad came into the waiting room. Calmly looking into my eyes, he said, "Everyone needs to go home and get some rest. I will call you as soon as your mom comes out of her coma. They are waiting for the swelling on her brain to go down so they can do surgery."

However, if the swelling does not go down within the next forty-eight hours she may have permanent brain damage. Thus, there is nothing you can do sitting around this hospital.

When my father finished I went into a state of shock, this was all my fault if I had not pressured Janis to call Steve none of this would have happened. How was I going to be able to look my parents in eyes ever again knowing the damage I had done.

CHAPTER XXIII

The Hospital

My father gruffly said, "There is nothing you can do here, son. I need you to go home and get some rest. I'll manage it from here."

Then he came over to me and firmly put his hand on my shoulder. "George," he whispered, "get Sally out of here. She doesn't need to see your mother like this. I think she will be better off waiting at home until after your moms surgery. Once the surgery is over and your mom comes out of her coma I'll call you."

"Son this is the hardest thing I have had to do my entire life. Just seeing you mom in a comma brings back many bad memories that I have tried to avoid for years. However, this time it is different because when you see your loved one on death doorstep you begin to doubt yourself and wonder if you action could have created the chaos that we now find ourselves in."

"Maybe I should have given you mom a break about her relationship with Steve, but with Steve in my face all the time it was hard. Sometime just seeing your mom smile when he was around and five minutes later she would frown up at me like I was the grinch."

"But, you know what I have discovered the last few hours son. When you love someone you love everything about them. No matter what things seem like you must know that the one you love loves you back the same way. And that is what your mother and I have son. I will never doubt her again."

"I had a moment of weakness, hopefully when you mom wakes up she can forgive me. Son it also made me think about how I was when you told me your were joining the navy. I should have been more supportive. Amid my shock, I forgot to tell you how proud I am of what you have accomplished in the short time that you have been in boot camp."

"Can you ever forgive me. Because I love you and I do not want to wind be estrange from you like you mother was from her father or I was from my father."

"Sir," I said. "You are a great father, and I could never ask for a better example than you. I know you were upset because you were concerned for me. But you do not deserve all the blame because I also assumed that you and mom were not true. However, right now we need to focus on mom. Just let me know what you need me to do."

"As I stated before, give me a few minutes and I will address Bill and I need you to go back to the rest of the family and stay calm. Tell them I will coming out to give everyone an update on you moms condition in a few minutes. I need you to leave me be for a few moments so that I don't crack up right in front of you."

Then after we talk I need you to get the rest of the family away from the hospital and take them home where they can relax. Thus, I turned around and saluted my dad as I slowly walked back to the waiting room with everyone else.

When Sally saw me she burst out "Where dad.? I thought you said you were going to get him. Is mom all right?"

I grabbed Sally, "Slow down, take a deep breath and let me say something before you blow up the whole room."

"I spoke with Dad, and he asked everyone to give him a few minutes and will address us on moms condition. I am asking everyone to stay calm. You know how long it takes to get answers when you are at the hospital. Everyone needs to relax. And Sally, when you see Dad, let him talk before you start asking a million questions."

We all sat on the edge of our seats, waiting for my dad. Several times I was tempted to return to my mom's room. But I knew that would only add to the chaos.

When my father finally entered the waiting room, Billy and Sally had fallen asleep. I quickly nudged them. When they saw their father, they hugged him and sat back, waiting for his words of comfort.

He looked at everyone, your mom is still in a comma, and they are waiting for the swelling on her brain to go down before they are able to do surgery. That is why I asked George to take you home and I will call him once you mom come out of her comma. Janis, you are welcome to stay at the house with the family.

I think it's about time we all respect your relationship with George. I am sorry if my crazy kids have been giving you a hard time. I have told George if they make any snide remarks or do anything to harm your relationship with my son it would make me and my wife very angry. Kids is that understood." They were shocked at the sternness in Toby voice all they could do is drop their head in shame.

After our father's speech, he returned to the ICU where our mom was. Sally wanted to go home, but when she went into the front room, she started having a panic attack. Every time she walked through the door, it was like she was reliving the scene of my mom's accident. All she could see was my mom lying on the floor bleeding.

Billy had gone completely silent. He would not speak to anyone. He put his headset on and spaced out.

When Janis saw how Sally and Billy reacted to being at the house, she asked me if I wanted to stay at her place since her grandparents would be gone for several months, and she would be by herself. It would be nice to have everyone stay at her place until Mom got better. I graciously accepted Janis, and we all went to Janis's house. I could not believe how at ease Janis made us feel. And I nearly forget about why I was even in the situation in the first place.

The next day, it was touch and go. When the swelling finally went down, the doctors were able to do the surgery on my mom. However, they did not know the extent of the damage to her brain. Toby refused to leave her side as he patiently waited for her to come out of her coma.

After my Mom's surgery, Janis shook me. "Your dad called and told me your Mom is awake and wants to see you and me. She said she had something to tell us before she sees anyone else."

I woke up Billy and Sally and told them the good news. "Hey, guys, Mom's awake and wants to see us. The doctors said she could have no more than two visitors at a time. Mom said she wants to see Janis and me first. Then you two can see her once we are done.

"He is waiting for us in Mom's room. All I can tell you is we need to put some pep in our step and get to the hospital because there is no telling how long Mom will be strong enough to see us because she still needs to rest."

I did my best to keep myself together until I saw my Mom. Plus, there was no telling what shape my dad was in because he had not slept the past few days. On the way to the hospital, the silence was driving me crazy, I could see the worried look on everyone's faces.

I grabbed Janis's hand as we headed to the sixth floor. I was surprised when I saw my dad waiting for us. I gave him a big hug and told him that Janis and I were prepared to visit Mom whenever he was ready.

I could see the weariness in my dad's eyes as he whispered in my ears, "Son, your Mom does not have much strength, but she insisted on seeing you and Janis.

After you talk to your Mom, you need to come to get me first. I will see how she feels about seeing Billy and Sally. Your mom needs to reserve her strength. However, I am not sure if she will be able to take the drama of seeing Billy and Sally.

"George," he said harshly, "It's hard seeing the love of my life like this. Everything is touch and go, and Mom may never fully recover. George, you, and Janis need to talk to her. The first thing she said when she came out of her comma was Toby, I need to talk to Janis and George. I have something important I need to tell them."

Then my dad looked at me and contemplated his next move.

"Sally, you, and Billy need to wait here while George and Janis see your Mom. While she was asking about both of you, she could only see two of you at a time."

"I need to get a little fresh air, and you must stay calm and wait for me to return. Then he walked out of the waiting room. Everyone sat there for a moment before Sally burst out crying. "George, I don't know if I can bear to see Mom in this shape. Why can't you and I see her first.? I am sure Billy would not mind waiting with Janis."

"Sis, you need to wait with Billy. Janis and I need to talk to Mom by ourselves. Once we are done, we will come back and get both of you, and you can go together to see Mom.

Billy, watch Sally and make sure she does not try to run away because I know Mom can't wait to see her."

Sally said, "Why can't I go with you and Janis to see Mom?"

"Unclog your ears, sis, there are no more than two people allowed in Mom's room. She said she wanted to see me and Janis. I think we should honor her request. I know it is hard, but it won't be long, and soon you will be talking to Mom."

Turning away from Sally, I turned to Janis. She was smiling as she said, "George, you know I love you and your family. I told you earlier I will do whatever you need because you are my past, present, and future. However, you and your brother are plain loco. Go see your mother with Sally and meet me in the car. I got to get out of this hospital before I become crazy like you."

I looked at Janis and said, "Can you just hold for a minute while I deal with my crazy brother? I really need your support. My mother would never let me hear the end of it if you were not with me when I go to see her."

Thinking that everything was fine with Janis, I turned around to address Billy. While I was addressing Billy, Janis quietly slipped into the elevator and made her way to her car, where she sat weeping, waiting for me, hoping I would understand that she could not take any more craziness.

I turned back to Billy. "Remember what I said, you need to look out for Sally. Billy, what did say to Janis? Everything was fine until you opened your mouth. Please think next time before you open your mouth because I must constantly explain to Janis how you are not really that bad."

"Billy you and Sally will talk after I see Mom.

I reached for Janis's hand as I continued to talk. Janis are you ready to see my mom?"

However, to my surprise, Janis had disappeared. I was about to chase after Janis, but Billy grabbed me by the waist. "Bro, let her cool off for a little. She'll be all right.

"George," Sally interjected, "bro, you need to calm down. You were making Janis nervous, and she bolted. I don't know what she is thinking, but you must forget about the rest of us right now. I know where she went, so you wait here with Billy and let me find her. We can fix this thing before it's too late.

While I am gone, the two of you need to calm down, especially you, Billy. You can be a pain at times, but I know you are a decent person. Think about how you feel because your wife is not talking to you. It is not a great feeling. Do you want Janis and George to end up the same way? Mom just got out of a coma, and she needs all our support. Dad is about to break, and if we don't make this right, Mom may go back into a coma."

Sally looked at Billy. "You must be the biggest dork I have ever known. You know what Janis means to George, and all you can think about is yourself. George, no matter what this knucklehead says I am glad you are with Janis. She is one of the sweetest people I know. We have become close since you left. I know she loves you and it hurts her when you are so oblivious to her feelings. All the commotion the last few days have been too much for her. Janis not only loves you, but she has also become part of the family, and you know how crazy we can get at times."

Billy, I suggest you get your ego out of the way and start acting like a normal human being, 'cause if you don't, you are going to find yourself all alone.

I kinda chuckled. "It ain't that bad, sis. I'm sure you can work your charm on Janis, and we will be fine."

Sally smiled. "You gotta promise me that if anything changes with Mom, you'll call me." Sally turned to me and gently kissed me on the cheek. "George, I am going to help you out this time. Don't think I am always going to be on your side. You got a lot to learn about love. If we work together, Mom will be fine. All I want you to do when you see Janis is tell her how you feel." She shook me. "For once in your life trust me. I will be back with Janis in a flash. Please let me work my magic."

I lightly tapped Sally on the shoulder and whispered, "Thanks, Sally. Don't worry, Mom and Dad will be fine. I don't know what I'd do without a great sister like you."

Then Sally took off toward the garage.

Billy put his hand on my shoulder as Sally walked toward the elevator. "Sorry, bro, I didn't mean to cause you and your lady any trouble. Sally can patch things up. Don't worry about Janis. She'll be all right. After you see Mom things will get better.

When Sally caught up with Janis, she was sitting in her car, weeping. Janis was weeping so hard that she did not recognize Sally at first, she thought she was talking to George. "Why does your family hate me so much? Why can't they see that I love you and I would never try to harm you?

Janis gasped when she finally realized she was talking to Sally began, "Janis please let me in, I know it's no excuse to take it out on you, but I promise you things will get better before they get worse. You are not an outsider, Janis, and I think it's going to be great having you as my sister-in-law."

Janis sat quietly looking at Sally. "Sally, you have been kind to me, and I appreciate your concern for my relationship with your brother. But he must show me that he loves me. He can make me feel like I am the lowest person on the face of the earth." Janis began weeping again, and all Sally could do was hold her, assuring her that her family did not have any ill will towards her.

Janis stopped weeping for a few minutes and asked Sally, "Do you really think George wants to marry me someday?"

"I know, Sally, he proposed to me on my front doorstep right before this craziness happened, and I don't remember what I said to him. It was like a hurricane hit, and his proposal got lost."

"Janis, if you feel like it, I will take you back to my brother, and the two of you can finally get some time alone. I think you will be surprised what my brother has to say because he is finally ready to let you know how he feels."

Janis smiled. "I think I'm ready. And don't think I will forget your friendship, Sally, it means so much to me."

"Janis," Sally said, "don't worry about Billy no matter what he says. Because right now, he is going crazy. I will take care of him. You need to focus on George because you deserve to be happy."

Stepping into the elevator, Janis grabbed Sally's hand and did not let go until the elevator door opened.

My mind was shot as Billy, and I waited patiently for Janis's return. When the elevator door opened, Billy sighed with relief as Sally and Janis stepped out laughing.

What Billy did next was a big surprise to everyone as he hit me on the shoulder. "Bro don't take too long with Mom. Janis has gotten you all tied up in knots. But Girl, if you break my brother's heart, I will come after you. All he ever talks about is Janis this and Janis that. Sometimes I want to stuff a pillow in his mouth. Remember that girl, because I don't take kindly to people moving in on my brother unless they are serious."

"George and Sally I am your older brother; sometimes, you are not very wise. Stop pretending you're the only one who cares about this family. Mom and Dad are going through a rough patch right now, and all the two of you care about is how we are treating Janis. Well, bro, you better step back and figure it out. Because right now, I am angry at the people who are messing with our parents. I have nothing against Janis. I want to make sure she is not part of the equation. You don't know if she even loves you, bro. As far as Sally is concerned, you need to leave her out of the picture. Can't you see she is afraid of losing Mom and doesn't want to lose you?"

When Billy finished talking, I quickly grabbed my brother's head and put him in a hammerlock. "Fooled you, bro," and threw Billy on the floor. While I had Billy in a hammerlock, I looked at him and said, "I'm not sure why you would say something cruel to Janis, but I'm not going to allow you to interfere with the woman I love. I suggest you back off. I appreciate Janis, and I think it's time for you to straighten up. Billy, you owe Janis an apology."

I was shocked when Janis came over to me and tickled my ears. "George, let it ride because I am ready to finish our conversation from yesterday. Billy's a dork. He'll come around."

I looked into Janis's eyes and melted as I eased up on Billy. After I let go of Billy, he took advantage of the situation and grabbed me to leverage himself as he jumped up. He was ready to fight.

"You need to chill out, George. You don't have to worry about me. I get the point. You're in love with Janis and we all need to accept that. But if you want to fight some more, I'm ready."

"Have you lost your mind, Billy? You know you can't beat me. I don't want to hurt you, but if you insist, I will make sure your mouth stays shut for a long time."

Janis came to his rescue again. "Ease up on him, honey. Billy's a pussycat who thinks he can roar like a lion." She burst out laughing and leaned over to Sally and whispered, "You are right, Billy is rough around the edges, but I never realized George was so crazy."

Sally nudged me. "I think it's time for the two of you to see Mom." Janis smiled and looked at me. "Are you ready to talk to your mom? After we see her, we can have some time alone, right now we need to focus on your mom."

I grabbed Janis's hand and turned to them. "Sally, Billy, the two of you must wait until I get back because we have unfinished business. But Mom is more important right now," I said as the door silently closed.

When I finally got to my mom's room, I was totally surprised to see my mother so alert. When she saw us, she smiled. She looked at me, I have something important to tell you that will affect the rest of your life."

"George, this is all my fault. If I had only told you about Steve when you were younger, none of this would have happened."

"Mom, don't cry. It is not your fault Steve is a jerk."

My mom sat up and smiled. To my surprise, my mom wanted to talk to Janis, and she motioned for her to come near. Then she asked

Janis to bend down as she whispered "Janis, I am only going to ask you this question one time.

Are you in love with George or did Steve get to you, and are you a part of Donna's plan to destroy my family? I know we have talked, and I have gotten closer to you. But if you don't love my son, I am begging you to let him go. Because I know he is going through wondering if he should ask you to marry him. If you are a part of Donna's plan, please don't leave my son high and dry. It will break his heart, but at least he will have some closure."

Janis began to cry. "Ma'am I am so sorry for Steve and what he did I would have never thought he could be so cruel.

Then my mom pressed Janis to answer her question. "This is not about Steve. He is a part of my past, you had nothing to do with what Steve did, he is the one who betrayed me and my family."

"What I want to know is do you love my boy?"

Janis smiled, "I love him with all my heart; I want to be with him and have a family and grow old together."

My mom mustered up all the strength she had and said, "Girl, I want you to look me in the eyes and tell me you love him. I will know if you are playing games or if you are serious."

Janis did not hesitate to say, "Ma'am, I highly respect you and would love to be a part of your family. If I must give up my love to ensure Steve and Donna are stopped, I will. Ma'am, I would never knowingly harm George or anyone in your family, I was furious when I found out about the trap that Donna and Steve set for me. I wanted to leave and run as far away from this place as possible.

However, I loved George so much that I could not fathom him not being in my life.

Then my mom face lit as she hugged Janis. Please stop I don't know if I can take anymore. I am sure once I get out of this hospital you and I will have some more time to talk, but right now I am getting a little tried."

Please believe ma'am I am truly sorry for what Steve and his friend Donna has done to you and your family. I was so happy when George came home from boot camp. All I wanted to do was spend some time with him before he had to go back to the navy. The past few days together have been crazy. When it's time for him to leave, just knowing he still wants me to be his wife has made me the happiest woman on the face of the earth."

"You have made me very happy, Janis, and I believe you will make a great addition to my family. Sally would love to have another sister. And don't worry about Billy. He will warm up to you. Right now, he needs to straighten out his own mess with his wife.; before he has a foot to stand on."

"Now let me speak to my bonehead son."

Janis smiled as my mother motioned for me to come close. Then she leaned over and kissed me on the cheek.

"Son, you must spend some quality time with Janis before returning to the navy. You need to let her know if you want her to be in your life. Have you asked her to marry you yet? I kind of blushed. Yes, ma'am, I was about to ask her when all this chaos broke out. I can't think about Janis right now. Too much is going on, and I must ensure you get better. Dad is going crazy, and Sally and Billy have gone off the deep end."

My mom put her hand over my mouth. "Son, I will be all right. Your dad will be fine, and Billy and Sally will make it. I want you to promise me that you will spend as much time with Janis as you can for the next week. I will straighten out everyone else. And if you decide she is the one tell her, make sure she knows how much you love her.

Everyone else can see it, now it's time for you to show her."

Now I think it is time for you to go get Sally and Billy for me she said as she hugged both of us and said, "The doctor said I should be able to go home in a few days. I suggest the two of you have some fun and see me at the house before you return to duty."

Now get out of here before I begin to cry. I don't expect to see you again until I am better." Then she closed her eyes for a moment and started breathing a little erratically.

I panicked and turned around to call the nurse when my mom

grabbed my hand. "Son, I am all right. I need to get my strength back. Once I've talked to Billy and Sally, I'll feel better."

Then she quickly changed the conversation, and we all laughed as I started talking about boot camp and how I missed Scott.

"That's my boy, always got to find a way to bring Scott into the conversation. You will be all right, and these few months of separation will only bring you and Scott closer together."

All I could do was stare at my Mom in amazement it like she knew just what I needed to hear.

Suddenly my dad came around the corner and chimed in. "Dear, I think you should leave George and Janis alone. I am sure they can work things out for themselves. It is their life, and we should not be butting in." He looked at my Mom. "Dear, I love you very much, but you gotta give George some space on this one. It is not often a man gets to be with the girl of dreams."

He hugged Janis and smiled at me. "Son, please do not let this one get away. I know your Mom and I have poked around in your business for too long. You are a grown man now, and you need to make your own decisions."

"Before all this craziness Janis and I were talking about our future together. Pops, if everything Mom is telling me is true, you don't have to worry about me anymore because as they say love conquers all. Mom, I think you should see Sally and Billy because they are really worried about you. And when I leave next week, you are going to have to cut them some slack."

My dad spoke up very clearly. "I know I don't say it enough, but we are proud to have a son like you. And if you are in love with Janis, I think she would make a fantastic addition to our family. Don't worry about Sally and Billy. They are always a little crazy." He looked at my Mom sternly. Your Mom and I will deal with them.

My Mom smiled and shook her head. She had never seen my father so forceful. Finally, she knew that he would protect her and the family. She said, "Janis, you are welcome in my home any time. Even if things don't work out between you and George, you will always be a part of our family."

Janis smiled. “George, let’s give your mom a little room.” Then Janis grabbed my hand and we slowly backed away from Mom’s bed.

I was beginning to relax as I shook myself back to reality. It was hard to maintain the façade, yet Janis could not know I was on to her, and I had to act like everything was fine. But I knew had to wait until after I spoke with the commander before I made any plans for our future. That is why Janis and I needed to be alone for a while.

Before I left my mom’s room, I turned to my dad. “If anything changes, call me. I will drop everything in a heartbeat. I am glad I was able to talk to both of you.”

Then my dad nearly pushed into out of my mom’s room. As my mom sat up and smiled, “Now, you two lovebirds, get out of my hair—time for me to see your crazy brother and sister. I got a few things I need to tell them. I will ensure they help your dad because he needs to rest. I will be home in a few days, and then we will all get together and send you off properly.”

“But I am ordering you to grab hold of that pretty little lady and show her the time of her life while you can.”

“Sure, thing, Mom; I will stay with Janis for a few days. So, if you need anything, you know where I’ll be”

My dad chuckled, “You kids have some fun I’ll hold down the fort.” My dad assured me if there were any changes in my mom’s condition I would be the first one he called.

Then I gently reach out to Janis and grabbed her hand as we silently walked back to the waiting room. Now I was ready to deal with Sally and Billy.

CHAPTER XXIV

Janis Confession

Since my dad was with my mom, I had to let Billy and Sally know that Mom wanted to talk to them. I was sure my dad would make sure they did not put too much pressure on Mom.

When the door opened, Billy and Sally sat on the seat, hoping to see Mom. When Billy saw us, he blurted out, "What did you do to mom? I thought she was ready to come home. Dad said that after the two of you saw mom, we could see her. What's up, dude? You're not mom. Why have you got to hide her from her own children? It's bizarre that mom asked to see you and your baby doll before seeing her own kids."

I was stunned by Billy's reaction, and the first thing that came out of my mouth was, "I am not sure why you treat Janis funny, but I am not going to allow you to interfere with the woman I love. So, I suggest the two of you back off. I appreciate Janis, and I think it's time for you to straighten up. Billy, you owe Janis an apology."

Billy looked at Janis and put his head down. "I am sorry if I offended you, Janis. I went crazy after my mom got hurt."

I looked at Sally. "Sis, this is one time I need you to be strong. You need to go with Billy and talk to Mom. Because if you don't, she will worry about you even more. Plus, I need time alone with Janis.

We need to discuss several things, and we haven't really had much time together since I got home.

Before you go, I want to thank you for being a good sister and a friend to Janis. Because I know there is a lot I don't understand about women, but you are my lucky charm." I looked at Sally and said, "I will never forget this, sis; I love you."

Sally nodded her head and followed Billy to Mom's room.

Finally, Janis and I were alone, and I could tell by the way Janis's face lit up that she was glad we were away from the chaos, and we could finally breathe for a few minutes. It was time for me to deal with our future. It felt awkward knowing that Steve and Donna had used Janis to get to me. But I could tell that her feelings for me were real, which was something no one could take away.

"Janis," I whispered, "I need to talk to you about many things, and I know I only have a few more days before I must leave.

Let's get me out of this hospital. We need to get some air. Honey, you are the only person I want to be with right now. You give me hope, and I don't ever want to be without you by my side."

"I know it has been crazy the past few days, but I am utterly and hopelessly in love with you. If you don't know that by now I said as I put my head down and the tears flowed down the corner of my face, "I don't think I will be able to live with myself."

As far as my family goes everyone regrets the harsh things they said to you. Since Steve's attack, my family has bonded together.

You heard my father and my mother they both will welcome you with open arms. Sally will always be there for you."

However. in the end if you don't feel comfortable around my family I will not force you to stay with them. I will figure somewhere else for you to stay. Because the bottom line is I love you and want you to be my wife. And if that means I must be estranged from my family so be it. They will have to earn our trust and I will be with you the entire time. My only question for you is are you ready to take the leap with me to become my wife?

I am still waiting for your answer. We have been overwhelmed by all the chaos and you never gave me an answer when I proposed the other night."

Janis smiled, "I know that I have not made it easy on you the last few days. But I am certain I want to be your wife."

Janis grabbed my hand. "George, I think it's time you and I finished our conversation. Then she whispered in my ear. My answer is yes you dork. If you don't know by now that I have been waiting for you to pop the question you are really a lost puppy. Plus, you need to relax a little your Mom said your family can take care of themselves for a few days.

When Janis said yes I went crazy, I grabbed her and hugged her so hard she almost lost her breath. When I saw her face turning colors and nearly passed out. I quickly loosened my grip and started giving her CPR because I thought she was dying."

Suddenly Janis started laughing as she pushed me away. "That's enough tiger we can save that for later I think it is time for us to go get something to eat."

I was glad Janis was oblivious to the fact that I was in agony over whether to stick with the plan or tell her the truth. However, when I looked into Janis's eyes and saw how overjoyed she was to be alone again, her kind words made my heart melt like butter. "Honey, I am so glad that your mother is better."

I turned to Janis and said, "The rest of this trip is ours, why don't we just go to your house and order a pizza for tonight. We can kick back and relax in front of the TV and watch a couple of movies." Then tomorrow maybe we can go to the beach and have some fun.".

Janis lit up, there is a couple of movies I have been wanting to watch while we snuggle on the couch."

After the pizza and the first movie Janis drifted off to sleep, I carried her into the bedroom, and I had no choice but to call the commander. I needed to update Commander Johnstone or May about the recent information regarding Steve's attack on my parents. Plus, they needed to know that Janis had accepted my proposal.

There was no doubt in my mind that Janis was an innocent bystander and that she loved me. Thus, it did not matter what May, or the commander said I was going to marry Janis at the appropriate time when I came back from my first tour of duty.

When May picked up the line, I barked at her, "Lady, what is wrong with you? Why didn't you call me back? I have vital information and I need to talk to the commander right now."

"Hold on a second, mister, before you say anything else you will regret. I did not find out anything about Janis until yesterday. It seems like Donna had an invested interest in setting you up with Janis because Janis is the daughter of one of the most influential military officers in the United States military history. I have not been able to verify the info because of the secrecy surrounding Janis's father."

May continued, "It seems like Donna was extorting Janis's father to get a hold of the plans for Project Light Shield. When someone tried to kill him, he fled the country instead of falling into Donna's trap. No one has seen him since."

"Donna's Sister Candice fooled everyone when she married Janis's father. She lost over one hundred pounds, died here hair, and changed her identity to Betsy Boston to throw people off. She wanted people to think Candice was dead. However, she made a mistake by using her mother's maiden name. Her scheme nearly worked until her son joined the military. Because the navy started snooping around, that is when she gave Janis's grandparents legal guardianship.

"When Janis's grandparents adopted her one of the conditions of the adoption was that changed her last name from Maggie Golden to Janis Wanderley."

Candice hoped that changing Janis's name would protect Janis. From her sister Donna. However, when Candice's son joined the navy, Donna figured out that Candice was still alive. Not only was Candice still active, but she was involved in helping Janis's father disappear.

And when Betsy met with your mother it blew Janis's cover. That is why Donna contacted Steve and was putting pressure on Janis to marry you.

Donna told Steve that if he convinced Janis that he was a good friend of her father's and he would be able to contact him if she were a good girl, he would set up a meeting with her father."

Once Betsy found out that Donna was on to her she disappeared, and Janis has not seen her since the meeting with your mom. But, to make Donna think that she was still in touch with Janis, she would call Janis every week. However, she explained to Janis that she had gotten a new job and was traveling a lot so she would not be able to see her in person.

This made Donna angry because Betsy knew how to cover her tracks and she had been unable to find her. She was certain that Betsy had warned Janis's father that Janis was in danger.

"While Janis's father seem to be hiding, he was never far away. He watched Steve come along. And he maintained his distance as Janis's grandparents introduced her to Steve, and he became the father figure she never knew.

When Steve told her that you were the key to finding out where her father was, she became elated. Steve was about to set up a meeting with her father at her wedding.".

"From the beginning, Steve had manipulated you because Janis was the most beautiful girl in your school. And everyone was trying to figure out how you were able to sweep her off her feet. You were one of the biggest nerds in the school. However, with Scott by your side, people left you alone. While he was a nerd like you, he was also one of the most popular boys in the school because of his athletic skills. He was a star football, baseball, and basketball player. He helped your school achieve national recognition with his winning shot at the state tournament when you were in tenth grade.

However, because he was a nerd and hung around with you, Janis, and Cindy, people left you alone.

"However, when Scott slowly began messing up in sports, eventually, he got benched. Yet you stuck with him until he became normal again towards the start of your senior year. When your senior year began, he was a scholar and jock again.

Everyone was tripping when you decided to join the navy. Everyone thought the two of you would end up at Harvard or Princeton, with

Scotts abilities in sports, and your abilities in science, and literature, you would bring them back to prominence.

"When Mr. Peterson found out that you were joining the navy, he immediately went and told Scott's father. He was afraid to talk to your parents because he felt like it would destroy their lives. Steve played dumb with Mr. Peterson and acted like he was concerned about Scott's future.

However, Mr. Peterson threw out a bomb when he told Steve that not only are you joining the navy, but Janis has also fallen in love with you, and Cindy was in love with Scott. He was not sure which one of you would pop the question first.

"Steve thought it would be disastrous for you because he could see Janis ripping your heart wide open. He felt like she was using you to overcome deep issues about her childhood, which could destroy your relationship. He didn't know what the issues were, but they could be a major factor in your thought processes before you jumped off the deep end."

"Cindy and Scott, on the other hand, would make a great couple. Therefore, you would be fine if the four of you stayed together. However, he felt like the idea of you joining the navy under the buddy plan seemed flawed. M. Peterson saw the navy as a big issue for you. Why didn't you go to the naval academy?

Therefore, it seemed like the buddy plan would destroy your future. Plus, Scott would have to prove that he would not revert to the dork he was at the end of his junior year in high school.

While Steve listened to Mr. Peterson and acted like he was going to find out what was going on with his son, he assured him he would find the underlying cause. Steve was on cloud nine because he felt overjoyed that his plan was working and that you were joining the navy. So, he contacted Donna, and they immediately stepped up their plan to destroy the NSA."

"May, that's old news. Why am I now finding out about Donna's relationship with Steve, Janis, and my mom? I should have known about Donna and Steve's relationship with my mom before she had to break down in front of me while telling me that I had a brother that

I never even knew existed. At first, it was hard for me to believe my mom would have an affair with Steve because I thought she and my dad were rock solid.

Suddenly, it seemed like my parents were about to get a divorce. Because I opened a can of worms when I found out about my brother. Then Steve tried to move in on my mom he nearly killed her.

The last few days have been touch-n-go and she was lying in a hospital bed in a coma. Finally, this morning she woke up and you tell me it is not my fault and I need to calm down.

"May, I am about as calm as I can be under the circumstances. But there is no amount of talking that will soothe my mind. Ever since I joined the navy my life has the commander has told me to focus on leading the PTF. The question I have is at what point do we sit back and say enough is enough. How many of our loved ones must die or be reminded of their past indiscretions."

She tried her best to calm me down. "You need to slow down, lover boy. You are only thinking of yourself, what about the rest of you team. What have they gone through. Yes, it seem chaotic right now, but the only way to stop the terror is to band together and fight the terror. John and James both told you the more you dug up the ugly it would get.

James even told you might not like what you see in the mirror. It may seem like we have a perfect life, yet with people like Donna, Steve, and Commander Revile running around the terror will only get worse. If they are willing to drug their own children, and injury those they love mentally and physically someone must stand up and fight back. While it might seem like we are weak now. We will stop their terror and the world will know peace.

What your parents, Janis, James, John are going through will become reality if we don't band together. If we let them get to us before the battle has even begun we have lost. We must remember our goal, stay calm as we rise above the terror and create a new reality far from their world of terror.

Look at the courage Janis had when they wanted her to betray you It seems like Janis has been given a raw deal but her love for you is far stronger than anything that the enemy has. Thus, they think they have the upper hand by pressuring Janis into marrying you. It may seem like Janis is playing their game. Yet, she is not. She truly loves you. They failed to seduce her, she would rather be with you and your family then be associated with Donna and her group of terrorists.

She is only acting like she is under their wings. They tricked her into thinking that if she helped them, her father would be able to escape hiding. But she saw right through their plan and realized she wanted no part of the plan.

She now understands that her real love is the only way ever to see her father again. The commander applauds her effort and is on board with you getting married at the appropriate time. He feels like that is an integral part of the plan that will draw them in. Your love is a weapon hiding in plain sight.

I stopped May "So that is why she was weeping in my arms last night. And Janis kept mumbling in her sleep. "*George, I will always love you, but it is better if I just disappear until all this craziness is over. If we get married, I will not be able to stand the pressure of having to live with your family and not knowing if I will ever see my dad.*"

"May, I feel like a moron for not believing her. She is trapped like her father, and she is caught up in a plan she has no control over.

"Janis feels like she is ruining my life. Yet, I cannot see my life existing without her. I want to be happily married. But, knowing that she is obsessed with finding her father and marrying me. It is almost impossible for her to beat the odds. Because in the end, she may not be able to reconcile the two."

When Janis talked about leaving me in her dreams, I was shocked that she would even consider such a dreadful thing. Leaving me, thinking she was protecting me. That would be a disaster I am almost certain Scott would go off the deep end and think it was his fault because of how he treated me in boot camp. Thus, in the future, Steve and Donna would come after all three of us and try to destroy us because we ripped their plan to take down the NSA to shreds.

"I have a confession to make. I know you said the commander

approved of my marriage to Janis. I proposed to Janis the day Steve attacked my mother, and she said yes, not only to wait until I get back from my first tour of duty, but she also agreed to live with my family unit I returned. I realize that I told you I would wait to talk to the commander. But, after the incident with my mother, I felt like I had no choice but to make everyone think we were getting married when I returned from my first tour. It was the only way that I could see to protect everyone. I am glad that the commander is on board with my proposal to Janis. I suggest you remind the commander if he wants me to be the leader of the PTF, he needs to give me some slack. I have already turned my back on my best friend, Scott. How much more do I need to do to prove myself?

Janis and I have been in love since the day I met her at Scott's house, and I refuse to turn my back on my love for Janis."

That is why I am so glad Janis accepted my proposal.

May was silent for a minute. "George, it seems like you were in a conundrum. Since she has agreed to wait and marry after you return from your first tour, that will give us enough time to track down Donna and commander Revile. At the same time, both you and Janis can save face."

"Thank you for having my back. I will never forget it."

"However, George I know you are excited but there is one stipulation you cannot reveal you are in the PTF until the appropriate time. That is the only way everyone can remains safe."

"Don't worry May, I will keep my lips sealed. I am grateful that Janis and I will marry soon."

"I got to go May; I will call you again as soon as things calm down a little. Once again thanks for having my back."

No problem man I look forward to hearing from you soon. Go get her tiger."

After hanging up the phone I went back into Janis's room and began shaking Janis.

"George, what's wrong with you? Can't you let a girl get a little rest?"

"Janis, a lot has happened since last night. And I know I have a tough time talking to you because you are the most beautiful woman I have ever known, inside and out.

"I am so glad you will be my wife, and you decided not to run away from me because that would not have worked anyway. I would have tracked you down. My fair lady my heart is in your hands, and I can't live without you. You asked me if you were a part of my future and if I wanted to be with you. I don't want to play any more games."

Then I grabbed her hand and made her look at the ring I had put on her finger before everything happened with my mom. "When I gave you this ring, I pledged to be with you for the rest of my life. We may not have said the actual vows yet, but I feel like you are already my wife.

Then I started to shake her again, but Janis would have no part of it as she grabbed me and shook me. "George, there is something I want to tell you before we celebrate. Janis started to cry, "I have not been completely honest with you. I am sorry for putting pressure on you to marry me."

When you left for boot camp Steve introduced me to a crazy lady named Donna. Steve told me that Donna had many friends, and she would help me find my dad.

However, Donna told Steve that if I convinced you to marry me before you went to your duty station that she would have a better chance of finding my father and that he would be able to safely return home. "At first, I played along with her. But when your mom mentioned Donnas name I panicked."

I went to Betsy and asked her if she knew Donna.. When I mention Donna to Betsy she told me to be careful. She told me she would trust your mom any day over Steve or Donna. And her main concern was me.

Betsy said, "Why is Steve so interested in you marrying George. Is this the first time he has pressured you to hook up with George, or has he been trying to put the two of you together since the first day you met at his house?"

"You need to ask Steve why it is so urgent that you marry George.

Because it seem to me like if Donna knew where you dad was Steve would have mention it when he first met you."

Then Betsy nudged me, but all that should not matter, because I can tell by the look on your face that you are madly in love with George. So don't marry George because you want to see your dad. Marry him because you love him."

Then she laughed, "Janis if that crazy boy doesn't see how much you love him he is blind and not worth a nickel. But, if he comes around and lets you know how much he loves you I say you'd be a fool to say no."

Don't worry about your dad, girl. I feel he never left you stranded and will show up when you least expect it. Remember, he was my husband. And if Donna or Steve knew him before he disappeared, I am sure he would have given them a way to contact him long ago. Because I know your dad loved you, and he would have never disappeared if he felt like you were not safe."

I am almost certain your dad is not far away, and he would never let anyone harm you. It sound to me like this Donna lady is trying to use you as bait to draw your father out in the open.

"The day before your father disappeared, he was acting strange. He asked and told me. Janis has already lost her mother, and I cannot bear the thought that something had happened to me. Therefore, it would be too much sorrow for her to take if anything happens to me. Let Janis know I am not far away and will not leave her alone forever. He asked me to ensure you were safe if something happened to him.

I thought your father was crazy, until he whispered his secret;. I shook my head, as he told me I could never tell anyone until he contacted me. Then he asked me again to protect his daughter."

There is a good reason he has stayed hidden for so long. Betsy sternly said, "I do not trust anyone who would try use you to bring the Captain out of hiding.

You need to stay close to George and his family. They will keep you protected until your dad feels like it is safe for him to come out of hiding to be reunited with his precious daughter."

My dear girl, there is a reason your dad is still hiding, and I believe there is still a whole network of people who want to harm you and your father. Thus, if you stay where your father put you, you will remain safe. Because once he reveals himself, it could endanger the one he loves the most."

"Janis, that is you."

"Now my dear girl don't ask me any more question about your dad and tell me all about that handsome young man of yours because if you don't snatch him up I'm sure someone will."

After talking to Betsy, she seemed to vanish, I have tried contacting her and all her numbers have been disconnected. It is almost as if she has become a ghost.

Thus, the next day I went to Steve and wanted to ask him more about Donna and why your mom warned me that if I had anything to do with Donna she would do everything within her power to convince you not to marry me. When I saw him I was about to approach him Then the phone rang, and I heard him talking to Donna on the phone in his den.

I knew Steve did not see me, so I tried to get closer so I could listen in on what they were talking about. When Steve mention that everything was on schedule and that he had given Scott the drugs before he went to boot camp, my mouth dropped wide open, and that he was confident that you would ask me to marry you while you were on R&R after boot camp.

I could not take it, so I walked to the den and knocked on the door. When Steve saw me he, said "Give me a second Janis, I am on an important phone call. Then he closed the door in my face. After he finished his conversation, he tracked me down.

CHAPTER XXV

George Engagement

"Daughter he said I was talking with Donna a little while ago and she said she had sent a message to your father. It seems like he wants to meet George and discuss your plans. He seemed very excited about meeting your future husband. When George returns from his first tour we can arrange a meeting between the three of you."

You will let me know when George asks you to marry him because I want to make sure I am at your wedding and if your dad does not show I would be glad to fill in for him and give you away.

When he said he wanted to give me away chills began to run down my spine. All this pressure to force you to marry was getting out of hand. Because I did not want to make you marry. I love you and I believed you would ask me in your time. I know I want to see my dad, but I would never force you to marry me.

"That's why I have been acting crazy. George, I love you and I want to be your wife, but I understand if you want to wait, or if you have found someone else."

"Baby," I said with confidence, "Forget about all the craziness that has happened since I left for boot camp. You are the prettiest woman I have ever known, and I don't care what anyone else thinks you have made me the happiest man alive by saying yes.

I know that we may not be able to get married until after I return from my first tour of duty. I have already asked my mom and my dad if you could live with my family until I return." I know this may come as a shock to you, but we have a few more days to discuss all the details.

You said yes to being my wife that was the ball game, and no one will be able to tear us apart. What do you think Mrs. Catwell you want to hold my hand for the rest of your life. And if you don't mind I could use one of those earth-shattering kisses about now cause I am ready to fly."

Janis lit up like a firecracker and kissed me so hard I nearly passed out. As I was lying on the bed limp, she was about to scream. Then I got up and twirled my head around. "That's what I'm talking about, baby," as I jumped up and hit my head on the ceiling and was out of it for a few seconds.

When I opened my eyes, Janis was staring at me with me deep blue eyes, and she whispered, "George, can we take it a little slower this time? Because if you act up the next time I kiss you, Steve will know we are playing the odds against him."

"Janis, don't worry, it won't happen again. I only needed a little bit of spark to break everything wide open. Because all this is like a dream, and I need a few minutes to clear my mind. I cannot believe you said yes, and we are about to start our lives together." Why don't you go take a shower I'll wait for you and then we can go somewhere to celebrate before we have to deal with my family.

While Janis was in the shower, I went outside to clear my head. While I was clearing my head, I called May.

"George, I thought you told me you were going to call me tomorrow or the next day. This better be good cause I have a lot of things to get done before I talk to the commander."

"May Janis and I are about to get married. I was thinking about just going to the courthouse and making it official. Maybe you can help me find an apartment somewhere in San Diego."

"George, get a hold of yourself. You are moving too fast. Didn't you tell Janis that you could not be married until after your first tour of duty? What did you do? Have you gone completely crazy?"

"Yep, I'm crazy and I am in love. I can't wait it's time for me to put my foot down now before I waste away. What do you think Ms. May? Is it possible that we can make this work out before I go to Mississippi?"

"George, you know that's not possible you will be blowing your cover and destroying the PTF. The only way things will work out is if you defy Donna and refuse to marry Janis until you come back from your first tour."

"Thus, Donna will think she has the upper hand. My friend if you deviate from the plan no one will be safe.

Tell me you did not tell Janis you are getting married today. That would be a big glitch in our plans.

"I know you are crazy about Janis but if you don't string Donna along and give her just enough information to keep Janis safe, we are all dead. You would be leaving Janis a broken field. Knowing if she ever finds out the reason for delaying your wedding, she may hate you for the rest of her life. You know this is the only way to bring her father home safely, and we'd better hope this plan works. Because if Donna gets her claws into Janis's father, she'll take him down, along with Janis and your family."

Then I laughed, "Got you, girl, now you know you are not the only one who is crazy."

"Everything is set, and you can tell the commander not to worry about the situation. Regardless of all the traps and snares set by Donna and Steve, everyone knows Donna made Janis a pawn and was trying to trap her. Thereby drawing out Janis's father."

"The more Steve pumped her head with the idea of me being with someone else, the angrier Janis became. He almost had Janis think I might threaten her father's life. He said the only way to protect her father was to marry me."

"He made her believe our marriage would be the key to her father coming out of hiding. When Steve mentioned her father, it pushed Janis off the deep end. Then when Steve hurt your mother Janis was in an awkward position and was torn by Steve's actions and was having a hard time understanding his motives."

"Whether Janis is part of the plan or not, Donna has set the perfect trap to draw out Janis's father, because she feels like you are going to break Janis's heart by refusing to marry her before you go overseas. Plus, Steve is somehow controlling Janis's emotional state. And he continues to act like Janis's friend. He knows Janis's father is worried about her marrying you and he would do just about anything to throw a monkey wrench in your plans. Janis's father has become increasingly frustrated because while he has been close to Janis he has not been able to be there when she most needed him."

"Thus, he would come out of hiding to ensure that his daughter's wedding is perfect, and everything will change the moment you are married. Donna feels like Steve has the upper hand if can control Janis's destiny. It seems like the groundwork to trap you and Janis's father was about to blow the roof down."

However, Donna is no fool and knows if Janis's father does not buy into your love. Donna could wind up blowing any chance of Janis's father coming out of hiding. And that would push Janis right into Steve's hands. Thus, giving him complete control over Janis's emotions and allowing him to put enormous pressure on Janis.

And just like Steve thought, he could make a move on your mother, which nearly killed your mother, and he would eventually break up your relationship with Janis.

However, that would only infuriate Donna after all her hard work to find Janis's father and set the trap to bring him out of hiding. And without Janis's father coming out of hiding, she still would not have access to the plans for *Light Shield*." Thus, she would take that anger and target Steve, destroying any hope of you and Janis having a life together.

Remember, George; you are in a highly volatile situation. Are you ready to withstand all the pressure it will take to protect Janis and your family?"

"Girl, you got it all wrong. Why does everyone think that when I announce that I plan to marry Janis when I return from my first tour of duty is a death sentence.? Janis and I were meant to be together, and nothing can keep us apart."

"Stop talking. You are overthinking the situation. All you need to do is your job. There are only a few more days before I go to Mississippi for training. You need to make sure to communicate with the commander. And convince him that my love for Janis is the key to trapping Donna and Steve and bringing everything full circle."

May, when Janis told Steve that I proposed to her, he was overjoyed. And the first person he informed was Donna. Thus, the timing of our wedding when I return from my first tour of duty is brilliant."

"I know it might seem like a risky proposition, but I believe Janis is innocent and she needs to be protected. That is why I have made the arrangements for Janis to stay with my family until I return. That will give you enough time to clear Janis and set the trap for Steve and Donna. Because without Janis in my life I know I will not make it."

"Yes, it seems like Janis is Donna's pawn, but the game is starting to get interesting. Since Janis is on our side, we are about to checkmate Donna. You need to make sure you stick to your end of the bargain. Because my plan finally allows me to control my destiny. And alleviates some of the pressure I have been under since I met commander Johnstone.

May grumbled, "Dude, I will inform the commander immediately regarding your present situation, and he will get back to you before you leave for Mississippi. You need to slow your roll. Donna and Steve must still feel like marrying Janis will bring Janis's father out of the woodwork.

"Captain Golden is aware of the trap Donna and Steve have set, and he has managed to circumvent the trap by contacting Commander Johnstone. While his location is still unknown, he has been sending Commander Johnstone riddles regarding Janis and you. He has been closely watching his daughter and knows she is in love with you, and his hints have been quite revealing.

"Thus, Commander Johnstone has been working diligently to

solve the riddles because he does not want Donna and Steve to trap you and destroy your lives."

"Meanwhile, Steve has been pumping Janis's head with the idea that she needed to marry you before you left for your training. He made her feel like you were about to break her heart."

"Yet, Steve did not know that the two of you were in love. And the more he told Janis you were a threat to her father's life; the angrier Janis became."

"You are right on top of it May" I stated firmly. "Janis told me all about the tricks that Steve has been using to play with her mind. But she knew I would never harm her or her father. And after talking to Betsy Janis let me know she felt like if she let me go, she would never know the true story about why her father abandoned her when she was five."

"Stop talking George," May replied." The commander is aware of the situation, we are all tired of playing games, with Donna, and if Janis is innocent as you have stated she will be protected when we smash through Donna's evil plan."

"George, you need to be ready to take Donna down along with the rest of the jokers who have been trying to destroy your happiness for years. Janis's heart will be broken if we don't get it right. Are you ready to deal with the consequences, my friend?"

"Yes, ma'am, remember to reiterate to the commander that everything will occur once I return from my first tour. This should give us time to weed out Donna and Commander Revile and finally allow Janis to have some peace."

"It is the only viable plan I see working to draw Donna out into the open. It would be a win for the agency. I am almost certain I can explain the situation to Janis once we are married. Janis is a very reasonable person. And I not only love her, but I also trust her to do the right thing."

"In the end, Donna will be placed behind bars where she belongs. Janis's father will be captured too. Thus, he can present the evidence to clear himself of any wrongdoing. Because he has the proof that

Donna framed him after he stole the plans to Light Shield to keep them safe from Commander Revile."

"May replied, "Slow your roll, mister; remember, I still must speak with the commander. He has been out of the office since you left and should return tomorrow to give me your final orders before you leave for your training. I suggest you cool your jets.

"It's too late. Why do you always have to be so hard on me, May? It's my family and my friends whose lives are in jeopardy, not yours. If I make the wrong move, Donna will have beaten us all. I am not willing to give her the satisfaction. So can you cut me a little slack?"

May laughed. "Well, honey, if you tell me, you miss me and send me one of them sweet kisses through the phone, I'll ease up a little. It looks like you and I got a shot at real happiness."

"You're crazy, lady. There's no way I am going to drop everything to be with a lunatic like you. Can't you see my heart is being smashed by all these secrets that I have had to live with for so long? And now you tell me my sweet Janis is being used to get me and my family. I don't know how much more I can take before I explode."

"I'm sorry, George. I was trying to lighten the mood, but there are a lot of people who are concerned about you and want to see the best for you. We are a team, and when one member of the team is in pain, the whole team is in pain. Sure, the other boys may not show it the way I do, but they are concerned too."

"I get it, May. I should not have gone off on you, but there has been an overabundance of information that has been dropped on me within the last six months. I never realized that this assignment would be so tough. And the weight of so many people trusting me is almost insurmountable. Tell me what you think I should do."

"George, take Janis out tonight and relax. I will make sure that I get back to you within a few days. Hopefully, by then your mother will be better, and the commander will have an answer on how we can make Steve pay for what he did to your mom and Janis.

The most important thing to remember is that you have friends who will back you up. I agree with your assessment. The only choice to keep everyone safe is for you to marry Janis once your tour is over.

By waiting to marry Janis, you will be protecting Janis and your family, and Janis's father will be able to finally step back out into the light. While the commander did not give me any further instructions he told me he trusted that I would make the right choice for everyone concerned.

"However, if Donna runs free, everyone's lives will be in danger. Thus, the main objective is to shut down Donna terrorist network. Then the two of you will be able to have a normal life. Finally, your love will flourish, who knows might have those six kids Janis wanted."

After hanging up the phone, I tried to get some sleep. It was useless!

Why did I think I had the right to unload my secrets on Janis's shoulders?

Why not tell Janis the truth? Then I would know if she was part of the deception or if she was being used.

Yes, I could have the NSA take her in for questioning. If she wasn't conspiring with Steve and Donna, then I would know that she was the woman I was meant to be with for the rest of my life.

I put my head down again and started trembling.

When Janis entered the room and saw me trembling, she began to giggle. "George, you know how to make a girl feel. And whatever you have to say, it can't be that bad. I have known you all my life, yet sometimes you seem to go a little overboard. I'm certain whatever you must tell me it will be all right. Calm down a little. I ain't going anywhere until we talk."

"George we finally, have a chance to talk about our future. "I know it has been crazy the past few days but, George, I am utterly and hopelessly in love with you. If we don't get things lined up before you leave, I don't think I will be able to live with myself."

My mind was gripped with terror when I began to realize that I might be crossing the line if I really told Janis how I felt. Yet I knew that if I said the wrong thing I would be falling into Donna's trap.

All I could do was put my head down and several tears dropped down the corner of my face. "Janis, we will always have time to talk about our future together, but right now I just want to relax and have some fun."

Janis replied, "George, if there is anything I can do to help you deal with the enormous pressure that you are under, please trust me."

I started to stutter, "Janis, I have something I need to tell you, something I'm afraid that if I tell you, you'll hate me, for the rest of your life."

Janis playfully hit me. "I could never hate you. I might get a little upset, but I could never hate the man that I want to be with for the rest of my life."

I gently gripped Janis's hand, looked into her eyes, and said, "Honey, Janis," in a faint voice, "you are right. We needed this fresh air," and I placed my cheek next to her cheek and did not say a word as I closed my eyes for several minutes and we danced to the sunrise.

When the sun began to rise I was staring a Janis and silently gazing into her eyes. The silence sent chills running down Janis's spine. She had never seen me look so serious, and it scared her.

"Janis, please have an open mind"

Before I had a chance to finish my sentence, my phone rang. I looked at the number and saw that it was the commander calling

"Janis, I need to take this call, then we can go to our favorite spot for breakfast, where I hope that we will be able to talk and resolve all this craziness that has been happening since I got home."

I was disappointed when it was May. "How are you, my friend? I hope you are ready for the good news."

Then Commander Johnstone got on the phone. "George, you, and May are doing an amazing job. It seems like your relationship with Janis has caused quite a stir in the NSA. I could not understand the connection, but when I found out who her father was, we were shocked."

"Janis father was part of the program to develop Light Shield, his disappearance coincided with James' father's disappearance."

"It seems like James's father and Janis's father were partners from the beginning and they got mixed up with Commander Revile, who had ties to Mr. J. and Donna."

"When Janis's father found out about you and Janis, being in love he tried to contact Janis. However, Steve has been hovering over her so much that he could not risk it until he was sure she was not surrounded by his enemies."

"I think your plan to become engaged to Janis is brilliant, then when you added the icing to the cake that you would not be able to see her again until after our mission. It was a stroke of genius when you decided to have her stay with your family for protection. somehow you told her you'd pick up where you left off and sort everything out.

By having Janis stay with your family, you have eliminated the threat of Steve and Donna controlling the situation. "Now they will have to figure out a way to get past your father and his connection with General Armstrong."

"Toby is very wary now, and I am certain it will be a long time before he allows Steve near your family after the incident with your mother. While Janis will still be able to contact Steve, she will be able to control the situation."

"I am glad you are deciding to marry the girl, because she is innocent in all of this. And the girl has truly fallen for you, according to Cindy, Scott's girlfriend. Don't be surprised, once we learned about their friendship, we tapped Cindy's phone, and 95 percent of the conversations were about you and Scott. Janis even told Cindy about Steve. However, she never mentioned Donna to Cindy. I think she has been trying to escape Donna's and Steve's grasp, because she told Cindy that Scott's dad had set you up but what he did not realize was that she had fallen hard for you, and she wanted to get away from it all so the two of you could start a life together."

"George, I heard you already proposed to Janis, and she said *yes."* I am glad you took charge and finally popped the question. Everyone is happy for the two of you. However, you must remember that you will be gone for a year before you can get married. Since she is willing to wait for you, then everything is a go."

"Thank you, sir. I am glad that we had this conversation. I hope it leads to Janis finding some happiness too. And her father will finally come out of the woodworks after Donna and Steve are out of the picture."

After I spoke with the commander, I returned to Janis and told her to get ready. We were going to our favorite place for breakfast, lunch, and dinner.

Finally, we were alone and having fun, as we finally discussed our future. The next few days were like being in heaven. Everything was finally on an even keel.

"Janis, you are my light in the middle of all the darkness that has surrounded me the past few days, and I know I am the luckiest man alive. I know it may seem like a long time, but I will write and call you when I can. Remember, after my first tour of duty is over, I am coming back for my bride."

I leaned over and kissed her on the cheek. "I need to be with the one I love more than anything else right now. I need to spend time with you now that my mom is doing better. The rest of the family can take care of things."

I could not take it any longer as Janis looked at me with her sweet eyes melting my heart once again

"Janis," I said as I held her hand, "Janis I know you said you would wait for me. But I wanted to marry you today. Because every second you are not my wife there is a cloud over my happiness. What do you think you want to make it official, or do we have to wait until I return from my first tour of duty?"

We can go to city hall and make everything official. All we need is a witness. Someone we can trust not to tell anyone. And then when I get back from my tour we can have a wedding if you want.

Janis grabbed me and kissed me. "I told you, George, I would wait for you. You are really a dork.

We don't need to get married today. We can have our wedding when you return from duty. All I wanted to know was if you loved me. And you have proved your love to me"

Janis's face lit up as we took off toward her house.

Then Janis began to cry. "I just want to spend time with you.

Knowing you still want me to be your wife has made me the happiest woman on the face of the earth."

While Janis was in the shower I got a call from my father, and he let me know my mother was being released from the hospital.

When Janis stepped out of the shower I grabbed her and kissed.

"All right mister, I know you missed me, but you can slow down and let me put some clothes on."

Janis gushed as I said, "You look beautiful, just the way you are. And I can't wait to tell you the good news.

Janis smiled, "I can see you are excited. Can you tell me because I am freezing and want to get dressed sometime today?"

I bust out laughing, "Sorry, dear, but my dad called and told me my mom was out of the hospital, and I was hoping we could visit my family after breakfast.

I looked at Janis. "I told my mom we were engaged, but we have not set a date yet."

Janis answered. "That sounds good. Because that will give everyone time to prepare for our wedding."

"My dad even suggested that I ask you if you would like to stay with family until I got back from my first tour. My mom thought it was great idea she thought you could use the support. My parents are very excited about the idea of you staying with them. They said Sally was already cleaning up my old room for you. They have assured me you will not have any more problems with my family."

Janis looked worried and said, "I am afraid your mother, Billy, and your dad will treat me like I am an outcast. The only one in your family who speaks to me is Sally. And after your mom's accident, we have become distant. She has barely talked to me

The other day, your dad told me it was all my fault, that Steve went crazy and if I tried to become your wife, he would never speak to you again.

He suggested your friendship with Scott, Steve, and me was a bad influence in your life. If it weren't for us, you would have never joined the navy.

CHAPTER XXVI

Final Day of R &R

He started ranting about how Steve nearly broke up his marriage. George, let me go with you. George, I am begging you to put me in the rear of the plane, and when we land, we can be together. I won't cause any trouble."

I looked at Janis and calmly said, "Girl, why are you freaking out? I told you; I must go away for about a year. And once I have completed my first tour, we will be married. But if you can't wait for me there is nothing else, I can do. Everyone regrets the harsh things they said to you. Since Steve's attack, my family has bonded together."

"Yes, I know some harsh things were said, but my father did not mean what he said. He was upset with Steve, and he thought you were part of Steve's plan to destroy my life. But when he saw how you were with Mom at the hospital and how you treated me with the utmost respect, it broke his heart the way he had treated you. Janis, I am asking you to trust me and give my family a chance. They can be very loud, rude, and downright obnoxious, but when they care about someone, they will drop everything to make sure that they feel safe and secure."

After the incident at the hospital when Billy saw how much I loved you, he dropped to his knees and begged me for forgiveness.

Janis chimed in, "George, please leave Steve out of the picture. Everything is raw right now. I don't know what happened between your family and Steve, but he won't even talk to me. I tried to see him yesterday and tell him the good news about you and me, but he slammed the door in my face and said he did not want to see me anymore."

George replied, "Janis, 'I said adamantly. It may be a long time before Steve talks to you again because he was hurt that you would choose me over him. You ruined his plans, and now he knows his life is in danger."

"I know my father has forgiven Steve for the problems he created for my mother. My father told me that he was blessed that my mom was still alive and that you would be a part of my life. Yes, he said some horrible things when he was angry because of the accident. He has taken full responsibility for his part in my mother's accident. If he can forgive Steve after all that has happened, I am sure he will welcome you to our family.

"However, if I have learned anything in the past few weeks, it is to forgive and have hope. Steve will come around, and all those that want to hurt him will soon be dropping like flies because one thing that is hard to break is my family's love.

"Although Steve will need to get his priorities together if he wants to be around my family in the future, and he must get away from Donna. Her hate, thirst for revenge, and jealousy would drive anyone insane. Janis, I don't care how long it takes for me to prove my love for you and those you care for. If it takes me until my dying breath, in the end I will know I was the luckiest man alive because I married the most beautiful woman in the world, and our love endured the test of time. I am begging you don't worry about Steve or my family anymore, because what affects you affects me. I only want to be able to wake up with your smile by my side for the rest of my life.

"Janis, everyone knows where I stand when it comes to you. If they mess with Janis, they are messing with me, and I cannot be a part of a family who does not respect my future wife.

"My mom went through the floor when I told her I finally proposed. She was elated by the news of our impending wedding. I am certain my mother told everyone about our engagement. Everything has changed since the incident with Steve. It changed our perspective on what it means to be a family and how much we mean to each other. Sally will be so glad to have another sister, and hopefully, with your influence, my brother Billy will finally grow up and reunite with his wife. You are going to have a wonderful time with my family, you'll see."

Janis nearly burst into tears as she hugged me and kissed me. "George, this is the nicest thing anyone has ever done for me. When you called me your wife, it made me queasy. I love you. And now I know that you are truly ready to settle down when you get back from you first tour,

"I know I am getting ahead of myself because I never even asked if you wanted to stay with my family unit until I return to marry you. However, I will feel so much better if you're staying with my family since you are going to be alone because of the issues with Steve. And with Scott being gone, I know you don't have anyone to look out for you. Are ready to become my wife even though we haven't said I do?" I smiled and said, "I do want you to be mine for the rest of my life after my first tour is over."

"Janis, you are my light in the middle of all the darkness that has surrounded me the past few days, and I know I am the luckiest man alive. I know it may seem like a long time, but I will write and call you when I can.

I could not contain myself, when I spoke with my mother as I reached over and hugged Janis. It's time to let the world know how much I love you. And I blessed beyond measure soon everyone will know you are my wife. And if they don't like they can take a hike. Janis you are my dream girl and always have been. I may have been dorky at one time, but you have made me lose my dorkiness. When I look into your eyes it send chills down my spine, then while I hear you sweet voice all my trouble disappear. Knowing that I will soon be walking together with the most, beautiful lady in the world not only on the outside, but also the inside.

Thank you for saying yes to my proposal it has put a fire inside me that I never knew existed. Now I can finally express myself without the fear of rejection. Because, my old self had no confidence, but you have made my heart leap for joy, and I will never doubt our love again."

Then before I could say anything else, Janis bent down and put her hands over my mouth. When she kissed me. The sweetness of her lips made me feel like I was standing on the top of Mount Everest.

My face was red as a beet as blushed right before I blurted out, "Remember, Sweetie Pie, after my first tour of duty is over, I am coming back to make you my bride. Your sweet kiss just sealed the deal; and now I have the courage to face the world.".

"I told my dad we would try to meet everyone for lunch at the house. And I could say my final goodbyes before you take me to the airport. Plus, I needed to make sure everything is all right with my mom."

However, I wanted to take you to a special place for breakfast before we meet with my family. When my father agreed to let you use his car to take me to the airport, I nearly went into a state of shock. My father has never let anyone touch his car, not even my mother. But, when he told me I deserved to ride in style with my beautiful lady, I knew you would be protected until I return in about a year."

Janis took my hand and smiled. "Let's go get some breakfast. I am famished. But you got to let me pick the place this time. Because I got a one last surprise for you before we meet your family."

I was so captivated by her sweet voice and glowing face I just nodded my head as she reached into my pocket and grabbed the keys open the door and pushed me into the drivers seat.

Let it rip honey, before I knew what hit me we were flying down the freeway, Janis had opened the moon roof of the car as we went into the tunnel, and she stood up and started screaming I'm in love with the most handsome dude on the planet. And her word just bounced off the walls of the tunnel and smacked me in the head.

I was completely caught off guard. Usually, Janis was very quiet and unassuming. Suddenly she was declaring our love to the whole world. Suddenly she told me to make a sharp turn onto a small dirt road after we exited the tunnel. I was going bonkers.

Janis was losing her mind. What had I done?

Then she suddenly slid over jumped on my lamp and slammed on the breaks as we skid into the parking lot of *Lezzert Brunch.* This was crazy, I knew we had at least an hour before the doors opened. What were we going to do until than Janis grabbed my hand.

Come on Honey man, let's get some breakfast and spend our last moment s with some delicious waffles, bacon, and eggs.

I looked at Janis, "you know they aren't even open yet. Janis smile don't worry about that I already got everything arranged. Then she did a special knock on the door and the door opened. As the chef stepped out and hugged Janis. Then he came over to me and hugged me.

"Welcome my friends, I have already prepared your meal and while you are waiting we have already put some blueberry scone and caramel macchiato on your table."

I looked at Janis, "George that is my friend from school when I told him I was getting married he told me to pick a day and he would cook a special meal for me and my lover. Just sit back and relax while we have a grand meal before we meet you family."

"Then I heard our favorite song and Janis said "Let's dance while we wait for our food. I want to hold onto you as much as I can before you take off to sail the seas. I want you to remember this day and think about all the fun that we will have once we are married.'

For the next couple of hours, we danced and ate. Then her friend came to our table, I think it's time for you have you final dance because I am about to open the doors to my customers.

Then the chef brought us a desert to take with us he whispered something into Janis ear and her face lit up. He turned to me "Sir anyone who can make Janis light up like you have is welcome to my restaurant any time. And if you need someone to cater the wedding just let me know for you and Janis it will be free."

I thanked the chef as we made our way to the car. "Janis you drive the car to the house, it time for me yell into the wind. Dear that was the best surprise of my life. Thank you so much. I can hardly wait until I say the words I do. You have made me the happiest man on the face of the earth."

Janis smile as she slid behind the wheel, and we drove through the tunnel. This time I stood and start singing *John Denver's song my sweet lady.* The echo from song felt like it was shaking the foundation of the tunnel. or the first time in a long time, I felt like I was king of the hill.

However, when we pulled into the driveway I nudged Janis. We are at the house are you ready to become part of my family." Janis burst into tears.

She grabbed my hand and whispered, "Just hold me for a moment before we go in cause it is going to be so hard for me when you leave this afternoon. Remember no matter what happens I will always love you.

After I wiped Janis tears we silently made our way to the front door. Suddenly the door flew open and Billy rabbed Janis. "Welcome to the family, everyone is waiting for the you in the front room. Mom and dad are stoked to see you. Sally and I will go down stair and play some pong while you talk to mom and dad. Then we will eat lunch."

"When we got to the front room everyone started clapping. My Dad blurted out, "glad to see you two in the sunlight. It's been a couple of days. George you, stunned us all when you popped the question?"

Billy punched me in the shoulder. "It's about time, you moron."

When my mom saw me and Janis, she tried to get up off the couch, but my father told her, "Don't overdo it, honey. I know George and Janis are glad to see you."

My mom motion for Janis to come over. She saw the glow on her face, and she smiled, "So glad to have you as part of this crazy family."

Janis smiled Then I turned to my mom and whispered, "Janis is really going through tough times after the incident with Steve. She feels like everyone blames her for what happened."

My mom looked at Janis and put her arm on Janis's shoulder, "Janis, Steve is the one who created all this chaos, and you had nothing to do with it.

All I know is anyone who makes my son as happy as you have will always be honored and welcomed in my humble home." Then she took my hand and said, "Don't worry, son. I am going to take Janis under my wings and make sure she's safe."

My dad hit me on the back. "I don't believe it, you asked Janis to be your wife."

Sally heard my dad call Janis my wife. She came out of hiding and burst out smiling. She looked at Janis. "Janis, you'll be staying with us in George's old room until he gets back from his first tour. That's the least we can do for my new sister."

Then everyone started clapping again. "Janis, Janis, Janis."

My father restated what Sally said, "I am ashamed of my son not having everything prepared for his bride. I'm not going to let you out of the house until you say you're going to stay with us till George returns."

Janis became overwhelmed by my family's reaction to our engagement. She burst into tears of joy. My father put his arms on her shoulder.

"Are you all right, daughter? That big buffoon of a son, he didn't hurt you or something. 'Cause if he did, I'll whip him into shape."

Janis just shook her head and said, "No, sir, I'm just so overwhelmed by your kindness. And I want to thank you, because George is the love of my life, and he has a very remarkable family. I will gladly accept the invitation to stay while George is gone."

Then I asked Janis to excuse me for a minute because I needed to talk to my dad.

After we stepped outside, I asked him, "Sir, is everything all right? I know it hasn't been easy for you but give Mom a chance. She is crazy about you and would be lost without you. I don't care what Steve did in the past, Mom will always prefer you.

I know Steve is a touchy subject because Janis is so close to him it had been hard for her phantom Steve's betrayal, Dad, can you make sure the rest of the family looks out for Janis. Now that Steve and Scott are gone she is all alone.

Did you know she has never really had a family before."

"George, I have never been prouder of you than I am right now. You have grown into an honorable man. And I will make sure that Janis knows that we are glad she will become a part of our family. Whatever happened between me and Steve is in the past. He will never bother you mother again. I can understand that he had feeling for your mom, but he took it to far."

As far Janis relationship with Steve we will all give her time to work through things. I sure when Scott comes home for R&R he will cheer Janis up. Plus, it will great see your old friend. Steve is the one with the problem not Janis or Scott remember that they are both your friends for life and they both were ambushed by Steve and his association with that crazy lady Donna."

"Son, you don't have to ever worry about me and you mom again, because I am sticking with her until death do us part. Billy is going to straighten things out with Lilly and the next thing you Sally is going find the love she deserves. Then I saw a few tears flowing down the side of his cheek. Now, get out of here before I start crying," he said, as he handed me the keys to the car.

As soon as my dad and I came back into the house, my mother whispered, "Son, if you don't already know it, I am proud of you, and I am sorry for doubting you. You are going to make a great sailor. Promise me you will be careful, because I don't know what I would do if something happened to you. Don't worry, Mom, I'll be careful. But I will miss everyone." Then I hugged my mom and told her I had to talk to Billy and Sally before I left."

I think just went to the basement to play some ping pong."

I looked at Janis. "You know I can't leave without saying goodbye to them. Did you want to join us in a couple of games of ping pong before I leave?"

Janis looked at me, "That's all right you go have some fun, I will stay here with you mom."

When I saw Billy and Sally, I laughed. "Why did you two take off so quick, you know I wanted to see everyone before I left.

Then Sally put down her paddle and came over and hugged me. "I thought you would never talk to us again after the way we treated Janis at the hospital."

Billy threw his paddle on the table. "George, you always gotta show up at the wrong time. I was winning. Ain't going to be fun anymore. Sally is going to start crying and talking about how she's gonna miss you."

I smiled. "You ain't gotta worry about her, bro. Sally is not going to be lonely without me around because she is going to have a new sister. Her and Janis will bond and have great fun planning our wedding next year."

Billy burst out laughing. "Pay up, Sis; I knew there was going to be a wedding next year. It's about time, George! I am so glad I don't have to listen to you blubber about how beautiful Janis is anymore."

"That's enough, Billy," I said, "both of you need to chill out. I want you to make Janis feel like she is part of the family. If I hear you are giving her any trouble, I will give you a knuckle sandwich when I return home."

Sally smiled. "You don't have to worry about me or this bozo, because if he steps out of line, I will personally take him down. I really like Janis, and I am honored to have her as my sister. I always wanted a sister."

Bro you need to stop worrying so much. We got you back. I am glad to see you happy. And I know that Janis is a big part of that. I just wish I could talk to Lily like you talk to Janis. It like she lights up when she is around you. I know I love Lily but, I guess I don't have the *it factor* like you."

Then Sally smacked him in the head. "Billy what is the matter with you, dropping you problems on George. You are almost as a big of moron as George." Just go tell Lily how you feel, because she loves you she just want to hear it from you."

"It's time for us to all go back upstairs and have some lunch. After lunch George is going to the airport. We need to make Janis feel welcome. Because once George is gone we are all she has."

"You know her grandparents are on vacation in Europe, and all the craziness with Steve. She need our support."

When we came back upstairs the first thing Sally did was grab Janis hand. "Sis why don't you help me get the food on the table. And as for the rest of you bozos you need to get to the table.

"Where did dad go I thought he was up here with you mom."

Suddenly, he came around the corner, "Did I hear someone calling my name. Can't a guy get a break for a minute I had to take care of some business."

Sally looked at my dad, "glad to see you could join us, I need you to my get to the table, while Janis and I get the food.

My dad face lit up like a Christmas tree. "It's about time, girl because I thought we might just starve, and I was going to have to give George some money to take Janis out before he left."

Sally shook her head as she turned to Janis "Welcome to the family, now you see the types of idiots I have to deal with every day. I am so glad that I am going to have someone sane to talk with while George is out galivanting all over the world for the next year."

Sally, just watch yourself or I will have to teach a lesson in manners. I know George will be crying knowing that he doesn't have to listen his sassy sister while he's sailing the ocean blue"

Then my mom spoke up. "You men will never learn. Let just sit down be thankful for Sally and Janis working so hard to feed your belly's."

I could not believe the feast that Sally and Janis brought from the kitchen. I was amazed it was the first time we had all sat down together since I began R&R. And for the for the next few hours, we laughed, joked, and had a wonderful time.

When time came for me to leave, I did not want to go. I felt like I was ready to start my new life with Janis right now.

Then my dad stood up, "Son," my dad said as he patted me on my back, "It's time to go now. You get that fine lady into my car and let her take you to the airport. I am sure you two would rather spend your last moment with each other rather than all of us clowns."

I hugged everyone and took Janis's hand as we made our way to the car. I watched my family waving at us until we turned left and roared down the road toward the airport. About thirty minutes later, we pulled up to the curb at the airport, and I popped the trunk to get my baggage.

I went around to the other side of the car and opened the door for Janis. "Janis, this is not goodbye this is the beginning of our life together."

Janis started weeping. "Please, I don't want you to leave me. I don't know if I can last a year without you. Everything has changed since your visit, and without you or Scott around, I am going to go crazy."

"Janis don't worry. You saw how overjoyed my family was when we told them we are engaged. I think the closer it gets to my returning, the happier we will all be. It is going to be hard for me to be away from you for so long. Yet when my dad told me he would make sure that you were safe and he was glad you decided to stay in my room, he told me to get used to the fact that it will be your room too. I told Sally to make sure that you and Cindy feel welcome in our house any time of day or night."

"Billy assured me that he would keep his smart remarks to himself. My mother said she was going take you shopping and help you with all the details of our wedding next year. She said she knows we haven't planned that far ahead, but once I get back, she wants us to be ready. My mom and Sally are super excited. It almost made me jealous. They told me I better not mess this up or they would never forgive me."

Janis put her hand over my mouth. "George, hold me and whisper sweet nothings in my ear until you get on the plane."

When I grabbed her, she was trembling and weeping. All I could do was wipe the tears away as I whispered, "Honey, you are the moon and the earth to me. The time we are apart will soon be a distant memory when we visit the White Cliffs of Dover, the Eiffel Tower in Paris, and the Leaning Tower of Pisa on our honeymoon that will only be the start of our journey together. I wish we could say our vows right now."

CHAPTER XXVII

Janis Father

I got down on my knees and handed Janis a piece of paper. On the paper was a poem I had written to her. I told her not to read it until she got home. Don't ever forget that I will soon return to sweep you away."

Then I got up a kissed Janis for the last time before I got in the line security line and waved goodbye. Janis grabbed me and hugged me tightly. "Janis, you gotta let go. It's time for me to get to my plane. This last kiss will keep me every night as I lie down to sleep. And when I wake in the morning, your face will be my sun, helping me make it through the day."

Although Janis stood near the security gate weeping, after she finally let go of me, she said, "George, thank you for loving me. I will wait until you get back. And as far as Steve and Scott go, I will do everything I can to fix my relationship with them and prove to your family that Steve is not as bad as everyone thinks."

"He may be a jerk at times, but he has the heart of a king. He was there for me when my father left. Steve and Scott are like family to me, and I want to fix the problem between him, and your dad. Give me some time to figure out what happened. I am sure that they will make up and move on with their lives."

I smiled at Janis. "That's why I love you so much.

You have the biggest heart, and you are one of the most beautiful people I have ever met."

Janis waited at the entrance until she could no longer see me, then she went back to the car and was ready to leave the airport.

Janis's heart was heavy as she made her way back to her house to get to pack and get ready to move in with my family. She did not know when she would see me again. With everything that happened in the past few weeks, she wondered if she was going crazy.

She had put her life on hold while I was away for a year. The day before I return from boot camp she had finished her first semester at the university. Now that I was gone, nothing seemed to matter.

All she could think about was how lonely she was going to be without having me around. Somehow, she had to focus on the future.

Getting her degree in economics had always been a priority in her life. The study of the economy had always fascinated her.

Thus, she decided to put all her efforts into her studies when her classes started in a few days. She hoped her studies would take her mind off her aching heart. She would focus on working at one of the financial institutions near her school. They had promised her that if she did well in her classes, she would be working at Charles Schwab or Ernst and Young. She realized it would take time and effort, but she felt like it would help her stay sane.

The thought of working was a much-needed distraction, and she turned the radio on and began listening to her favorite song. Her mind was so preoccupied that she did not even see the strange man sitting in the back of her car until she got to the stop light, and she was about to get on the exit ramp.

"Don't scream, Janis, because if you draw any attention to the car, both of us will be dead," the man said

"My dear little girl, I see you hooked a real keeper. It sounds like he is swooning in your charms."

Janis said in a panicked voice, "Mister, who are you? If you lay a hand on me, I will make sure you are put away for good."

"Easy, girl, I am not here to hurt you. But I am here to warn you about the mess you are about to get into if you marry George. I know you think you know him, but he is one scary man. I don't know who is worse, him or Steve, the guy you consider to be your father.

You must know anyone who is a friend of Donna's must be a complete whack job. So, before you go off the deep end, you need to take me to the nearest restaurant so we can get something to eat and discuss how you are going to help me finally have peace in my life for the first time since you were a baby."

"Sir, I don't know whom you think you are, but I am not afraid of you. And if you are not out of the car before I get off the freeway, I am going to roll down my windows and scream."

"I thought you might say that, so go ahead, dearie, try to roll down the windows or try to open the door and see what happens."

Janis stopped the car. She tried to roll down the windows, but they would not budge. She tried to open the door, but it was stuck.

"Janis, I told you I am not here to hurt you. We need to go somewhere and talk. Once we have talked, I will be out of your hair."

Janis nodded her head. "There is a Denny's about a mile up the road where we can get something to eat. After we eat, you promise to let me go?"

The stranger smiled. "Janis, I told you I would let you go. I will be watching you to make sure that no one harms you.

When George steps over the line, I'll send my best men after him in heartbeat because I ain't going to let anyone mess with my girl."

Janis looked at the stranger like he was some crazy old man who didn't want her to be happy. When they finally got out into the light, she saw his face and almost fainted. "Papa, is that you? Is that truly you?"

The stranger looked at Janis and said, "Calm down, dear, we don't want to make a scene."

"Why are you here, Papa? It's been almost fifteen years since the last time I saw you, Matter of fact, the last time I thought I saw you was when Betsy took me to Granma's house. Not to long after Grandma Adapted me I meet Steve and his son Scott.

"Steve told me told me that he had meet you before you

disappeared, and he was afraid you might be dead due to the crazy circumstance surrounding your disappearance. He told me he would help try to find out what happened to you. And if there was any chance that you were alive he wanted to reunite us."

"Papa, you were gone, and I had nowhere else to turn. I met George, my future husband at Steve's house and it was not until recently Steve tried to introduce me to this crazy lady named Donna. Donna told Steve that since your disappearance she had been tracking you and she feared for your life that is why she wanted me to marry George, because she felt like that was a way we could be reunited."

"Janis, calm down for a minute. I gotta get something to eat and I will explain everything."

Janis pulled into a parking space near the door and said, "Here is Denny's. Let's get something to eat."

Janis's father smiled as they got out of the car.

After he had ordered a coffee and a Grand Slam, he looked at Janis and smiled. "Girl, you have gotten so big. I really wished I could have been around to watch you grow up, yet I had to disappear to protect you. However, if I would have known Donna was gonna find you, I would have taken you with me.

I know how close you and Steve are. Once I found out that Donna had hooked you up with Steve, I nearly blew my cover. There were so many nights I would sit outside your grandparents' house ready to snatch you and take you away from all the drama. Yet, I knew I could not risk it until I saw you with George last week.

When George proposed to you, I knew I had to get you to safety before someone tried to kill you. That is why I am here today. I must get you to a safe location in the next few weeks or we may all wind up dead."

"After seeing you and George together, I made some calls, and when I found out he was Sergeant Toby Catwell's kid, I was elated because I knew he would keep you safe due to his connections with General Armstrong. But I was puzzled by Steve's response to your engagement with George. And my unction was correct when I checked up on Steve; it seems like he has been a busy man. When he attacked George's mom, I knew it was too dangerous for you. My dear girl, you don't have to worry about him anymore. I made sure that Steve is out of the picture for good. I know you may not understand, but you are going to have to forget about Steve."

Once his food came, he stopped talking for a few minutes and gulped down his Grand Slam and cup of coffee. Then looked at Janis and smiled.

Janis looked at her dad as if he had broken her heart. "Why can't I be with George. He is the love of my life, and I am sure I will be safe with George's family. Just because they are chasing you does not mean I am in danger. Because I don't think Steve will be stupid enough to try and visit me while I am staying with Georges family."

"Why do you want to destroy the only happiness I have in my life.? I have not seen you in years and you suddenly show up and expect me to just disappear with you and forget about George. That ain't going to happen."

Why can't I be with George? Is it because of a stupid mission that you went on fifteen years ago. And then abandoned me. I had nothing to do with your choices. So, after we eat I don't ever want to see you again if it means I can't marry George."

"No, I didn't say that dear girl. I am letting you know everything is not as it seems. George does not realize that I am your father, and if he ever finds out he may never want to see you again. I am the one who designed the PTF. George thinks Commander Johnstone picked him to lead the squad. Yet he does not realize I am the one who had him placed on the secret task force. He is under my tutelage, I can't let his love for you destroy the inevitable.

"I hope you understand, Janis, I cannot even claim you as my daughter because I have a whole new name, and no one must know about my past. Once my true identify is known, I will either be a champion of freedom, or I will be considered the biggest traitor this county has ever known. I know you love George and you have said you are going to marry him when he returns from his first tour.

However, you will have to break your relationship off for everyone's safety. You are currently a distraction, and George must move on. You mustn't distract him, and act like you need your own freedom until Donna and the commander are captured.

"He will always love you. And when the time comes, the two of you will be married. But I am begging you to let me protect both you and George. Daughter, I know I am asking a lot of you not to contact George before he returns from his first assignment. You must trust me. I am going to take you to a safe place where I can train you.

Once you have dumped George and you have completed your training, I will disguise you and you will be right in front of George's face as a part of George's team, where you will find out the specifics of your part of the mission. And when you understand you will be right by his side without him even knowing, you will thank me for keeping everyone safe.

"The two of you will always be together, dear. And when the battle is over and we have taken Donna and her goons down, you will be able to reveal yourself, and I will give you my blessing to marry George.

George is kinda of a dimwit when it comes to relationships. Therefore, it will take him some time to start a new relationship. Your new persona will steal his heart, and he will forget the old Janis until the time comes to show him what you are truly made of."

"Darling, my great friend Commander Johnstone has decided to make you one of George's key allies in the PTF. When you are properly trained and ready, you will be right in front of George's face, and no one will know your identity except me and the commander."

Once you write George a *dear John letter*, it will break his heart. And he will become more focused on the mission. That is when you will go undercover. No one will ever suspect your new cover, you become will be inseparable, and he fall in love with you all over again.

Janis gasped. "You are going to put me in front of George's face? Don't you think he will figure out something funny is going on? I don't believe I could be right in front of George's face without him recognizing me. I'm sure I will say something that would tip him off."

Janis's father laughed. "Girl, after your training, your foundation will be so strong that no one will know who you are until the proper time. And once you reveal yourself, George will be flabbergasted and drop to his knees and propose to you. The only difference this time is I will be there to watch you walk down the aisle."

"Remember, I love you. And in the next three weeks, I will be back to get you prepared for the greatest adventure of your life. Please give me a chance to help George become the hero he is meant to be."

Janis began to weep. "Pops don't tell me you are going to leave again. I really need your guidance, comfort, and love."

Janis's father put his hand over her mouth. "Janis, I will always be with you, and George's family will become yours. Whenever you feel lost or lonely, think of our conversation today. I will return soon.

"Janis, your cover is already in place. And once I return, we can finally begin your training. It may take three months, but I am sure you will adapt, and your dream will come true. You will be with George every step of the way.

After you're trained, we will be together permanently. You must keep this meeting our little secret, because if anyone finds out I have contacted you, they will try to kill you and anyone you love."

Her father leaned over and kissed her. "Before I go, there are four men that you can trust, General Armstrong, Captain Silverton, Commander Johnstone, and George's father Toby Catwell.

In a few minutes, Toby will come through the door. I want you to go with him and stay with George's family until I return for you."

Before he said anything else, he jumped up, grabbed the bill, and paid it as he ran out the back door of Denny's. He broke into a car and hotwired it, and he zoomed out of the parking lot onto Broadway.

The incident with her farther threw Janis into a state of shock. As she sat at the table contemplating what had happened, suddenly Toby burst through the door and faintly said, "Janis, there you are. I have been looking all over town for you. I'm glad you are safe," he said as he hugged her. "I am not even sure how I can explain it to you, but you need to come with me. I'm afraid there has been a terrible accident since you dropped George off at the airport." He grabbed Janis and dragged her to his car and pushed her into the passenger seat.

Janis was truly scared by the silence as they made their way to the house. When they got into the house, Sally, Billy, and George's mother hugged her.

"Janis, you need to sit down and watch the evening news with us. It seems as if our friend Steve was attacked today, and as his attacker left, they shot him three times. I am surprised you didn't hear the news."

"Steve is still alive, but he is in critical condition. And he asked me to bring you to the hospital as soon as you got home."

Janis stood in the front room for a few minutes thinking about what her father had told her about Steve. She did not realize that taking Steve out of the picture meant someone was going to try and kill him. Janis looked at George's family strangely and she fell to floor. The pressure of meeting her father and Steve's untimely accident had caught her off guard. However, before she hit the floor, Toby caught her and carried her over to the couch. He told Billy to get some icy water.

Billy ran to the kitchen and got a bucket of icy water. When he returned, his father ordered Sally to put some sheets and towels on his chair. He transferred Janis from the couch to his chair. Once she was in the chair, he told Billy to dump the bucket of water on Janis.

Janis jumped up from the chair right after the water hit her in the face. "Where am I? And why did you throw a bucket of water on me?"

"Janis don't get crazy on me. I told Billy to pour water on you because you passed out. I need you to be alert so that I can take you to see Steve at the hospital."

"Steve's in the hospital?" Janis shouted. "Why didn't you tell me? I must see him right away."

George's father looked at Janis like she was a crazy woman, and he followed her to the car.

"Billy, take care of Sally and your mom. I'll be home after we see Steve."

Billy saluted his dad. "Righto, Pops. Mom and Sally will be fine. Take care of business, and we will see you when we see you."

Moments later, Janis was rushing into the emergency room to see Steve, but they would not let her see him until one of the doctors came out.

"What is wrong with you people? He was asking for Janis's when he got here. Let the lady through."

The doctor rushed her to Steve's room. "Ma'am, he's been drifting in and out, and I am not sure how much longer he has to live. We tried to remove the bullets, but one of them is stuck in his temporal lobe and we cannot operate due to the swelling. And if the swelling does not subside soon, he will die from the pressure on his brain."

Steve reached out his hand to Janis. "Is that you, Janis?" Steve said. "I must tell you something before these doctors take me to the operating room."

He pulled her head down next to his mouth and whispered, "Donna is coming for you, so you better find a place to hide. I think if you stay with George's family you will be safe, but you cannot go back to your grandparents' house or my house. She must not know where you are. I will have your grandparents notified that you are safe, and that is all they need to know because they must not know where you are for the next few weeks. I'm going to tell them you are living with Betsy. Keep a low profile and stay with George's family until he gets back from his first tour. George's parents will know what to do to keep you off Donna's radar

"Janis, you must stay alert, because if Donna finds out you are marrying George everyone will be worse than burnt toast, as she will try to destroy you. Somehow you must get a hold of your father. He is the only one who knows how to get you to safety. I beg you not to underestimate Donna. She will stop at nothing to achieve her goals." He pecked her on the cheek. "I am so sorry for getting you mixed up in this mess. Please try and get a hold of Scott for me. Cindy should know how to contact him. Tell him I'll always be proud of him. He needs to stick with you and George like glue."

"Tell Cindy if she loves my boy. She must go to him and tell him. I would have been honored to see her as my daughter, like you, Janis. I know I have made many mistakes, but having you become like a daughter to me was never one of those mistakes. That is why I want you to get as far away as you can before Donna tries to erase you.

Let Toby know that I wish we could have met under different circumstances, and that I am sorry for all the troubles I have caused him and his family. I wish I could have been a better friend. I know I do not deserve any pity. Tell him he is blessed to be with some like Tammy. I'm so sorry I put you through all of this. I thought I could trust Donna, but I was wrong. She has deceived me for years, and now all those who are close to me are going to pay the price unless they get to safety."

Steve said in a somber voice as he let go of her hand, "You must leave and never come back. I am almost certain I won't make it through the night."

Steve called for the doctor. When the doctor arrived, he whispered something in his ears. Then the doctor escorted Janis back to the waiting room where Toby was waiting for her."

"Janis I am not sure what Steve just told you but, I think it is better for you to return to my house. If you need anything from you house I will figure out a way to get it for you. But right now, you are not safe until I can figure out what is going on."

I think all this has something to do with what my son is involved in. I will make some phone calls until then you will be safe with the family."

I will wait with you until you are ready, but you need to understand that all this happened because Steve was tied up with the wrong people. He may be sorry now, but he made his choice and I want to ensure that I will do everything in my power to keep you unscathed."

About three hours later, the doctor came out. "Janis, I'm afraid to tell you that Steve did not make it. Is there someone who can contact his son?"

Janis quickly replied, "I will make sure he is notified. If you need anything else, please don't hesitate to call me. I am going to go home and rest."

Immediately after talking with the doctor, Janis called Cindy.

At first, Cindy did not realize it was Janis on the phone because she was crying so hard.

She almost hung the phone up until she blurted out, "Cindy, Steve is dead. Can you contract Scott or notify someone who can?"

The next day Cindy went to the recruiters office and told them the situation. She gave him Scott's name and asked her if they could contract him regarding his father's death. She said all she knew was that he was on some type of secret mission near Alaska and that she did not know how to contract him.

The recruiter assured her he would get a message to Scott. After several days he contacted Cindy to let her know that he has sent the message to Scott Commanding Officer. Once he received the message, he nearly lost it as the officer of the base told him that he would not be able to leave until the *USS Carl Vinson CVN-70.*

Once the *Carl Vinson* arrived, they would be able to fly him to Hickam AFB, and then to McChord AFB. They told Scott he could take forty-five days to take care of the arrangements for his father's memorial services.

For the next few days, George's family did their best to comfort Janis and Cindy. Toby took care of as many of the arrangements for Steve as he could. However, he knew they would have to wait until Scott arrived to make the final arrangements.

When Scott arrived at the airport, Cindy and Janis were waiting for him. When Scott saw Cindy, he raced over to her and hugged her. He turned to Janis and pecked her on the cheek.

"Thank you for being there for my dad. I know he considered you as his daughter, and I am grateful for your kindness. Janis," Scott said, "can you give me and Cindy a few minutes? I'll have Cindy get you when we are done." Then he took Cindy by the hand and made his way to get a cup of coffee.

Scott turned to Cindy. "Girl, I don't want you to worry about anything. I talked to the CO of my ship, and they gave me forty-five days to take care of all the arrangements for my dad. Since it is only going to take a couple of weeks to make the arrangements for my dad's funeral I wanted to know if you would be willing to go with me to San Diego and help me get settled in before I go on my first tour.

"I know we won't have much time before I meet my ship in the Philippines next month. But I thought you might like to join me in San Diego for a few weeks before my tour, which should be for less than a year. Then I will be home for eighteen months before I must go on another tour. Cindy, what do you think? Would you like to see where I am going to be stationed for the next four years?"

Cindy's face lit up. "Can you give me a few days to think about it?"

"Sure thing." Then Scott asked her to find Janis. "I must make a phone call and finish some of the final arrangements for my dad."

She immediately went back to the gate and found Janis, who was waiting patiently. "Janis, can you believe it? That meathead Scott asked me to go with him to San Diego for a few weeks. He wanted to show me his place where he is going to be stationed for the next four years. What should I do? I thought he was going to ask me to marry him first."

Janis laughed. "Hold on a second, Cindy. Scott is crazy about you, but are you sure this is what you want to do? You can convince him to stay around here, and when he needs to get settled in Toby, Billy, and the rest of us can help him move into his new place."

CHAPTER XX VIII

Steve's Death

Cindy put her head down. "It was not what I expected. It's kind of like eloping. I just thought we would be married before I went to San Diego with him.

Janis and smiled. "I guess we will never understand the men we love and why they are such dimwits at times. Since I am staying with George's parents, I have asked them if you could join me until after Scott takes care of his business and leaves for San Diego. You can let Scott know you will be staying with me at George's house. I think it's a done deal." Janis looked at Cindy like she was out of her mind. "Whatever you got to do is fine with me."

Suddenly, Scott came speeding down the walkway. "There you are, I'm sorry about all that, Janis, but it's kinda crazy right now. I have a lot on my mind. I need to get home and start cleaning up the house. It might take me a few days, but when I get done signing all the paperwork, I will be moving to San Diego. I'm sure Cindy told you I want her to accompany me the San Diego.

"Right now, everything seems strange, but I am hoping that within the next few days, I can clear things up and finally be able to breathe. It's no pressure, Cindy, but I would like you to join me in San Diego before I return to duty. I have many things that I want to discuss with you. Please, Janis, don't think I am leaving you out because you are like my sister, and I know George would want you to be taken care of.

The first question I need to ask is do you have a place to stay? I know you are staying at your grandparents' house. I am not too sure you are safe there. Do you got food, is there anything I can do?"

Janis was shocked by Scott's abruptness. "I have been staying with George's family. I thought he would have told you that. I also asked them if Cindy could stay with us while you're in town."

Scott stopped. "Janis, you are so right. I should have realized that George would make sure you are taken care of. You see, it's been difficult the past few days because I have been getting messages from all directions.

They would not allow me to receive any mail or phone calls while I was on a secret mission in Alaska. Cindy's message was the first contact I have had with the outside world in a month, so I have been digging through a month's worth of messages. Thank you for picking me up at the airport, but I already have a rent a car. And now that I know where both of you will be, I will meet you at George's house later. I must go downtown and talk to my dad's lawyer."

As Scott started walking toward the exit, Cindy yelled, "Hey, mister, wait for us. You don't want to leave your favorite women stranded."

"Okay, sweetheart, bring them sweet lips over here so I can get home sometime today."

Janis laughed as Cindy ran toward the exit.

Scott kissed her and then he softly whispered in her ear, "Cindy, please go with Janis. I need to take care of business and it may be a while. It will be boring. Plus, you would be a distraction. I know the lawyers are going to talk fast, and everything would just fly over my head because all I would be able to think of is you and me in my sweet apartment in San Diego."

Janis poked Scott. "All right, mister, that's enough in public. You need to get a room somewhere."

Scott laughed. "Make sure you get my sugarcane home safely, and I'll meet you at George's house."

When they got to George's house, they parked and knocked on the door. Sally answered the door.

"Janis, Cindy, we are going to have to get you a key. You should not have to ring the bell every time you come home." When she did not see Scott, she looked at Janis. "What you do with Scott?"

Janis looked at her blankly, then she blurted out, "Scott went to see his dad's lawyer. He said he would hopefully be back to join us for dinner. You know Cindy will be staying with your family until Scott takes care of his father's business. Then Cindy and Scott might be going to San Diego until he returns to his duty station."

Sally hugged them both and said, "I am glad that both of you will be staying with us. I don't understand how men can be such morons at times. First George, now Scott.

What is it about men? They don't seem to have any brains when it comes to women."

When Toby heard Janis and Cindy, he came to the door. "Is there anything I can help you with? You got baggage that I can take to your room? Cindy, we made up the guest room for you."

"Toby," Cindy asked sweetly. "Do you think you can call Scott and let him know that you will help him with the rest of his arrangements for Steve?"

Toby smiled. "Now I see why Scott can't wait to make you, his wife.

It is so hard to resist such a charming young lady's request. Scott is like a son to me. I will do whatever I can to help him out."

Sally harshly spoke to her dad, "Thanks, Pop. You need to move out of the way so us girls can get everything set up for Cindy. While you call Scott, I will get the quest room ready. Let's go, girls, we've got a little work to do to fumigate Cindy's new room. My dad means well, but he is the biggest dimwit of them all when it comes to women."

Toby felt bad. He should have let Tammy get the room ready. She would have, but he's had her on lockdown since she got back from the hospital. It's only been a few days, and he wanted to make sure she rested for at least a week like the doctor suggested. Thus, he made sure she was careful until she sees the doctor next week.

As they took off to make sure Cindy's room was clean, Toby called Scott. "How are you, Scott? I wanted to let you know that I am here for you, and if there is anything me or my family can do to help you out, just say the word."

Scott replied, "Sir, thank you for being so kind to me. I heard what Steve did to your wife, and I am sorry. I would have given him a piece of my mind if I had been here. My father could be such a pain at times. However, I know he regretted his actions because the two of you meant the world to him. Considering everything that happened while I was away, you have already helped me more than I expected. And when you asked me if I needed anything, I was shocked. Right now, there is not a lot you can do."

You are already taking care of the two people who mean the most to me, which takes a load off my mind. Now it is time for me to finish with the lawyers. There are documents I need to dig up. The rest of the arrangements were already stipulated in my father's will. Once I clear everything with the lawyers and fulfill my father's last wishes, I will have a memorial for him and then I will be moving to San Diego with Cindy."

Then he said, "Sir, can you keep a secret?"

"Son, anything you need," Toby replied.

"Cindy does not know I want her to be my wife before I move to San Diego. I am waiting for the right time to propose to Cindy. I was hoping we could get married as soon as I finish all my dad's business."

Scott took a deep breath and said, "Sir, after I propose, do you think your wife would be willing to work with Sally and Janis to help Cindy.

I know Tammy needs to rest, but I think the three women can do all the heavy work while Tammy would be like a manager and directing them to pull off the perfect wedding in your backyard.

However, you must keep this a secret until I ask Cindy to marry me tonight or tomorrow afternoon?"

Toby was silent for a few seconds when Scott told him that he was moving with Cindy to San Diego. Why was Scott so ready to marry Cindy while his son George was not doing the same thing with Janis? "I am glad for you and Cindy. The wedding sounds like a great idea. I am sure the girls will have a blast setting everything up, but my dimwit son should have done the same thing with Janis.

"Scott, is everything all right between you and George? Because I know you talk about everything, and it surprises me that you do not want to wait to have a double wedding with George when you return from your tour."

Toby laughed. "My son is a complete nitwit when it comes to women. When George told me he was engaged but they had not set a date yet, I could hardly believe my ears. I know the fool is in love with Janis.

Toby asked Scott again. Scott are you sure everything is all right between you and George"

Scott smiled "Mr. C, I assure you there is nothing wrong between me and George. We will always be friends. The time I spent in Alaska made me think about what is important in my life. I am not afraid to move on with my life. I thank God for your son because he made me realize that I could not wait to marry Cindy until I returned from our tour. While George and I discussed getting married together, everything went sideways when I transferred to Alaska. Now that Steve is gone losing my dad and my girl is unacceptable.

"Sir I need and want Cindy by my side for the rest of my life. The thought of her waiting on me is now a moot point. It's time for me to move on with my life and be true to myself. Cindy is the most important person in my life right now, and that's why I hope she will marry me. Sir, I am ready to settle down and have kids. I have already asked her to come with me back to San Diego where the *Carl Vinson CVN-70* will be stationed.

"Toby, as far as George is concerned, I am not sure what his reasons are. If you ask me, your son is afraid of commitment. But if he said he will marry Janis next year, so be it. I cannot wait for a year to be with my baby. George always has been a little bit of a dimwit when it comes to women. Don't worry about it. George is crazy about Janis. But from what I've seen lately, he may lose Janis if he is not careful."

"Scott, you are making the right choice. You have made me incredibly happy with your decision to marry Cindy. And when you're ready, I'm sure my wife would love to help plan a grand ceremony in our backyard for your wedding. It is the least we can do for you."

Your wedding will be one of the highlights of my life. I only wish I could contact General Armstrong and see if he could cut George lose for a couple of days to be your best man.

Toby hung up the phone as he wished Scott the best. He was relieved to find out that the events of the past few weeks had not damaged George's friendship with Scott. Toby still felt like there was something that Scott was not telling him. Because, like Janis, he felt something fishy was going on that George was hiding from him.

While he knew the importance of George's mission, all he could think about trying to do was fix Janis and his son's relationship. He wanted to call General Armstrong and find out what was going on.

But it would be detrimental to George's mission with the PTF. Plus, with the current situation with Steve and his wife, he felt like it was best to leave well enough alone. He had plenty of time to figure out what was going on with George. Right now, he wanted to be there for Scott and Janis until his son came to his senses.

Scott was a constant reminder of my relationship with Janis. Steve and Scott were the ones who had introduced me to Janis. And due to the recent revelations about Steve's past relationship with my mother, he felt like I was dissing Janis. Somehow, he had to get across to me that Steve had no part in setting me up with Janis. What made matters even worse was that I had not even tried to contact Janis since I left.

My father was quite upset, and he wondered what was wrong with his idiot son. He could not sit back and watch me destroy the best thing I had going in my life. It is not Janis's fault that Steve was a bad fellow. And certainly, if I could forgive Steve, he felt like I should forgive Janis. Things were truly getting out of hand.

Especially since Cindy had left several messages for me to call Scott due to Steve's death, everyone was wondering why I refused to return Cindy's calls."

Toby was furious; he thought he had raised his son not to be so compassionless. He felt like I should have known how close Janis was to Scott's father, and she truly needed to hear my voice.

After taking care of his business with his father's lawyers, Scott headed to the house to pick up Cindy for dinner.

When Toby saw Scott, he approached Scott and said we need to talk. "I know you told me nothing is wrong with you and George. But things are not adding up. Janis has waited by her phone for the past three days, but it never rang. I have watched the tears flowing down Janis's face. I need some straight answers.

He was sure I had contacted him, and hopefully, Scott could tell him how to get a message to his son. He felt like I should be with his friend in his time of need. Yet, with every attempt Janis made, I refused to respond.

Scott brushed Toby off, "What is the matter with you and Janis? George and I are fine. I just wish you would give George and me a break," he said angrily. "You both need to stop worrying about me. You think your son is being a little brat; you think you understand our relationship, and it can be very exhausting for both of us.

Please stop your constant bickering and fighting it does not help matters. I don't want to hear what you think anymore. George and I are friends, and that's all you need to know," he said as he forcefully hit the wall in the pantry. George can take care of himself.

Then Scott once again covered for me, telling Toby that he had talked to me. You and Janis need to chill out. George called me yesterday and told me he was sorry about my father's death, and that he wanted to be with me but could not get away. He had just taken two weeks' vacation and his school would not let him leave. And unless the death was in his immediate family, there is no way they would let him leave until after he completes his training."

Scott continued, "He won't be able to leave after training because they are sending him directly to the USS *Carl Vinson CVN-70* in the Philippines.

"Toby, you were in the army for over twenty years. You know how the military can be sometimes. George was talking about going AWOL so he could be here. I told him to calm down, and that everyone understood how he felt. I let him know I understood his pain and told him I appreciated him wanting to be here, yet it is not worth him ruining the rest of his life. Sir, George will be home after our first tour, and I will be by his side when he walks down the aisle with Janis."

I know that George needs to talk to Janis, yes, he is a jerk at times, yet he's wanted to marry Janis since the day they met. You know he has two left feet when it comes to Janis. I told him last night that he needs to get his foot out of his mouth. If he doesn't, someone will sweep Janis off her feet.

Sir, give him a little time. He will soon show everyone how serious he is. We both knew joining the navy would change our lives. Neither one of us wanted to hurt the ones we loved. Give him a chance. He will blow your mind away when he returns from our first tour."

"That is all you need to know right now. It has been a trying time for both of us, and if you love your son like I know you do, you and Janis need to stop bugging me about him. It is bad enough that he is not here, but the two of you don't need to make it harder by putting a guilt trip on him."

Now, let me go. I do not want to miss my dinner with Cindy tonight. Hopefully she will say yes when I put a ring on her finger. Please wish me the best of luck. The events of the past few days have been overwhelming, and the only things keeping me going are my friendship with George and the fact that I am going to marry my gal before I return to duty."

Toby patted Scott on the shoulder and told him he was glad his son had such an honorable friend. After, my father smiled, and he looked at Scott and wished him the best of luck. "If there is anything I can do to help the two of you, let me know."

Then made his way into the front room. When Janis saw him, she immediately stopped him. Let me let Cindy know you are here. Then she disappeared for a few seconds. When she returned, she noticed Scott's knees were rattling. "What's up, Scott? Thought you were coming to take Cindy to dinner later this evening. You can come in and sit down, and I'll wait with you while Cindy is getting ready."

Then she giggled a little when she saw Scott was shaking. "You need a hug, my friend. I heard you talking to Toby. I am so proud of you. You are the closest thing I have to family. And you don't need to worry about Cindy. All she has been talking about today is whether she is going to go with you to San Diego or not. It's time to tell Cindy how you feel, slugger. 'Cause if you don't, I will find a pool stick and take you out back. Remember how I first met George?"

Scott burst out laughing. "Janis, thank you so much. You always seem to know just what I needed."

"When you pop the question, I know what her answer will be, so you can relax. When she comes down the steps, just be yourself and wrap your arm around her and peck her on the cheek and tell her you got something important to ask her at dinner."

Then Cindy suddenly appeared. "Get your gruffy hand off my man, girl, your time is coming, but I'm ready to rock and roll tonight with my honey. I heard he was taking me to some swanky restaurant tonight. He said he had something important to tell me. Does it have to wait? Because it better be something extraordinary." Cindy winked as she gently slapped Scott. "Buddy, you'd better be glad I'm still stepping out with a two-timer like you."

Scott's face turned beet red as Janis gave him a gentle peck on the cheek. "That's all right, girl, you can have him. He's too short for me and look at them chubby legs." Then they both burst out laughing.

"You two have already embarrassed me enough. Janis don't wait up. Cindy and I may see the sunrise if you don't mind moving out of the way while we have some fun. Cindy can spill all the beans sometime tomorrow."

"What's that," Janis playfully said, "you have her home by midnight because she's got a big day tomorrow."

Cindy said, "Scott, you know Janis is my new guardian and she has me on lockdown."

Scott shook his head. "You two are crazy. Janis, after this I don't think you have to worry about Cindy disclosing information." And he stunned everyone by grabbing Cindy's hand and getting down on one knee.

"What is wrong with you, I can't wait any longer. Cindy, I ain't got no time to wait for dinner. I am ready right now. Cindy, will you do me the honor of being my wife in two days after Janis and George's mom get the wedding plans done?

Then after the wedding, we can have our honeymoon at our new home in San Diego. We can have about six kids and live the rest of our lives together. What do you think?" Scott said as he put the ring on Cindy's finger. "Do you love me? I ain't moving until you tell me something, 'cause those sweet words coming from your silky voice will make me the happiest man in the world."

When Cindy saw how serious Scott was, her face lit up like a rose. She could hardly contain herself. "Yes, Scott, I'd be honored to be your wife. Get off your knee."

He slowly got up as his knee loudly cracked. He leaned in to give Cindy a kiss, and she burst out into tears. "Scott, I don't know what to say. This is so overwhelming. I thought you had to take care of the arrangements for your dad. I don't want to be in your way."

Scott looked Cindy in the eye. "Honey, you will never be in my way. I need you by my side for the rest of my life.

Don't worry, girl, I only have a few more things to do. All the final arrangements should be made within the next two days. Therefore, I figured you, Janis, and George's mom could have things ready by Friday to plan a small wedding in George's backyard. We can have a nice reception and then start our new life together. I am asking you to come with me to San Diego for three weeks to have our honeymoon before I go on my first tour. Tomorrow is going to be a wonderful day."

Then Scott put his hand around Cindy and said, "This is just the beginning. Let's have some fun. Ma'am," he said to Janis, "don't wait up, but I promise to bring her home at a decent hour."

After Cindy left for dinner, Janis went to her room and stuffed her head into her pillow and began to sob uncontrollably. What was wrong with her? Why didn't George want to marry her before he left for his tour? George told her she had to wait until after he returned from overseas. Something was wrong with George. Why didn't he tell her he wasn't ready to settle down?

She would have understood better than the silent treatment she had been getting for the past month. Well, it didn't matter. She was not going to rain on her friend's parade, she thought as she cried herself to sleep.

Cindy could hardly wait to start her new life with Scott. For the next few days, she made Janis's life horrible. However, Janis knew why George did not call her or his family. Everything was falling into place just like her father had said. She knew that she would have to write George a Dear John letter. And when he refused to respond to her calls, she felt like her father would be returning soon to take her into hiding.

Thus, Janis bury her frustration and acted like she was excited for her friend Cindy. However, when she was alone the tears flowed. Then every time Janis would bring up the subject of George, Scott would say that once the training was over, he was hoping to see George. Once they got situated in San Diego, he would try to contact George to set up a meeting with him after he finished his training in Mississippi. Scott was trying his best to encourage Janis.

Therefore, he continued to act like he could contact George, and George would be able to get a seventy-two-hour pass, which was normal for sailors who were going to be flying to meet their ship in the Philippines. However, nothing had been normal with George since boot camp, and Scott had seen the way they treated George about coming to Steve's memorial.

Scott doubted that he would be able to pull it off since George had already had R&R before he went to Mississippi. Also, he did not know if George's graduation from A school would correspond with Scott's vacation time. All he knew was that he would only be in San Diego for about three weeks before meeting his ship in the Philippines

CHAPTER XXIX

Scott's Revelation

The last word he received was that George was going to have to fly straight from Mississippi to the Philippines to meet the *Carl Vinson CVN-70.*

Scott was heartbroken when his father could not see him get married. Before joining the navy, Scott genuinely believed they would have a double wedding after boot camp. Yet the navy had messed everything up when they stationed him in Alaska and sent George home on R&R. It did not make sense to him, but he felt like he had no choice but to roll with the punches.

However, once he married, Scott stopped covering for George. The first person he chose to come clean with was Janis. Because inside, he felt for Janis, and he knew George was a complete airhead when it came to her. When Scott told Cindy he needed to catch up with Janis before they left for their honeymoon. She barely noticed he was missing as she was on cloud nine and ready to start her new life with Scott.

When Scott walked into the living room, he bumped into Janis, and before he could even get it out of his mouth, Janis smacked him and frowned at him. "What is the matter with you, Scott? This should be the happiest time of your life, and you are still trying to stick up for that idiot George" The smack did the job as he looked at Janis and said, "Right back at you, girl, I know you are excited for Cindy and me, yet you are still letting that goon George dictate your happiness."

Then he looked at her and said, "this would be a double wedding if it had not been for the navy messing up our R&R after boot camp.

"Janis, I know you are worried about George, don't be. George is a big boy now, and he is head over heels in love with you.

"You have no idea how George constantly talks about you. George is one of the biggest knuckleheads I know, and he does not want to admit he misses you."

"Janis, he wants you to become his wife. Everyone knows you will be his bride and have at least three kids running around. George loves you, yet he still does not know how to communicate those feelings with you."

"You can be assured that once he gets on board his new duty station, he will start contemplating his poor choices. By the time his tour is over, he will be ready to run into your arms and make you his wife.

He smiled. "I'm sure you heard his famous stutter when he finally told you he would marry you. Because all you must do is blink your eyes to make his heart do a swan dive. This does not exclude George from being a complete dimwit regarding women. He talks like he's so strong, yet as soon as he sees that twinkle in your eyes or hears your sweet voice, he falls apart."

Scott wanted to tell Janis the truth about what happened in boot camp, but he did not want to destroy her illusion of his friend. That's why he was playing along with the navy's game. Yet, it was gradually destroying their friendship. Thus, he was wary when he talked to Janis because he did not want to disclose to much information.

However, he knew that George was a little cuckoo. When he talked about his first tour in the navy, it had made him so anxious that he even got upset with Scott for a couple of weeks, right before they went to boot camp.

"Janis, I know you wish he would tell you how he feels, but he is a complete emotional wreck when comes to you. You are his quicksand. He loves you and feels like his world revolves around you. All through high school, all he talked about every day was being married to the most beautiful woman in the world and how he felt so unworthy of your love.

Yet when it came time to pop the question or talk about getting married, he always froze up. George is afraid you are going to turn him down if he asks you to marry him. He has a complex. To him, you are like a princess, and he is a frog. It is a miracle that he proposed to you.

Janis began to blush as Scott kept talking. "Janis, he knows that you two will be happy and are meant for each other. Trying to get past that awkwardness and get through his big lunkhead is like trying to get a camel through the eye of a needle. when he is around you. he just goes crazy. However, it is inevitable, my dear friend Janis. If you got him to agree to marry you when he comes back from overseas, you have already won the battle."

I know it may seem like a long time, but before you can snap your fingers, you and George will be married, living next door to me and Cindy until we both decide if we want to reenlist or buckle down and make a whole new life with our beautiful wives."

Then she looked at Scott and hugged him. "I hope I have not been too hard on you, but we were all put in a dangerous situation when the two of you joined the navy. I will play nice with Cindy, and I am glad you have grown up and realized the value of finally settling down with Cindy. She is my best friend, and I know she loves you, so I wish you the best. Don't worry anymore about me and George. We will work things out.

Scott turned to Janis, I am glad we cleared that up I need to back to Cindy, but I will see you again before I leave. Scott returned to the reception and him and everyone was enjoying themselves as they dance the night away.

Finally, it came time for them to leave and Cindy threw the bridal bouquet she noticed Janis was missing. When she mentioned it to Scott he told her not worry about Janis told me a little while ago that she was not feeling to good and went to her room to get some rest. She told me to knock on her door when we were getting ready to leave. Just wait right here I'll go get her she said she wanted to congratulate you before you left.

Scott went to Janis's room and knocked on the door. When Janis opened the door he gave her a big hug and let her know they were getting ready to leave for San Diego. "Janis, I can assure you that George will contact everyone as soon as he can. I know George. He told me he could hardly wait until his tour was over so he could hop a plane and fly home to marry you."

Janis looked Scott's square in his eyes, "Scott, I appreciate you trying to comfort me, but I would prefer you stop lying to me. I am not oblivious to the fact that you are covering for George. Can you please just let me know if my suspicions are correct? Something is off because every time someone talks about George you seem to go into panic mode."

Suddenly Scott got quiet and became edgy because he did not want to make his friend look like a total Fruit Loop. Then a light went off, and Janis blurted out. "Scott, it's not about him joining the PTF and leaving you behind, is it?"

Scott put his hand over Janis's mouth. "Don't say that again, because if anyone hears you talking about George being in the PTF they will know someone has leaked top-secret information to you. Who is it? Because they have put yours and George's life in jeopardy."

"George and I have been given separate duty stations, and our paths will not cross again until the appropriate time. If George's family ever found out about it, they would panic, and it could blow our mission out of the water. I did not want to tell you this, but since you already know about the PTF, I am hoping you keep your mouth shut for all our sakes."

"No one is supposed to know about the PTF because it was not created until after we graduated from boot camp. I was supposed to be a part of the team. I messed up when I took the enlistment exam. However, no one knows it, but I have become a member of the team, just in a different location than George."

"You said you wanted the truth. That's all I know. If George proposed to you and said he would be back for you after his first tour, and then he put you with his family to ensure your safety while he was gone, he is telling you how deeply in love with you he is. And he would freak out if anything happened to destroy your relationship.

The truth is he has become an integral part of the PTF, and he cannot veer away from his mission. If he would have married you, his mind would be nothing but mush. All he would be thinking about is the next time he could be with you."

Then Scott begged Janis to be patient with George and assured her that once George figured out where he stood with the PTF he would marry her in a heartbeat. The separation from him and the uncertainty of his mission has left him in a strange place. When he returns from his first tour, he will be if far better shape.

"Janis, I should have been trapped like George, but for some reason, they allowed me to take forty-five days' leave to take care of my father's last wishes. When I found out I was coming home, the first thing that came to my mind was I was going to marry Cindy."

"Steve had been very fond of Cindy, and my father would have wanted me to move on with his life. So that is why I married Cindy as soon as I got the chance. Janis, I am the luckiest man in the world to have a dame like Cindy by my side."

"Janis, I truly hope the navy lives up to their end of the bargain and allows me to see my friend again soon. However, if George is not on board the *USS Carl Vinson CVN-70,* when I finally reach my first duty station, I've decided it is time to move on. I will not be able to cover for George anymore, and he is going to have to answer for his own actions. Until then, Janis, I owe it to my friend to cover for him. Because no matter how far apart we are, one day we will join hands and take on the world together.

"I have no idea what the navy has in store for me or George. The PTF has changed both of our perspectives on life. However, one thing it will never change, Janis, is George's love for you. I don't care if you are separated for a year or ten years, he will always love you. When you look at me and Cindy, don't get jealous. The way I feel for her is the same way George feels about you. You will be happy,

Janis, and one day you will understand and look back at these dark days and laugh.

Janis started shaking. Her father had told her not to tell anyone about the PTF. She had broken her promise. Now she found out that both Scott and George were in the PTF. She was really freaking out. Why would her father withhold the fact that Scott was part of the PTF? Her father told her that Scott was not a member of the PTF, which caused friction between George and Scott. Was Scott collaborating with Donna behind the scenes? Had the burden of his father fallen upon his son?

However, Janis could tell that Scott missed his friend George. And if it were up to her, she would have Scott reevaluated to become a member of the PTF, working alongside George instead of at a separate location. Then she thought to herself that her father did not know as much about the PTF as he was letting on. To her, they were using Scott as a decoy to take some of the pressure off George. That's why he was sent to Alaska and George was sent to Meridian Mississippi for his storekeeper training. For some reason, they were trying to keep them separate.

Then Janis said, "Thanks for the honesty, but you can never tell anyone else what you just told me. Because if someone captures you and you give them the info as easily as you did me, we would all be dead."

Scott looked at Janis and said, "I never thought about it that way. I figured George must have told you, so therefore it was all right for me to tell you."

Janis said, "Why would you think George would reveal the fact that you were part of the PTF? The George I know would never open his mouth because he knew that it would instantly put both of you in danger. How do you know I am not a spy for this person they call Donna, and was sent to trick you into divulging the plans of the PTF? It sounds to me like the location they are sending you to is far more secret than what they have planned for George."

"It looks like he is the one on the frontline and you are going to be the last line of defense. Thus, your location is secret. Now, if I were a part of some conspiracy, I would get you to give up the location and Donna could take you all down. And it would prove George's theory that I never did love him."

"However, my friend, I will never reveal my source to you. Because the way it looks is that the PTF is trying to confuse Donna and throw her off the track However, Steve told me to stay with George's family because he knew I would be safe. If he knew you were a part of the PTF, he would roll over in his grave. He told me right before he died Donna had deceived him and he had done some horrible things."

"George begged me to look out for you and not blame him because he was the one who got both of us in this dangerous situation. He said that when I saw you to warn you about Donna and keep you away from any task force they were trying to use to take her down because he said she would not hesitate to have you sitting at the bottom of Davy Jones's locker next to Victor."

"Since you are already involved, it is imperative you keep your mouth shut, because as they say loose lips sink ships."

Now that we have talked I think it is time we get back to your wife and I will drop you off at the airport. I will ask George dad if I can use one of their cars. Now, go get you wife. Be happy Scott. Don't worry about me or George both of us will be all right. Scott quickly left out of Janis room to get Cindy.

When Janis came downstairs she caught up with Toby and asked him to borrow the car to take Steve and Janis to the airport. Toby smiled and quicky tossed her the keys.

Suddenly Janis found herself in a familiar situation when she dropped Scott and Cindy off at the airport. Janis found herself wondering if she could hold out until George returned next year. Every day she waited by the phone hoping he would call her. She would go to the mailbox expecting a letter. Suddenly, a month had gone by, another month had gone by, and after three months Janis was ready to figure out a way to contact George.

After their honeymoon Scott flew to the Philippines to meet the *Carl Vinson.* After Scott left Cindy started calling at least two time a week asking her if she wanted to come visit her for a few days in San Diego. Janis told her she it was kind of hard for her with her schooling and her new job. Cindy said she understood and would still call her to to stay in touch until their men got home next year. Then hopefully they would be able to come to Janis wedding.

The one-day Cindy called, Janis and she was extremely excited. "Janis, I got a letter from Scott. He asked me if I had been in contact with you and begged me to tell you to hold on a little while longer because he knew George was going to be a changed man when he got back from his tour of duty."

After hearing the good news from Cindy, she forgot about the letter that her father had asked her to write to George. All she had to do now was wait for a about another year and all her dreams would come true. And every day she was becoming closer to Sally.

She felt like she was a part George's family and even Billy had started to warm up to her and just as George said. Billy reunited with his wife, and they were happy.

While Cindy continued to call her twice a week and tell her about the amazing adventure Scott was having. He told her about all the various places he had seen since he left, and that for the first time in his life, he felt like he was accomplishing something. The hardest part for him was not being able to share the experience with Cindy.

Janis did not know whether Scott was still covering for George or if he was telling the truth. Therefore, she refused, to believe Scott and she was not going to let him off the hook until she physical saw George.

However, Scott continued to protect George, because he felt like they would soon be back together, and the time apart would mend their friendship. He did not want to drive a wedge between George and Janis because they were the only family he had left since Steve's death, and he had promised Steve that he would look out for Janis.

Scott felt like all Janis needed was to give George a little space and have patience, because the more he develops his own path, the more he'll realize how much he needs his friends. One day he'll put his foot in his mouth and his thick skull would get the hint. And when that happened, Scott wanted him and Janis to be by his side

Scott continual defense of George reprehensible action really bothered her. Why was Scott was acting like George's mouthpiece? She felt like Scott was making things up to keep her off guard. It did not matter how shy George was she knew he could speak for himself. And for him not to communicate with her was unacceptable.

She knew George's training was only supposed to be three months. When he did not contact her, she felt like she needed to take things into her own hands and figure out a way to contact him. However, she hesitated because the words of her father continued to haunt her.

Thus, the only person who seemed to be on George's side was Scott, and his excuses were an insult to her intelligence. She was beginning to worry that George had forgotten about her. She started throwing herself into her classes and was starting to feel like she needed to gain her own independence.

She hated to admit it, but it looked like her father was right. If she broke up with George, it might jar him to the point where he would reach out to her. However, it might also permanently damage their relationship.

While she was still debating writing the letter because she did not want to break George's heart, it was having the opposite effect on her, and he was breaking her heart due to his silence.

She was slowly beginning to realize that it might be the only way she could turn the corner in their relationship. If George felt like Janis was going to leave him. Maybe then he would drop everything and come home to marry her.

Janis became very conflicted, and she felt like she was living in a dreaming. The past few months could not be true. She knew George loved her. Surly he had his reason for not responding to her calls, and letters.

However, the more the days went by, the more she erased the conversation with her father. It was driving her insane, it did not make sense! Why did he have to show up after she had dropped George off at the airport. He had abandoned her for eighteen years. Now, when she was about to get married to George, he shows up and tells her a strange story and asks her to hold off marrying George.

She was beginning to fell abandon all over again and what remaining sanity she had left was gone.

She knew if her father returned, she knew she would have no choice but to dump George and everyone would go crazy, blaming George for all the problems between the two of them.

Could Janis believe she was going to be closer to George than she had been her whole life. The way things were playing out it seemed like Scott was oblivious to of PTF and how it might ruin all of their lives. And once Scott found out that she dumped George he would go crazy, because he was so close to Janis and George.

While Janis did not want to believe the reason for George's indiscretions. She slowly began to accept that her father might be right. Because so far everything he had predicted happened. Steve was hurt, thus moving him out of the equation. George and Scott were both acting strange. It almost seem like they had not talked since boot camp. And Scott was just playing game with Janis mind, because he missed his friend George.

Suddenly she began to understand why she had to write George a Dear John letter. He had refused to respond to her calls. Now the only thing she had left was to wait for her father to return so Janis could begin her training. Was she ready to change her life up and begin the challenge of being right in front of her lovers face without him even recognizing her?

While this seemed impossible when she dropped George off at the airport and few months ago. She was freaking out because when her father returned in a few days she would go into hiding. She would be in hiding unable to reveal her identity.

Maybe her father was wrong. Her letter might drive George insane and he would drop everything and rush back home and elope with her like he said he wanted to do in the first place.

Janis weighed all of her options and she finally broke down and wrote the letter to George, but her heart would not allow her to mail it to him, because she desperately hoped there was another way to get through to his thick head so that they would be together.

After writing the letter she a great sorrow in the pit of her soul. Her father better be right! The idea of deceiving all those she had grown to love was crazy. Would her father live up to his end of the bargain? She excited about getting to know her father. However, she did not know when her father would return. He had told her he would be back soon. Could she trust him to keep his word? He had abandoned her for over eighteen years. Why was this time going to be any different?

She started to doubt her father's true intentions. Why would he try to break up her relationship with George? And why would he even have the audacity to ask her not to marry George?

Was her father right? Once she broke up with George, it might jar him to the point where he would reach out to her. While she was still debating writing the letter because she did not want to break George's heart, she was slowly beginning to realize that it might be the only way she could turn the corner in their relationship. If George felt like Janis was going to leave him, she hoped he would drop everything and come home to marry her.

The troubling part was that her brother Scott would not let anyone speak against George. He had to know there was a possibility of her not hooking up with George. Why was he so staunch quick to defend George. She had a feeling that Scott was still holding on to the idea that love conquers all. He had seen their relationship blossom and he did not believe it would ever fade. He kept begging Janis to give George a little space and have patience.

He told her the, more he develops his own path the stronger their relationship will be. One day he'll put his foot in his mouth and his thick skull would get the hint. And when that happened, Scott wanted to ensure that both he and Janis would be there for him.

However, what Scott would never have suspected was that Janis's father was one of the main characters in keeping the three of them apart. It seemed like he had taken everything to the next level and would stop at nothing to keep his daughter safe. Sure, it may have seemed like he'd left her alone. But he had never left her. And he knew every step she made, and as he had told Janis, he was about to take her away and hide her from everything and everyone while he trained her on how to survive. And he was going to put her right in front of everyone's face and they would not even know who she was.

Janis had no idea that her life was getting ready to change, but her father had already started the process and it would only be a few more days before she would have to go into hiding. His archenemy, Donna, was beginning to close in on the truth. he had to get her to safety.

However, he did not realize George was drifting apart from Janis. And while Steve was out of the picture, George was still wary of Janis. Thus, even if he tried to take Janis away from Donna's web, it created a rift between George and Janis and threatened their relationship.

Within the Light's Shadow

The Road to Peace

Kenneth Kirkwood

Within the Light's Shadow II: The Road to Peace

After, George Catwell completes Boot Camp his first duty station is onboard the *USS Bunker Hill CG-52* as member of a secret NSA unit. While Scott is assigned onboard *USS Carl Vinson CVN-70* as a decoy.

As the leader of the PTF George, and his team May, James, and John must set up a secret unit called the PTF to protect Captain Silverton and Commander Johnstone from terrorists as they navigate the *USS Bunker Hill CG-52* from San Diego to Australia for a secret peace conference.

INDEX

D

E

G

H

J

L

M